Ania,

Enjoy the journey!

JEFF J. PETERS

M000199470

CATHADEUS

BOOK ONE OF THE WALKING GATES

JEFF J. PETERS

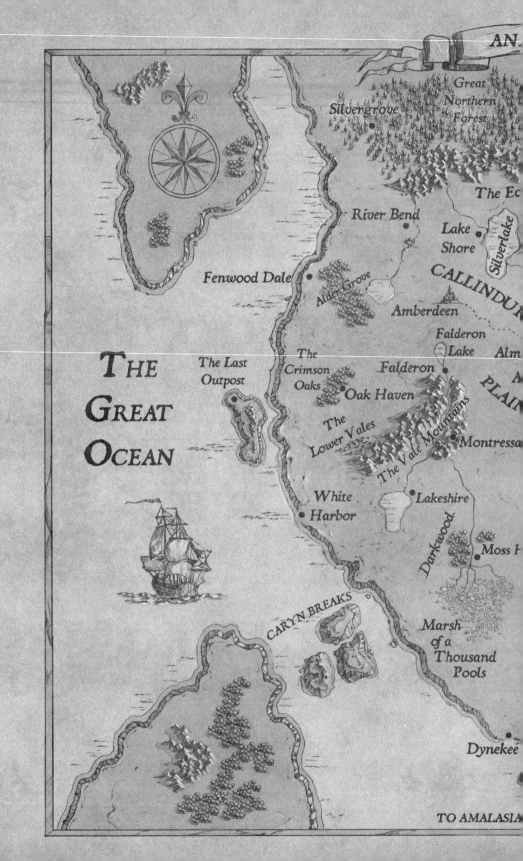

CATHADEUS © copyright 2018 by Jeff J. Peters, LLC. All rights reserved. No part of this book may be reproduced in any form whatsoever, by photography or xerography or by any other means, by broadcast or transmission, by translation into any kind of language, nor by recording electronically or otherwise, without permission in writing from the author, except by a reviewer, who may quote brief passages in critical articles or reviews.

Cathadeus is a work of fiction.
Names, characters, places, and events are products of the author's imagination.
Any resemblance to actual names, characters, places, or events is purely coincidental.

ISBN 13: 978-1-63489-072-4
eISBN: 978-1-63489-073-1

Library of Congress Catalog Number: 2017942525
Printed in the United States of America
First Printing: 2017

Cover design by Steven Meyer-Rassow
Cover art by Jorge Jacinto

www.jeffjpeters.com

837 Glenwood Ave.
Minneapolis, MN 55405
www.wiseinkpub.com

To order, visit www.itascabooks.com or call 1-800-901-3480. Reseller discounts available.

To my boys, for their pure enjoyment

To my wife, for her endless love, patience, and companionship

And to my master teacher, for helping me to find my voice

Thank you

PROLOGUE

Sunlight touched the southern peaks of the Dragon's Spine as Thrag completed his patrol. The morning was cold and snow still covered the ground. The exposed parts of the dwarf's face were chilled and steam appeared whenever he breathed—but he didn't care. He loved being in the mountains, and the sharp biting feeling on his rough skin was preferable to the heat in the mines.

Wiping the ice crystals from his beard, he lit his pipe and took a long draw before exhaling. The light crept into the clearing, and he turned to leave but stopped abruptly. A dozen yards away, barely visible in the snow, a dark shape broke the pristine white. Thrag covered his pipe and checked about. Convinced he was alone, he retrieved the small object and rolled it around in his hand, feeling the rough cuts from the crude instrument that shaped it. Even before he looked down, he knew what it was. A totem.

Moving quickly to the nearby river, he scouted its banks. He picked up a trail and followed it until he smelled their campfire. Two large, muscular beasts stood behind the flames and slightly to one side, another lying further back and to the left.

Minotaurs.

They occasionally entered the Spine to hunt, wearing totems for protection that never worked, and his kin always defeated them. There hadn't been any significant intrusion in almost six hundred years—not since the Breath of the Dragon wiped out their valley.

"So what ya doing in the mountains?" Thrag mumbled to himself, studying their bull-like faces. They had furs and leather jerkins covering their human bodies, and their weaponry was too advanced for a hunting party. *Sentries*, he concluded. *But for what?*

He needed to find out and report in, and they were too dangerous to be left alone. Unstrapping his giant battleax from across his back, he loosened the throwing weapon in his belt. Clenching his jaw, he readied to charge, then stopped. He couldn't see into the trees. Normally, he wouldn't care, but this time he had to be sure. Someone had to report, and something about this already had his beard on edge.

Turning around, he put his back against the boulder where he hid and called. A long, peaceful sound echoed among the rocks. He knew the Mins would hear it, even though he was downwind, but he wasn't worried—he'd been a ranger for more than sixty years and could imitate nature's calls. His sound was strong and true, riding the wind between the mountain pines and craggy valleys before fading away. He repeated it a few more times, then waited. As expected, the Mins ignored it. Minutes passed, and he watched the trees. Then a branch moved. Against the wind. His companion was closer than he'd thought, as usual.

Time to go.

Thrag burst from the rocks, hurling his smaller ax at the Minotaur on the right as he sprinted across the clearing. The weapon hit the beast square in the forehead, felling him. The other Min grabbed its weapon and brayed loudly. Thrag leapt up onto a stump directly opposite the fire, using the smoke to obscure his approach, and launched himself at the beast. He came through the screen with his battleax held high above his head in both hands, yelling as he appeared. The creature raised its halberd to block the strike, but Thrag's ax smashed into it, splitting the shaft in two. The Min stepped back to steady itself, but the dwarf wasn't slowing. He landed in front of it, bringing his weapon around and striking diagonally across, hitting the Min below the knee and severing its leg. The creature bellowed a horrific call, falling onto its newly formed stump. The third Min was up now, a spear in hand and coming to the fight. It pulled its arm back preparing to skewer the dwarf, but a dark form hit it from behind, sending the creature hurtling past Thrag. The dwarf ignored it. He thrust the top of his weapon straight up, hitting the crippled Min under the chin and jolting its head back. Raising his battleax again in both hands, Thrag struck down with his formidable strength, burying the blade deep into the Min's chest, killing it.

He turned to look for the remaining beast. It hung from the massive jaws of a giant, sleek, charcoal-gray leopard standing eye level beside him.

"About time you helped," Thrag admonished, looking into his companion's enormous eyes.

The leopard gently lay the dead Min down on the ground without making a sound and stared back at the dwarf.

Thrag rocked his head from side to side. "Well . . . thanks," he said.

He cleaned his weapons and searched the camp, uncovering more tracks. Following them through the trees, he found another trail leading to the old ruins.

Crossing the flattened outer wall at dusk, Thrag hid among the long shadows and intricately carved broken stone buildings that had been cut from the mountain. He moved carefully between the fallen rocks, stopping at an open courtyard. Giant columns circled the perimeter, portions of the ceiling they once supported visible among the snow. Three heavily armed Mins stood in the center, their backs toward him, facing a man dressed entirely in black armor. Beyond them, two smaller servants waited, hoods covering their faces.

". . . finish preparing yourselves. We attack at first light," he heard the man say over the Mins' heavy breathing.

It would take Thrag two days to return with reinforcements. *Not enough time*, he thought. He'd have to stop them himself.

He crept closer, then signaled to the leopard, and charged.

Throwing his ax at the middle creature, he hit the brute in the back of the head, splitting its skull and knocking him down. A brief feeling of pride flickered across his thoughts at his consistent throws, but he pushed it aside as the leopard shot past him, grappling the Min on the left. Thrag raised his weapon, preparing to strike the last beast when a crackling filled the air. Green light hit his body, encircling him and clouding his vision, freezing him in place.

Magic, he thought as his muscles shuddered. He could resist. He knew how—but this was strong. Then he realized his mistake; the figures behind the man weren't servants. They were witches.

A sudden, intense cold penetrated his chest as a curved sword pierced his body. Thrag yelled out in pain. The man in black stood before him, smiling wickedly. *Not a man*, Thrag scowled. *An elf.* Two black eyes stared back at him with malice.

The elf withdrew the sword from Thrag's chest, and the dwarf fell to his knees. He signaled for his companion to flee. Then the elf struck again, a single quick and deadly motion that severed the dwarf's neck, dropping his body to the ground.

CHAPTER

1

Braxton Prinn sat at the wooden table, moving his eggs around his plate drearily; his light-brown hair was a mess of unruly curls, and his normally focused green eyes were bloodshot and glazed. He knew today was Merchant Tide, the two-day market event that started each new week, and that his mom would be expecting his help. But time had slipped by last night working on a rover deer's hide. It was the first time he and his friends had anything of real value to sell, and he was excited about the money it might bring. Now, though, he was tired and sore, his few predawn hours of rest insufficient for the upcoming day's work.

The front door opened, and a blast of cold air blew in, causing Brax to shiver. The long-sleeved shirt and leather tunic did little to protect him from the frigid morning air. His older brother stood in the opening, his woolen cloak dripping with rain that glistened like tiny crystals, reflecting the dancing firelight. Beyond him, the inky darkness of predawn hid the yard outside and the village beyond. Penton wiped his muddied boots and removed his blacksmith's gloves, shaking his long black hair before hanging his cloak on a nearby hook.

Shutting the ironbound door, he walked over and sat opposite Brax, placing an oil lamp carefully on the crimson-oak table.

"Late night again?" Penton asked cheerfully.

Brax nodded, smelling the heavy scent of their dad's smithy on him. "At least we finished on time."

"Finally!" Penton glanced up at the ceiling. "Hopefully you won't keep waking me anymore, going to bed so late."

"You're one to talk," Brax replied. "You've been waking me every week for the last four months! What is it that you and Gavin do after Merchant Tide anyway?"

Penton leaned across the table. "Drink brew and dance with young women." He beamed. "Something you might consider in a couple of years, when you come of age."

"Not likely."

Penton laughed. "Seriously though, I hope you get what you want for the rover."

"Thanks." Braxton poked at his cold breakfast. "That's up to you and Phin now."

"Why don't you come with us? Neither of you've been to Amberdeen, and I know you'd rather be with her."

"I'd like to," he admitted. "But I need to help at the Gate, and I promised Dad I'd pick up the monthly supply from Rusk."

Their mom walked in and set a plate of warm muffins down on the table. Brax grabbed a couple and juggled them to avoid burning his fingers.

"How's Dad managing?" she asked Penton.

"Good, just adding a few last-minute things from the storeroom."

"Maybe you should go and help." She looked back at the kitchen window. "You know he shouldn't do any heavy lifting."

Penton started toward the back door, then stopped and grabbed the plate of muffins before hastily retreating out of his mom's reach.

Brax's mom smiled. "Ready to go?" she asked kindly, kissing him on his messy curls.

He got up and unhooked his wool-lined cloak from next to where Penton's still dripped. Tying it about his neck, he retrieved the wicker basket by the fire, pushing the rover deer's silver-white hide and small, curved horns further down into its already bulging contents. Hauling the container onto his back, he headed to the kitchen. His mom was waiting for him, her hood pulled up and a small leather bag slung over one shoulder. She lit an oil lamp, opened the back door, and hurried out into the rain. Braxton took a breath and followed her into the dark.

They turned left and headed down the partially hidden trail, passing through their little gate and out onto the dirt road. Their weak light spilled across the street, barely revealing the house opposite, its occupants still sound asleep.

"Are you not going to Amberdeen today?" his mom asked, as they continued toward their village.

Brax shook his head. "I need to meet Rusk and then help in the smithy."

"I can manage alone, you know. You don't have to stay."

"I know, but I need to help Dad. I promised as much."

His mom smiled. She knew he never missed helping her.

They walked for over a mile before reaching Oak Haven's plaza, listening to the sounds of their footfalls on the wet cobblestones as they crossed to the center. Two guards came into view, their dark, cloaked forms standing on the lower steps of the Walking Gate to avoid the rain. Giant crimson-oak pillars extended from the platform behind them, disappearing into the mist, the edges of the roof they supported barely visible above the men.

"Jen." The first guard nodded at seeing Brax's mom. It was Janton Roe, of the night watch.

"A damp market day," the other man added, holding a long spear upright, its diamond-shaped point catching the lamplight.

Brax's mom returned the greetings and headed up the stone steps to the marble platform. He followed behind her, feeling the guards watching him.

"At least the snows have stopped." Brax unstrapped the large basket and turned toward his mom. She knelt on the cold floor, drying and clearing off the water and other debris that had blown in with the storm. Braxton hated seeing her like that and it bothered him that she worked as a servant to the Gate Keepers. He wished she'd take the trials to join their inner group. But he knew she'd never agree. She never did.

Pulling a towel from her bag, he dropped down beside her. "I'll do it," he said, avoiding her eyes.

His mom stood up. "It's an honor to help, Brax," she reminded him, opening the basket.

They continued for the better part of an hour, cleaning the platform and surrounding steps, placing silk cushions around the large octagon crystal inlaid in the floor. Sunlight crept in from the horizon as Braxton returned from the well. The rain had stopped and the sky was clearing, promising another bright spring day. A small group of villagers had gathered in front of the Gate—their crops, crafts, and other articles for sale carefully wrapped in bundles they held or carried on their backs. Penton was in line, holding a little wooden pushcart filled with tools, weapons, and other items from their smithy. Their dad leaned heavily on his cane beside him, providing instructions for selling their metal work.

Brax's mom filled some cups from the decanter he was carrying before setting it down on a wooden table. "Thanks for all your help today." Her blue eyes looked up at him. "You'd better head down now, though. You know how Terran gets about anyone who's *not supposed to be up here*." She deepened her voice, imitating the big man.

Brax grinned and quickly kissed her cheek. Retrieving the wrapped bundle from the basket, he hurried off the platform.

Twelve Gate Protectors had replaced the evening watch, presiding now over Merchant Tide. Armed with swords and long spears, their chainmail vests covered leather tunics and dark green cloaks draped over their shoulders, a white octagon on their breast.

"Morning, Captain." Brax ran down the steps. He could feel Terran's penetrating gaze boring into his back.

Weaving among the merchant tables and away from the growing line of travelers, he reached their meeting spot. Phinlera's slim form entered the plaza and ran toward him.

"Morning," he said. "For a moment there, I thought you weren't going to make it."

"What, and miss my chance to visit Amberdeen, earn money, and travel with your brother all in the same day?" She winked. "You must be joking. I hardly slept!"

Braxton avoided her eyes and flushed at seeing the middle button missing from her tight shirt. Phin didn't seem to notice and continued jostling around excitedly, her enthusiasm contagious.

A shrill trumpet sounded, causing Brax to jump and look back at the Walking Gate. Eight robed figures approached the temple, their heads bent low and their hoods pulled up.

"You'd better go," he said, handing Phin the rover deer's pelt and horns, along with several copper coins. "Good luck, for all of us."

Phin flashed him one of her brilliant smiles and pushed a strand of long black hair away from her face. "Don't worry so much." She tucked the coins inside her worn vest. "It'll be fine. Besides, Pen's agreed to help me, remember?"

"I know. Just be careful. Amberdeen's a big city."

She gave another wink of her brown doe eyes and hurried off toward the Gate. He watched her energetic movements as she joined the line, seeing her laughing with his more muscular brother.

Brax wound his way past Oak Haven's vendors to the receiving end of the Gate. Crops, tapestries, baskets, crafts, and a variety of homemade food and drink were laid out throughout the plaza, awaiting visitors to Merchant Tide. He checked the tables and carts for anything new, before continuing to his familiar spot near the inn.

The Keepers took their positions up on the marble platform, sitting around the crystal. Braxton watched his mom serving those around her, helping each member get seated and providing refreshments before their work.

Another trumpet quieted the crowd, and the few morning songbirds and continual dripping of rainwater were the only sounds in the open rotunda.

The Gate Keepers started summoning their spirit magic, and an orange glow of hazy, ethereal light floated up from the crystal. Then other colors began to appear and mix together, swirling and sharpening as each new Keeper added his or her own distinctive magic. After several minutes, a rainbow column of light extended from floor to ceiling, merging to form a single pillar of magical white energy. The radiance grew brighter until Braxton was forced to look away, listening instead for the signal that would announce the Gate's opening. A final trumpet echoed across the plaza, and he looked back to the now golden light illuminating the platform and opening the Walking Gate.

Villagers ascended the steps, passing between the wooden pillars and under the peaked and tiled roof, depositing four copper coins into the collection box before moving toward the column. Brax listened to them speak the name of the town they wished to travel to before entering the light. Most, like Phin and Penton, were heading to the capital city of Amberdeen, with a few destined for the mountain city of Montressa, or Dynekee to the south.

He heard his brother, followed by Phinlera's slightly nervous voice, as they departed Oak Haven. Simultaneously, travelers started arriving through the southern end of the Gate's column—visitors coming to buy, sell, or trade their wares. Their village seldom saw large numbers of travelers, except in the reaping months or at the Crimson Festival for the annual allotment of red wood harvested from the neighboring forest.

Only a few people appeared from the light, and there were long gaps between visitors coming down from the Gate. After almost an hour of watching people mill about in the plaza, Brax recognized the short, stocky form of Ruskin Tryn arrive on the platform. Thumping down the stairs, the dwarf headed over to where Brax stood waiting.

"Well met, young Braxton," he said, his gruff voice matching his rough exterior. A stout hammer, which Ruskin referred to as "Fist," hung by his side, and his sleeveless green tunic had a crouching badger sewn in with silver thread, which the dwarf wore proudly.

"Morning, Rusk." Brax grasped the dwarf's calloused hand, the strength of which always surprised him, even though he knew his friend lightened his grip when greeting him.

Unslinging his large pack, Ruskin handed it to Brax. "This is for your dad."

Used to their monthly exchange, Brax braced himself for the heavy weight and grabbed the pack with both hands. As usual, he dropped it to the ground as soon as the dwarf let go.

Ruskin laughed, tucked his long braided beard under his belt, and headed to the tavern. "I'll see you at dinner," he called back, without turning around. "Got some business at the inn."

Accustomed to Ruskin's routine, Brax adjusted the metals and tools in the bag before hoisting it onto his back for the long trek home. The portal would be closing down soon; the strain of maintaining the energy needed to keep the column active limited the time it remained open. The Keepers would retire to their lodge, returning at sundown tomorrow to reopen the Gate for another hour, allowing travelers and villagers alike to return home. His mom always stayed longer though, cleaning and packing up. It was the same start to every week, and Braxton knew it well.

Not seeing her on the platform, Brax was transfixed by the golden swirl of spirit magic emanating from the Walking Gate, exaggerated now by his lack of sleep. Shapes materialized and disappeared as light reflected to and from the column, creating images that didn't exist—circular shadows from the mixture of both natural and magical light.

A face suddenly appeared inside the column. Large, broad, and grotesque, it was covered in thick brown hair, with deep-set black eyes above a rectangular snout. An evil grin revealed sharp, curved teeth and two long horns pointed outward above the creature's small ears, reminding Braxton of a large bull's head. It had intelligence in its eyes, though, and it watched him intently.

Brax blinked, dispelling the image. He searched the light for any sign that the face had been real. The swirling magical energy continued to flow, shapeless and ever-changing, but nothing more appeared.

He was still trying to make sense of what he'd seen when the sounds around him began to fade, as if someone were silencing the familiar noise from the busy plaza. A ringing filled his ears, not from any outside source but from somewhere deep within him. Above all else, came the clear and unmistakable sound of his mom's voice inside his mind.

Braxton, run!

He stood paralyzed in Oak Haven's small plaza, shocked by the fear she imparted and her speaking in his head. The steps leading up to the receiving end of the Walking Gate were only a few dozen feet away.

"*Guards!*" The shrill and penetrating sound of his mother's voice cried out. Everyone within earshot turned in surprise at the unexpected alarm.

Hearing the panic in her call, Braxton sprinted toward the Gate, all thoughts of the vision in the column giving way to his need to reach her. A loud whistle blew on the other side of the platform, simultaneously summoning the guards and sending people scattering in every direction.

Brax had barely reached the bottom of the steps when three large forms emerged from the Gate. Standing more than a foot taller than him, their massive humanoid bodies were covered in dark hair, with oak-sized legs extending from torn pants and wide, shoeless feet. Bare chested, their arms ended in hands that could cover his face. One of the beasts held a giant sword aloft while the others grasped even longer spears. It was their bull-like faces, however, that drew Braxton's attention—exactly like the one he'd seen moments earlier in the light.

The creature closest to him looked down and brayed loudly, raising its spear. Braxton froze, recognizing its destructive intent. Something struck him from behind, and nausea spread through his body as all sound and light began to fade.

He fell, collapsing into darkness.

CHAPTER

2

Crackling from the fireplace broke into the silent void from which Braxton slowly emerged. He opened his eyes, trying to focus on the giant oak beams running the length of the ceiling. He was in the main room of their cottage, on a makeshift bed of blankets that had been hurriedly thrown down. A cloak was stuffed under his neck, and his feet faced the fire.

The low hum of voices gradually drifted into his consciousness. Turning toward them, he stopped at the sudden pain that stabbed the back of his head, causing his eyes to water and his nausea to return.

"Aaahh," he groaned, reaching behind his head and finding a wet cloth.

"He's awake," he heard Ruskin say.

"How do you feel?" His dad limped into view, leaning on his cane. The sleeves of his blacksmith's shirt were rolled up, exposing muscular arms, and he still wore his work trousers and heavy boots.

"I thought for a minute that little tap from Fist had killed ya." Ruskin appeared next to his dad. "Thought you were made of tougher stuff than that, my boy."

"You're lucky Ruskin knocked you out when he did," his dad said. "Or you'd be dead."

"Standing perfectly still for that thrown spear." The dwarf smiled, trying to make light of the situation.

"What . . . what happened?" Brax rubbed his head, trying to remember.

"There was an attack at the Gate." Fear and doubt reflected in his dad's normally strong and reassuring eyes. But it was more than that. A deep sadness hung from his features, as if every line had been chiseled deeper and all happiness he'd once known had been drained from his dark and drawn face.

"What is it? What's happened?" Brax tried to sit up. His throbbing head and nausea forced him quickly back down.

"It's your mom . . ." His dad cleared his throat.

"She was injured in the attack," Ruskin completed sadly. "She's not well."

"*What?*" Braxton sat up abruptly. The pain in his head clouded his vision, and his stomach threatened to lurch, but he bit his lip hard and resisted lying back down.

It was then that he noticed the still form of his mom lying beside him and felt his heart wrench. Her face was a ghostly white, and her usually warm features were devoid of life. A large bandage soaked with blood crossed her chest. She was on a mattress that had been dragged from his parents' small bedroom, little bits of straw still lining the path to the common room.

"Mom?" he called, but there was no answer. "No!" A wave of anger shot through him, followed by a profound sadness beyond anything he was prepared for. He leaned over her bed and cried.

His dad patted his shoulder. Brax continued sobbing, not caring what the men might think.

When he'd cried himself out, he felt small and weak. The world had suddenly become a much larger place, and he was ill-prepared to deal with the extent of its reach. He wiped his face on his sleeve and looked up.

"I know," his dad said slowly.

Ruskin shook his head. "It could have been worse, if she hadn't warned us . . ."

Braxton wanted to hit the dwarf. *How could it possibly be worse?* But he didn't say anything and just glared at him instead.

"Your mom raised the alarm barely in time," Ruskin continued. "Terran was able to react, and the Protectors responded. Had she not yelled out when she did, we would all have been surprised. And you, young Braxton, would be dead."

"They attacked the Gate Keepers," his dad clarified. "Two of those beasts went straight for them, killing three members almost immediately. The Protectors were on them in seconds, allowing the rest of the Keepers to get away. Your mom helped them escape, but they were dazed from being pulled out of their magical link. One of those monsters went after her, but thankfully Ruskin was there and occupied it long enough."

"Not before your mom took the full brunt of an attack, I'm afraid." Ruskin shook his head, looking disappointed.

"She saved the others by putting herself in front of that creature's weapon. Luckily, Rusk was able to fell the beast and save your mom. Otherwise she'd be dead too."

Brax's heart lifted. "Then she's not . . . ?" He trailed off, unable to say what he feared.

His dad took a deep breath. "No, but she's gravely wounded, and her condition hasn't changed in almost three hours."

Brax rubbed his eyes. "What were those things?"

"Minotaurs," Ruskin responded, "and their history is a sad, sad story." He scratched his beard, his eyes distant as he gazed into the fire. "Unlike the dwarves, elves, fairies, and other pure creatures that come from the spirit realms, the Mins—as they're more commonly called—were created. More than six hundred years ago now, when the Alchemists started experimenting on the races of the old world. They used their magic to fuse and mix the life forces of various creatures together in an effort to create a race that would serve them. Thousands died in those experiments, tortured by the infusion of a foreign species into their own being. It was an awful, destructive time, one that should never have happened."

He dropped down heavily into a chair by the fire.

"Eventually they started perfecting their mixings, learning from each failed attempt. At first they created the orcs, a combination of elves and pigs; these were stupid, useless creatures, capable only of squabbling among themselves. Other combinations were tried. Centaurs were formed from men and horses, but were so proud a race, they couldn't be subverted to the Alchemists' will. The ragi were dwarves with lion heads—too strong or too stubborn to be subdued. There were many others, but eventually they created the Mins. A combination of men and bulls, they are strong, unafraid, and vicious." Ruskin spat a piece of meat he'd been chewing on into the fire and watched the flames, deep in thought.

"Why'd the Alchemists create them?" Brax asked.

"They wanted slaves, workers they could control and who'd serve them unquestionably," the dwarf explained. "The Mins were exactly what they were looking for. The equal of several men, they're capable of carrying huge weight with little rest, and their human essence gives them just enough intelligence to carry out most tasks. The perfect slaves."

"What happened to them?" Brax continued, unsure he wanted to know the entire story.

"The Alchemists pushed too hard, breeding great armies of Mins to use in place of human soldiers. They forced them to fight one another—brutal battles in which thousands died, fighting over the smallest land disputes for the Alchemists and sometimes for sport."

Ruskin walked over to the table and poured himself a drink.

"It was a terrible time, a useless waste of life. Maybe that's what caused the earth to awaken." He took a long swallow, refilled his glass, and returned to his seat.

"The volcanoes of the Dragon's Spine erupted," Braxton's dad clarified. "The Breath of the Dragon, they called it. Peaks all along the mountain blasted fiery plumes high up into the air, releasing oceans of lava that swept down into the valley of the Alchemists, transforming their once-lush forests, rivers, and meadows into a barren wasteland."

"Everything was destroyed," Ruskin said with a smirk, as if the destruction was deserved. "All their great cities, their temples, and the paved stone roadways that connected their settlements. All the great achievements of the Alchemists and their Min slaves were consumed by the fiery ocean. Even the Alchemists themselves, frightened and locked away in their towers, couldn't escape."

"What happened to the Mins and the other mixed races?" Braxton asked, engrossed now in the tale.

"Most died along with the Alchemists, but a few survived the devastation. The Mins fled into the Ridge, but the ogres living there fought them off. Shunned by society, they wandered around for years until, desperate and homeless, they returned to the Breaker Dunes. They live there to this day, foraging around in small groups led by the strongest bull. And to my knowledge, they've never crossed the Calindurin before. That is, until now."

"Something must have forced them out of the valley," Brax's dad added. "Otherwise they'd never have left. The Mins hate the other races and haven't left the Dunes in almost five hundred years."

Ruskin nodded. "Something's changed, all right, and that's what worries me. As you said, Thadeus, they hate the other races, and they're too stubborn to band together. Something or someone has overcome their fierce nature and convinced them to invade the West. What we have to do now is find out why."

CHAPTER

3

Braxton knelt by his mom's makeshift bed, her deathlike sleep unchanged. He stroked her blond hair, pushing the strands back from her lifeless face and tucking them behind her small, delicate ears. The history of the Mins still filled his thoughts, and the images he created of the attack on his mom rolled over and over in his mind like a relentless sea.

He tried focusing on something else. "Which Gate Keepers died in the attack?" he asked, interrupting the quiet conversation between Ruskin and his dad.

He could feel them looking at him, but he kept his eyes on his mom's face.

"It was Arren Bo, the Gate Leader, who we lost first," his dad said. "Young Kyler Olms, the newest member, who joined the Keepers only last summer, was also taken. I still remember how excited he was to have been accepted. And . . ." He paused. "Nenra Reed."

Brax looked up, shocked. "Gavin's mom?"

His dad nodded. "I saw him after the attack. I fear it's going to take him a long time to recover from this loss."

"Worse yet," Ruskin interjected, "with three of their number dead, and especially your Gate Leader gone, there's no way you can open your Walking Gate again. Not unless you have some new initiates waiting to take their place."

Brax's dad shook his head. "From what Jen had told me, there isn't anyone far enough along in their training to join. I'm afraid it's going to be a long time before we can reopen our Gate."

"That's going to be bad for your economy, especially if you can't sell the crimson harvest this year."

"I know. I think Oak Haven is in for a rough time ahead."

Brax thought about the impact the attack would have on their village. Without a connection to the outside world—and the ability to buy, sell, and trade via the Walking Gate—Oak Haven would never survive.

He turned to his mom, tears welling up in his eyes. What would become of their family if she didn't recover? He tried pushing the thought from his mind, thinking instead of Phinlera and how she'd be unable to return home quickly if their Gate was closed. Would his feelings for her change during their time apart? Or would she—as he feared—develop an attraction toward his brother? As the realization of the possible outcomes from the day's events continued to unfold, Braxton fell further into despair. He lay his head down on the bed next to his mom's.

Braxton.

He sat up quickly, expecting to see his mother's smiling face and bright blue eyes looking back at him, recovered from her wound. But her features remained unchanged, and she was deathly pale. Had he imagined her speaking? Was his desire to have her back so desperate that he was creating voices in his mind?

Braxton, can you hear me? Her call was louder than before but still inside him.

"Mom . . . is that you?" He stared at her face, trying to understand where her voice was coming from.

Yes, Brax, it's me. Oh, I was so worried you wouldn't hear my call, especially after the attack on the Gate. Listen to me, Braxton. I don't have much time, and I need your help. The only chance for my survival is to take my essence back to Arbor Glen. Please, Brax, you must do this! Take off my pendant and return it to my tree. Do you understand?

"What tree? Where's Arbor Glen? What essence? Mom, I don't understand!" He started to panic at the desperation in her voice.

Your dad will explain it to you, but you must hurry. You need to arrive in nine days, before the start of a new cycle. Remember, Arbor Glen. Find Bendarren. I love you. Good luck.

"Mom, wait—where's Arbor Glen? Who's Bendarren?"

There was no answer.

"Mom!" he called frantically, willing her to respond, his face mere inches from hers.

His eyes filled with tears. "Tell me what to do." But other than the sound of the crackling fireplace, the room was silent.

"Braxton," his dad said quietly.

He looked back. His dad and Ruskin stood behind him.

"Tell me what she said, son."

"I . . . I don't know," he stammered. "Something about taking her essence, or her pendant, to a tree in Arbor Glen. That she needs my help, that I have to find someone named . . . Bendarren. But I'm not sure. It all happened so quickly, and she spoke faster than normal. Dad, I don't understand. What's going on?"

His father didn't respond. He walked over to the table and poured himself a drink, took a long, slow draught followed by a deep breath, and then sat down in a chair by the fire.

"Listen to me very carefully. I need to tell you something that may be difficult for you to hear." His dad's face was serious now. "Your mom is an elfling." He let the words hang in the air for a moment before continuing. "They're a small, reclusive race who live in Arbor Glen, a hidden glade deep within the greater Arbor Loren forest. We met, as you know, in the elven city of Almon-Sen, more than nineteen years ago this spring. But what we've never told you is that she's one of their race, who left her people to live with me and bear human children."

"What!" Brax stood up, feeling dizzy. "How can that be?"

"I know it's hard to accept," his dad replied. "She worried you'd feel ashamed if you knew, considering how the mixed races are treated. We planned to tell you when you were older, but it doesn't matter now. She's still your mother, and she needs your help. If I understand correctly from what you've said—and what I heard you say back to her—she's transferred her essence, or her life force, into her rose pendant. You need to carry it back to Arbor Glen. I should really be the one to go, but my old leg won't make the journey." He forced a weak smile. "With Pen away in Amberdeen, you must do this Brax."

"Me?"

"There's no one else," his dad said.

Brax glanced at Rusk.

"Ha!" Ruskin responded. "The elves won't let a dwarf into their kingdom. Not now."

His dad took another deep breath. "If you don't go, Brax, your mother will die."

These last words hung in the air like a thick fog, palpable and real. Brax ran his hands through his hair. He paced the room and shook his head, trying to grasp that his mom wasn't human but some sort of elven subrace, and that she might not survive. Frustrated, he stared down at her, wrestling with his emotions. His whole life had been suddenly turned upside down. It was all so unreal. Regardless of her background, though, he knew what she meant to him—and that losing her would be unbearable. He promised himself that, no matter what else happened, he'd find a way to bring her back.

CHAPTER
4

Braxton spent a restless night tossing about in the loft he shared with his brother. Visions of his mom's wound haunted him, and his self-doubt constantly threatened to crush his weak resolve. He cried repeatedly at the thought of losing her, despite her recent words. It was a few hours before dawn when he finally slept, exhausted from the day's events and his previous night's lack of sleep. His dreams provided little comfort, though, each one a new variation on some failed attempt to carry his mom's essence to Arbor Glen and ending with a look of anguish on his dad's face, his eyes telling Braxton that he knew he would fail, and that he should have sent Penton instead.

The first rays of sunlight touched the rooftops when his dad woke him.

"Time to set out," he said, shaking Braxton awake.

Brax got up, thankful to be rid of his dreams, and dressed. He stuffed some clothes into his travel pack, grabbed his hunting bow and remaining arrows, and headed downstairs. His dad and Ruskin were at the table, talking quietly. A steady fire showed they'd been up for several hours, or perhaps hadn't slept at all.

Brax dumped his pack at the base of the stone steps and walked over to his mom's bed. Ignoring the conversation of the two men, he knelt down beside her and felt her hand. Removing the towel from her forehead, he rinsed it in the basin on the floor and gently placed it back on her brow.

"I love you, Mom," he said quietly and kissed her cheek. "I won't fail you."

"Go and get something to eat," his dad encouraged. "You're going to need your strength."

He returned a few minutes later with a cold breakfast—a small wedge of cheese, a piece of sausage, and some of his mom's day-old muffins—and dropped down beside her, eating mechanically, forcing the food down.

"We've laid out the most direct route to Almon-Sen," his dad said as he and Ruskin walked over. "Rusk will be traveling with you. I need to stay here with Mom."

Braxton could see the disappointment in his dad's face at not being able to travel.

"If anyone can tell us about the Mins—or the reason for this suicidal attack," Ruskin added, "it's the elves. They live right on their doorstep and watch them closely."

"What do you mean, suicidal?" Brax asked.

"Well, killing the Gate Keepers meant closing the Gate, and they must've known we'd never just let them walk out of town alive." Ruskin smiled grimly. "It was a one-way journey, my lad, and the Mins would've known that before they began."

Brax realized that the dwarf was right. The Mins had no way of escaping once the Gate was closed.

"We won't get any answers until you reach Almon-Sen," his dad said. "It's a four-day walk to Falderon and another three-day's ride to Arbor Loren. The weather shouldn't be a problem, so with any luck, and if you travel fast, you should get there in plenty of time."

"Why don't we just ride from here and get there even sooner?"

His dad nodded. "That would've been ideal, but Rusk needs a horse. There aren't many in our village, and with the Gate closed, everyone will have to travel now to get supplies, which puts horses in high demand. We've been checking all night, and no one's even willing to sell us a mule. Besides, I don't think our townspeople are going to be too pleased to discover your mom's an elf. Not after all these years of living beside them as a human, so they're not exactly going to jump at the chance to help us. Anyway, Rusk knows someone in Falderon who'll give him a horse. You can ride Obsidian together until then. He's big enough to carry both of you that far at least, if you don't push him."

"Getting to the elves isn't a problem," the dwarf commented. "Getting into their city . . . now that's going to be a challenge."

"Why do you say that?" Brax asked.

Ruskin took a bite from a chunk of bread he was holding. "If the attack on the Keepers was more widespread than just Oak Haven, which I'm guessing it was, the elves have probably closed Almon-Sen. They know how to protect themselves, and it starts with preventing outsiders from entering their kingdom. Letting in a dwarf and a human boy is going to require some careful persuading."

"We'll get in," Brax said, determined not to fail. "If I explain that my mom needs help."

"Maybe. We'll just have to see what the mood is when we arrive. Anyway, we need to get there first, and that means leaving soon."

"I have something that might be of use to you, Brax, if you can learn to use it." His dad limped over to the table, motioning for him to follow. He unwrapped the leather ties of a deerskin bundle and separated the skins, revealing the most exquisite sword Braxton had ever seen.

The golden cross-guard was made of a metal he didn't recognize and tapered away from the dark wooden grip, cut in relief, with a deep-red strapping spiraling down to a rounded pommel. But it was the blade itself that captured Brax's attention. A beautiful unicorn's head was engraved near the hilt, its horn extending down the center and its long flowing mane continuing over the guard in strands of white chain.

"It's called the Unicorn Blade," his dad said, lifting the sword from the skins and holding it aloft. The long silver shaft glistened in the firelight, reflecting its sharpened edge. "It belonged to my father."

"A spirit sword!" Ruskin sounded surprised. "I never knew Tyrrideon was a Wielder."

"Grandpa Ty?" Brax asked. He knew his grandfather had served the Empire and could remember listening to stories of his adventures whenever he'd returned to their village.

His dad nodded. "He gave it to me before he died. And he was more than a Wielder, he was their captain for seven years."

"What's a Wielder?"

"An elite group of swordsmen who serve the king," the dwarf said dismissively.

"They're his own personal unit," his dad explained. "Responsible for carrying out the king's orders at the highest level, and with the greatest secrecy."

He placed the weapon back on the table. "There were nine swords originally, but only six remain. Five are carried by the current King's Squires—which is their official name—who serve young King Balan in Amberdeen. The sixth, however, is right here." He placed the weapon back on the table.

Ruskin leaned over the Unicorn Blade. "This is amazing craftsmanship." He picked it up and continued to admire the sword, turning it over and running his fingers down the side. "It's much heavier than I expected. Unnaturally so. There's some magic at work here." Holding the blade in his bare hand, he turned the hilt toward Brax and offered him the weapon.

Braxton looked at the dwarf. Then he reached out and gripped the handle.

Ruskin's deep-set eyes watched him, his face expressionless. He let go and the full weight of the sword fell upon Brax's forearm, causing the tip of the weapon to drop down and hit the floor.

Ruskin laughed, and his dad smiled too. Feeling a bit embarrassed at his lack of strength, Brax grasped the sword in both hands and raised the end of the blade, his arms straining with the effort.

"We'll have to work on that while we travel," the dwarf said, heading to the door. "I need to refill my ale skins and get some pipeweed. Shouldn't take long." He left the cottage, leaving Braxton alone with his dad.

His father turned to him. "While you're gone, remember to trust in your instincts, and in what you feel. Don't follow anyone too blindly. Ruskin is a good guide, but you carry your mom's essence with you now, and the Unicorn Blade. Let those guide you."

Brax nodded, not quite sure he understood.

"Take this," his dad said, reaching into his pocket and pulling out a small deerskin purse. "It's not much, but it should help. Spend wisely, and be careful."

"I will, Dad, and I won't let you down—or Mom."

"I know. Just do what you can, and we'll live with the outcome."

Brax nodded again, not wanting to think about what failure might mean to him or his family.

"Now, go pack some food," his dad suggested. "You leave in an hour."

CHAPTER

5

The sun was still climbing toward midmorning when they heard the galloping horse behind them. Braxton rode atop Obsidian, the large black draft horse his dad used to turn the forge, and Ruskin sat behind him, grumbling about preferring to walk.

They stopped and watched as the approaching rider grew closer, the sounds of his horse's hooves announcing him long before he could be seen.

At a couple hundred yards away, Braxton recognized the horse as Cinnamon, the auburn mare belonging to Gavin Reed. Having grown up without a father, Gavin had spent much of his youth with Brax and Penton, often accompanying them on hunting trips and other outdoor expeditions.

He drew up alongside them, a cloud of dust settling in around him. His curly, sandy-brown hair was unkempt, and his face was strained and pale, his eyes bloodshot and red, evidence of the grief he'd suffered at losing his mom in the attack.

"I'm going with you," he stated firmly. "I want to find whomever is behind this and repay them personally."

"We're not pursuing them," Brax replied. "We're heading to Arbor Loren to save my mom and to see if the elves can tell us why the Mins attacked."

"But you know where they are." Gavin looked at Ruskin, holding his jaw tight and clenching his teeth.

Ruskin took a deep breath. "Revenge is a terrible thing to live with. It's a beast that consumes you. Besides, you're a militia guard now. You swore an oath to protect Oak Haven, and you've a duty to its people."

"I've a greater duty to avenge my mother," Gavin snapped, leaning in closer toward the dwarf. "I don't care about the militia, or Oak Haven, for that matter. I'm going after them, whether I ride with you, follow from behind, or go on my own. You can't stop me. Nobody can. And they can lock me up for deserting if I ever come back."

Ruskin eyed Gavin, weighing him up, then nudged Brax. "What do you think? This is your trip. You decide."

Braxton understood the anguish his friend must be feeling—the same pain he'd felt when he thought his mother was dead. It was something he wondered if the dwarf could ever understand.

"Let him come with us. He's as much right to know who's behind this as I do. Besides, we may need the extra help."

Ruskin made a *hmph* sound and kicked the side of Obsidian to get him walking again, shaking his head and muttering something about harboring a criminal.

"I want to make it to Falderon quickly—assuming no more interruptions," the dwarf commented, emphasizing his disapproval of Gavin joining them.

Bear, Gavin's large elkhound-wolf mix, caught up with them a few minutes later as they continued along the road, panting heavily as he ran up next to Cinnamon. Standing well over three feet tall at the shoulder, he had a thick mop of black, brown, and gray hair and a head resembling that of the forest creatures for which he was named.

Braxton smiled at the elkhound's appearance. Somehow, having Bear along brought a sense of familiarity to their journey. For a brief moment, he felt as if they were just off on another hunting trip rather than an expedition to save his mother's life and uncover the reason for the Min attack. But then the enormity of what he was trying to do crashed in on him again. He sniffed and looked away.

They paused briefly in the midafternoon for a lunch of bread, cheese, and some salted and dried meat Braxton had brought with him from the cottage. The path east was surprisingly empty, devoid of the normal traffic of farmers, tradesmen, and merchants who frequented the road between their village and the larger towns. They passed several farms, but no one worked the fields, despite the sunny spring weather. The residents, it appeared, had either deserted their homes entirely or locked themselves away tightly inside.

"The attack must've been more widespread than just Oak Haven," Ruskin commented. The dwarf's rough voice reflected a deepening concern.

At the end of the second day, they stopped by a copse of tall pines next to a creek that meandered down from the Vale Mountains. Yellow wildflowers were visible in the fading light as evening's shadows crept across the broad fields thick with spring grass.

Gavin started a small fire, cooking something that spread an enticing aroma across the little clearing. Braxton was tying up Obsidian for the night, when Ruskin came over.

"We need to practice with that sword of yours." He held a thick branch in one hand, smoothing it over with his hunting knife to form a short, debarked staff.

Braxton nodded, found his pack, and unwrapped the Unicorn Blade. Gavin looked up, but didn't say anything. Brax was grateful that his friend didn't ask any questions. Carrying the heavy sword to one side of the clearing, he stood facing the dwarf. He knew he needed to learn how to use the weapon, and, although tired and hungry, this was as good a time as any to start practicing.

Ruskin held up the staff, and Brax strained with both hands to lift the blade and cross swords with his dwarf tutor. After holding their position for a moment, Ruskin flicked his wrist down and sent a stinging pain searing across Brax's left thigh.

"What was that for?" he yelled out, rubbing his leg.

Ruskin chuckled. "Just wanted to make sure you were paying attention. Now, let's try again."

They practiced for the better part of an hour. Brax's movements were slow and uncoordinated with the heavy blade. He could barely stand from the strain of wielding the sword, and the numerous hits from Ruskin's staff were still stinging his arms and legs, when the dwarf finally called a halt.

"That'll do." He stepped back and tossed his staff to the ground. "I'm getting hungry."

Braxton collapsed next to the fire, his body aching. His stomach rumbled from the lack of food, encouraged by the scent of Gavin's cooking. His friend handed him a bowl of stew, which he gulped down, before noticing a weak smile on Gavin's face for the first time since joining them.

"He gave you quite a workout."

Brax nodded and continued eating, dipping some bread into the bowl to sop up the gravy.

"Ha! I took it easy on ya 'cause I knew it was your first time," Ruskin retorted. "I don't think any of the Mins will be quite so gentle."

Brax knew he was right, but his body hurt from where he'd been struck multiple times, bypassing his weak attempts to deflect the strikes. Frustrated and tired from the exercise, he felt his eyes keep threatening to shut. They finished their meal and turned in early. Despite the pain from the many welts and bruises on his limbs, Braxton fell quickly asleep.

It was a little past midnight when he woke with a start. Something had pulled him from his sleep. He sat up and looked around the clearing. Ruskin and Gavin lay still, their rhythmic breathing evidence that neither had heard whatever had alerted him. Even Bear was asleep next to the dying fire, something Brax found odd, considering the elkhound's superior senses.

He listened for a moment, straining his eyes to pierce the darkness that surrounded their camp, but nothing moved. Bullfrogs drummed their nighttime song near the little stream while closer by crickets hummed. An owl hooted in the distance, causing Brax to jump, but, otherwise, the night seemed undisturbed. He lay back down, reassured by the ongoing chorus that would have ceased in the presence of movement, when he heard the voice.

"You should pay more attention to your senses, young Braxton."

He shot up, the hairs on the back of his neck bristling as he looked across the dying fire. He was about to call to the others when the visitors entered the clearing. There, standing before him, was his grandfather Tyrrideon, his hand resting gently on the mane of a beautiful white unicorn, its presence radiating a faint inner glow. His grandfather smiled, showing a familiarity that immediately put Brax at ease. He wore a pair of green pants that extended to his knees, with his calves and feet bare, and a loose-fitting cotton shirt with broad sleeves that ended at his elbows. Two small interlocking circles, one above the other, were embroidered in golden thread at the center of his otherwise plain covering.

"Grandpa Ty?" Braxton asked, scrambling to his feet.

"Yes, it's me, my boy, come to see how you're doing."

"But how . . . how is this possible?" Brax stammered. "You . . . died years ago!"

"Never mind that," his grandfather laughed. "I've come to introduce you to someone." He looked at the unicorn and gently stroked its face. Its soft white hair shimmered in the moonlight, radiating the glow Brax had noticed earlier, its silver horn a spire of brightness that parted and held back the night. He'd heard of such things in legends before and always believed they belonged to myth rather than reality. Yet now this magnificent spirit-creature stood before him, as if having stepped out of a dream and into his world.

"Her name is Serene, and it is her essence that resides in that sword you tried to use tonight. She's here to see if you're worthy of that gift."

"Gift?"

"Yes, the gift of being able to use her weapon. You see, Braxton, each spirit sword contains the essence of a spirit being, and it is that purity that keeps their Wielders balanced. They were gifts given to the first human king when the world was still young, intended to help his governing and ensure that the race of men grew up with spirit guidance—that their egos were kept in check. To use one, you must first join with the creature from which it came. Only then can you truly learn to wield it. Serene is here to see if that honor should pass to you."

"What must I do?" he asked, unsure what his grandfather meant.

"You need to let her join with you, Brax. She will look into your innermost thoughts, feel your deepest emotions, and see your greatest desires. If you prove worthy, she will pass the honor she once bestowed on me to you, and your life will never be the same."

Braxton stared at his grandfather, still not believing he was real—that he was actually talking to him—this man who'd taught him how to string a bow and skin a deer. His thoughts wandered to the times he'd spent listening to tales of his grandfather's many adventures, the places he'd traveled to, the—

"Are you ready to begin?" Tyrrideon asked, causing Braxton to jump.

Brax nodded, despite his nervousness.

The unicorn stepped closer. The flames of the campfire glowed at her approach, outlining her face. Then she appeared right inside his mind, filling his vision and blocking out all other thoughts. He reacted instinctively, pushing away with his will, trying to get her out of his consciousness. But she occupied his entire awareness, a distinctive impression he could more than see—he could *feel* throughout his body, as if she were standing completely inside of him. He shook involuntarily, unnerved by the experience, and tried to dispel the intrusion.

The image vanished.

Beloved child, came the clearest and most beautiful voice Braxton had ever heard. The unicorn stood motionless on the other side of the fire, her dark eyes focused on him. It was she who was speaking, he realized, communicating directly within his mind.

You must allow me to enter freely. I will not invade your thoughts or create this joining unwelcomed. However, without this connection, I cannot allow you to use the blade that is my extension.

"It's all right, Brax," his grandfather said. "She won't harm you, but if you do not wish it, say so now. She'll withdraw, and we'll go no further."

"No." He took a step forward. "I want to learn to use the Unicorn Blade. I need to." He hesitated. "I'm sorry. I didn't expect any of this." Taking a breath, he tried to steady himself and stop from shaking. The entire experience had been extremely unsettling. He waited a moment before closing his eyes and focusing. "I'm ready to try again."

Serene's face reappeared in his mind, but this time, he resisted his natural reaction to push her away. He allowed her to move deeper and deeper into his thoughts, opening to her presence, willing to trust in this creature. A rush of warmth filled him, making him feel strangely uplifted, as if he had the courage to take on the whole world and knew he'd win. The bruises and aches from sparring with Ruskin vanished. He felt bigger and stronger, like he'd actually grown. All thoughts and sorrow at losing his mom faded, and a feeling of absolute joy flowed through him. It was unlike anything he could have imagined, and he wanted it to stay with him forever.

They started slowly then, random thoughts and memories crossing his mind. He saw himself as a small boy playing in the kitchen, his mom cooking nearby, and with his boyhood friends, running in the fields. He remembered wrestling with Penton, learning to spar with swords, and then with his dad, practicing with his bow. The images flashed through him, each one going by a little faster than the one before, each causing an emotional reaction he sensed was being watched. He relived the attack of the Mins, seeing the face that was bent on killing him and feeling the fear it invoked. His mom appeared, lying on her makeshift bed in their little cottage, and his dad's lined face, sorrow expressed in his eyes.

An uncontrollable sadness erupted inside him, and Brax burst out crying. He regained control of his emotions, and the visions continued. He saw the Mins again, and an intense desire for revenge burned through him like an unstoppable flame. Instantly the images stopped, and his mind went completely blank. For a long time he floated, weightless, lost on an endless black sea, devoid of all sound, sight, and emotion, until warmth returned to him, slowly at first, but building steadily. He could see Serene's brilliance blocking out the void, and light entered his mind.

He stood in the fields outside Oak Haven with Phinlera next to him, holding his hand and smiling up at him. Looking at her, he felt a joy he never knew possible and laughed out loud—a rich and wondrous sound. He clung to that vision, admiring her face, seeing the way her hair was pushed behind one ear, the light catching its highlights. Her beauty. He loved Phinlera completely in that moment and felt those same feelings reflected back from her. Giving himself over to it completely, unequivocally, he wanted it to continue and never end.

Gradually, the vision began to fade, and Brax grasped at it within his mind, trying to solidify the image that was disappearing like water through his hands. When it vanished, he stood there feeling small and alone. He kept his eyes closed for several minutes, battling with his emotions, until painfully, he looked up.

Ruskin, Gavin, and Bear were still asleep. Grandpa Ty and Serene stood on the far side of the camp. The fire had been refueled somehow and burned brightly now. Braxton, however, felt cold. With the warmth of the connection to Serene gone, he felt frail and incomplete, as though the larger and better part of himself had somehow been removed. Rubbing his arms, he shivered, then looked at his grandfather, who smiled broadly.

"Congratulations, my lad," he said. "You passed."

CHAPTER

6

The sun was rising when Braxton awoke. He looked around the clearing expectantly but saw no sign of his grandfather or Serene. The fire had died out, and Gavin, Ruskin, and Bear remained asleep, the dwarf's snoring breaking the quiet of a new day. Brax lay in his bedroll wondering if he'd dreamed the whole experience of the night before, until he sensed Serene's presence within him. He recognized her immediately, watching his thoughts and actions, feeling his emotional response. Reaching out slowly, awkwardly, he connected with her, and that same euphoric sensation washed over him, bringing with it the warmth from before. She didn't say anything, and he chose not to ask any questions, understanding now the depth of their connection. He reveled in that joining, realizing for the first time since leaving home that he was no longer alone on this journey.

"Thank you," he whispered.

He got up and bathed in the stream. The cool water made him feel alive, filled with a new sense of purpose. The spring air smelled fresh with a light sweetness from the budding wildflowers growing along the banks. It invigorated his lungs, like smelling air for the first time after being locked away in some dusty cellar. He looked out across the fields. The grass was a vibrant green, and the few trees there stood like giant sentinels among the emerald sea, their branches uplifted in praise to the brilliant sapphire sky. Everything seemed clearer. Colors were intensified, and the experience itself was almost tangible, as if he could drink it in, quenching an unknown thirst.

Returning to the camp, he found Gavin and Ruskin preparing a warm breakfast. The aroma of sausages, tomatoes, and mushrooms enticed his senses. Bear trotted over to him and licked his hand, and Brax scratched the elkhound's fur. His companions seemed well-rested and even cheerful after the seemingly uneventful night, completely unaware of Brax's experience.

"With any luck, we should reach Falderon tomorrow," Ruskin said as they broke camp and set out toward the Vales.

"Promises to be a good day." Gavin looked up at the sky, his dark mood noticeably improved.

The morning passed much like the one before, with Brax and Ruskin riding together, next to Gavin, and Bear running alongside them, moving steadily east. They stopped briefly for a quick lunch before setting out again in the early afternoon. The sun was dropping when they dismounted and approached a stand of wild oaks tunneling the road.

Draw my sword, child.

Braxton jumped at the unexpected sound of Serene's voice in his mind as he walked Obsidian, causing the stallion to jolt his head and pull the reins free. Brax patted the big horse's neck. Bear growled a low guttural sound, stopping a few paces ahead of them. The hair on the back of his neck was standing upright and his head was bent low, pointed toward the oaks. Ruskin, however, continued walking.

"Rusk!" Braxton called out, drawing the Unicorn Blade from across his back.

The dwarf stopped and glanced briefly over his shoulder. Gavin, sitting atop Cinnamon and accustomed to Bear's signs, already had an arrow notched in his bow.

A dozen ragged looking men emerged from the woods, armed with an assortment of weapons. Dressed in tattered clothing, they looked as if they hadn't bathed in months, if at all.

"Damn dog, we would've surprised you lot if your mangy mutt hadn't smelled us out," the rogue closest to them said, spitting on the ground. He was a thin, ugly man of about Braxton's height, in his midthirties, with greasy black hair matted down on one side. A large sore on his cheek looked infected and oozed into the stubble on his chin. Obviously the leader of the gang, the other men crowded around him, leering and chuckling greedily.

Ruskin rolled his shoulders. "Good." He tapped Fist in his hand. "I've been needing a bit of exercise. I'm looking forward to this."

The leader's smirk dropped from his face, and the rest of the band became uneasy.

"You won't be so confident when I run this through ya," the man retorted, brandishing his sword. His men, gathering courage from their leader, moved closer.

Brax ran up to Ruskin's side. The dwarf glanced at him doubtfully but looked back at the brigands before they registered his concern.

"Get 'em, men!" the ugly bandit shouted, lurching forward. Ruskin casually stepped aside, raised his hammer to parry the leader's attack, and then swung underhand to hit another man in the groin, dropping him like a heavy sack.

Chaos erupted as the other bandits rushed in, two of them going for Braxton. Serene reacted immediately, her energy surging through him and forcing him left. In a single movement, he blocked a downward strike from a tall man, then swung his magical weapon against the full force of the other foe's sweeping strike, splitting his staff in two. Continuing around in a circle, he ended with the edge of the sword against his original opponent's neck, barely cutting into him. It all happened so quickly that Braxton was almost as surprised as his two adversaries, but he recovered his composure before the men recognized what had happened, and smiled a warning at the taller man. The brigand dropped his sword and hastily backed away.

Braxton, however, felt nauseous from the sudden rush of energy. He knew he couldn't rely on Serene to help protect him again and that he'd have to learn to fight on his own. Taking a breath to calm his stomach, he sliced through the air, feeling how light and nimble the Unicorn Blade felt now—not heavy and cumbersome like the night before.

He looked about. The bandit leader and two of his unfortunate thugs were collapsed in front of Ruskin. The dwarf had his powerful left arm wrapped around the neck of a fourth man, who, despite being slightly taller than Ruskin, was being dragged around, flailing wildly in equal attempts to cut Ruskin with a dagger and breathe. The dwarf didn't even seem to notice, and just looked around for another victim. Two other bandits lay dead, pierced by Gavin's arrows. Bear stood prone over one gang member, shaking the man's forearm, the dagger he'd held long since discarded. The thug's other hand covered a nasty gash on his face that was bleeding profusely. The remaining few brigands, surprised by the state of their group, backed away.

Ruskin went after them, the bandit at his side now completely purple in the face.

"Rusk, let them go," Brax called out.

The dwarf stopped, seemed to think about it for a moment, and then, realizing he still held the unfortunate man under his arm, gave a sudden squeeze. A sickening crack echoed across the road before Ruskin released his victim, who fell limply to the ground. The retreating men stared wide-eyed, dropped their weapons and surrendered.

It was late by the time the bandits, under the watchful eyes of the dwarf, had finished burying their dead. Brax felt sick at seeing the bodies, unaccustomed to so much death. When the men finished, Ruskin tied them into a sitting position against one of the oaks lining the road, their legs bound and their mouths gagged.

They spent the night in the brigands' camp, which they found hidden among the trees. By morning, the thieves were hungry and thirsty, and they begged for something to eat. Feeling sorry for them, Braxton and Gavin took turns feeding and watering their captives.

"We'll send a patrol for ya once we reach Falderon," Ruskin said as he checked their bindings and replaced their gags. "If you're still alive in a couple of days, you can look forward to a lifetime in the Empire's dungeons.

Assuming, of course, the wolves don't get ya first." He grinned, picked up his pack and swung it over his shoulder, then started off down the road.

Brax and Gavin glanced at each other, trying to decide if leaving the men tied up was the right thing to do. After a moment Gavin sighed, mounted Cinnamon, and headed off after the dwarf, Bear following behind him.

Braxton thought about the bandits' predicament, and whether to ungag them or at least leave them something to eat or drink. But he couldn't figure out how to let the men feed themselves without also untying them, which would undoubtedly lead to raiding farms or harassing travelers. Eventually he felt he had no choice but to keep them tied up.

"I'm sorry for the life you've chosen," he said, taking up Obsidian's reins and following after his companions. He could feel the eyes of the men boring into him and heard their muffled calls. Resisting the temptation to turn around, he hurried to catch up with the others.

"I thought you might let 'em go," Ruskin said over his shoulder when Braxton met up with them. "That would've been a mistake."

"Maybe, but tying them to those trees is as good as sentencing them to death. Wolves are bound to smell them out before long."

"You don't know that for sure. Besides, it's only a day to Falderon. If they can last through the night, they should be fine." He paused, waiting for Braxton's reaction. "Remember, lad, that only by the hardship of life's lessons will they possibly be forced to seek another way. If we allow them to make a living on travelers and farmers, they'll never change."

"I guess you're right, but it doesn't make it any easier."

"They should be all right," Gavin added, standing beside him. "I don't like it either, but what choice do we have?"

The dwarf looked at Braxton. "We have something more important to discuss. You fought well last night. Too well for someone with such little experience. Take off your shirt."

"What?" Brax asked, shocked.

"You heard me. Take it off. I want to see your chest."

"Why—what for?"

"I'm not walking into Falderon with you carrying that sword around like a banner, attracting attention from every guard or militiaman within a hundred yards. Now take it off, or I'll do it for ya." He took a threatening step forward.

"Fine." Brax felt frustrated with the dwarf. He unhooked the Unicorn Blade and dropped it to the ground, then pulled his shirt and tunic over his head, further ruffling his hair.

"Happy now?"

The dwarf stared at him. Gavin let out a low whistle.

"What?" Brax looked down at his body. In the middle of his chest, two small interconnected circles, one above the other, had been burned into his skin like welts from some branding iron. They looked exactly like the ones he'd seen on his grandfather's shirt. He stared at the mark in surprise, running his fingers over the raised edges.

"I thought as much," Ruskin commented, breaking the silence. "The Chosen Cross. The mark of a Wielder."

"A Wielder?" Gavin choked, looking at the dwarf. "How could Brax possibly be a Wielder? You must be joking."

"That sword's adopted you, my lad," Ruskin said, ignoring Gavin, "and I'm not sure whether to congratulate or pity you."

"What do you mean?"

"The life of a Wielder is like no other." Ruskin shook his head and looked down for a moment, scratching his boot in the dirt. "You have a long, hard road ahead of you, I'm afraid."

"How can Brax be a Wielder?" Gavin looked quizzically at their guide.

"It was my grandfather's sword," Brax explained, picking up the scabbard and unsheathing the Unicorn Blade. He held the weapon in front of him and ran his other hand down the side, admiring its craftsmanship. A rush of warmth flowed through him and the energy pulsated inside his body, bringing with it that radiant feeling. It vanished a moment later, leaving Brax feeling chilled by its sudden remission.

"Get dressed," Ruskin said, bringing him back to his senses. "We're going to need to find a way to hide that sword before entering Falderon, or someone's bound to recognize it. That would be a problem."

"Why's that?" He resheathed the blade.

"Anyone found carrying a spirit sword is to be taken immediately to the king, a diversion we can't afford. We need to keep this quiet and that mark of yours hidden. Don't draw the weapon in the city unless you're absolutely forced to defend yerself, and make sure you're alone when changing. Avoid the public baths as well. Oh, and no women."

Braxton flushed. He pulled his clothes back over his head and hurriedly tucked his shirt into his pants. Reslinging the Unicorn Blade, he picked up Obsidian's reins and mounted the saddle. Gavin, sitting atop Cinnamon, eyed him.

"What?" Brax asked.

"You're full of surprises today, aren't you? I hope that sword brings you good fortune," he said, extending his hand.

"Thanks, Gav." Braxton shook his friend's grip. "For now though, I just want to make it to Arbor Loren."

"Don't be surprised if things don't work out quite the way you expect them to. That's a big responsibility you carry on your back. I only wish you'd had it during the attack on the Gate. Things might have turned out differently."

Braxton realized he hadn't thought of that before. Could Serene and the Unicorn Blade have protected his mom, or saved Nenra Reed or Arren Bo? He wondered about the events of the Min assault and whether having the sword might have changed the outcome. His life had been so simple a week ago—focused on his interest in Phinlera and the joy of hunting in the nearby forests of a place he once knew. Now he seemed thrust into a larger world, a new land to which he was unaccustomed and suddenly forced to comprehend.

The ground rose steadily as they entered the foothills, changing from grasslands to rough, hilly outcroppings. The farms and homes they passed seemed abandoned. Livestock wandered around uncared for, and wolf-ravaged carcasses lay rotting in the sun. The sight and smell made it difficult to eat, but Ruskin seemed unaffected, eagerly consuming their lunch and drinking liberally from his ale skin.

When he'd finished, the dwarf pulled some furs from his pack and handed them to Brax. "Cover up that scabbard, and wrap the hilt and crossbar. Make sure to hide the unicorn insignia."

Braxton cut the furs into strips, tying overlapping bands around the handle to camouflage its identity.

Refilling their waterskins from a nearby stream, they set out again, climbing steadily upward. It was midafternoon when they finally saw Falderon perched atop a plateau in the Vale Mountains. The walled city sat at the very edge of a steep cliff overlooking a sapphire-blue lake. Colored roofs rose above the protective barricade, and the spires of a great worship hall reached upward like an appealing arm toward the sky. Two watchtowers flew the Empire's banner of a silver lion's head set upon a purple background, adjoining the double wooden gate that faced westward toward Oak Haven and the sea.

Standing on the road that meandered down from the entrance, Braxton felt a sense of relief at reaching their initial destination. Anxious now to enter the city, and eager for knowledge of how widespread the Min attack had been, they picked up their pace and headed toward the gate.

CHAPTER

7

Crossbow-armed archers stood along the stone towers and walls adjoining the closed western gates of Falderon, peering out toward the setting sun. A few looked down cautiously as Braxton and his companions approached, assessing their threat on the city.

A dozen yards away, two guards emerged from the side door at the base of one of the towers and headed toward them. Chainmail vests covered their long white shirts that extended down over leather leggings, and they wore round slightly pointed helms.

"State your names and your business," the older guard called out, planting the butt end of his spear firmly in the ground and raising his left hand, signaling for them to stop. He had brown hair jutting away from under his helm and a curly beard streaked liberally with silver. The other man stood next to him, holding a halberd with both hands.

"We're from Oak Haven, heading to Zambini's," Ruskin said casually, stopping a few feet away and giving their names. "We seek refuge for the night."

"Submit your goods for inspection." The guard moved forward, signaling for his companion to take up a defensive position in front of the gate.

Ruskin walked over to Obsidian, unhooked his pack and dropped it to the ground, unstrapping the bindings and opening the top. Following his lead, Braxton and Gavin dismounted and did the same.

The guard peered into their packs, poking at their belongings with his spear, pulling out a few clothes here and there, and generally looking the travelers up and down. Bear growled when he got too close to Gavin, and the man eyed him cautiously.

"Keep your mutt back," he snapped.

Gavin pointed to the ground, and the elkhound lay down, watching the guard as he rifled through Cinnamon's saddlebags.

After a few minutes, the man seemed satisfied and signaled to the other guard, who banged on the side of the gate with his fist. Slowly, the giant door opened just wide enough to let them through.

"Why so tight?" Ruskin asked, closing his pack.

The guard spat in the dirt. "It's those damn Mins. Attacked our Gate. We're not taking any chances."

"They hit Oak Haven a few days back. Took out their Keepers." Ruskin jerked his head toward Braxton and Gavin.

"Amberdeen and Montressa got hit as well. Appears to have been a planned assault. The king's ordered everyone into the cities, and travel is restricted now to escorted watch. You'll have to stay in Falderon until a patrol arrives—if you can find room."

Brax's heart dropped at the thought of not being able to continue quickly. He worried about reaching Arbor Glen in time and getting his mom's essence safely to her tree.

The dwarf mumbled something and picked up his pack.

"Wait," Brax called out at seeing Ruskin heading toward the gate. "What about those men we tied up?"

Rusk sighed, shook his head, and turned to the guard. "We met a band of amateurs who tried to relieve us of our goods a day's walk back. We beat 'em around a bit then tied them to that clump of trees that tunnels the road. The boy here's worried they'll become wolf grub before long and wants 'em rescued." Not waiting for a response, he glanced at Braxton. "Satisfied?" He continued toward the gate, grumbling to himself.

The guard looked amused. "We'll send a patrol in the morning to pick them up."

"Thanks," Brax said, leading Obsidian after the dwarf. Gavin smiled and patted Braxton on the back as he walked past.

Entering the city, they found it congested with travelers, farmers, and residents of every kind. Tents of various shapes, sizes, and colors—as well as lean-tos, small sheds, and other makeshift housing—had been set up to accommodate the increased population from the surrounding countryside. Small corrals along the main road held cattle, sheep, pigs, horses, goats, and other farm animals the villagers had brought. Those who couldn't afford to pen their livestock simply tied them to their tents or slept with them. People were everywhere—in the streets, alleyways, and courtyards—anywhere they could find a place to sleep. The local residents and storeowners had even converted their front porches into rooms, where groups or families huddled together with what few possessions they carried.

"We'll be lucky to find lodging," Gavin commented, as he and Brax caught up with the dwarf.

"Zambini's will have room," Ruskin replied, not bothering to stop.

They followed the dwarf down the main cobblestone road away from the gate and into a large round plaza from which three more roads fanned outward. The rotunda, like the streets, was packed with farmers, merchants, wagons, and soldiers, and the various inns and stores they passed were filled with customers buying goods or seeking accommodations. Ruskin didn't seem to pay them much heed and just pushed his way through the sea of people.

After winding through the crowds for almost an hour, they turned onto a narrower road that led to a little square on the north end of the city, stopping in front of a green two-story building with a white thatched roof. Like the other inns and taverns, this one was overflowing with visitors eager to find a bed or hot meal for the night. Above the door, a large metal symbol of a pipe and barrel was affixed to the wall below the words:

ZAMBINI'S INN AND PUBLIC HOUSE

Gavin offered to stay outside with Bear and the horses while Ruskin and Brax entered the crowded tavern. The rectangular common room had a tall, peaked ceiling, with a second story overlooking the lower floor, and a large glowing fireplace. A dark wooden counter extended opposite the entrance where people crammed together, buying food and drink. Tables, benches, cots, and chairs covered every open space, and barmaids moved about, carrying trays of frothing tankards, loaves of bread, and bowls of steaming stew, filling the inn with an enticing aroma.

Scanning the place, Ruskin convinced a couple of drunkards to give up their table by simply pulling them off their bench and leaving them lying on the ground. He waved down a barmaid and sat fidgeting until she returned with several tankards of ale. Draining three of them quickly, he called to the deeply tanned girl who'd introduced herself as Kalendra, and told her to fetch Zambini.

Braxton had just returned from delivering a drink to Gavin when a tall dark-skinned man with closely cropped, curly black hair strode over to them. A rich, collarless, blue silk shirt was buttoned to his neck, with long sleeves fitted tightly about his wrists, and tucked into leather pants. He smiled broadly upon arriving at their table, his white teeth contrasting against his skin.

"Welcome to Zambini's, my friends. How may I be of service?" he asked, surveying them closely.

Ruskin had the hood of his traveling cloak pulled up and his head bent low. "We want your best drink, your best food, and your best rooms, in that order. All on the house."

The other man's smile faltered, and, for an instant, a cunning look flashed through his eyes. Recovering quickly, his expansive smile returned and he laughed aloud.

"My friends, nothing would please me more than to satisfy your needs, but these are trying times. I can therefore offer you no more than a bowl of my best stew, some of my finest ale, and meager accommodations in our common room. All at a fair price."

"Don't try to con me, ya pirate," Ruskin said, standing up and pulling back his hood. "Your fair price is at least twice what you paid."

"Ruskin, you old scoundrel!" Zambini roared, embracing the dwarf. Separating, they clasped hands. "What brings you to Zambini's?"

"Ah, we're heading east. I'm escorting this young'un to Arbor Loren." He gestured toward Braxton.

"You going to the elves? That I never thought I'd see."

"Me neither, but I promised his father." Ruskin introduced Brax. "For now we need a room, some grub, and a few supplies, if you can spare 'em."

"I wasn't lying, my friend, when I said these are desperate times. The inn's full, but for you, I will give you a room in my own house."

"Good. I'd like to see Brennah again. There are three of us, a dog, and two horses." He sat back down and drained another ale.

Zambini sighed. Having already committed his home to the dwarf, he knew he couldn't refuse him now. "I'll find room for your horses. Bring them around back."

"Thank you, Mr. Zambini," Braxton said.

Ruskin choked on his drink. "Don't call him Mr. Zambini, or he'll get an even bigger opinion of himself." He wiped his wet beard on his sleeve. "Besides, this pirate likes my company, don't you?" Ruskin looked slyly at the man.

Zambini's smile returned. "That I do, my old friend, that I do."

They followed their host down a hallway that divided the busy kitchen on one side with several closed doors on the other, and into a packed storeroom at the rear of the inn. Without stopping, Zambini opened the back door and led them through a cobblestone courtyard enclosed by a row of stables on the left and a low wooden wall that extended around from the back of the tavern. A small, whitewashed cottage with a thatched roof sat opposite. Its painted, green door matched the inn, and a single oil lamp burned brightly above the entrance. Colorful window boxes with pink flowers were visible in the fading light, and a brick chimney emitted a spire of smoke that drifted off toward the Vales.

Zambini opened the door to his house, and let Brax and Ruskin into the modest front room. A large round table sat in its center, and a warm fireplace burned nearby. Three closed doors covered the back of the cottage, and an open hall led off to the left.

"Welcome to my home," Zambini said with a flourish as a young, slightly chunky woman with long blond hair and striking blue eyes joined them from the kitchen.

"Ruskin!" She rushed over and embraced the dwarf.

"Hello, Brennah, it's nice to see you," Rusk mumbled, engulfed in the bosom of the taller woman.

She released him and stepped back. "Come and sit down. You're staying for supper, of course?"

"Wouldn't miss it if I was within ten leagues of your kitchen." Ruskin rubbed his hands together.

An hour later, after stabling the horses, they sat around the table enjoying a delicious meal of roasted beef, potatoes, wild vegetables, and warm, freshly baked bread. Endless wine from Zambini's cellar was complemented equally by the bountiful quantities of food from Brennah's kitchen. It was an outstanding meal, and Braxton ate more than he had since leaving Oak Haven. Gavin generously complimented their hosts as well, and even Bear seemed content, falling asleep in front of the fire.

Zambini's twin four-year-old boys, Kudu and Bendwhalie, had joined them too. Both had their dad's curly hair but with lighter brown skin from their mother's influence. Kudu had deep green eyes, while Ben had inherited his mom's startling blue color. They were a constant source of motion—wrestling, running, or playing around the house, each trying to outdo the other. Ben appeared stronger, but Kudu seemed quicker, easily escaping and taunting his brother.

Hours later, Braxton lay in the warm embrace of Brennah's hand-knitted blankets on a soft, comfortable mattress, watching the night's shadows spread across the whitewashed wall. A bright moon shone over the floor, highlighting Bear's intermingling fur as he lay asleep on the rug between the two beds. Gavin's light snoring sounded from the other side of the room, and Brax smiled at the ease with which his friend found sleep, despite recent events.

Sleep that continued to evade him.

His mind was a turmoil of thoughts and fears, challenging his strength and resolve, questioning his ability to see his mom's essence safely to Arbor Loren. It teased his false sense of courage gained from touching the energy in the Unicorn Blade, telling him it was a passing whim, a chanced occurrence, a fleeting event. That he was overstating his capabilities. He called out to Serene, seeking her calm reassurance. But there was no answer, and the resounding quiet only refueled his doubts. Frustrated, he thought of Phinlera, and wondered if she was safe. He knew she could defend herself. Her father had been the Captain of the Guard back home and had taught her how to fight with a sword and bow from when she was very young—before he left on a military campaign and never returned. Still, Brax worried about her safety, and being away with Penton, even though he knew his brother was helping. Eventually, hours past midnight, he fell into a restless sleep of false securities and endless hopes, the light of his many desires always seemingly just out of reach.

CHAPTER

8

Braxton woke to the sound of rain splattering against the window. He got up, dressed quickly, and tidied up his bed, as Gavin had obviously done before leaving sometime earlier. Wandering into the front room of Zambini's cottage, he found it deserted. The fire was burnt out and the pale light of a cloud-filled morning filtered in through the windows.

Brennah emerged from the kitchen, carrying a bowl of steaming oats and a plate of warm muffins. "I thought you could use a hot breakfast," she said kindly. "Did you sleep well?"

"Yes, thanks." He seated himself at the table. "I'm sorry I'm so late. I must have overslept. When did the others leave?"

"Not to worry, dear. The men left at first light, and your young friend departed shortly afterward. Said he was going to look for supplies, so I don't expect you'll see him anytime soon."

Brennah sat opposite Brax, enjoying a muffin as he consumed the oats. Kudu and Bendwhalie came running in and started wrestling on the floor. Brax smiled at them, remembering how he and Penton used to do the same when they were young.

"Your boys never stop moving, do they?"

"They're a handful, all right." She watched fondly as her two children rolled around on the large woolen rug in front of the fireplace. "You might enjoy a hot bath in the inn," Brennah suggested, looking up at Braxton as she cleared his plate and headed back to the kitchen. "Zambini just refilled it with clean water this morning, and I believe the fire's still hot."

"That sounds wonderful. Where is it?"

"Oh, just go in through the back door. It's on your left. You can't miss it."

A half hour later, Braxton relaxed in the hot, soothing waters of the bath. The room was about twice the size of the bedroom he and Gavin shared, with a stone floor tilting gradually toward an inlaid drain opposite the door. The large four-foot-deep barrel in which he soaked could easily have seated a half-dozen people. Resting atop curved metal legs, it was raised above the hot coals of a recessed fire pit.

Braxton felt his muscles relax and the tension in his arms and shoulders evaporate. The steam clouding the room filled his lungs, creating a warm, drowsy sensation despite his recent sleep. He was just standing to reach for the soap from a nearby cupboard when the door opened, and in walked the barmaid Kalendra, a pile of fresh towels in her arms. For a moment they both froze, looking at each other. The girl's eyes dropped down his body, and Braxton scrambled to grab the remaining towel from the cupboard and wrap it around his waist.

Kalendra, an attractive girl of about Penton's age with shoulder-length brown hair and dark green eyes, smiled as he desperately tried to cover himself.

"I thought you might need these," she said, breaking the awkward silence. "But I see you're . . . pretty well-stocked already." Her eyes ran over him, and a bemused smile crossed her face. Then a slightly inquisitive frown creased her brow, and Braxton realized she was staring at his chest. He looked down at the Chosen Cross. His heart dropped, remembering Ruskin's warning. Desperately trying to find something to cover the mark, but seeing his clothes out of reach, he grabbed the bottom end of the towel that had been floating in the water and pulled it up. Realizing then that he was exposing himself, he dropped down quickly, making a loud splash and spilling water onto the floor.

Kalendra stifled a laugh, walked over to the cupboard and put the towels on the shelf. She returned to the doorway and stopped to look back at him. "See you later," she said with a wink, then quietly closed the door behind her.

Braxton chided himself for being so careless. He climbed out of the tub and dressed quickly, dampening his clothes with his still-wet body. Hurrying back to the cottage, he avoided Brennah and spent most of the day in his room, pacing back and forth, trying to determine what to do. Maybe Kalendra hadn't recognized the rings. Perhaps she thought them to be burns in his skin, or the result of an accident, or some strange birthmark. But ultimately he kept coming back to the same conclusion. What if she recognized them for what they were? What if she understood?

Frustrated, he forced himself outside and walked around the courtyard. He visited the horses, brushed them down, and added bedding to their stalls. Finally, accepting that what had happened couldn't be undone, he refilled Obsidian and Cinnamon's haynets and returned to his room.

Gavin was there, tired from his long day. "The Min attack was much more widespread than we thought," he said when Brax entered. "Every town with a Gate as far down as Dynekee was hit, and all at the same time too. Whoever was behind this was certainly well-organized. The Empire's on full alert now, and the king's got patrols out searching every farm, glen, and nook for the Mins."

"That's going to make it hard for us to get to Almon-Sen." Brax dropped down on his bed, despondent.

"No word yet on whether the Mins hit the elves," Gavin went on. "Apparently there's been no communication with them since the Gates closed, but it may be too early to tell, now that all messengers are by horseback."

Brax nodded, his hopes lifting a bit. With luck, maybe they could still make it to Arbor Loren in time. He kicked off his boots and lay down, thinking about the journey ahead. They still needed to get to the elven forest, gain passage to Arbor Glen, and find this Bendarren, all in the same time it had taken them just to reach Falderon.

A wave of panic washed over him as he worried they weren't going to make it. Clutching at his mom's pendant, he shut his eyes tightly.

I am with her, child. Make the journey.

Braxton jumped at Serene's voice, dispelling his dark thoughts. Hearing her in his mind brought an immense peace, but knowing she was helping his mom provided an even greater comfort.

"Thank you," he muttered.

"What?" Gavin looked up from the supplies spread out on the floor.

"Nothing." Brax wiped his face and got up. "Let's get something to eat."

They returned to the tavern and found a table near the fireplace to enjoy their supper. Kalendra came over as soon as she saw them, smiling at Brax.

"Nice to see you again," she said, looking him up and down with a sly wink. Gavin eyed them suspiciously but didn't say anything. He ordered the evening meal and a couple of ales.

"What was all that about?" he asked once she'd left.

"Nothing." Brax glanced about, but then seeing his friend staring at him, admitted to his encounter with the barmaid. Gavin roared with laughter at the embarrassing tale, and Braxton felt himself flush.

"Seriously, though, Brax, you need to be more careful. You don't want to end up in Amberdeen."

"I know, I know. I just got careless. It was all so unexpected. I'm not used to anyone paying me attention. It won't happen again, I can assure you."

They were finishing their meal a half hour later when Zambini strode over.

"Hello, my friends," he said with a broad smile. "How'd you enjoy the evening's fare?"

"Excellent as before." Brax cleaned his plate with the last of their bread, and Gavin nodded, his mouth full.

"I've been meaning to ask you." Brax finished chewing. "How do you know Ruskin so well?"

"Oh, we've known each other a long time," Zambini replied, avoiding the question.

"How'd you meet?" Gavin pressed.

Zambini's smile faded. He looked at them for a moment then scanned the room. "It was on a merchant's ship off the southern coast of Andorah," he said, sitting down and pouring himself a drink. "I was no older than you are now." He nodded at Brax. "Understand, my friends, that I was sold by the Hunters when I was very young, and life as a ship's slave was all I knew. It was how I thought life was supposed to be—at least until I met our dwarf friend.

"The slavers had just taken on a new load of captives from Kharnus and were several days south of the city when this frenzied little man, and two others like him, appeared on deck. He looked like an escaped slave himself, all in rags with a dirt-smeared face and long hair and beard that were knotted and unkempt. They'd snuck aboard in port, hiding themselves without food or water for three days in the lower hull. How they survived, I still do not know."

Zambini shook his head. "They attacked the slavers and their shipmates with a ferocity I'd never seen before nor since. Three of them taking on seventeen hardened sailors, each warriors in their own right. Men whom I'd seen fight before. But this one little man—the one the others called the Badger—fought relentlessly. Like a maddened dog!" Their host grinned. "It was the first time I'd ever seen a dwarf in battle, and I was shocked at the ferocity with which he attacked those men. When they'd finished, none of the slavers were alive. But one of Ruskin's companions had been killed too. The dead sailors they simply tossed overboard, but their fallen comrade they carefully wrapped in the captain's finest sheets and buried him at sea.

"I had fought against the dwarves myself, thinking them to be just another band of pirates raiding our ship's supplies. But Ruskin, my friends, hit me on the head with the side of his hand as if swatting a gnat on the wall, and I dropped to the deck unawares. When I awoke, he and his companion had freed all the slaves, and Ruskin was questioning them thoroughly.

"Later I learned he'd been a scout from the Dragon's Spine. He'd led a party of a dozen young dwarves on their first expedition across the Valley of Wind, from Dûrak-Thûhn to Lake Shore. They were unfortunate to have encountered a large caravan of Hunters who, despite losing many men to this Badger, had captured the young ones and taken them as slaves to be sold in Kharnus, leaving Ruskin for dead. He tracked them all the way to the coastal city. And from what I understood, he single-handedly sought out and killed every one of those Hunters. Unfortunately, he discovered that the younger dwarves had already been sold to numerous merchant slave ships like mine."

Zambini stopped and took a drink from his cup, then refilled it slowly. Gavin and Braxton waited impatiently, eager for him to continue.

"Well, my friends, for the next fourteen months, Ruskin sailed our ship, the *Sea Nymph*, all around the Endless Sea and to the Great Ocean, searching for the young ones he'd lost. The slaves he rescued became his crew, and I became first mate. He treated me better than anyone had before, even giving me a room and some possessions to call my own. And he paid me, and the others, with the money we took from the coffers of the ships we sank, keeping none for himself. Ruskin wasn't there for riches but relentlessly searched for every young dwarf he'd lost. He left a trail of burning ships and dead bodies in his wake. All were saved . . . except one. A dwarf boy, the youngest of their original group, died of scurvy, a terrible and painful death."

Zambini shook his head, pausing for a moment. "This one he lost, the one he always referred to as Pup, was Ruskin's only son." He stopped to let the weight of his words sink in, taking another drink.

"Losing him was a terrible blow to our dwarven friend, and Ruskin howled with grief. He almost tore the ship apart with his bare hands." Their host smiled wryly, remembering the scene. "Eventually we sailed to Dynekee, where he burned the *Sea Nymph*, the only home I'd ever known, and set us free upon the land. Me he took with him, along with the dwarves he'd rescued, and brought us here to Falderon. He left me in the care of a human family he knew, while he returned his brethren to the Spine. Then he disappeared for many years. Eventually he started showing up again to check in on me. I think in his mind he adopted me as a replacement for the son he'd lost. For his Pup."

Their host looked around proudly. "Years later, I opened this inn. I wanted to share the profits with Ruskin, but he wouldn't have it. Occasionally now he stops by, and I always help him in whatever way I can. I owe him my life, my friends." Zambini looked serious for the first time. "Everything I have, all that I've gained, is thanks to that Badger. You are fortunate to have him with you."

CHAPTER

9

The following morning Brax paced around their room, waiting for Gavin to get dressed. He worried about the number of days that had passed and whether they'd make it to the elves in time, despite Serene's reassurance that she was helping his mom.

They'd gone to bed late the night before, talking about Ruskin's past and what it must have been like to have lost his only son. Brax could hear the agony in his friend's voice when Gavin compared it to losing his mother— lying there in the darkness of their little room—and hoped he wouldn't have to share in that pain.

They had just started breakfast with Brennah and her boys when Ruskin returned, thumping in heavily from the misty courtyard. Standing in the doorway, he shook the rain off his matted hair and long beard, sending flicks of water flying in every direction. Zambini was with him, and they joined the others at the table as Brennah hurried off into the kitchen to fetch something for the dwarf to eat.

"The town's locked up tight," Ruskin reported, draining a morning tankard of Zambini's ale and talking now through a mouthful of sausages. "I was able to get myself outside the gate to take a look 'round, but there's no way the three of us slip by on horseback, or on foot for that matter."

"We have to," Brax said, anxious to continue their journey. "I need to get to Arbor Loren. I can't wait for a patrol to arrive."

"We won't make it a hundred yards." Ruskin took another drink. "There are guards everywhere and groups of bandits raiding the farms beyond, fighting among themselves over pillaging the better homes. Worse yet, those damn Hunters are about, taking advantage of unfortunate folk. I hate those slavers." He shook his head, muttering something into his beard.

"You got out." Brax stared at the dwarf, annoyed that he was unwilling to try.

Ruskin leaned closer. "That's because dwarves have an affinity with the mountains and know how to disappear among 'em. You, lad, will stand out."

"I don't care. I have to try."

"And get caught." Ruskin shook his head. "A lot of good that'll do your mom."

"He's right, Brax." Gavin put a hand on his shoulder. "We should wait for a patrol."

"I don't have time to wait." Brax stood up, knocking over his chair. "My mom is dying!"

Ruskin looked at him. "You can't help her if you're in prison or in Amberdeen."

Zambini frowned, but didn't say anything.

Brax paced the room, weighing up his chances of getting past the guards, the bandits, and the Hunters. Even with Serene's help, he knew he'd never make it alone. Reluctantly, he looked back at the dwarf and nodded.

Ruskin glanced at Zambini. "See if you can find out when the next patrol's coming. I'm off to bed." He got up and disappeared into Brax's room. A moment later, they could hear him snoring.

Brennah walked over and quietly shut the door before returning to clear the table. Zambini finished the rest of his drink, kissed his wife, and headed back to the inn.

Seeing the rain had stopped, Gavin suggested they take advantage of the clearing weather to find some additional supplies. Brax knew his friend was trying to help by distracting him. He took a deep breath and agreed.

He found it helpful to be outside, wandering among the many local stores and numerous makeshift bazaars that filled the streets and plazas of the crowded city. The cool air cleared his mind and calmed his nerves, helping him to relax. Bear followed behind them, weaving his way between villagers and occasionally startling them as he brushed up against their legs.

It was late afternoon when they returned, depositing their few purchases at the cottage before heading to the inn for something to eat. Gavin sent Bear to the stables, and the elkhound happily ambled off to find his favorite napping place on the hay in Cinnamon's stall.

As nightfall approached, the rain started up again and Ruskin entered the rear of the tavern.

"Zambini tells me a patrol's expected tomorrow," he said, passing by Brax carrying a heavy crate up from the cellar, and not bothering to stop. "I'm going for a drink."

"That's great news!" Brax's spirits lifted at the thought of finally being able to leave. He put down the load they'd been helping Zambini move for the past few hours and followed the dwarf to the common room, calling for Gavin to join them.

Finding a table near the entrance, they sat talking about the patrol's expected arrival. The main hall of Zambini's was overflowing with visitors seeking an evening meal or liquid relief from their misfortunes brought on by the Min attack, aggravated further now by the arrival of the late-spring rains. Braxton's muscles hurt from the strenuous work he'd done. He rubbed his shoulders, stopping to enjoy a small mug of trill—a local mixture of wild berries, cream, and locally brewed ale.

Kalendra brought their dinner, and Brax hungrily consumed the meal, listening to Ruskin and Gavin discussing their travel plans, when Zambini came over.

"Good evening, my friends," he said loudly. "How's the supper tonight?"

"Suitable," Ruskin grunted, indicating for him to sit.

Braxton slid over to make room, and Zambini sat beside him, pouring himself a drink. He took a long swallow, surveying their surroundings, then added quietly, "If my people are correct—"

"You mean your spies," Ruskin corrected.

Zambini grinned. "The patrol should arrive by midday tomorrow.

They're bringing much-needed supplies to Falderon, along with a group of travelers from Amberdeen and the neighboring farmlands—those caught away from their homes during these unfortunate attacks."

"How long will they rest before going south?" Ruskin pressed, his mouth full.

"No more than a single night; they should depart the following morning. But my friends, you'll need to gain permission from the patrol's captain to join them, as many will want to go. Priority will be given to those citizens stranded away from their homes and to merchants transporting food and drink. Travelers will be the least welcome."

"That could be a problem for us," Gavin said. "When will the next patrol arrive?"

"Not for another two weeks, I'm afraid. Travel is very much restricted now." Zambini looked worried. "This could be bad for the inn's business."

Ruskin eyed him slyly. "It's a good thing your stores and cellar were stocked full before the attack. How is it again that you happened to be so well-prepared?" He leaned forward emphasizing his point.

Zambini bent back. "My old friend, you wound me. Fortune smiled upon Zambini. I chanced upon a wagonload of goods at slightly below merchant costs a few days before these unfortunate events began. I simply could not pass it up." He smiled, raising his hands.

"Goods that you're now selling at triple normal prices to your own townsfolk." Ruskin jerked his head toward the inn's guests.

"I'm only doing what's naturally good for business. It would be a shame for me to not enjoy some small profit from my good fortune. And I assure you, I'm only charging the absolute minimum to provide for my family."

"Where will the patrol go once it leaves Falderon?" Braxton interjected.

Zambini turned toward him, still smiling from his exchange with the dwarf. "This one will go to Dynekee, stopping a few days in each town before returning to Amberdeen. It is most unfortunate, my friends, but you'll not be allowed to leave the column before the next town. I do not know how you're going to travel east."

"We first need to join them," Gavin clarified. "We'll then figure out how to leave them. Any ideas?"

"I've taken care of that for you." Their host reached into his doublet pocket and produced a small folded parchment. "These are papers identifying you as merchants traveling to Montressa." He handed them to Ruskin. "They should pass the captain's eye."

"Thank you," Braxton replied. "You've been so very helpful and generous. I only wish I could repay your kindness."

Ruskin rolled his eyes. "Oh please, don't play into this old pirate's feigned sympathy. Besides, he owes me one, don't you, Zambini?"

"That I do my friend. But all the same, it's a pleasure to help those in need. Now, I must get back to my other guests." He got up, smiled at them, then walked over to a nearby table and started up a conversation.

"Well, that was nice of him." Gavin turned to Ruskin. "What do the papers say?"

The dwarf unfolded the parchment and began reading, mumbling to himself, his chin buried in his beard.

Braxton rubbed his aching muscles. He glanced around the warm, smoky, and very noisy room, seeing Zambini's guests enjoying the fruits of his well-timed purchase. Sleep tugged at him, and after a few minutes of fighting the feeling, he began to drift.

The presence of someone leaning right over him suddenly brought Brax fully awake, alerting his senses, and a cold, almost spiteful shiver ran down his spine. Startled by the intrusive sensation, he looked back, expecting to find someone standing right behind him. But there was no one there.

"You all right?" Gavin asked.

"Yeah, I . . . I'm just tired." But he continued to search the room.

In your mind, Serene said, surprising him. The high-pitched ringing returned to his ears as all other sounds faded away.

What? What's in my mind? Then he felt it, the sensation of being watched, and that same cold feeling invaded his consciousness.

Someone is entering your thoughts, Serene said calmly. *Take a breath and quiet your mind, child. I will hold them.*

Braxton's mind raced at the idea of another person entering his thoughts. But he closed his eyes and took a deep breath, smelling the scent of the crowded room, exhaling fully, and trying to calm his emotions.

Focus on awakening the spirit magic. Summon it to your call. Feel it radiate throughout your body.

Not quite understanding what she meant, Brax tried remembering what it felt like to connect with Serene, calling the energy to him, willing it to return. It responded, pulsating inside of him and spreading out to fill his body, bringing with it that same uplifting feeling. Then he felt it, a foreign presence on the right side of his awareness—as though someone, or something, were pressing just behind his ear. Panicking, he pushed at it with his will, trying to force it away. Instantly the energy faded and the pressure on his head intensified. They were getting through.

CHAPTER
10

*C*alm yourself, child, Serene said. *I will not let them harm you, but you must focus your mind. Do not allow fear to take hold, or it will weaken you.*

Braxton took another breath, trying to banish his fear, giving himself over completely to the energy.

Good, Serene encouraged. *Now see yourself within a great sphere of light, like that of your midday sun, and join it with the energy.*

He concentrated as best he could, envisioning himself standing in a ball of brilliant sunlight, engulfed in its radiance, remembering what it felt like to have the sun's warmth on his face. He could sense Serene moving in closer and focused on combining the energy and the light together. Then his mind illuminated, as though a great and vibrant beacon had been lit, and his thoughts became clear and calm. A flowing energy band was attached to the right side of his head, like a small, transparent tube, connected to his consciousness, moving back and forth in a rhythmic motion caught in a magical wind.

Take hold of that band, child, and push the light deep into its opening.

Following her guidance, he sent the energy toward the tendril, imagining a great hand reaching out to grab the rope-like connection, its grip clamping down upon it. A sudden and forceful pull came back in response. The presence on the other side was trying to pull free.

Do not let go, child. Send the light into the connection.

Excited now, Brax sent the combined light and energy into the opening, a feeling of exhilaration rushing through him. The struggle from the opposite end intensified, but he continued extending the brightness farther and farther into the connection. Slowly, he started moving toward it, being drawn into the enlarging tendril, and he felt himself begin to leave his body.

Serene, help me! he called out frantically, holding onto the edges of the growing energy tunnel that he could see now clearly in his mind, not wanting to get pulled in.

I am here, she said. *Go with the light, child. I am with you.*

Her voice calmed his fear. He held on for a moment longer, then let go, giving himself over to the pulling sensation that was drawing him into this strange connection, trusting completely in Serene. He floated around the room, above the people in the tavern, weightless and detached. Blurry images of the inn's patrons drifted by, as though Braxton were looking at them through water or distorted glass, all the while moving farther down the energy tube.

It ended as quickly as it had started. He stood in a circular room made of smooth stone walls, the opening to the tunnel from which he'd just emerged behind him, large enough now for someone to stand in, but still of the same flowing energy. Unsure what to do, he looked around. His end was filled with the brightness from the light he'd created, and it warmed and comforted him, boosting his confidence. It stopped, however, at the center of the chamber, where a deep, dense blackness hid the rest of the room. It seemed unnatural, this dark, like some unimaginable void that prevented the light from extending.

"Send the light into the darkness," he heard Serene say out loud. Turning, he saw her standing there.

"Serene!" He rushed over and wrapped his arms around her long, graceful white neck.

She moved her head up and down, allowing him to enjoy the warmth of her presence. "Send the light into the darkness, child," she repeated.

He stared at her blankly. "What is this place? What's happening?"

"You will see in a moment, but you must do as I say. There is danger here. Send the light into the blackness, and banish its presence."

Concentrating as best he could, he summoned the energy into a great ball, combining it with the light. Taking a moment to ensure the two were inseparably joined, he turned toward the middle of the room and pushed outward. A burst of visible light flowed from within him, extending into the room and dispersing the void. There, standing before him, was a man, previously hidden by the darkness. Taller than Braxton, he was well-groomed, in his midthirties, with straight black hair and a closely cut beard and mustache that covered his chin, connecting at the corners of his mouth. He looked slightly nervous as he stared at Braxton, apparently unaware of Serene's presence.

"Well, you're younger than I'd thought," he said, in a deep, calm voice. Then, before Brax could respond, he moved his arm in an arcing motion, and the darkness enveloped him again, like a black curtain falling between them.

Instinctively, Braxton sent out the light, peeling back the dark cover like a wind whipping clothes up on a line. But this time, the man was ready for him and he pulled back his covering, hiding himself once more. For a few moments, they engaged back and forth in a mental battle, one trying to illuminate the darkness, the other trying to hide within it.

"Focus your mind, child. You are stronger than him," Serene said.

Stopping, he felt his opponent's sense of success as the dark lay between them. Braxton pulled from deep within himself, summoning the energy and light back in a great rush of combined spirit magic. And it came. Stronger and with a renewed sense of purpose. Focusing on its blending, he took a slow, deep breath and calmly released it, concentrating more on illuminating the room than trying to disperse the dark. Instantly the blackness vanished, and the entire room was bathed in the brilliant light of the magical energy. The man on the other side, stripped of his cover, looked very nervous. He turned left, then right, his small, dark eyes looking for a place to hide or a corner of the room from which to draw his veil. But there were none. The light was complete. Realizing he was beaten, he stopped and looked at Braxton.

An image appeared to the man's left, as though the right wall of their room had become partially transparent and Brax was looking through it into a dark dungeon. The man moved about anxiously, and Braxton could feel him tugging at his mind, attempting to get free, trying to break their connection.

The dungeon-like picture became clearer, and this same man was standing in a cell in front of the barmaid Kalendra. She was kneeling on the stone floor, her dress torn, her right shoulder exposed. Crying. Her long hair hung loosely down and across the side of her face.

"Tell me about the boy!" the man yelled, smacking her with the back of his hand.

Slowly she looked up, and through sobs of pain and fear, retold of the previous day's event. How she'd walked in on Brax taking a bath at Zambini's and had seen his naked chest and the two interlocking circles.

When she'd finished, the man stared at her, then walked over to the door of the cell, stopping by another much bigger man.

"When you're finished with her," he said quietly, "kill her." The big man smiled an evil grin, exposing awful yellowed teeth. The well-groomed man glanced back at Kalendra before exiting the prison, closing the door behind him. He stood there for a minute, deep in thought, then turned and walked down a short hallway to a flight of stairs. Ascending rapidly, he emerged through a concealed door behind an enormous barrel in a wine cellar. Making sure he was alone, he left the room and entered the cathedral. He crossed the main worship hall, stepping over some commoners sleeping on the floor and shaking his head in disgust, before ascending another flight of steps to a small library. There he seated himself behind an elaborately carved wooden desk, laid out some parchment, and wrote:

Your Grace,

I may have discovered a Wielder, hidden in a farm boy come out of the west! He arrived in Falderon two days back.

Will report once confirmed.

Your faithful servant,
Zacharias

Pouring hot wax from a nearby candle onto the parchment next to his name, he took the ring off his right hand and pressed it into the wax. He let it dry for a moment, rolled up the parchment, and left the room.

The image suddenly disappeared as Zacharias pulled against their connection with such force that Braxton stumbled forward. Zacharias dropped to his knees, his face down. When he looked up, Brax could see blood streaming from Zacharias' nose and the corners of his mouth, leaking into his beard.

The ground began to shake.

"Time to go, child," Serene said, and Braxton felt himself being pulled back toward the tunnel's opening.

"Wait, I have to save Kalendra!" He turned toward Zacharias.

"No, child," came Serene's stern reply. "You must go, now. You cannot save her here, but there is another way."

A moment later he was in the tunnel, floating around Zambini's inn. He emerged back in his body, the tendril detaching and disappearing.

Braxton opened his eyes, lifting his head from the table, seemingly having fallen asleep.

"Finally awake, are we?" Ruskin commented.

He stood up, ignoring the dwarf, and looked around. His head spun from the motion. A man stumbled toward the door, blood pouring from his nose and mouth. Brax rushed to cut him off, but Zacharias shoved a young barmaid into him. They crashed backward over a nearby table, ale and stew spilling everywhere. When Braxton looked up, Zacharias was gone.

CHAPTER

11

Shaken by the experience at the inn, Braxton left Zambini's as soon as he'd cleaned himself off and felt it possible to get away without attracting too much more attention. He knew the others would follow, knowing they couldn't discuss the experience in the crowded tavern. He crossed the courtyard to the cottage and paced back and forth in his little room.

Who was that man? he asked Serene.

Someone who has lost his way, came her quiet reply.

Tell me more; I want to know where he is.

The one you call Zambini can tell you of him. For now, calm your mind and clear your energy of the experience.

Not quite sure what she meant, he took a deep breath and filled himself with the vision of the light he'd summoned. He washed his face in a basin of cool water Brennah had set up on the nightstand, and then reached out again.

What was that image I saw?

A recent memory, Serene answered. *You entered his mind, child, and in so doing saw the thoughts closest to his consciousness. Ones he had recently experienced or considered. In this case, of events earlier in your day.*

And Kalendra, where is she now? How can I help save her?

It will be all right, child. Tell the others of your experience, but do not reveal me, for they know not of our connection, and you should keep my presence quiet for now. Be guarded, beloved one, and keep the sword that is my extension close, for he will come for you again, this one who has lost his way.

She stepped back from him then and wouldn't respond to any more of his questions. Braxton returned to pacing, playing over and over in his mind all that had occurred, focusing on every detail, trying to understand what it all meant. He felt a wave of excitement at realizing he'd stood his ground against Zacharias, defeating his attempts to hide in the veiled darkness. The wondrous energy still flowed through him. *How far could the spirit magic be extended*, he wondered, and what other experiences awaited him? Panicking, he realized Ruskin was right. For better or worse, he'd stepped onto a much larger path, into events he didn't understand and couldn't explain, and he knew it was changing him.

Gavin knocked and opened the door.

"They want to talk to you," he said.

They returned to the main room of the cottage. Ruskin sat by the fire lighting his pipe. Bear was curled up asleep on the rug, and Zambini stood at the hearth, his hand on the mantel.

Brennah got up from the table as they entered. "Can I get you something, dear?" She handed Kudu the small basket of skins they were working on.

"Some water, if you have it." Braxton sat opposite the dwarf and Gavin joined Bendwhalie threading beads near his brother.

Ruskin puffed a few times on his pipe, watching Brax intently. "What happened at the inn?" he asked. "And don't leave anything out." He eyed him suspiciously.

Brax took a long drink from the cup Brennah handed him. The cool water quenched his parched throat and cleared his mind. Then, slowly, he began retelling the event with Zacharias, saying that he must have used dark magic to enter Brax's thoughts. He skipped over mentioning the energy tube and his own use of the spirit magic, focusing on seeing Zacharias' memory, careful not to disclose his connection with Serene. He stopped to take another drink and to monitor their reactions, giving himself pause before continuing. The others listened quietly, allowing him to retell the full experience uninterrupted. When he finished, nobody spoke.

"I know this one," Zambini said, breaking the silence and walking over to sit by his wife. "I met him once, many years back. He is, I am sure, the captain of the Scarlet Brotherhood here in Falderon."

"Who are they?" Gavin asked.

"A spy network with military ties, which I've long suspected serves the bishop. Now it's confirmed." He shook his head sadly.

"Why would the bishop have a secret spy or military network?" Braxton looked at Zambini and then at the dwarf. "And what's that got to do with me?"

"Understand, my friends, that the bishop is a powerful man. He is the direct spiritual advisor to the king and overseer of all the worship halls throughout the Empire. While he openly supports the Wielders"—Braxton looked down at that moment to avoid Zambini's gaze—"he secretly works to usurp their power. The King's Squires, like the bishop, answer to no one but the king, and that threatens the bishop's power. They alone have the authority to challenge him on spiritual matters. The king is young and easily swayed. Without the Wielders to guide him, the bishop would have ultimate control over our ruler and thus the Empire itself."

Zambini got up and poured himself a drink from the decanter next to Ruskin, who'd been quietly making little smoke rings float to the ceiling.

"Which brings us to Zacharias' note," their host continued shrewdly. "Why would he think our young friend here is a Wielder?" he asked of no one in particular, taking a sip from his cup.

"Because he is." Ruskin stated.

Nobody spoke as Zambini looked first at Ruskin, then at Braxton, his eyes focused, masking his thoughts.

Be careful, child, do not underestimate this one, Serene said quietly.

"Show him your chest." Ruskin waved a hand casually toward Brax.

Is that all right? he asked Serene, grateful for her presence.

It is too late now; you have no choice but to trust him. He is a good man with much heart, but he may find a way to profit from this knowledge.

Brax watched Zambini. Their host's face was completely blank, hiding his emotions, calmly sipping at his drink. Only his eyes told Braxton he was in the presence of a masterful negotiator—one whose mind never stopped thinking or calculating.

He got up, lifted his shirt and revealed the Chosen Cross.

"Oh, you poor dear!" Brennah exclaimed, causing Braxton to jump. She crossed the room, put her arms around him, and drew him close. He remembered how his mother used to embrace him that same way. Closing his eyes, he stood there in Brennah's arms, her maternal scent filling his senses. Then slowly, he reciprocated the embrace, burying his face deep into her shoulder, accepting her surrogate affection. When he pulled away, he looked back at Zambini.

Their dark-skinned host, with whom he'd now entrusted his life, eyed him before turning to Ruskin. "As much as I learn about you, my old friend, you always manage to surprise me every time you visit." He smiled at the dwarf. Then he faced Braxton and inclined his head. "It is an honor to serve you."

Ruskin choked on his drink. "You're not getting all soft on me, are you, Zambini? I thought I'd taught you better than that."

Brax stared at them. "What about Kalendra? Can you help her?"

Zambini's smile dropped. "This is another surprise to me." He shook his head and sat at the table. "How is it that she knew you were a Wielder?"

Braxton quickly retold of the incident in the bath, downplaying the details to avoid any embarrassment. "I didn't think she'd know what it meant. I was obviously wrong."

"She must've been feeding information to the Brotherhood about the goings-on at the inn," Zambini said. "I took her into my service three years ago because I knew her mother years back. I must admit, I never expected her to betray me." A deep furrow creased his brow, and a look of disappointment flashed through his eyes. Braxton realized that he was hurt as much by Kalendra's ability to fool him as he was by her spying on the inn.

Brennah glanced at her husband. "Don't be too hard on her, dear. You don't know the full circumstances under which she revealed this information. Perhaps it would be best to find her before making any more assumptions."

"Good advice," Ruskin said.

Zambini nodded, but his face still showed deep thought on the matter, and Brax could tell the barmaid's betrayal ran deeper than he let on.

Gavin stood up. "I'm willing to help rescue her if needed."

"Me too," Brax added.

"No, you won't." Ruskin looked at Brax. "You're staying put. I don't want you leaving the inn, or the cottage, for that matter."

"I'll see what I can find out tonight," Zambini commented. "If she's not already dead"—he looked at the others—"we may be able to help her."

CHAPTER

12

On the morning of their third day in Falderon, Braxton woke early yet again, worried about Kalendra and anticipating the patrol's arrival that would allow them to continue on their journey. He pulled on his boots and quietly strapped the Unicorn Blade to his back, hoping not to wake Gavin. Bear stretched and padded over to him. Brax rubbed the elkhound's ears, glad to have him with them.

He left the cottage as the sun was rising, a gray glow burning through the mist that had settled in on the city. Barely able to see more than a dozen feet ahead of him, he crossed the courtyard to the inn. The moist fog seeped into his clothing, causing Brax to shiver in the cool morning air. Ascending the back stairs, he passed through the doorway and down the hall into the common room. The main area of Zambini's was unusually quiet, most of the patrons still asleep on their makeshift cots brought in after dinner. Brax found a secluded spot near the fireplace and stoked the embers into a low flame that cast a dim light across the room. Locating the cook, he returned a few minutes later with a warm breakfast and a small mug of trill.

As the inn's guests started to rise, and the hall began filling with visitors and regulars alike, Brax headed back out toward the cottage. The rain had started up again, coming down in sheets. He bent his head low and scrunched his shoulders, preparing to dash across the seemingly distant courtyard in hopes of avoiding being drenched by the sudden downpour.

He'd just left the porch when Serene's warning echoed in his mind.

Draw my sword, child!

Stopping, he slid on the cobblestones, ignoring the pelting rain and reached for the blade, unable to see beyond a few feet ahead of him. He'd barely pulled the sword free, when a large form emerged from the fog, racing toward him. Braxton raised the Unicorn Blade awkwardly in an attempt to block the unexpected charge. But his opponent barreled into him, knocking him backward and sending him sprawling onto the ground. The spirit sword slipped from his grip and skidded away. He lay stunned for a moment, a brief wave of nausea flowing through him.

"Well, that was easy," a deep voice said with an evil chuckle. A man towered over him, his sword pointing at Braxton's throat.

Brax lurched toward the Unicorn Blade, but the man was ready for him.

"Oh no, you don't." He thumped a heavy booted foot down hard on Braxton's forearm, pinning him to the ground and sending a wave of pain shooting into his hand. The big man reached down and lifted Brax easily, gripping him by his clothes.

"Hey, boss, I've got your little runt. Now what?" His fetid breath washed over Brax's face, exposing his yellowed teeth. Braxton recognized the man from the image of Kalendra's cell.

Zacharias and four other guards appeared, materializing like ghosts out of the fog. Dressed in dark crimson shirts and black leather pants, they held short, curved swords. Three of the men had their hoods pulled up, concealing their faces, but the fourth man—an ugly thug with a curved nose and scarred chin—had his long, greasy hair exposed to the rain, pasted down now to his wet head.

"Krag, watch the inn," Zacharias ordered, and the ugly man moved quickly toward Zambini's.

"Now we'll see if you live," Zacharias added, watching Braxton from under his round-rimmed hat, "or if you die here and now. Hold out his arms!"

The big man grabbed Braxton's wrists and forced them apart. Zacharias lifted Brax's shirt, exposing his bare chest, finding the Chosen Cross.

Serene, help me! he called out.

Zacharias looked up at him, his eyes wide. He'd heard Braxton's call.

Send the energy into the big one's arms, Serene responded. *Help is coming.*

Frantically he summoned the spirit magic as best he could and sent it into the man's hands, pushing at him with all his might. Howling in pain, the man dropped Brax, stepped away, and shook his hands in response to the shock he'd received.

Taking advantage of the distraction, Braxton dove for the Unicorn Blade, sliding across the wet cobblestone floor. He grabbed the sword and rolled over onto his back, raising the weapon against the man he knew would be pursuing him. Having recovered from his shock, the large thug jumped at Brax, but then hung in air, as if frozen in time, a look of surprise on his face, the spirit sword piercing his chest. A dribble of blood fell onto Braxton's hands and the man's eyes rolled back as his full weight crumpled toward the ground, pulling Braxton and the Unicorn Blade with him.

"Grab him!" Zacharias barked, backing away as the remaining men rushed forward.

A series of whizzing sounds pierced the air, and two of the thugs fell backward, a small dagger protruding from each of their necks. Lying on his side, the Unicorn Blade still piercing the big man, Braxton looked back at the inn. Zambini stood at the top of the stairs, with Kalendra behind him, her clothes torn and stained, and her face heavily bruised. Krag, the man who'd been sent to watch the door, was dead, his throat slit. Zambini pulled another dagger from his boot and picked up the dead man's sword, ready to fight.

The remaining guard hesitated, looking first at Zambini and then at Brax, unsure what to do. A piercing howl emanated from the fog. Bear smashed into the man's back, knocking him forward several paces. The elkhound's jaws gripped the man's neck. Yelling with pain, the guard struggled to get free, then lay still.

The sound of boots on wet stone echoed across the courtyard. Brax turned to see Zacharias running toward the stables. He leaped up onto a pile of barrels and scaled the wall, disappearing from view.

Pursue him! Serene's voice shot through Braxton's mind.

Scrambling to his feet, he pulled the Unicorn Blade free, his gaze momentarily falling on the limp body, and followed his adversary, scattering barrels into the courtyard as he cleared the wall.

"Wait!" Zambini called, but Brax didn't stop. He chased Zacharias down the side street. Turning this way and that, Zacharias darted first down one path and then another, crossing alleyways and pushing over carts and people to get away.

Brax's heart pounded and his head throbbed, but he pursued his prey, anxious not to let him escape. For a minute, it reminded him of hunting deer back home in the Crimson Oaks.

He narrowed the gap as Zacharias began to tire. Realizing his opponent was gaining, Zacharias darted into a small alleyway between some shops and headed toward the open market. A wave of panic washed over Brax as he realized he was going to lose him in the throng of villagers in the plaza. Intuitively he pushed out with the spirit magic, knocking Zacharias off balance. He stumbled and crashed into a nearby tent, causing it—along with a row of hanging wicker baskets—to collapse on top of him.

Brax slowed to a trot and exited the alley into the crowd milling around the commotion. He scanned the area for his adversary and noticed a city patrol approaching. Zacharias was hurrying away through the villagers. Braxton was about to pursue him when a familiar voice called out.

"Braxton. Braxton Prinn!"

Turning in that direction, he saw Phinlera bounding toward him. She threw her arms around his neck as she arrived. "How in the world did you get here?"

"Phin!" He hugged her in surprise. Then he broke from her embrace and looked around for Zacharias. But all he saw was the crowded plaza and more city guards heading his way.

Zacharias had escaped.

CHAPTER

13

After the fight with Zacharias and the Scarlet Brotherhood, the little cottage behind the inn was brimming with people. Penton and Phinlera were there, along with a young girl. The patrol had arrived earlier than expected. Starting several hours before dawn, north of Falderon Lake, they had made the mountain climb in the cool early morning, driven on by their captain's eagerness to reach the walled city.

"Her name is Cassandra, but we call her Cassi." Penton looked fondly at the six-year-old girl. She had long blond hair that hung loosely down her back, and her blue eyes were bloodshot and circled by dark rings that detracted from her otherwise sweet and innocent face. Her dark green jumper was stained and covered a dirty white blouse that had a slightly ruffled neck, which Brax imagined must have looked quite pretty once. Her leather shoes were scuffed and in much need of repair.

"Pen and I had split up to try to find a place to stay when we arrived, seeing how crowded the city was," Phinlera explained.

"Not ideal, I know, but the best plan for finding refuge for the night," Penton added, seeing Brax's questioning look at leaving Phinlera alone.

"Cassi's father was killed by the Mins when they attacked Amberdeen," Phin said quietly to Brax. "Right in front of us too. It was a terrible sight." She looked down and swallowed hard, wiping her eyes with the back of her hand. "Anyway, Penton saved her when she ran to her dying father's side. He promised the man we'd see her home safely to Montressa, and she's been with us ever since. Your brother's a good person, Brax. He allowed Cassi's father to die in peace."

Kalendra was also in the cottage, sitting at the table in front of Zambini and Ruskin.

"I didn't know what the markings were," she said defensively. "I walked in on Brax taking a bath and saw the rings on his chest. I mentioned them to Caryle, someone I'd been seeing for a few months. He took me to Zacharias right away and told me I had to tell him. I never knew he was a member of the Brotherhood. I swear it, Uncle!" She looked up at Zambini.

"I knew those two were related when I first saw them," Phinlera murmured to Brax.

"No, I don't think so. She just calls him that because he knew her mother and took Kalendra into his service at the inn."

Phin nodded, but looked unconvinced.

"I'd never betray you, Uncle, never!" Kalendra sobbed at Zambini's scrutiny.

Brennah, sitting next to her, pulled her close, comforting her. She gave her husband a stern look as he towered over them that spoke volumes about whose side she was on.

They continued retelling their experiences. Gavin got up and went outside when Braxton mentioned Nenra and the attack on the Keepers. Brax struggled with his own emotions as he relayed the wound their mom had suffered, getting up and hugging Pen at seeing tears on his brother's face. When they separated, he showed him the necklace, and told of their urgent need to reach Arbor Loren. He mentioned the Unicorn Blade as a gift from their father and revealed the Chosen Cross, skipping over meeting Grandpa Ty and his connection to Serene. When Brax finished, Penton paced the room.

"I should've been there!" he exclaimed.

"It wouldn't have changed anything, lad." Ruskin puffed on his pipe, sitting now by the fire.

"Maybe, but you don't know that for sure, do you? I could've helped. I might have made a difference!"

"We were all taken by surprise and felt useless. Don't blame yerself for something you can't change."

Penton nodded, reluctantly. He sat back down, his face in his hands.

"It's taken me a long time to accept this, Pen," Brax said. "And I still can't get over it. But it's helped to know that Mom's alive, and we still have a chance to save her. If we can just get to the elves in time."

His brother looked up. "You're right. I want to go with you. I need to help with this."

"Of course. We can all do it together." He looked around the room.

"I can't!" Penton snapped. "I promised a dying man I'd see his daughter home safely."

Braxton looked at Cassi, who seemed to understand that she was somehow the cause of his brother's frustration. Seeing all their staring faces, she ran toward the door. Zambini caught her before she could get away and lifted her up, holding the struggling girl in his arms.

"Let me go! Let me go!" she yelled, and began to cry.

Pen got up and took Cassi from Zambini. "It's all right, I'm not mad at you. Please understand, it's not your fault."

Burying her face into Penton's shoulder, she sobbed for a long time. Braxton watched his brother quietly comforting the girl, talking in soothing tones and rubbing her back. It occurred to him how much Cassi's safety meant to him, and how much Penton had changed in their time apart. He'd always been the carefree older brother; now he seemed grown up, matured by an experience and responsibility he couldn't change and an oath he couldn't break.

Pen looked at him. "I need to see her home safely first. Then I can help."

Braxton nodded.

"May I suggest," Brennah interjected, "that perhaps Pen and Gavin take Cassi by horseback to Montressa and then follow the rest of you to the elves? As they'll be riding and you'll be on foot, you should arrive at about the same time anyway, or at least within a few days of each other."

For a moment nobody spoke. Brennah's solution seemed so simple that none of them could find any reason to argue with her.

"I'm not sure Gavin will agree." Brax looked at his brother. "He was pretty focused on avenging his mom."

"I'll go," Gavin interrupted, standing in the doorway.

"We already have papers for two adults and one child to travel with the patrol to Montressa," Phin said, looking at Gavin, "so the guards won't know if it's me or you traveling with Pen and Cassi."

"And we have the merchant papers Zambini provided that should get the rest of us out of Falderon." Brax looked around excitedly. "We can then escape the column and head east during the night."

Penton shook his head. "It won't be that easy. The captain of the patrol, a man named Breem, is no fool. He had the guards randomly check everyone's papers at various times between Amberdeen and here to ensure no one left or went missing. They even caught a couple of villagers trying to escape back to their farms and put them in chains."

"We were checked three times," Phin added.

"Then we'll have to outsmart him," Ruskin said with a cunning grin.

Zambini looked at the dwarf. "I'll check to see when the patrol's leaving. Come on, Kalendra, we'd best get back to the inn."

The barmaid looked up at him and smiled, stood and hugged her uncle. A minute later they left and headed across the courtyard.

Brax and the others spent the remainder of the day preparing to leave Falderon, wrapping supplies and storing them in a wagon Penton fetched from the entrance. "It was Cassi's father's," he explained. "We rode it down from Amberdeen and stored it when we arrived."

When they'd finished, Brax sat with Phinlera behind the inn, talking together and happy to have her back in his company. The rain had blown south, and a warm sun had emerged to dry out the cobblestones and shrink the remaining puddles. Gavin and Penton joined them an hour later. At Penton's arrival, Cassi came skipping out of the cottage, her face washed, and her long hair combed and pulled back in a pretty pink ribbon that Brennah had given her. Her green jumper and white blouse had been cleaned and restored to their original condition.

They passed the afternoon talking about happier times and joking lightly. Everyone avoided speaking about current events, hiding their fears of what they all knew still lay ahead. When the sun sank beyond the western horizon and long shadows fell across the courtyard, they headed back into Zambini's for their last meal in Falderon.

"Oh, I almost forgot," Phinlera said, as they sat in the common room enjoying a warm supper and Pen had left to get them something more to drink. She reached into her leather tunic and withdrew a small bag of coins, which she handed to Brax. "Open it!"

He untied the strings and poured the coins onto his palm.

"Seven crowns!" Phin exclaimed. "That's two silvers and three coppers apiece. I get the extra for making the trip." She winked, nudging him playfully with her elbow.

Brax looked at her for a moment.

"For the rover deer! The whole reason I went to Amberdeen, remember?"

"Oh!" He looked down at his hand, remembering the pelt that he, Phin, and their friend Janson had worked on for so long. A few weeks ago, all he could think about was the money they'd earn from the silver-white hide and beautifully curved horns. Now it seemed empty and hollow, and the coins felt cold. Funny, he thought, how life changed so quickly.

"That's great, Phin." He tried to sound enthusiastic, but he knew his words were shallow. He looked up at Gavin, who nodded in quiet understanding.

"Your brother helped a lot," Phinlera went on, still excited. "I was willing to settle for half that, but Pen bartered with an old noble like a seasoned merchant. It was great!" She laughed and returned to her supper.

"You did well," Brax said, tucking the coins away.

They finished their meal and headed back to the cottage. Zambini stopped by to let them know the patrol was leaving at sunrise. Brennah gave them some fresh muffins for the trip, along with generous quantities of dried meat, bread, cheese, and sausages. They refilled their waterskins from the rain barrel outside the kitchen and packed the rest of their supplies.

Braxton was just setting out his makeshift bed by the fireplace when Cassi came over.

"Your friend's very beautiful," she said.

"She is pretty, isn't she?" He watched Phinlera talking with Brennah.

Cassi giggled. "She gave me a gift. Now I don't have to be sad anymore."

"Oh? What was that?"

She covered her mouth shyly with both hands. "She told me you'd ask, but I promised not to tell. I just wanted to thank you for sharing her with me." She skipped off to the little room Braxton and Gavin had shared, but which had now been claimed by the girls, leaving Brax to finish making his bed and puzzle over her words.

CHAPTER
14

Braxton, Phin, and Ruskin sat together in the back of the wagon, lined up with the other hopeful travelers waiting to leave Falderon. Penton rode up front with Cassi, guiding the long makeshift reins attached to Obsidian, Cinnamon, and an old mule that had belonged to Cassi's father.

They'd stopped an hour before sunrise at the back of the column, which now extended from the main gate all the way to the city square. The patrol's guards strode down the line, inspecting papers, searching belongings, and forcefully removing stowaways discovered among the travelers.

"They're coming," Gavin mumbled as he walked around outside with Bear, checking the strappings of the bonnet Ruskin had added to their carriage that gave the wagon a gypsy look.

"Papers!" a guard called out as two men approached, their chainmail clinking as they moved. Penton unfolded the parchment and handed them over. The man started reading, then stopped and looked up.

"Zambini's?" he asked, and Pen nodded. The guard looked back at the documents. Then he held out his left hand, keeping his eyes on the papers. Penton gave him a small coin purse that Zambini had provided, and the man stuffed it in his pocket without looking up. He handed back the papers, and the clinking of their armor passed by as the guards moved on to the next in line.

"That seemed to go well," Phinlera said.

Ruskin made a *hmph* sound, then lay down on his side, facing away from them, and soon began snoring.

A little after sunrise, a horn sounded, followed several minutes afterward by the sudden lurch of their wagon, signaling the patrol's departure from the mountain city. The ironbound wheels creaked as they rolled along the main cobblestone road from the central plaza. Braxton and Phinlera tried to minimize their jostling, but despite their best efforts, bounced around in the back of the wagon. The movement didn't seem to bother Ruskin, though, whose sleep, if anything, seemed to deepen with the moving sensation. They continued for several minutes, approaching the walled perimeter and passed through the main gate.

A cold shiver ran down Brax's spine as they crossed the threshold marking the outer limits of Falderon. A moment later, they were free, and Braxton breathed a sigh of relief. He looked at Phinlera, glad to have her with him and to finally be continuing on their journey.

They traveled south for over an hour, climbing the outer edge of the Vale Mountains along the winding road east of the Rolling River. Gavin and Bear joined them in the back of the wagon.

"Pen thinks the captain will keep us moving until noon, before stopping," Gavin reported.

Ruskin woke up, sat behind Pen, and started asking him questions.

"What's the setup at night, and how often do the guards patrol the outer perimeter of the camp? Do they spread their tents among the travelers or pitch them together?"

Penton and Phinlera took turns answering, trying to remember as many details as they could from their trip down from Amberdeen. Each added pieces the other had forgotten, building upon their companion's responses in hopes of providing the dwarf with as much information as possible. In the end, Ruskin seemed pleased and soon began describing ways they might escape, each plan taking advantage of a particular weakness he perceived in the patrol's defense.

Braxton listened quietly, looking out ahead to where the guards were positioned among the serpentine line. The front of the column was led by the man Pen identified as Breem, sitting proudly atop a large gray horse of a similar breed to Obsidian. He had straight black hair that reached to his shoulders and a long purple cloak with the silver Imperial Lion embroidered at its center that glistened whenever it caught the sun. Behind him, two men rode alongside each other, one holding a banner that matched the symbol on their captain's cloak. The other had a large curved horn strapped to his back.

Four mounted guards followed these initial three, wearing mail and carrying a shield and a long spear held upright that had a purple pennant near the tip. At various intervals among the travelers, two similarly armed men rode together, occasionally breaking rank to ride up or down the column. Merchants, though, made up the bulk of their group, with families, farmers, and a few other citizens scattered here and there along the line.

They continued climbing south for several more hours. Brax could hear the water's occasional bubbling coming from somewhere off to their right. Near midday, the horn sounded another deep note, and the guards organized themselves into a defensive position, as the patrol stopped for a brief rest. By nightfall, they had traveled halfway to the river's source, high up in the Vales, stopping for the evening at a clearing alongside its banks. Campfires soon flickered here and there as merchants and other travelers prepared meals or built fires for the night. Brax and the others ate a warm supper from the food Brennah had provided along with wild mushrooms that Gavin found growing by the water, washed down with ale from a small keg Ruskin had lifted from Zambini's cellar.

When they'd finished, they took turns walking around the campground, their hoods pulled up and their heads bent low to avoid eye contact with the guards. The site was set up in a rough half-circle formation, with the open end facing the river. Five gray rectangular tents formed the outer perimeter, with the first and last resting on the rocky banks. Large campfires illuminated the spaces between the housings, clearly delineating boundaries for the travelers. The captain's tent, along with one other, sat in the center of the encampment with the horses picketed at the river. Patrols moved about the outer edge in a steady procession. The remaining throng of more than a hundred farmers, villagers, merchants, and their associated children and livestock were scattered randomly within the protective area, with the wealthiest families and their wagons positioned closest to the middle.

Braxton and Phinlera were just returning for a second time when they passed within earshot of the captain. The sun had set hours earlier, and most of the travelers had already turned in for the night. The guards continued their silent patrol, passing between the fires that limited their vision into the darkness beyond to only a few feet away. Brax glanced at Breem, who was standing outside his tent talking with another man whose back was toward them. The nearby campfire illuminated the side of Breem's face, accentuating his hooked nose and square jaw as the light danced across his strong features. A thick black mustache hung down past the corners of his mouth, and deep lines reflective of the man's age and years of service furrowed his brow.

As they continued toward their wagon, Brax noticed the captain becoming increasingly agitated with the other man, raising his hands and gesturing left or right. Breem stepped closer as the conversation turned to arguing. The patrol's leader was clearly disagreeing with whatever the smaller man was saying, shaking his head as both voices grew louder. Brax and Phin were just getting close enough to have a better view when they heard Breem's deep voice bellow, "Enough!"

The conversation broke off, and the two men stood facing each other in angry silence. When the second man turned to leave, the light from the fire fell across his face.

Braxton's heart dropped as he recognized Zacharias.

CHAPTER
15

"We need to go now!" Brax exclaimed, as he and Phinlera burst into the back of the wagon.

"What's wrong?" Penton stood up.

"Zacharias is here." He told them of the argument they had witnessed.

"I thought I saw him standing in the shadows by the gate when we left Falderon," Gavin commented. "But I wasn't sure."

"I think he was watching for me." Brax remembered the feeling he'd had as they left the city. "I don't know how, but he knew I was in the column."

Ruskin swore. "Get your things. We're leaving."

Penton shook his head. "You won't make it past the guards. You should stick to the plan and wait until after the midnight change."

"No time," the dwarf answered over his shoulder.

"We'll need a distraction," Phinlera said, hastily stuffing a few stores into her pack.

Ruskin turned to face them. "This will do." He held a dark yellow bag in the center of his palm, no bigger than an oversized coin and about twice as thick. He pushed at it with his thumb so the others could see it contained a rough, sand-like substance that appeared to move away in response to the pressure he applied on it. The sack was sewn shut, and it reminded Brax of the small beaded bags they used to sell to children back home during Merchant Tide.

"Just throw this in the fire near the horses—by the tent on the north side."
He handed it to Pen. "It'll create what we need." He glanced at Brax and
Phin. "Be ready when it does."

Penton gently bounced the object up and down in his hand.

"Be careful with that," Ruskin cautioned. "It took me almost your lifetime
to make." He looked at the sack, clearly disappointed at having to give it up.

Brax, Phin, and Ruskin crouched in the shadow of a merchant's wagon
near the southernmost tent of the guarded perimeter. A partially cloud-
covered moon cast a flicker of light across the bubbling river, accentuating
the darkness in which they hid.

After a few minutes, Ruskin handed Brax his pack, left their concealment,
and walked over to the two guards by the campfire. Brax and Phin watched
as the dwarf began conversing with the men. A sudden and loud explosion
erupted from the northern end of the encampment and a flash of light
lit up the sky. Braxton and Phinlera jumped at the unexpected sound as
burning timbers flew in every direction, a few igniting a nearby tent. The
eruption spooked the horses, which broke their tethers and bolted through
the campground, smashing into tents and making them collapse. Chaos
erupted as merchants, families, and guards ran in every direction, a few
shouting that they were under attack.

Ruskin reappeared next to Brax and Phin. "Come on!" he yelled above
the commotion, leading them back to where the guards were. One lay
unconscious on the ground; the other was nowhere to be seen.

"I told you to be ready," the dwarf snapped over his shoulder. Not waiting
for a response, he led them away from the river and into a cluster of nearby
boulders. They moved hastily from one clump of rocks to another, before
dropping down into a gully and disappearing around a large granite base.
Unaccustomed to the mountainous terrain, Brax and Phin stumbled often,
losing their footing and sliding down the broken rock. It was impossible

to see in the darkness that engulfed them. Even Phinlera with her usually superior vision had trouble, and within minutes, the two of them were hopelessly lost. Ruskin reappeared and guided them away at a fevered pace, distancing themselves from the commotion on the road.

They descended the Vales for over an hour before the dwarf allowed a brief rest. Stopping in a narrow ravine, they hid under the protective cover of a fallen rock shelf that created a natural roof against the occasional light of the moon. Brax tended to his bleeding cuts and rubbed his bruised shins, which reacted painfully when touched. Sweat ran down his back, emphasized by the weight of his heavy pack and causing his shirt to stick to his skin. Used to chasing deer back home in the Oaks, his stamina was well-developed, but he found himself panting from the exertion across the uneven terrain, and from the sheer effort of keeping up with the dwarf's hectic pace. But at least they'd escaped.

He looked at Phin. Her hair was matted down with perspiration, but her eyes shone brightly with excitement, and she smiled back at him. Even now, unkempt, she looked beautiful, her features barely visible in the dim light of their makeshift cave. But he could tell she was getting winded, her chest rising and falling in rapid succession, the frequent stumbling across the loose mountainous rock taking its toll. But she wouldn't complain. She never did. Considering herself equally capable, she'd press on. He found her boundless energy and determination to keep up with him infectious.

Ruskin, by contrast, wasn't even perspiring. His breathing was calm, even slightly relaxed, and he barely drank from his waterskin when they stopped. Brax knew this was the dwarf's domain and that he loved being out in the rocky terrain and open air; he could probably continue for days without tiring.

"We wouldn'ta had to run for it if ya'd been paying attention," he commented as they sat together in the dark.

"We were a bit surprised by that explosion," Phinlera said defensively.

"You could've warned us," Brax added. "What was that thing you gave Pen, anyway?"

Ruskin grinned. "An ancient dwarven secret. I hate having lost it," he said more seriously, "but it served us well."

They turned northeast and continued for most of the night, pausing infrequently for a brief drink or to catch their breath. Ruskin paced about whenever they stopped. Occasionally he'd leave them to rest for a while and silently disappear into the night, like a wolf slipping away into the darkness, only to materialize again out of the deeper shadows when they'd regained their strength, leading them on.

It was during one of these resting periods that Braxton remembered what Cassi had said.

He sat down next to Phinlera. "I've been meaning to ask you. What did you give Cassi?"

She looked puzzled. "What do you mean?"

"Back at Zambini's, the night before we left."

"I didn't give her anything."

"You must've," he pressed. "And she seemed pretty excited about it too."

"No, nothing. Are you sure she wasn't talking about Brennah?"

"Pretty sure." He relayed the conversation.

"Well, I didn't give her anything," Phin repeated, tying her hair back.

Brax looked questioningly at her. What could she have possibly given Cassi that she'd want to keep secret? He mulled it over for several minutes, growing more and more frustrated at her refusal to admit she'd given something to the young girl. He was about to confront her again when Serene's calming voice entered his thoughts.

The gift, child, was from me.

He was stunned. He was so sure Cassi had meant Phinlera. He started to ask Serene if he'd understood her correctly when Ruskin returned. Brax followed behind the other two, thinking over Serene's words as he trudged through the gloomy darkness, his surroundings reflective of his mood. It suddenly occurred to him that if Cassi had meant Serene, she must've seen her.

But how could that be? he thought, perplexed. *How could she have possibly seen Serene?*

He called out to her.

Put it out of your thoughts, child, she said firmly. *It is not of your concern, and you need not ask of it again.* She pulled away, and he could feel her energy withdrawing.

For a long time, he thought about what it meant, despite Serene's advice to let it go. He couldn't understand how Cassi could have seen or spoken with the sword's master, or why Serene wouldn't talk to him about it now. He wished he could see the young girl again—he'd have much to ask her. Finally, accepting he wasn't going to get any answers, he began thinking instead of his mom and Arbor Loren. He knew they wouldn't reach the elves tomorrow, their ninth day since leaving Oak Haven. Serene had said she was with his mom, a thought that relieved much of his fear. He only hoped it would be enough. He clutched at her pendant under his shirt, drawing comfort from the wooden carving pressed against his chest. This riddle he understood, he thought. This one he could help answer.

By early morning, they'd traveled a far distance from the river, down the Vales and into the Windwailed Valley. The rain had started up again, promising another gray day. They spent a few wet hours trying to sleep in a stand of hemlocks tucked at the mountain's base. Water trickled down Braxton's back, seeping into his clothing and making for a dismal morning. He thought of being back at Zambini's cottage, lying by the fire and enjoying Brennah's excellent cooking. It was a memory he knew he'd recall often over the coming days. At least they were free of the patrol and heading toward the elves, a realization that brought a ray of light in this otherwise dreary day.

At midmorning, Ruskin woke them from their restless sleep, and they set a steady pace toward Arbor Loren. Travel was easier now, with Braxton and Phin more accustomed to the open terrain, able to keep up with their dwarven companion.

They reached the western foothills of the Calindurin Plains after sundown and had just entered some rocky outcroppings when Serene's warning brought Braxton to a sudden halt.

Draw my sword, child.

"Rusk!" Brax called out, dropping his pack and reaching over his shoulder for the Unicorn Blade, cautioning Phinlera with his other hand.

But his warning came too late. The earth opened up beneath Ruskin, and they could hear the sounds of snapping branches mingled with the dwarf's cursing as he disappeared into the pit below. A band of a tough-looking men emerged from behind the rocks and scattered trees. Wearing leather jerkins and olive shirts, they carried weapons of one sort or another, a few holding nets or ropes tied into wide loops.

Braxton felt a sinking feeling in his stomach as he realized they'd encountered the one thing Ruskin had hoped to avoid. The Hunters.

CHAPTER

16

A s the slavers closed in on them, Phinlera stepped up next to him, her dagger and short sword drawn, ready to fight. Braxton wanted to yell at her to get back, to turn and run, but he knew she'd never listen. Fearing for her safety, he panicked that something would happen to her.

Calm your mind and focus the energy. Serene's voice broke into his thoughts.

He took a breath, smelling the cool air, and summoned the spirit magic, feeling its warm sensation awaken to his call. The lead Hunter was almost on top of them when he unleashed it, sending out a wave of energy that hit the first few attackers, knocking them back a dozen feet or more. The other men stopped short, seeing their companions flung through the air. Taking quick advantage of their hesitation, Braxton leaped forward with the Unicorn Blade held high and brought it down upon the surprised thug closest to him. Regaining their composure, the rest of the Hunters charged in.

The closest dropped instantly, a dagger protruding from his chest. Phinlera appeared by Braxton's side, bent down quickly, and retrieved the thrown weapon, before raising her sword awkwardly to parry the attack from another brute.

Braxton swung at a third Hunter, but the man deflected the blow.

Use the energy, then go left.

"What?" he asked, unaccustomed to hearing Serene's voice in the heat of battle. A heavy thud struck his right temple, followed by a deafening bolt of pain that shot through his head, scattering his thoughts. Nausea filled his stomach, and his eyes flooded. The world began to spin as the ground leaped up, swallowing him into darkness.

He awoke to the irregular motion of Cassi's wagon and the creaking sound of iron-rimmed wheels cutting their path through uneven ground. The hard wooden floorboards pressed against his cheek, and his head bumped every time their carriage fell into one of the many recesses along the rough trail. He kept his eyes shut, breathing in the fresh morning air that had a strong pungent scent of newly cut straw. Trying to roll over onto his back, he found his arms and legs numb and unable to move. A throbbing sensation filled his mind, and his stomach threatened to heave. He lay there for a while, allowing the queasiness to pass. Finally, determined, Brax gritted his teeth, opened his eyes, and sat up.

Morning sunlight struck his face, forcing him to blink until he was finally able to squint at his surroundings. He was surprised to see the expansive Calindurin Plains. Then he realized he was in a cage.

Three sides of his little mobile prison faced the central Andorah valley, but the front was boarded up, blocking his view of the driver and whatever beast pulled them on. Straw littered the floor, and, except for two dark bundles near the wooden wall, his cell was empty. He looked around, trying to remember what had happened but couldn't recall anything from the day before. It took him a moment to realize the dark shapes were actually the crumpled forms of Ruskin and Phinlera, lying bound and unconscious.

He moved toward them, but his body refused to cooperate, and a painful throbbing stabbed at his temples, mocking his efforts. Each attempt produced the same futile results, causing his nausea to return. He lay on the decking, trying to settle his stomach, focusing on his surroundings. Gradually his mind began to clear, as if being pulled from some long, dreamless sleep.

Swallowing hard, he tasted a bitter flavor in his parched throat and felt a soft, smooth object pressed against his tongue. Rolling it around in his mouth, the taste intensified. He spat the object onto the straw and stared at the small white pebble, trying to connect it to something familiar. It was only then that he realized his hands were bound and his ankles strapped together with tight leather cords that cut into his skin. Sitting up abruptly, he struggled against his bindings before giving up. Somewhere in the back of his mind, he remembered Serene and frantically called out to her. But the effort only intensified the pain in his head, reviving his nausea, and causing him to collapse back down.

When the sickness passed, and he was able to swallow without retching, he slid over to Phinlera. Pushing at her with his shoulder she rolled over. Her eyes were closed, and her face looked pale and drawn. Sweat ran down her brow, and a deep purple bruise covered her right eye and cheek. Braxton swore, turning away and chiding himself for her injury.

When he'd finished wrestling with his emotions, he began calling to her, nudging her with his elbow. Gradually she began to stir, as if returning from some distant world, and he coaxed the white object from her mouth.

"Where are we?" she said at last, still lying on the floor, her voice weak and dry.

"Somewhere out in the Calindurin." He sat up and nodded toward the cell bars. "We've been captured."

She turned toward him. "What about your mother?"

Panic flooded into Brax as he realized they were no longer heading toward the elves. He looked about frantically, trying to determine how far south they might have gone, or how much time had been lost, searching for clues among the few landmarks he could see. But nothing looked familiar. Rubbing his chin into the side of his neck, he loosened his shirt, and breathed a deep sigh of relief at seeing the leather strap, knowing his mom's pendant was safe. He only hoped Serene was protecting her.

Phinlera sat up against the backboard, more coherent now. She wet her lips and swallowed hard. "We should wake Ruskin."

Working together, they helped the dwarf eject the pebble from his mouth.

"Asphidel," he said, once he'd regained consciousness. "It's a drug that keeps the body in a state of dreamless sleep, weakening your ability to think rationally. Comes from a plant in Amalasia. A favorite tool of the Hunters." He spat in disgust.

Braxton knew about the southern continent but had never met anyone or seen anything from Amalasia.

Ruskin glanced around. "Looks like they're taking us to Kharnus. Probably to be sold as slaves." He swore again, annoyance furrowing his brow.

"We need to figure a way out," Phinlera said, trying to sound hopeful.

Braxton looked at Ruskin. "Any ideas?"

"Maybe." He nodded slowly. "When the guards come by."

"I haven't seen anyone," Brax admitted, turning to face the cell door at the rear of the wagon.

"They'll feed us now that we're awake. They won't let their prisoners die— no profit in it. And that gives us an advantage."

They continued traveling south, seeing no sign of the Hunters. Occasionally they'd hear voices approaching from the front of the wagon, but no one came into view. Wrestling with their bindings without success, they formed a back-to-back circle and Phinlera's nimble fingers worked at undoing the knots around Ruskin's hands. She was just starting to loosen the thick cords when the wagon came to an abrupt halt, throwing them forward onto the floor.

A fat, brown-haired Hunter appeared alongside them.

"Well, our guests have awoken early, I see," he said in a dry, sarcastic drawl. His loose-fitting, deep-red silk shirt was tucked into black trousers that puffed out at his legs, and he wore a scarred leather chestpiece. A falchion extended from his belt, its curved blade extending out behind him as he walked. In his hands he held the Unicorn Blade.

Braxton's heart sank at seeing the spirit sword in the Hunter's possession, and he swallowed against the lump forming in his throat. The man continued to the back of the wagon, unhooked a large metal key ring from his side, and opened the barred door. Leaping up the single step, he stood over his prisoners.

"Let's see if what they say about you is true." He stared down at Braxton, ignoring the others. Unsheathing the Unicorn Blade he admired its craftsmanship. "In all my many years of traveling, I've never actually seen a spirit sword. It's heavier than I'd expected." He balanced it in his rough hand. Then he sheathed the blade and bent down, dropping the weapon. Grabbing Brax's tunic with both hands, he yanked him upright, pulling his shirt loose and revealing his bare chest.

"So this is the answer to all the riddles." He eyed the Chosen Cross and laughed. "You're going to make me a very rich man, my young friend."

Braxton squirmed, but the Hunter held him in place.

"What's this?" he said with a puzzled look. He grabbed the pendant from around Brax's neck and yanked it free, dropping Brax heavily to the floor.

"Leave that alone!" Phinlera yelled. She twisted about, trying to break her bonds.

"Easy, missy," the Hunter cautioned. "I'll deal with you in a minute. You'll be a nice distraction for a while." He looked at her with an evil grin, eyeing her body up and down.

Slumped on the decking, Braxton saw his mom's pendant in the Hunter's hand, and his mind snapped. He kicked out with his remaining strength, catching the man behind the knees and knocking him to the ground. Instantly, Ruskin's muscular legs closed around the man's neck, holding him in a tight grip. He struggled frantically, trying to force the dwarf's limbs apart in order to gain some precious air, but Ruskin didn't budge. All the while the Hunter had been focused on Braxton and Phinlera, Ruskin had been carefully working at the knot Phin had loosened, finally managing to get free. He held their captor in place now, his legs closing like a vice, slowly squeezing the life out of the man. The Hunter's face turned a deep shade of red, then faded into a dark purple as the air he so vitally needed was denied him. Then he lay still.

Ruskin jumped to his feet, like a badger springing back to life. He pulled out the man's falchion and cut their cords, bringing much-needed relief to their numbed limbs.

Quickly retrieving the pendant from the dead man's hands, Brax tied it around his neck. He grabbed the Unicorn Blade and jumped from the wagon, following after the other two sprinting toward a clump of trees to the west. As he ran, he chanced a look back at the row of a dozen or more covered and prison-celled wagons, standing together, forming a winding line south. Hunters moved about the carriages, but nobody seemed to notice their escape from the rear of the column. A moment later they entered the trees.

They'd lost their packs, their food, and their waterskins, and the only weapons they had were the Unicorn Blade and the falchion Ruskin had taken from the dead Hunter. But at least they were free.

CHAPTER
17

As soon as they entered the copse of pines, a shrill note rang out behind them. No one spoke; they all knew what the alarm meant. Running through the dense trees, they brushed past saplings, twigs, and the long grasses of the undergrowth. Another horn sounded ahead of them and farther west. Without slowing, Ruskin turned north.

Clearing the thicket, they sprinted east along the far side of a hillock that blocked sight to the wagons, and then turned north again into the foothills. A horn signaled back at the pines, answered by the one out of the west, closer this time. A third followed moments later far to the north, echoing through the hills, and Ruskin swore.

"They're herding us like dogs." He increased their pace.

Keeping to the sides of low knolls or within the small pine forests that littered the foothills, they dashed across the open spaces between rocky outcroppings. Their flight continued for over an hour, followed periodically by the sounds of their pursuers tracking them. Ruskin urged them on, twisting and turning in response to the sounds of the Hunters, trying to lose their pursuers. At times, it seemed to work, but they'd invariably hear the horns again as their enemy picked up their trail.

"We're widening the gap," the dwarf said at one point, noting the lengthening time between signals. But Brax and Phin were starting to tire. When they came to a small gully, they called for a halt. Ruskin continued up the narrow ravine without slowing, guiding them toward a cluster of trees on a hill at the far end.

"We'll rest there, just to catch your breath," he said, slowing his strides to help ease their muscles.

Brax eyed the hills as they continued up the canyon. They rounded the bend on the eastern side when heavy, weighted nets forced them quickly to the ground. Voices shouted and they were pinned in place. The three struggled to get free, but exhausted and outnumbered, they soon found they couldn't move. A long horn blew, and the nets lifted long enough for the Hunters to bind them.

They were taken to the hillock fronting the pines near the top end of the ravine, guarded by a score of Hunters. Most were outfitted like the ones they'd seen before—brown leather jerkins over olive shirts tucked into black pants, and holding an assortment of weapons. Eight of the men wore tight-necked green vests, without shirts, and knee-length pants with bare feet. Taller and slimmer than the rest, they grouped together on the hill away from the other Hunters, holding slings and seemingly more at home out here in the central plains.

Their captors encircled them, their weapons drawn. No one spoke as they watched Brax and his companions, preventing any chance of escape. The falchion and Unicorn Blade lay on the floor, several feet away, guarded by a large man.

"Now what?" Ruskin asked, breaking the silence.

The big Hunter walked over and struck him across the jaw with his gloved hand, causing Ruskin to look back with loathing and spit blood.

Braxton realized that Serene hadn't warned him of the impending danger, and he called out to her urgently now.

It is all right, child, she said calmly. *I am here.*

Why didn't you warn me? He summoned the spirit magic.

Keep your mind at peace. The energy subsided as though responding to her words.

What's going on?

Patience, child. You need to wait now. She pulled away, breaking their connection.

The sound of cantering horses entered the canyon as half a dozen men rode toward them. They watched the group approach, led by a tall, muscular Hunter wearing a dark mustard-colored shirt under a thick leather tunic. Four spear-armed guards rode behind him. The man's presence seemed to cause the others in the ravine to back away, obviously recognizing their leader. It was the person next to him, however, that drew Braxton's full attention. He held his breath as he looked into the face of Zacharias.

"Is this what you wanted?" the Hunter asked after they'd dismounted. The two men walked toward the prisoners.

Zacharias nodded, watching Braxton. "You led us on quite the chase. Your dwarven guide is to be commended. For a while there, I thought you'd slipped past our net."

The Hunter leader made a *hmph* sound.

"The bishop is most interested in meeting you," Braxton's adversary continued, ignoring the other man, "and I'm looking forward to introducing you."

"What about my payment?" the Hunter asked.

Zacharias watched Braxton for a moment, then walked back to his horse. He untied his saddlebag, withdrew a large sack, and handed it over. "You'll get the rest when we're in Amberdeen."

The tall man nodded, weighing the sack in his hand, then began yelling orders to his men, mobilizing them.

Serene, help me! Braxton called out, realizing they intended to take him to the capital city.

Zacharias turned sharply toward him. "Karas!" he yelled in alarm, and the leader barked a quick response. The Hunters stopped and faced their prisoners, with weapons drawn.

It is all right, child, Serene repeated calmly. *Be patient and clear your mind, for he can hear you, this one you know. A decision is being made. Wait.*

Nobody moved.

Zacharias took a few cautious steps forward. "Bring me his weapon!"

The Hunter who'd hit Ruskin handed him the Unicorn Blade, then backed away.

For a moment, no one stirred.

A rush of air broke the silence as a thick bolt hit Zacharias in the shoulder, flinging him back a dozen paces or more and pinning him to a tree.

Good! Serene exclaimed. It was the most excitement Brax had heard her express, and he jumped at the sudden response. *Awaken the energy now, child, then wait. Focus on the ones by the horses.*

He called upon the spirit magic, summoning its full strength. It responded instantly, as if lying just beyond his consciousness, awaiting his call. He held the energy, trying to stop its power from releasing, barely able to contain its strength. But he waited.

The Hunters all faced the trees. There stood the largest man Brax had ever seen. Easily a foot taller than everyone else, with shoulders twice as wide, a broad head, and a flat, square chin. His smooth-rimmed leather hat was pulled down over his long hair, casting a shadow across the man's face. In one hand he held an enormous crossbow, which Braxton guessed was the source of the bolt that still pinned Zacharias to the tree. His other hand grasped an ax that looked small for the man's size, but which Braxton imagined would've required most of his strength to lift. Standing at the edge of the forest, he watched the Hunters.

"The mountain man!" one of the sling-wielding men exclaimed, and he and the others in his group backed away, obviously familiar with this newcomer.

"Hold your ground!" the muscular Hunter barked, stepping forward. But the tanned men ignored him, turned, and fled, disappearing among the rocks. The leader of the Hunters swore, then looked at the big man.

"You've interfered with our business for the last—" he started to say, but stopped short as the ax stuck in his chest, knocking him to the ground.

The remaining Hunters in the gully surged forward, then halted abruptly as the mountain man dropped his crossbow and drew an enormous sword from across his back, which he held aloft in both hands, ready to strike. The wide-eyed Hunters stared at the massive weapon. Taking quick advantage of their hesitation, their big opponent stepped closer and swung his sword in a low arc, decapitating the man closest to him.

Now! Serene's voice echoed in Brax's mind.

He turned as best he could and released the full force of the energy on the guards at the horses. The power of the spirit magic broke upon them like a pent-up storm, its thunderous burst flinging the unfortunate Hunters back several yards and causing a loud thunderclap to echo down the ravine, startling the horses. The unexpected sound, along with the sight of the mountain man, their dead leader with the ax still buried in his chest, and their decapitated companion, was too much for the remaining Hunters. They turned and fled, leaving Braxton and his friends alone with the giant man. Their rescuer stepped up to them.

"I am Sotchek," he said in a deep, resounding voice. "And I offer you my help."

CHAPTER
18

Braxton couldn't thank the big man enough and introduced himself and the others. Sotchek didn't respond. He drew a hunting knife from his belt and cut their cords.

"We're making for Arbor Loren," Brax continued, rubbing his wrists. "Any help you could provide would be most welcome."

Ruskin grumbled at the request, but nodded his agreement.

Sotchek looked up at the sky. The others followed his gaze and could see a few sparrows and some crows flitting about above the trees, and another bird far overhead, a tiny dot against the azure background. They couldn't understand what the big man was staring at so intently.

"We need to go." Sotchek picked up the Unicorn Blade and falchion, and handed them to Braxton and the dwarf.

Phinlera bent down next to the decapitated Hunter, swallowing hard at the sight of the man's body still oozing blood. She peeled back the fingers of his hand and claimed his small curved sword for herself.

"I hate to steal from the dead." She stood up quickly and looked at them. "But I need a weapon."

Braxton nodded, seeing the uneasy look on her face. His eyes fell unwillingly on the man's severed form, and he turned away.

Sotchek walked over to the dead leader and retrieved his ax before rolling him over with a booted foot to lie facedown. He picked up the sack of coins that the man had dropped, tied it to his belt, and strode over to where Zacharias was still pinned to the tree.

"He's alive," he said, a broad hand pressed against Zacharias' neck.

Ruskin checked him as well. "Barely. His breath is weak. We should just take his head and be done with it."

"No!" Braxton stepped closer, the thought of more killing bothering him. "Let him go."

Sotchek pulled the thick, spear-like bolt from Zacharias' shoulder and walked back to the forest, leaving Zacharias in a crumpled heap.

"There are more Hunters coming. We should go. Now." He picked up his crossbow and disappeared among the trees.

Braxton, Ruskin, and Phinlera stood looking at one another, trying to decide whether to follow their rescuer or make their own way north. A second later, they ran after the mountain man.

They found him waiting for them, a large pack strapped to his back, the crossbow secured to it, and the throwing ax hanging loosely in his belt.

"This way," he said, then faded away into the forest.

For the remainder of the day and into the night, they followed their new guide, running periodically to keep up with the man's long strides. He changed direction often, leading them through groups of pines, down gullies, and up the small streams that dotted the foothills of the Calindurin, all the while moving northeasterly. They occasionally stopped to catch their breath or to drink from the waterskin Sotchek carried. Each time they paused, their giant friend studied the sky, as if inspecting a detailed map.

"They're still following," he said, during one such break late in the day. He looked at Braxton. "You carry a large price on your head. Or perhaps, like me, it's your half-blood they fear." Without waiting, he turned and led them on.

It was approaching midnight before they finally stopped, finding shelter in a small cave that Sotchek had obviously frequented before. He moved aside some thick brush to reveal an opening in the rock.

"We'll rest till dawn. I'll keep watch." He handed Ruskin a small pack, along with the waterskin. "Get some rest. We have a long walk tomorrow."

He slipped away into the dark, leaving them alone in the cavern. Ruskin got a small fire going near the back wall, lighting their evening home and bringing much-needed warmth to the night.

"Talkative fellow," the dwarf said sarcastically, handing out some bread and cheese he found in the sack. "But I'm glad he happened upon us when he did, or we'd be near the Ridge by now."

Braxton furrowed his brow. "There's something about him, though, that doesn't make sense, as if he's not quite comfortable in our presence."

"I noticed it too," Phinlera agreed. "He's obviously spent a lot of time alone, but he seems friendly enough—for now at least."

"I couldn't care about his manners." Ruskin chuckled. "If he can get us to Arbor Loren without any more delays, I'm happy to have him lead us."

The two nodded and consumed their cold meal. They settled in next to the fire after they'd finished and soon heard the dwarf's snoring echoing in the cave.

Phinlera rustled around on the hard stone floor, trying to get comfortable. "I want to ask you something."

Brax looked at her from where he lay. "What is it?"

He could see the light dancing off her features, accentuating her cheekbones and reflecting in her bright eyes. He smiled, admiring how beautiful she looked. She responded warmly, causing his heart to leap.

"I want to know about the sword," she said more seriously.

He didn't respond right away. "I've been wondering if you'd ask me."

"I'm just not quite sure I'm ready."

"What do you mean?"

"I've known you for a long time, Braxton Prinn. But lately you've done things I've never seen before, or even imagined could be done, and that scares me."

"It scared me too, at first," he said quickly, "but I'm getting used to it now, and I think you should know."

She rolled onto her back and stared up at the smooth rock overhead, watching the firelight dance around on the ceiling, remaining quiet for a while.

"I want to know," she said at last. "I want to know how this has changed you."

Braxton looked at her. "I want to tell you," he said. "I need to tell someone, and I want it to be you. Not here, not now. Maybe when we get to Arbor Loren."

She nodded. "I just don't know how it will change things—our friendship, I mean, and that's what scares me."

He sat up. "It doesn't have to change anything."

"Maybe," she said softly, "but you can't be sure."

He thought about it for a long time as they lay in their little cave out in the Calindurin. Had the sword changed him that much? Was he no longer the boy who'd left Oak Haven a week ago? He knew he'd grown. He knew he'd taken on an experience he could never have imagined, and carried with him a greater responsibility now. But had it changed who he was inside? His feelings for Phinlera or the life he hoped they'd create together? He lay thinking about it in the dark, until, a few hours before dawn, sleep beckoned with its warm embrace, and he drifted.

Braxton awoke to the cool feeling of morning air blowing into the cave as Sotchek roused them. The fire was burning brightly, with a pot of meaty broth bubbling above it, wafting an enticing aroma throughout their otherwise cold, dark home. Their new guide handed each of them a small wooden bowl and they took turns helping themselves to portions of the food. The hot breakfast was a welcome treat—a mixture of vegetables, wild mushrooms, and small pieces of meat Brax hadn't tasted before. It satisfied their stomachs with a warm, soothing sensation, strengthening their bodies and banishing their sleep.

"I was able to direct the Hunters west," Sotchek explained as they ate. "Today's walk should be easier and will gain you much ground."

"Thank you," Braxton replied, looking up from his bowl. "You've helped us so much. We're in your debt."

The other two nodded, consuming their meal.

"You said last night," Brax added after blowing on his food, "that I, like you, am a half-breed. I'm uncertain what you meant." He'd been thinking about it since wakening and wanted to know more about their large friend.

Sotchek scrutinized him from his deep-set eyes hidden beneath bushy eyebrows. It made Braxton feel uncomfortable, as if the bigger man was looking right through him. He turned toward the fire, using the food as an excuse to look away.

"You have elven blood," Sotchek said at last.

"Why . . . do you say that?"

"You may look human, but your breath is from the forest."

No one spoke; they all stared at Sotchek.

Brax nodded. "Yes. My mother is elvish."

"Are you going to Arbor Loren to see her?"

"No. To save her. She was injured in an attack by the Mins, and I need to get to the forest to find help."

Sotchek stirred the stew in silence.

"You said you were a half-breed," Braxton pressed, "but I imagine you're not elven."

Even as the words left his mouth, he knew he'd gone too far. The mountain man looked at him sharply, sending a sinking feeling down into Brax's stomach.

Be careful. Serene warned. *Do not insult this one, for he is quick to anger, and we need him as an ally, not an enemy.*

An uncomfortable silence settled over the camp as Sotchek stared at him. Braxton tried to act naturally, as if his question was normal, but his hands shook when he lifted his bowl. He quickly set it back down on his lap, hoping the big man hadn't noticed. Ruskin lit his pipe and puffed on it calmly, helping to ease the tension.

"This stew's excellent," Phinlera said, trying to help. "The meat's pheasant, right?"

Sotchek didn't respond or even acknowledge her question. He just continued staring at Braxton, unmoving, as if even his breath had stopped and his large form had become part of the surrounding rock. Brax felt his skin crawl, and the hairs on the back of his neck tingled in warning. He knew the other man could strike him from where he sat, and he'd be helpless to defend himself.

Serene, he called out nervously. *Help me. I never meant to insult him!*

Wait, she replied. *Do not speak further. Let him respond first.*

Braxton took a breath to calm his nerves, and even managed to drink some of the broth without shaking too much.

"It's grouse," Sotchek said, glancing at Phinlera, and causing Brax to jump and spill his stew down his shirt. The giant man's face lightened, and the crease in his brow subsided.

"I am part ogre," he continued, watching their reaction. "My mother, like yours, wasn't human."

"Oh," Braxton choked out, trying to act natural, but he knew his response sounded strained.

"My father was a trapper from Kharnus. He was attacked by a shale bear on the Ridge while hunting."

"Shale bears are vicious creatures," Ruskin interjected, taking the pipe from his mouth pointedly and shaking his head. "My clansmen encounter them often in the Spine. We know better than to wrestle with 'em."

Sotchek turned toward the dwarf. "I think it was the first time my father had met one. It took him by surprise."

"Mmm." Ruskin puffed on his pipe and nodded. "They do that in the Spine too."

"My mother's village was nearby. She came across him lying in a ravine after the attack and nursed him back to health."

"I thought your people preferred not to associate with the lesser races."

"That is true," Sotchek agreed, "but she took pity at seeing his broken form, all mangled and bleeding, and was cast out for doing so."

The dwarf nodded thoughtfully, as if fully understanding. Brax and Phin, however, kept quiet, unwilling to risk insulting Sotchek further on topics they knew nothing about.

"We'd better go." The big man got up.

They stood quickly, doused the fire, and gathered their belongings. Within minutes, they were on their way again, their new guide leading them toward Almon-Sen. Ruskin grabbed Braxton's arm as they left.

"That was foolish, lad."

"I know, I'm sorry. I didn't mean to insult him."

Rusk smiled at the pained expression on Braxton's face. "No harm then," he said, letting him go. "Just choose your words more carefully. We need this big fellow's help." He followed after Sotchek, leaving Brax and Phin to trail behind.

The day passed uneventfully, and they saw no sign of the Hunters or any other travelers out on the central plains. They stopped late again to shelter in a small group of valley pines, enjoying another stew of Sotchek's making. Braxton lay on a bed of fallen pine needles, worrying about the number of days that had passed since leaving home and wondering if his mom's essence was still with him. He reached out to Serene for some answers, but she didn't respond, and her silence only refueled his fears.

Sotchek woke them early the following morning, well before sunrise.

"This is where I leave you," he said, towering above them as they lay on their makeshift beds, his pack already secured and the camp cleaned. "Continue north until you reach the great road crossing the plains. Turn east, and it will lead you to the elves."

"Thank you for everything," Brax said, rising to his feet and extending his hand.

Sotchek looked at him for a minute, brusquely shook his hand, then turned and walked away. Brax watched him go, saddened by the sudden departure. He was about to return to the camp when Sotchek raised his left elbow, and a small sparrow hawk swooped down to land on his outstretched arm. A moment later they were gone.

They ate a cold breakfast from the sack Sotchek had left, then set out in the direction he'd indicated. By midday, they found the broad cobblestone "great road" winding through the plains, connecting Amberdeen to Almon-Sen. They turned east and walked for a few hours, eventually topping a small knoll that provided a panoramic view of their surroundings. In the distance stood the deep emerald forest of Arbor Loren. The trees extended for miles in either direction, from the far-off Dragon's Spine in the north to the tips of Tail Ridge Peaks in the south.

Braxton smiled at the sight, relieved, as if coming home—a home he'd never seen before but always knew existed. He let out a deep sigh, a breath he'd been holding since Oak Haven. It had taken them longer than expected to get there, and at times, he'd wondered if they'd ever make it, but now at last Arbor Loren was in sight.

"Hold on, Mom," he said quietly to himself. "Just a little longer. Hold on."

CHAPTER
19

A mile from the elven forest, Ruskin stopped and turned to Braxton and
Phinlera.

"Do you see 'em yet?" he asked, jerking his head toward Arbor Loren.

"See what?" Brax scanned the trees.

"The elves! Do you see anyone in those damn woods?"

Ruskin had been growing more and more agitated as they approached
the elven kingdom, his obvious dislike for entering their woodland realm
becoming increasingly apparent.

Braxton strained his eyes, searching. Accustomed to finding deer, birds,
and other woodland creatures back home, he was sure he'd see the elves if
they were there. But nothing moved—only the continual swaying of the
trees as the afternoon sun cast a golden light upon the canopy.

"I don't see anyone—just the trees."

The dwarf grunted in acknowledgment. "They've seen us by now," he
said, almost to himself, then started walking.

"Do you see anything?" Brax asked Phin.

"No people, but it looks like there's some kind of netting running
between the larger trunks a few layers in. Do you see it?" She pointed to
the left of the road.

He looked again as they continued, smiling at Ruskin's grumblings
about entering "these cursed woods" and how he never should've agreed to
go on this journey. He stared farther into the forest, beyond the outermost
perimeter and deeper into the emerald green. Then he saw what Phinlera's

sharper eyes had noticed—a silvery mist interspersed with layers of green and brown, like leaves caught in a gentle breeze, flowing between the large oaks in a rhythmic pattern. It covered the entire height of the forest and rippled like water, sparkling here and there in the sunlight. Patches of the woods seemed to appear and disappear so as to create the illusion of seeing farther into the trees than was actually possible. Brax watched as they drew closer, realizing he couldn't see past the outer layer of the forest. The netting formed an impenetrable barrier, preventing outsiders from seeing beyond a dozen feet.

"What's that layer of mist between the trees?" he called out to Rusk.

The dwarf stopped and looked at the forest, shaking his head before turning toward them.

"They call it the *feil*, the forest's shroud—magical weavings by the elves and trees or other such nonsense," he grumbled. "It blocks sight into Arbor Loren, and anyone who tries to pass through it becomes ensnared, like a fly in a spider's web. It's one of the reasons I hate this place."

The road continued on, reaching a small opening at the edge of the central Andorah forest that extended into the trees a hundred feet or more. The *feil* lay on either side, allowing their path to continue unhindered. Two giant oaks stood like sentinels beside the road as it crossed into Arbor Loren. Guardians to the entrance of the great elven kingdom, they extended above the canopy, with wooden platforms in their uppermost branches. At the end of the road, two more enormous trees, which Brax guessed to be fifty feet or more across and over five hundred feet tall, towered high above their neighbors, marking the gateway into Almon-Sen.

They crossed the threshold without stopping, passing the outermost watchtowers unrestricted. Still they saw no sign of the elves. Ruskin strode ahead confidently now, but Brax and Phinlera trailed behind, searching the forest and admiring its immense size. Braxton glanced at the trees encompassing them on either side of the road, each more than a hundred feet tall, their branches extending outward like giant's fingers to touch their neighbors. Where these overlapped, wooden tendrils intertwined, forming a continuous connection from one great oak to the next, creating an endless pathway wide enough for a man to walk upon.

As he marveled at the formations, he became keenly aware that he was being watched. Then he saw them. Elven bowmen standing motionless along the walkways like extensions of the trees themselves. The colors of their cloaks, like the forest around them, changed in response to the light filtering down through the canopy. He could feel their penetrating gaze from beneath their hooded coverings, sensing the intrusion, questioning their presence.

Approaching the great doorway at the end of the road, Brax noticed how, high above, the branches of the two magnificent oaks interconnected to form a path along which platforms were intermingled. Twenty feet from where their road ended, Ruskin stopped, unslung his pack and dropped it to the ground. He raised his hands to show he was unarmed. Braxton and Phinlera did the same.

"We come out of the west beyond the Vales." Ruskin spoke loudly at the entrance to the elven forest. "To meet with Bendarren. Our need is great, and we seek passage into your woodland realm."

There was no response. They waited, searching the great oaks, but no one appeared.

After a few moments, the dwarf added, "We carry the essence of one of your own, and it is urgent we find Bendarren. Grant us passage to Almon-Sen."

Still nothing.

"How is it that a dwarf knows the name of Bendarren Elestera?" came a sudden reply.

There, standing between the two great oaks, was an elven warrior, who seemed to materialize from the trees themselves. One minute they were staring at the forest, and the next he simply stood in front of them. As tall as Braxton, his ash-blond hair ran like liquid gold to his slim shoulders, sparkling whenever the afternoon light fell upon it. Intense green eyes accentuated his narrow face and high cheekbones that angled slightly toward a defined chin. Two small, pointed ears protruded from his hair, and a long, braided strand hung down from his left temple.

Ruskin bowed respectfully, then touched the fingers of his right hand to the center of his chest, then to his forehead, before extending outward, palm up, in a gesture of peace and greeting. The elf didn't respond but just scrutinized the dwarf. Braxton and Phinlera quickly followed Ruskin's example.

"I ask you again," the elf said, "how is it that you know the name of one of our people? For such things are rarely given." He cast his forest-green cloak over one shoulder, revealing a brown tunic inlaid with silver thread that glistened whenever he moved. His lighter green trousers were tucked into high, soft boots laced to the knees, and a longbow, made of a deep-forest wood, was strapped across his back, its white-feathered arrows protruding from a quiver above the opposite shoulder.

"We were sent to find him by one of your own. A young elfling named Jen Prinn fights death. The boy here carries her essence."

"That name no longer has meaning to us. She is an outcast woman who abandoned her people's deepest beliefs to join with a *human*," the elf said in disgust, looking Braxton up and down.

"That woman is my mother," Brax replied quickly, stepping forward, angered by the elf's lack of respect. "And she needs Bendarren's help."

"So, you carry her essence with you," he answered. "Very well. If you want to enter Arbor Loren and carry her disgrace upon your shoulders, that's your business. But proving what you say is true is mine. Before you can enter our kingdom, I will look into your mind and see if what you tell me is indeed the reason for your coming. If I find you speak the truth, I will allow you passage. If not . . ." He raised his right hand to show two fingers. There was a sudden *whoosh* in the air, and a half-dozen arrows rained down from the trees to land in a circular formation around the surprised visitors.

Ruskin backed away quickly, his hand instinctively going for the falchion. Then he stopped, realizing what he was doing, and lifted both hands again to show that he had no intention of fighting.

The elf seemed amused. "A wise choice." He turned to Braxton. "Do I have your consent?"

"You do."

Do not reveal me, Serene said. *Focus on the Min attack.*

He was about to respond when he realized the elf had already entered his thoughts. It was not abrasive or intrusive or clumsily done. Unlike the experience he'd had with Zacharias in Falderon, this was subtle, delicate, and artfully achieved. The elf was there before Braxton could react, moving through his mind like an extension of his own thoughts, a gentle breeze that carried with it a presence easily missed.

Frantically he tried to think of something to counter the intrusion and fixated on Phinlera. His desire for her ran plainly through his mind, and the feelings she awoke in him echoed louder than the ringing of a gong. He scrambled to control his thoughts, trying to hide his desires, but it was too late, and the elf smirked at Brax's feeble attempt to divert his attention. Braxton took several deep breaths. He closed his eyes and focused on blanking his mind, as Serene had taught him. For a moment it worked, and his mental canvas cleared, emptying his palette.

Well done, he heard the elf say. *Now I will talk with your mother.*

Before Braxton could respond, the elf's presence reached into the very depths of his mind to the exact place where his mom's essence waited. There he connected with her. It was a strange and intrusive sensation that Braxton fought to repel, but the elf brushed him aside, like clearing a gnat.

It's all right, Brax, he heard his mom say. It was the first time she'd spoken since leaving Oak Haven, and a wave of emotion welled up inside him. He sniffed and swallowed to remove the lump in his throat, relieved to find her still with him.

Hello, Gaelen. She turned her attention to the elf. *You seem well.*

So it is true then, he replied. *The elfling who abandoned us has returned.*

Braxton felt them connect then in a distant way, as if merely catching the echo of something he once knew. They conversed quickly, a strange and silent communication that transcended words but was rich in its distinct exchange of emotions and images. It was an entirely unique experience, having these two people communicate in his mind, using his body for their meeting place, catching only glimpses of the thoughts and feelings he couldn't see but could only feel. It reminded him of being back home in his bedroom, listening to his parents' quiet conversations when they thought he was asleep. Yet entirely different somehow, as if the feelings and pictures running through him carried a deeper meaning filled with expression and intent, relaying through emotions a complete history that words alone could never convey.

He could feel Gaelen's resentment toward his mom. Yet it was more than that—a sense of disgrace or even personal injury at her leaving them and abandoning their ways. But Brax understood why she'd had to go. Bendarren had foreseen the need for his mother to leave their woodland realm and to marry an outsider, believing that one day her offspring would return to Arbor Loren, changing it forever.

He witnessed how the elven mentor had visited her inside a beautiful oak covered with soft pink flowers, telling his mom to forsake her people, to separate from their immortality, and to leave the protection of their woodland home. He experienced the grief she'd suffered in accepting his words and her pain at separating from her tree, a life she'd loved beyond her own. Forbidden to disclose her directive, he endured her degradation by the elves when she announced her intentions, lived through her agony of departing from the forest she adored, and felt the abandonment of the people she loved. Overcome by her emotions as she rode away in that small wagon beside the man he now knew to be his father, Brax felt her entire life with his dad, and the sorrow for the life she'd lost—aware of its complex story through the burst of a single impression, like comprehending a detailed book by merely touching its cover.

The sheer sadness of her experience was a complete emotional drain for Brax. He wanted nothing more than to break down and cry for her loss, for the choices she'd been asked to make. But he was denied relief from the feelings bottled up inside him. He just stood there, a distant participant in their conversation, overwhelmed by the emotional echoes of their exchange, transfixed somehow by their joining, this elf and his mom.

When the connection finally ended, Braxton fell to the ground and wept. He cried for what she'd endured, for the weight she'd carried for so long and how well she'd hidden it from him. He wept for how deeply she'd loved her people and for her endless longing for her tree, wounds cut deeper into her consciousness than any physical harm the Mins could have inflicted. He felt connected to his mom in a way he'd never imagined possible, having within seconds shared her entire life's story, her very deepest regrets, reliving in their entirety all her emotional pain. For the first time, Braxton Prinn finally understood his mother.

I think at last I understand you, the elf said, when Braxton had cried himself out. He was speaking openly within Brax's mind, communicating with his mom. *You have suffered much in your choice, Jenlyrindien, but you are free now.* His voice was kind, entirely opposite in tone from their initial meeting. *It would be my honor to escort you back to Bendarren Elestera, and, more than that, to uphold your return to our people.* He inclined his head.

Thank you, Gaelen. Brax's mom's reply was both joyful and sad. *Then I am truly home.*

CHAPTER
20

They passed through the gates of Almon-Sen and entered Arbor Loren at last, twelve days after leaving Oak Haven. Gaelen led them beneath the great archway of enfolding oaks, giant guardians that watched their crossing like sentient beings, silently recording their passage.

Ruskin followed behind, his eyes flicking this way and that at every sound, like a badger suspicious of entering a trap, knowing his only way out was slowly closing behind him.

They continued among the trees and passed unknowingly into the *feil*. All light and sound vanished. Braxton felt completely alone, as if he'd been picked up and dropped into the middle of a dark and turbulent ocean that he could neither see nor hear, feeling only a peculiar current pulling him toward some unknown fate. He shivered in the silent void, aware that there was no longer any warmth left in the world. Fear and panic overwhelmed him, and he instinctively wanted to flee. He looked about for something with which to identify—a shape, a color, a sound—but there was nothing. Nothing to give him any reason for hope, and he floated about in the cold, naked and lost.

Then a light split the dark, bright and vibrant, dispersing the gloom. There stood Serene, her unicorn form surrounded by a brilliant and all-encompassing radiance, banishing the void.

Come, she said, stretching her head out to touch his face, dispelling his fear and calming his mind. He wrapped his arms around her long muscular neck, letting her lead him on, unaware and uncaring of the direction they went.

Feeling warmth on his face, Braxton opened his eyes and blinked. He stood alone in a beautiful glade of emerald green, with little white flowers growing in patches of sunlight that filtered down from the canopy. He breathed in deeply, washing away the darkness of the *feil*'s nightmarish experience. Phinlera appeared, stumbling amid her own visions he cared not to know. She thrashed about for a moment before stopping to look up at the sun. Ruskin emerged seconds later, swinging his arms wildly before realizing he too was free.

"I hate the *feil*!" he said.

"Come." Gaelen appeared from across the clearing. "We have a long walk tonight." He offered them his waterskin and several small, round cakes. Braxton felt as if he was tasting food for the first time. Rich earthly spices mixed lightly with the sweetness of honey filled his palate, enticing his senses and invigorating his body.

They left the glade following a trail that only Gaelen's eyes could see, allowing them to walk unhindered along the woodland floor. Winding among the giant oaks, they passed unaware to the south of Almon-Sen. Night descended, and an endless sky of twinkling stars burst above them, visible through the canopy. A chorus of night birds took up their callings, and an exquisite elven voice joined the choir from afar, gradually increasing in strength and cadence to come forward and lead the symphony. Walking behind Phin, Brax realized that the voice was not coming from any one person but from the perfect blend of hundreds or perhaps even thousands of elves all singing together. He'd never heard anything quite so beautiful, wanting both to laugh and cry at the same time. As the sound reached its climax, the spirit magic awoke. Pulsating inside of him and growing stronger, it flowed through his body in waves of rhythmic, uplifting energy.

The music began to fade, and with it, the energy receded. It left Braxton feeling exhilarated, as though he'd touched energy for the first time, reaching completely across the bounds of the physical world and into pure spirit, drinking from its endless spring.

He was still enjoying the wondrous sensation when he realized that the others had stopped walking and that Gaelen was staring at him. The elf smiled, a peaceful and radiant gesture. He nodded at Brax in apparent understanding, as if something he'd been struggling with was suddenly made clear. Then he turned and led them away.

Hours past midnight, they entered a small clearing deep in the heart of Arbor Loren. An enormous tree stood opposite, matching the ones guarding the entrance to the elven kingdom. A small cottage fronted the magnificent oak, its back disappearing into the trunk as though the home itself was an extension of the giant structure. Small platforms were visible among the varying levels of the branches, some with walls on one or two sides or protected by a low railing.

Standing among the wildflowers and bathed in the light of the moon was an elf, dressed in a beautiful blue robe of interwoven silver leaves. His straight, white hair hung down past his shoulders and a long, thin nose and narrow, pointed chin defined his features. It was his deep-blue eyes, however, that reflected his wisdom. Braxton realized that this was a man who knew much about the world, as if life's infinite history could be read from within his gaze.

He recognized him immediately. That same masterful presence he had felt during his mom's experience with Gaelen.

This was Bendarren.

Approaching slowly, their elven guide raised a hand, signaling for them to stop.

"Welcome," Bendarren said, his voice both firm and soft. "I am Bendarren Elestera, keeper of this grove. I've been awaiting your coming."

Braxton and the others introduced themselves. They bowed to the elf in imitation of Gaelen's lead and made the sign of greeting, ending with both arms open in a gesture of peace and friendship. The elven elder returned the motion, inclining his head.

Braxton stepped forward. "My mother is dying." He explained what had happened, taking a deep breath before describing her wound and unconscious state. Removing the necklace, he relayed how she had connected with him and her plea to return her essence to Arbor Loren. "This is the pendant," he said, holding it up for the elf to see.

Bendarren listened without interrupting. When Brax had finished, the elf let the silence hang in the air for a few moments before responding.

"You've done well to come this far, but Jenlyrindien's essence is fading, and her time is near. You must reach her tree in Arbor Glen and release her essence at first light, or she'll be lost to us forever."

He looked at Braxton for a long time, his gaze penetrating deep into Brax's eyes, as though seeing past his thoughts and into his very soul. Brax felt Serene move in the back of his mind and an unspoken word seemed to pass between her and the elf.

Bendarren bowed fully. "I understand now how it is that she still clings to life. It is an honor that you have come, and you bless our forest with your presence."

"Come," he said quickly, causing Braxton to jump. Turning from the glade, he led them back into the trees.

They walked for hours. Gaelen provided more cakes that felt warm to the touch, and they drank often from his waterskin. Braxton was surprised that he could keep up with the elves. They hadn't slept since their last night with Sotchek, and yet he was wide awake. The muscles in his legs felt stronger, as if he could walk all night without tiring. Whether from the elven food or the newfound exhilaration that flowed through him at finding Bendarren, he wasn't sure. They'd come so far and encountered so many obstacles that had threatened their success. But now their journey's end seemed near, and the anticipation of saving his mom was invigorating.

He leaned closer to Phinlera. "I can't believe we're finally here. That we actually made it."

A puzzled look crossed her face. "Did you think we wouldn't?" Phin always was the optimist.

"No," he said, a bit defensively, "but so much has happened since we left home. I'm just happy to be nearing the end."

She smiled at him.

Ruskin, by contrast, trailed further behind. He looked around nervously and muttered to himself whenever they stopped or when one of the elves spoke. Before leaving the glade, Bendarren had given him the opportunity to stay behind rather than take this last path, recognizing the dwarf's discomfort in the forest. But he'd refused.

"I vowed to stick with 'em," he'd said, jerking his head toward Brax and Phinlera. "I may as well go this last leg."

Braxton was grateful for Ruskin's company and for how much he'd helped them on this journey. He knew they'd never have made it this far without him, and that he owed his dad's friend a great deal. *Someday*, he thought, *I'll find a way to repay him.*

They continued throughout the night, consuming a steady supply of cakes. It was approaching morning when Bendarren led them over a small rise and into a large clearing dotted with gigantic oaks.

"This is Arbor Glen." He gestured about without stopping. "Home to the elflings."

Braxton looked around at each massive tree, their leafy silhouettes outlined against the brightening sky. The moon had moved on to another part of the forest, completing its evening journey.

Cresting a low hill, they stopped briefly in front of a bare and gnarled tree. Brax glanced at it absently. Unlike the neat bases around most of the oaks, a blanket of moss covered the ground and vines choked its trunk.

It must be dying, he thought to himself. He looked at Bendarren, eager to continue.

A deep sadness washed over him, and his mom's essence began to cry. *This was her tree*, he suddenly realized. This twisted old oak was once that beautiful form he'd seen in her vision. Its leaves and flowers were gone, and only this withered form remained, a dried husk of the beauty it once possessed. He dropped to his knees and wept.

"It is time now," he heard Bendarren say.

Braxton got up and wiped a sleeve across his face.

"What must I do?"

"I will guide you."

Following the elf's instructions, he unhooked his mom's pendant and held it against her tree, pressing it with his left palm. The elven mentor grasped his other hand. Braxton was surprised at the strength of his grip. Then Bendarren placed his open palm against the trunk, opposite the pendant, completing a half circle.

"Now, place your forehead against the oak. Close your eyes, and wait for the sun to rise."

Brax rested his head against the gnarled bark. He could feel where the sap had run down, and smelled the pungent scent of its damp and decaying form. But he waited.

His mom's essence came more into his consciousness. As she did, so did Serene. A wave of emotion flowed through him. He was grateful that his master was there, knowing she was helping his mom. He felt them move into the forefront of his mind. A moment later, Bendarren entered his thoughts.

There was a brief instant when the elven elder almost saw Serene, but Brax felt her divert his focus, and the elf turned toward the tree. A powerful energy emanated from Bendarren—a strong, vibrating presence as if from a much younger man. Braxton's palm pulsed where they touched, the energy flowing between Bendarren, himself, and the tree.

You have done well, Jenlyrindien. I am pleased. Bendarren spoke in that same emotional exchange that Gaelen had used.

Thank you, Father, his mom replied.

Braxton frowned. Was his mother really this man's daughter, or was it just a title she bestowed upon him? He wasn't sure.

Your sacrifice has cost you much, but you are home now. Rest, my daughter.

Yes, Father. I've longed for this sleep, but my life has been blessed by those who chose to walk with me. I am not sorry for the choices we made.

I am pleased, Bendarren repeated.

Brax's mom turned toward him.

Thank you, Braxton. Thank you for this.

"Of course, Mom." He spoke out loud. "I love you."

I know you do. I love you, more than you know. She began to cry, and he sensed, more than heard, *I will miss you.*

"What do you mean, Mom?" he asked. "You're going to be fine. We're at your tree. Bendarren is here."

I will not be going home, Braxton, she said after a pause, and he felt her tears flow.

"What! Why?" he called out. "I don't understand. I thought we made it in time."

The light is awakening, Bendarren interrupted. *It is time now, Jenlyrindien. Rest and be healed, my daughter.*

"What's going on? Mom?"

A burst of energy flowed into him from where his forehead touched the oak, and his body shook uncontrollably. His ears rang from a single, incredibly high-pitched note inside his mind, blocking out all other sounds. He knew the sun had risen. Then his mom's essence started moving into the tree.

"No! Mom, don't leave me!"

Listen to me, Braxton. Her face appeared in his mind. *My time has come. My body is beyond repair.*

He tried to pull away from the oak, but his head wouldn't move, and his left hand felt embedded in the trunk. He summoned the spirit magic, focusing on severing the connection.

Serene appeared, blocking his vision to everything but her white form standing between them.

Beloved child, you cannot stop this. It is her choice to make. Let her go.

"No!" he yelled, building the energy, feeling the spirit magic flow through him in waves.

Serene moved ever so slightly, and the energy dissipated.

Let her go, she repeated. *I am with her, child. Trust me.*

Braxton clung to the fading remnants of the spirit magic, knowing it could save his mom, but unsure what to do.

Trust me.

His heart pounded and the high-pitched ringing became a rhythmic pulsing in his ears. He held his breath, refusing to let go.

Then he exhaled, releasing all the tension in his muscles and his connection to the energy. The spirit magic vanished.

Thank you, Brax, his mom said. *I love you so much.*

"Don't go, please," he begged in a broken voice. "Don't leave me, Mom. I need you."

He could already feel her essence pulling away, and only an echo of her original presence still remained within him, until the pendant dropped from his palm.

"Mom!" he yelled out desperately.

Braxton, she answered, as if calling to him from some far-off place. *Braxton . . . Brax . . .*

Then she was gone.

CHAPTER

21

A woman's voice sang gently, a beautiful and peaceful sound, as if morning itself had woken and was singing praise to the coming of a new day. Braxton lay in a soft bed with white linens, the east end of his room open to the sun. He tried remembering where he was, but his mind refused to cooperate. A detailed scene of an elven girl bathing in a pool filled with water lilies was carved into the ceiling. He stared up at her and thought she glanced toward him, but then, just as quickly, she was frozen again.

The singing ended and the events of the previous night flooded into him. He remembered his mother being drawn into her tree and the pain at losing her returned. He already missed her presence—her singing, her comfort, her warm embrace. Most of all he missed the joy she always brought to him and his family. Now she was gone. Because of him. Because he failed.

He rolled over and cried.

After he'd pained for a while, he dressed and walked over to the railing. He was high up in the tree of Bendarren's home, overlooking the forest. He couldn't remember ascending its height last night, only lying beneath the oak into which his mom had withdrawn, calling out to her, begging her to stay.

Good morning, child, Serene said calmly.

"What's good about it?" he answered gloomily. "I failed."

Once you walk in the forest and breathe the morning air, perhaps you will find that all is not lost.

He watched the sun, feeling its warmth on his face. Small birds rose from the trees and danced in the light, swooping back and forth on a gentle breeze. Braxton admired their basic life, silently wishing his could be as simple.

Turning back, he descended the spiral staircase inside the enormous oak, emerging into the main room of Bendarren's home.

Phinlera sat at an intricately carved table, eating from a spread of fruits, berries, and honey cakes. She leaped up when she saw him. Ruskin was nowhere to be seen.

"Brax, come quickly, you need to see this!" She ran over and pulled him toward the door.

"Hey, Phin."

"Come *on*, Brax," she insisted, dragging him outside.

A wave of sadness welled up when he realized they were heading back to Arbor Glen. Following behind her, he knew he'd have to face this sooner or later.

It was late morning when they reached the enormous oaks.

Braxton! His mom's voice burst into his mind.

"Mom?" He jerked his head up, expecting to see her. The bare, dying tree was gone. In its place stood a tall, upright, magnificent oak, clad in leaves of a thousand greens intermixed with small pink roses. Vines no longer choked its trunk, and a few tiny white wildflowers grew at its base. It was the most beautiful sight Braxton had seen in a long time.

Bendarren stood beside the tree. "Good morning, Braxton," he said kindly. "Come and visit with us for a while."

He stumbled forward. "How . . . how is this possible?"

Oh, Braxton, I am so very proud of you, his mom's voice said again.

"Mom, is that really you?"

Yes, Brax, you saved me! You saved my essence and gave life back to my tree. Thank you. Oh, thank you so much for this.

"I . . . I don't understand. Mom, what happened?" Tears of joy ran down his face.

The one who walks with you healed me. I've been given life again, life within this form.

An immense happiness emanated from her presence, as though she were feeling joy and love for the first time—a wonderful and unconditional emotion for her tree and the life she held within it. Happy for her, he wiped his hand absently across his face.

Brax wondered what kind of life she could have now, how it would affect their family, and what his dad might say? But in the end, he wrapped his arms around her trunk, no longer smelling rot or decay, but a perfumed, springtime aroma.

"Don't ever leave me again," he said.

She folded her branches down to cover him. *I am home now and will always be here for you within this grove.*

He stayed within her embrace, talking with his mom, telling her all they'd encountered and how much she meant to him—all the things he'd never said when she was in human form. Eventually they laughed together, peacefully connected within their minds.

When she folded back her limbs, he stood back and admired her height. She looked magnificent with the sunlight filtering down through her leaves and upon her branches, displaying a myriad of colors. Phinlera grabbed his hand and squeezed it excitedly.

"Told you," she said smugly, nudging him with her elbow.

"Thanks, Phin. I owe you."

She leaned up on her toes and kissed him square on the mouth. Then broke away and ran into the forest. He was about to pursue her when Bendarren spoke.

"I am glad you are happy, Braxton Prinn. In time, your father will come to live here too. Even now, he is preparing for the journey."

"Thank you. Thank you so very much, for everything."

"I am grateful you have come." He waited a moment, then added, "Perhaps you could do something for me?"

"Anything," Brax said, happy to repay the elf's kindness.

"The Council of Elders will convene tomorrow in the forest's court in Almon-Fey. I would very much like you to accompany me there."

"I'd be happy to."

"Then enjoy your day, and I will send for you at nightfall." Bendarren smiled at his mom's oak, then turned quietly and disappeared into the forest.

Braxton and Phinlera spent the day in Arbor Glen, sitting beneath his mom's tree, the three of them conversing together, with Braxton relaying his mom's words.

I need to rest now, for I am tired and not quite healed, she said at last.

He got up and hugged her before leaving with Phin. The two of them wandered among the gargantuan oaks—the worries of the previous night gone. The elves offered them food and drink wherever they went, their hospitality as endless as the varied tastes of the bountiful fare they provided. Most were women and children, but occasionally, they'd see an elven man among the boughs. Unlike the weapon-clad soldiers at the entrance to Almon-Sen, they wore robes of forest colors or deep-blue or green shirts of the finest silks. No one carried weapons, and all tended to the stately trees that distinguished Arbor Glen from the rest of the forest.

Braxton sat alone with Phinlera in a small glade. "I want to tell you about the sword."

She looked into his eyes. "I would like to know."

He disclosed to her then all that he'd experienced in his connection with Serene and the raising of the spirit magic. He covered every detail, wanting to share with her the entire experience, happy at last to have someone to talk to. She listened intently, interjecting occasionally to ask a question or to clarify that she now understood why he had made certain decisions or acted in a particular way.

When he finished, she gazed at him. "This experience has changed you."

"In a good way, I hope." He laughed a bit self-conscious.

"I think so, but I'm amazed at what you've been able to do, Brax, and that these things are even possible to achieve. If it were anyone else telling me this, I wouldn't believe them."

"I know it's hard to understand, and sometimes I can't believe it myself, but I cannot change from this path, Phin. It's connected to me somehow, joined with what I am and who I'll become. I don't even know if it is possible to separate us, the spirit magic is so intertwined with me now."

"I know." She stared at him for a long time. "I can see it in your eyes."

They relaxed on the grass, looking up at the deep-blue sky, listening to the numerous sounds around them—birds and insects all calling to one another.

"It's so beautiful here," she said after a while. "As if the whole world's in balance. At peace."

"Yes, but I'm looking forward to going home soon."

Phinlera sat up. "Home? I don't think we'll be going home anytime soon."

"What do you mean?"

"Well, given everything that you've just told me about Serene and her sword, I think you have a long road still ahead of you before we'll see the familiar sights of Oak Haven again." She forced a smile. "She wouldn't have chosen you otherwise."

"I never thought of that." He sat up next to her. "I was always so focused on just getting my mom to Arbor Glen; I never really considered anything else."

She touched his hand. "I think it's time you did."

He lay back down. "Perhaps you're right. Maybe I should connect with Serene and ask her."

Phin grabbed his arm. "Know this. No matter what happens or what she says, I'm going with you. Promise me you won't try to go on without me."

He didn't respond.

"Promise me."

"All right," he conceded at last. "I hardly think I could stop you anyway."

"Yeah, and I'm still faster than you and a better archer too, so don't forget that." She poked him playfully in the side, making him laugh.

Braxton took a deep breath. He started to call to the sword's master when an elf in a long brown robe appeared from the trees.

"Bendarren kindly requests your return."

They looked at each other for a moment, then followed the elf into the forest.

CHAPTER
22

*B*eloved child.

Braxton jumped at the sound of Serene's voice. She hadn't spoken to him since the previous morning, high up in the little room of Bendarren's home, and she startled him now.

They'd walked for most of the night, following Bendarren's lead to Almon-Fey before resting in the capital city. Ruskin had joined them too. Having spent the day drinking and smoking at one of the feasting halls, his spirits had risen considerably.

They sat in the elven court, on wooden benches covering one end of the rectangular platform. Council members faced each other from across the front, seated on high-backed chairs of leather sewn into wooden armrests that lined both sides of the open-air structure. Bendarren had discreetly named each member as they'd entered—five on the left, four on the right, with one chair left empty—providing a brief background on their status in elven society and their duties to the court.

King Eilandoran was the last to arrive, directing the council from a beautiful white carved throne beyond the chairs and opposite the benches. He wore a golden vest inscribed with silver and a small wreath interspersed with tiny white gems that glistened from atop his long black hair. A cloak made of emerald-green leaves intertwined with golden feathers draped over his throne. He was asking for a report on the Breaker Dunes, when Braxton had heard Serene.

I need you to speak my words, she continued.

What . . . what do you want me to do?

Repeat to the court exactly what I say, and keep your eyes closed. Do you understand, child?

Yes.

Braxton took a deep breath, closed his eyes, and waited for Serene's words. The court continued on around him, the king's rich voice periodically rising above the others. Brax listened quietly to events he didn't understand, wondering why he was there. He'd saved his mom and was eager to spend time with her back at her tree. He asked Serene what to say, but she wouldn't respond, and he just kept thinking about his mom or returning home with Phinlera, sitting beside him.

"Our scouts have reported large groups of Mins massing in the western Dunes," Kael was saying. He was the Blademaster, Bendarren had explained, the finest swordsman in all of Arbor Loren. He strode around the court, confidently addressing the king and the council members.

"Many of our flyers have not returned," he said, "and I fear they're being shot down. Patrols were sent out, but only one of their number returned. He says they were attacked by Mins armed with ballistae and flocks of vipers coming off the peaks at Ben-Gar."

"This is a significant change in the Min attitude," Illian, the general of the elven army and a man of high distinction, stated. "First an attack on the Gates in the western lands, and now the massing of armies on our eastern border. Clearly the Mins are preparing for war."

"Why the sudden show of strength?" the king asked. "After centuries of peaceful coexistence within the Dunes, what has changed?"

It is the work of the Dark Child, Serene said. *Tell them,* she added to Braxton when he didn't respond.

Brax stood up, took a deep breath, and spoke Serene's words aloud to the court.

Everyone stopped and turned in shocked silence. A murmur rippled through the elves, an obvious combination of offense and surprise reflected in their quiet voices.

"You dare to speak at our court?" Kael retorted. "By all rights you shouldn't even be here. And what does a half-breed human boy know of such matters anyway?"

I know a great deal more than you, Kael Illyuntarie, came Serene's response, which Braxton relayed nervously, trying to steady his hands by holding them behind him. Interrupting the court was clearly an affront to the elves and one that Kael took personally.

"I should kill you where you stand for this disgrace!" the Blademaster snapped, moving quickly across the platform to Brax. "You're the son of an outcast woman who forsook our people's deepest customs, insulted our honor by marrying a *human*, and dirtied our blood. Her half-breed child dares to return, carrying her essence, and he has the indecency to stand here in our court and speak aloud like an honored guest!" Kael drew his sword. "I claim the right of Emari," he cried, turning toward the king and bowing deeply.

Eilandoran nodded slowly. The Blademaster stood right in front of Brax.

"This is a fight to the death, boy," he said flatly. He was so close Braxton could feel his warm breath on his face. "I hope you're prepared to die." He strode over to the right side of the court and waited.

Draw my sword, child, came Serene's calm guidance.

What? I cannot possibly defeat him! He's an elven Blademaster! He's way beyond my skill.

Yes, child, he is, but he is not beyond mine. Draw my sword, and step aside. This is something I will do.

Braxton took another deep breath, trying to steady his nerves. He reached a shaking hand over his head and grasped the handle of the Unicorn Blade. Kael chuckled at the sight of his nervousness. But as Brax's grip tightened, a massive rush of spirit magic flowed into him. Serene came forward into his consciousness so completely that she took over his entire physical form, beyond anything she'd done before. It was a strange sensation, as if a much larger and greater being had suddenly stepped right into his body. He pulled himself aside awkwardly in his mind, allowing her to take control.

His body straightened to its full height, which seemed small in comparison to her overlaying presence. The power of her energy flowed through him, awakening every muscle to her magical form. All fear, all doubt, all apprehension fell away like sand to a rushing wave, and the calm, euphoric feeling embraced him completely. His eyes stayed closed as she lifted his head and drew the sword. A ringing echoed across the court as the blade was released, silencing the assemblage. For a moment nobody moved, and Braxton could hear the blood pumping in his ears.

Kael rushed forward with incredible speed, striking a decisive upward blow that Braxton knew, alone, would have ended his life. But Serene had already raised her weapon, even before the attack came, and calmly deflected the strike, angling Brax's body sideways to the elf. Surprise rippled through the court as Kael's forward momentum moved him past his opponent. Braxton felt as if the whole world stood still. Then the Blademaster turned and struck again, moving his sword at lightning speeds—above, below, across—but each time, Serene deftly blocked his efforts. The two blades rang out across the awestruck audience. Repeatedly Kael attacked, darting left and right, swinging low, then overhead. He danced around Braxton in a blur to the wide-eyed Phinlera, watching in fear. But Serene continued to block his strikes as the two opponents maneuvered about the platform.

"Enough of this!" The words burst from Braxton's mouth after several more minutes of Kael's offensive. Then Serene struck back. She moved Braxton's body forward, his arm swinging so fast that Kael could barely deflect her attacks. He stumbled back from the onslaught of Serene's superior skill. After a half-dozen more strikes that pushed the elf completely across the court, Serene flicked Brax's wrist and Kael's sword flew from his hand, sliding away across the wooden floor. The Unicorn Blade ended with its point pressed against his throat.

"I am Elhunarie." The words came out of Braxton. "And this half-breed boy, as you call him, is my Chosen. I expect your loyalty and your counsel. Or has the Dark Child's influence so overshadowed the elven people that you forget your place?"

The silence was beyond anything Braxton had ever heard, as if the entire forest had suddenly been stilled; even the birds and insects were quiet. He could feel every eye staring at him, there within the calm serenity of Serene's protection.

"Now, listen carefully," she said, removing the spirit sword from Kael's throat and turning Brax to face the council members. "The Min gathering is not by chance. It is the work of the Dark Child, guided by the Witch Sisters of Dahgmor. They have gathered the tribes together and united them under a single banner, their banner, with the intent of destroying the elven people.

"The attack on your Walking Gates was intended to disrupt the western lands, causing each to close its borders to one another—a clever plan that has achieved its goal. The Dark Child knows this and is preparing for war. You have little time left before the full onslaught and power of the Min army is brought against your eastern border, and they are a number far beyond your reckoning. You cannot hold back this storm when it comes, and it will break upon your forest with a ferocity that even the *feil* cannot protect. You have this one chance. Attack before their army is at full strength. If not, Arbor Loren will fall. Even now you cannot defeat them, for they already outnumber you many to one. You need help. Call upon the allegiances of old. Only together can you hope to stop this tide."

She turned Braxton to face the Blademaster. "I require your assistance, Kael Illyuntarie. In exchange for attacking me today, you will train my Chosen, for he will need to face the Dark Child before the end, and he is woefully unprepared. I put him in your charge now. Make sure he is ready when the time comes, for I will not be able to aid him again as I have today.

"You have much to do, children of the forest," she said, moving Braxton to look at the council again, "and little time in which to achieve it. Heed well my words, or the beloved Arbor Loren will fall."

Serene pulled back then, her essence receding completely from Brax's body and the spirit magic dispersing as quickly as it had come. He convulsed, opening his eyes and dropping to his knees. Looking down, he retched onto the platform. Shivering uncontrollably, his body continued reacting to the unexpected energy change.

Phinlera ran to him and wrapped her cloak around his shoulders.

"You all right?" she asked, concern reflected in her voice.

"Get him some broth to drink," Bendarren shouted. "Quickly!"

He heard movement, and the elves handed him a small bowl of warm liquid.

"Drink this." Phin helped him raise it to his lips.

Braxton drank slowly, trying not to spill its contents with his shaking hands. The warmth of the broth soothed him, relaxing his body, allowing his energy to return.

When he looked up at the court, his eyes met stunned faces. The shock of what had occurred, and the warning that had been given, still overwhelmed the elves. It was Kael who spoke first.

"I owe you an apology," he said calmly, towering over Braxton and extending his hand. "My honor blinded me, and for that, I am truly sorry. I accept the charge from the one who walks with you and take responsibility for my actions. I vow to train and protect you."

Braxton smiled, took his hand, and shook it weakly.

"Thank you. I am honored to learn from a Blademaster."

"The honor is mine, young Braxton Prinn."

He walked over to a small table to the left of King Eilandoran, opened its single drawer, and withdrew a long piece of red ribbon. Kael stood there for a moment looking at the silk cloth. Then he turned toward the court and tied it around his right bicep.

There was an outcry from the elves.

"No, Kael, you cannot!" General Illian came to his feet. The council members voiced their agreement, and a murmur of discussion broke out.

Walking to the center of the platform, the Blademaster held up his hands for silence. "In response to my recent actions and foolish heart of late, I accept Balen-Tar." He tore the symbol of the golden eagle from his left breast and dropped it to the wooden floor.

The court erupted in protest. All of the gathered elves standing now, loudly voicing their disapproval.

"Be still!" King Eilandoran rose, silencing the court and the considerable crowd that had gathered from the forest. He turned to the Blademaster. "Kael Illyuntarie, long have you served Arbor Loren with grace, courage, and distinction. The elven people do not agree that you have been dishonorable, and neither do I." The crowd agreed. "However," Eilandoran went on, quieting his people, "this choice is yours alone to make." He paused to emphasize his words. "I ask you then, do you call Balen-Tar freely upon yourself? And I urge you to carefully consider the weight of your response."

"Great king of Arbor Loren, gathered council members, and honored guests to our kingdom." Kael walked around looking at those assembled. "Long have I served you, risked my life for you, and defended our homeland. And I believe I have done so with honor."

The elves murmured their consent.

"However," he continued, raising his voice above the court, "I cannot deny that which my heart now recognizes has brought shadow upon my actions. I therefore accept discommendation freely and will wear the cloth of Balen-Tar by my own choosing."

Surprise and disagreement broke out among the elves again. The king raised his hand, forcing silence. "Kael has made his decision. The family and bloodline of Illyuntarie shall henceforth bear the mark of dishonor."

Kael nodded, walked over to Braxton, and smiled at him weakly. "May the deeds of my future be greater than those of my past."

Then he turned and left the court.

CHAPTER
23

King Eilandoran dismissed the court shortly after Kael's exit, directing them to ready their armies and prepare for war. The elven kingdom seemed to come alive to Serene's message, focusing on the preparations for what lay ahead.

Bendarren, however, led Brax and the others to a small glade, where long, intricately carved tables had been arranged beneath the giant oaks. As they sat together, an elven attendant brought them a silver platter filled with fruits, pies, and warm cakes.

"Couldn't you find any meat?" Ruskin grumbled at noticing the lack of venison in the elven diet.

Brax and Phin, though, enjoyed the woodland fare and drank cool water from wooden goblets that never emptied.

"When Serene spoke to the council today," Brax said to Bendarren, "she mentioned she is Elhunarie. Can you tell me what that means, for it's a word I've not heard before?"

The elven master looked at Braxton and he felt a brief connection between Serene and the elf.

"Eons ago," Bendarren replied, "there were no trees or mountains. No animals or birds or people. Indeed, there was no life. No world. Not even the sun or the stars." He gazed up at the sky as if to emphasize his point. "There was just an endless void stretching on forever.

"Then a thought sprang from the darkness. The very first expression of life, and where it touched the void, light was created. And as the thought recognized its own self-creation, its own conception from nothingness, it grew in understanding of who and what it was. As it did so, the light expanded and became the great central sun."

Bendarren poured himself a drink from an elaborate silver decanter an elven maiden had just set down, before continuing.

"Then the thought looked out across the void and perceived that it was alone. And so it pulled from deep within itself and created shards of radiant energy that it sent out into the darkness—Children made in its own image, lesser thoughts born of the One. These great beings traversed the void, their light calling back to the source, saying, 'Father, there is nothing.' And the One heard his Children and conceived that there should be light to guide them. So he sent out smaller suns, great stars created to brighten the darkness and further separate the void.

"And some of the Children called back to their Father again, saying, 'Send forth a place where we can further your work.' And the One heard their call and saw that their intentions were good, and he created giant balls of fire from within his own expanding form, radiant spheres that burned in his own brilliance. These he sent out to touch the cold of the void. As they did so, their outer shells cooled and hardened to form great orbs of rock that held the fire of life deep within them. And the One said to his Children, 'Use these as your canvas upon which to create.'

"The Children worked with the rock, molding it into mountains and valleys. And where there were spaces left hollow, they filled them with water, cooled from the void. They pulled trees from deep within the life of the shell and set grasses and flowers to grow in abundance upon their surfaces. Then to their creations they sent forth animals and birds filled with tiny sparks of life taken from within themselves, just as the One had done, each giving willingly to serve their Father. And all that they created was beautiful and strong and abundant."

Bendarren stopped to take a drink from his goblet and eat one of the warmed cakes. Brax and Phinlera sat quietly, eager for him to continue. Ruskin, however, appeared disinterested in the elf's story and consumed large quantities of ale he'd discovered in the silver pitcher, stopping only to stuff more honey cakes into his mouth.

"Then," their elven guide said, "some of the Children desired to see what it would be like to walk in the valleys, to visit the trees and the animals, and to experience all that had been created from the power of the One. And so they divided themselves into twelve smaller forms of the Children they once were, lesser gods that could exist within the constraints of a physical world. These came down to walk upon the earth for the first time, calling back to the One and telling him of all that existed. How beautiful and plentiful it was. And the One was pleased with his Children and said to them, 'Create life that can walk upon the world to enjoy what has been created, and let it carry my seed, that it may know from whom it came.' And the lesser gods listened to their Father and toiled long and hard, pulling from the light within themselves, given by the One, working with the greater Children who'd remained above, and together they formed the races of the world.

"The first of these were the elves and dwarves, created to care for the forests and the mountains. Then other pure forms, like giants and dragons, were given to serve the land and the air. All carried within them the knowledge of their god parents and the abilities that had been given to them to care for the world they loved. And for centuries, the various races lived in peace and life existed in balance.

"Then a few of the lesser gods wanted to create a life that would grow more rapidly and experience a broader range of what the world could offer—lives that would evolve from a tiny existence into a great awareness, and that would traverse the world to experience all that the One could provide. And so they created humans. These they formed in small tribes that were primitive at first, but that had the ability, more than others, to grow and evolve. To ensure that they focused on their lives and world alone, undistracted, the gods hid from mankind the knowledge of their parents and their descendant from the One—blocked from human consciousness but kept alive deep within them, that they might discover it for themselves.

"Finally," Bendarren said, "the Children who had split into the lesser gods departed from this world, leaving it to grow on its own, watching it from the spirit realms, adjusting and aiding where needed. And for thousands of years, it flourished.

"Eventually, though, one of the lesser gods who'd helped create life thought that the human race needed guidance, as it had grown too rapidly and too wildly. And so he called together his brethren, and they pulled again from the light within themselves as their Father had done, and they sent forth another new life to walk upon this world. To these they gave full knowledge of the One, authority to rule over all other races, and the ability to understand and guide them, to counsel their need, and to vary creation so as to allow it to continue to grow. These that came were the Elhunarie—great masters sent by the lesser gods who split from the Children, born of the One."

"What happened to them?" Braxton asked, captivated by the story.

Bendarren smiled and ate some of the fruit, drinking from his water goblet and leaving Ruskin to finish the ale. When he'd paused long enough, he continued.

"Unfortunately, although the human race grew rapidly, they looked to the Elhunarie to solve all their problems, to provide for them, and to correct every hardship that mankind endured. In short, they became dependent upon the masters and worshiped them as gods themselves—'the gods within the four lands,' they called them. The Elhunarie decided then that in order to allow the human race to continue to grow through its own natural evolution, through its own self-experiences, that they, the descendants of the lesser gods, should depart this world. And so the Elhunarie left the earth, leaving the races to fend for themselves.

"Before going, however, they too pulled from deep within the forms they'd used to traverse this world, as guided by the One, and placed parts of their own essence into twelve relics. These are the spirit swords, Braxton, of which you carry the Unicorn Blade. These they gave to the leaders of men to help counsel the human race and to maintain a connection to the masters, through which guidance could still be given."

"I thought there were only nine swords," Braxton said.

"No, there are twelve." Bendarren took another drink from his goblet. "The number is significant, as it represents the twelve original Children that came from the One, the twelve lesser gods that divided from them, and the twelve Elhunarie who came to the earth. The last two of these are sometimes referred to as the Greater Council of Twelve and the Lesser Council of Twelve. The reason mankind believes there are only nine blades is because three of them are actually not swords. These were given to different races of the world, remaining unseen by the land of men even today. In truth they should be called the spirit weapons rather than the spirit swords, but that is not important."

Braxton wasn't sure he understood everything Bendarren had said, but he nodded anyway, and the elf smiled kindly.

"And who is this Dark Child?" Phinlera asked. "And the Witch Sisters?"

"The Dark Child is an elf," Bendarren said simply, seeing their surprised faces. "Born of Arbor Loren.

"Understand that elves do not experience any of the negative emotions carried by many of the other races of the world. We have no hatred or jealousy. Our strong do not victimize our weak, and greed and power are nonexistent within the woodland realm. To keep this purity and our immortality, one child is born to us every few hundred years who carries all the negative emotions of our entire race. All these traits that would destroy other nations are born within this one child, this Dark Child, and they come to us with these emotions intact.

"To keep the elven race pure, the Dark Child is sacrificed at birth, given back to the One so we may flourish as a people."

"He's killed?" Phinlera exclaimed. "That's barbaric!" Brax too was surprised that the elves, a nation known for its compassion and enlightened thinking, would commit such an atrocity upon one of their own.

"He or she is sacrificed for the good of the elven people, yes," Bendarren clarified.

"Then how could the Dark Child be the cause of the Min attacks on the west?" Brax was confused.

"A little less than a century ago, a male child was born to us with this trait. As is our custom, we prepared to return him at the moment of birth. Unfortunately"—Bendarren took a deep breath—"we failed.

"There was an attack on the ritual ceremony by two very evil creatures, the Witch Sisters of Dahgmor, ancient and magical beings of tremendous power. All but two of us in attendance that night were killed, and the Dark Child was taken by the Witch Sisters and raised in shadow. It is they, I suspect, who are the real instigators of the Min invasion.

"As the Dark Child has approached manhood," Bendarren continued, "all the evil emotions of hatred, fear, and power have begun to creep back into our people. I think your experience with Kael today, Brax, is an example of this. But you must not judge our Blademaster too harshly, for he is battling a much greater war within himself than you can possibly imagine. You see, Braxton, Kael was the only other elf to survive the attack from the Witch Sisters that night, and it was his charge to ensure our safety and thus the destruction of the Dark Child. Kael therefore carries not only the burden of failing to protect us, but also the knowledge that he has allowed the evil emotions that could destroy our nation to creep back into the elven people."

Brax and Phin both let out a deep breath, understanding now the reason behind Kael's initial attack and the weight of failure he must carry.

"Our Blademaster," Bendarren said, "has sworn an oath to find and kill the Dark Child. However, we've never been able to locate him. Now, it seems, Kael may get his chance at last."

CHAPTER
24

Awaken, child, Serene said, pulling Brax from his dreams.

He got up, tired from the lack of sleep and events of the night before. The elves, he'd discovered, had created a feast in his honor, a festival for the coming of an Elhunarie back into their forest. Despite their focus on preparing for war, they still found time to create a banquet for all to enjoy. Many had attended, arriving in periodic waves throughout the night, staying awhile to celebrate, and welcoming Braxton into their woodland realm before continuing with their night's duties. The event went on until late into the early morning hours, including much singing and dancing in which Braxton was obliged to participate. Even King Eilandoran had attended, staying just long enough for Bendarren to introduce him.

"We are honored by your coming," the king said before departing, surrounded by a group of attendants.

Brax, however, found the whole event uncomfortable. Unaccustomed to attention back home, he'd been suddenly thrust into a distinguished position within elven society, recognized now as the Chosen of Serene. It was an unexpected experience, and one he hoped not to repeat. While the dancing, music, and endless fare for which the elves were renowned awed him, he would've preferred to attend as just one of many rather than the honored guest.

It was well past midnight when he finally went to sleep. Bendarren had shown them to separate rooms at different heights in a guest oak adorned with silver leaves. Ruskin, however, had flatly refused to ascend the tree, settling instead for a makeshift bed on the floor of the ground level.

Brax admired the predawn light on the forest, standing now by the half wall in his room that seemed customary in the elven homes. He wondered if it would be the same wherever he went—if he'd have to endure a life of constant focus from those around him rather than the quiet anonymity he'd previously enjoyed.

Will home ever be the same again? He sighed heavily at how dramatically his life had changed. *But it was worth it*, he thought, *for his connection with Serene.*

He descended the wooden stairs inside the tree, listening to Ruskin's snoring growing louder as he approached the dim light emanating from below.

"Good morning," Bendarren said, as Brax entered the room. Kael stood beside him, the red cloth of Balen-Tar visible above his shirt.

The Blademaster inclined his head. "Are you ready to begin?"

It took Braxton a moment to realize what the elf meant, but then he remembered the training Serene had required of the Blademaster.

"I am," he said, trying to sound prepared, even though he still felt sleepy.

"Then I take you into my charge," Kael spoke proudly, turning toward the door and indicating for Braxton to go.

He guided Brax to a clearing outside the capital city just as morning's light broke through the trees. Braxton liked the place the elf had chosen— quiet and away from everyone else. He felt he'd met half the elven nation last night and was grateful to be alone with the Blademaster.

"Eat first," Kael suggested, handing him a wrapped cloth containing some small vegetable cakes and a few clusters of nuts and other forest grains.

The clumps were held together by a flavorful honey that energized him, clearing his mind and awakening him fully. Kael watched Brax consume the meal and drink from a waterskin the Blademaster handed him. When he was done, Braxton drew the Unicorn Blade, ready to begin.

"No, Brax," Kael said gently, raising a hand. "Put it aside for the moment."

He looked at the elf, then sheathed his weapon, unstrapped it from his back, and set it down.

"Take some deep breaths and fill your body with the morning air."

Brax breathed in the forest's crisp scent as Kael walked around him. Then he placed a hand on Braxton's stomach.

"Breathe so you push my hand away."

The Blademaster showed him how long to hold his breath, what to do with his chest and stomach, and how to fill his lungs completely. Brax felt as if he was learning to breathe all over again, as if he'd been doing it wrong his entire life.

Patiently Kael guided him through the movements, placing his hand against various parts of Brax's upper body, checking the rise and fall of his efforts.

"Good," he said at last. "Now, stand with your feet apart and place your right foot ahead of your left, like this."

For the remainder of the morning, the Blademaster taught him how to stand, how far to bend his knees, where to place his arms, and how to rest his weight on the front of his feet. All the while, he instructed Braxton on his breathing, clarifying the actions that needed correcting.

They stopped briefly at midday for another meal of forest berries, fruits, and cheese. Already fatigued, Brax drank liberally from Kael's waterskin. When he was done, the Blademaster showed him how to move forward and back on his feet, when to shift his weight, and how to feel his connection with the ground beneath him. He had Braxton turn left and right, got him to step up quickly onto a fallen tree by the clearing's edge, and then just as quickly drop back down. He taught him how to pivot in place more fluidly and how to recognize when his body was weakening.

Late in the afternoon, Kael pulled the log into the center of the glade and had Brax move forward and back across its length, balancing on the narrow trunk. He stopped Braxton at times to hold his weight first on one foot, then the other. The Blademaster touched parts of Brax's legs, pushed here and there on his muscles to show him where his weaknesses were, repositioned his feet, and instructed him on how to strengthen his posture, constantly reminding him to breathe.

When evening came, he tied a cloth around Brax's eyes and had him repeat some of the exercises blindfolded. Braxton found it much more difficult without the benefit of his sight or the confidence of knowing his surroundings. Kael, though, was an excellent instructor and taught him how to trust his body and his intuition, encouraging him at every turn. He helped Brax rely on other senses besides his sight and showed him how to gain awareness with his entire body.

By the time they stopped and Kael led him back to the guest oak, Brax was totally exhausted. Even though he hadn't swung the Unicorn Blade even once, his entire body felt drained. Every muscle ached from the intensity of the exercises, and yet he was sure the Blademaster had barely scratched the surface of what he knew. For a moment, he wondered if he was up to the challenge, but he thanked Kael nonetheless when they arrived and promised to continue in the morning. Seeing no one else around, Braxton crossed the empty hall, ascended the staircase to his room, and collapsed on his bed.

The following day, he returned with Kael to the clearing. Brax's muscles ached from the previous day's exercises, but he didn't complain. He knew he needed to learn to fight properly with the Unicorn Blade, and that time was not on their side. They repeated the actions from the day before, stopping at midmorning.

"Now," Kael said, "unsheathe the spirit sword."

Braxton felt a sense of exhilaration at his words, as if he'd finally earned the right to draw Serene's weapon. He grabbed the wooden handle and pulled it free.

Kael inspected his grip. Then one by one he started repositioning each of Braxton's fingers.

"You need to place your hands here and here," the Blademaster said, moving them apart. "This gives you strength, these fingers add agility, and placing your palm here adds balance."

For over an hour, he instructed Brax on just how to hold the weapon, what to do with his hands based upon the type of strike he intended, and which part of his palm to use. Finally, he showed Braxton how to swing the Unicorn Blade. When he did so, the movement flowed easily, as if the sword almost swung itself.

"You see, Brax, learning the basics is the key to becoming a master."

For several hours Braxton maneuvered the sword under Kael's direction. His body ached, but he didn't complain. The Blademaster had him swing the weapon in the same arc over and over until Braxton's muscles strained. All the while, he adjusted Brax's posture, kneeling down at times to move his feet or standing next to him and lifting his arms. Sometimes he stood behind Brax, adjusting his shoulders or aligning his hips. Occasionally he'd wrap his hands over Braxton's and perform the movements with him, guiding his actions, allowing him to feel the perfect swing. Throughout the motions, the Blademaster's primary instruction remained the same. "Breathe."

"Now," Kael said in the late afternoon when Brax stopped for a drink. "I want you to summon the spirit magic."

Braxton stared at him in surprise. He had no idea the Blademaster knew anything about spirit magic.

"If time was not an issue for us," the elf continued, "I'd have you practice for another month before proceeding, but that's not a luxury we have."

"What . . . do you want me to do?"

"Within your heart's center, bring up the energy that your sword's master has given you. Let it flow into every part of your body, every muscle, every thought, throughout your very essence and into the weapon. Feel the blade becoming a part of yourself, and allow the spirit magic to bind you."

Braxton stared at him.

"Is something wrong?"

"I . . . I just didn't realize you knew about the spirit magic."

Kael chuckled. "That energy is part of everyone and everything we are, Brax. It lives inside all of us. The sword, for you, is a catalyst—a doorway for finding what naturally exists in all beings. You are fortunate to have such a tool that has awoken its abilities in you. For most of us, it takes years to find."

Braxton nodded, not quite understanding. He closed his eyes and summoned the spirit magic. Instantly it responded, intensified by his recent exercises, and it coursed through him, bringing with it that same uplifting feeling. Enjoying the sensation, he directed the energy as Kael had instructed, guiding it into his limbs, pumping the energy outward throughout his body, strengthening his form. Then he sent the energy into the Unicorn Blade, connecting it through his hands. The sword reacted, lightening to his grip, intensifying the vibration, and extending an invisible tendril back from the pommel to the Chosen Cross on his chest, increasing the euphoric feeling.

"Good," Kael said. "Very good. You've used the energy before, I see. Your connection to it and the sword are stronger than I'd expected. Now repeat what we practiced."

Opening his eyes, Braxton replayed the actions, feeling the fluidity of his movements and the weapon. For a brief moment, he seemed to glide along the forest floor—almost as if moving without intention.

When he stopped, he looked back at Kael, waiting for further instruction.

"You've done well, Brax, better than I'd hoped for." The Blademaster nodded his approval. "We'll stop here for today and continue again in the morning. And tomorrow, we'll duel."

CHAPTER
25

When Braxton arrived at the guest oak, he was energized from the day's experience and the remaining spirit magic still flowing through him. Unlike the night before, he felt exhilarated, as if he'd drunk from some wondrous spring of life that gave him unlimited energy. Even his aching muscles felt better. He understood now how the elves could go for days without tiring.

Entering the familiar wooden building that had become his elven home, he was surprised to see Penton and Gavin laughing with Phinlera. His brother got up as soon as he saw him.

"There you are!" He walked over and hugged Brax.

"Pen!" Brax exclaimed, returning the warm embrace. "When'd you arrive?"

"Oh, we made it to Almon-Sen yesterday morning, but it took us a while to convince the elves to let us in and even longer to find out where you were staying. We only got here an hour ago."

"Good to see you," Gavin added, extending his hand after the brothers had parted. Braxton shook his grip, then bent down to scratch Bear, the elkhound trotting over from under the table to nuzzle him.

Ruskin puffed away on his pipe, a mug of ale in one hand.

"They were just telling us about their journey," Phinlera explained. "Come, sit and listen. Have you eaten?"

"No, I'm starved. Kael's been working me hard." He turned to introduce the Blademaster, but the elf was gone.

"Come on, Brax," Phin called again.

He stared at the door, disappointed at not being able to introduce Kael or thank him for the lesson. He joined the others and helped himself to some stew and bread that had been laid out.

"I saw Mom today," his brother said as Braxton began eating. "We spent a long time together, and she told me what you'd done. You saved her life, you know."

Brax shrugged and took a quick drink, tipping his head back to hide his emotions.

"I know you miss her," Pen continued. "I do too. But, in a way, I think she's happier now. And we can still talk with her and feel her presence. If I close my eyes when I sit under her tree, I can almost feel her right beside me."

"I know," Brax said weakly.

"Tell 'em about the patrol," Ruskin interjected.

"You should've seen it." Pen laughed. "We threw that little pouch of Rusk's into the fire, and seconds later it exploded across the entire camp."

"Yes, we saw." Brax grinned, remembering the scene.

"How could we miss it?" Phinlera added.

"But what you didn't see was how the colors in that bonfire changed to the most amazing iridescent blues and purples, or how the exploding red-hot timbers ignited the tents and spread like wildfire across the camp, as if they were alive. It was incredible!"

"It was pretty amazing," Gavin agreed.

"I meant tell 'em about the patrol's leader," Ruskin clarified.

Pen nodded. "After hours of having his men chase down horses, the patrol's captain—Breem, you'll remember—rounded us all up and interrogated everyone personally. He was furious. He wanted to know where we were, what we saw, and if anyone had come in or out of the camp. His eyes bulged so much when he spoke, I thought they were going to pop out and roll across the table."

"Your friend Zacharias didn't like us much either," Gavin added.

Braxton looked up, his smile fading.

"He sat in on all the questioning and told the captain we were lying. I think if he didn't hate Zacharias so much, Breem would've had us whipped right there and then. Anyway, the soldiers tore through our bags and food crates as if they'd gone mad, looking for something to implicate us, but they never found anything. And the guard we bribed was nowhere to be seen."

"Good thing too," Gavin said. "Otherwise we'd probably both be dead by now, or at least in chains."

Pen continued. "The next day, everyone was checked every hour, and the guards moved among us so frequently that it felt like we were being herded like cattle. One even rode in our wagon for a while. And we had to sleep with the soldiers too. It took us twice as long to get down to Montressa. Poor Cassi was so scared, I thought she was going to turn us in." He laughed.

"What happened to her?" Phinlera asked.

"We eventually got her home safely. She lives in one of those small rooms in the public housing on the south end of town. When we explained to her mom what had happened, she was so grateful to us for bringing Cassi home that she wanted to give us everything they owned—which wasn't much. Anyway, if we ever go back there, we have a place to stay. It'd be nice to see them again."

Brax was only half listening. "I hope letting Zacharias go doesn't prove to be a mistake," he said turning to Phinlera, who nodded. He told the others of their last encounter with Zacharias and meeting Sotchek.

"I told ya we should've just taken his head and been done with him," Ruskin commented.

"It was kind of you to let him live," Pen added. "I just hope you don't regret it."

"Me too," Brax said, looking worried.

They continued talking into the next morning, laughing occasionally as they retold their respective stories, catching everyone up since separating in the Vales. It was late again before Brax finally got to sleep, and he was still tired and stiff when Serene awoke him at dawn.

Time to go, child.

He rose and dressed. Although drowsy and sore, he was excited to see Kael and to continue his training. He thought about how much the elf had taught him already in such a short time. And today would be extra rewarding. Having the opportunity to practice his swordplay with a Blademaster was indeed an honor, and one he could never have imagined. Growing up in Oak Haven, he'd always heard tales of the legendary elves and their renowned skill with both sword and bow. He'd often pretended to be one of them, play fighting with Pen, using broom handles as weapons. He'd never dreamed he'd get a chance to practice with one of them. Now he was going to test his skills with their best, and he couldn't wait.

Grabbing the Unicorn Blade, he hurried down the steps of the giant oak, but even before he reached the great room, he knew something was wrong. Maybe it was the lack of Ruskin's familiar snoring, or the absence of elf song. Mostly, though, it was just a feeling, a distinct impression that something had changed.

"What's going on?" he asked when he entered. Ruskin was fully dressed, talking with Bendarren by the table, a green traveling cloak pulled around his shoulders and the falchion tucked under his belt

"It's the Mins, Brax," Bendarren said calmly. "They're on the move."

"Yeah," Ruskin added. "And they're coming this way. All of them."

Braxton looked at Bendarren. "What're you going to do?"

"There's a Walking Gate in a small village in the mountains at the base of the Dragon's Head," the elf explained. "A very old Gate, one of the first ever made. It has long since been forgotten by most people, lost from memory and knowledge of such things, but it is there nonetheless. There was a council this morning, and it has been decided that a small patrol will travel to the Gate and try to open it. If we can reach it in time, we may be able to send in an army behind the Min line."

"I'm going with 'em," Ruskin said. "At least as far as the Dragon's Spine anyway. I need to convince King Tharak to send down a regiment to help. Not an easy task, I might add."

Braxton felt a sudden loss at the idea of parting with the dwarf. They'd been through so much together and traveled so far, and he owed his life to Rusk. He wasn't prepared to say goodbye. Not yet.

"The rest of the elven army is marching to our eastern border," Bendarren continued. "War, it seems, has finally come to the forest."

"What can I do to help?" Brax asked.

Ruskin exhaled audibly.

"The council is sending one of our elfling people with the patrol," Bendarren said. "And, like your mom, this is the first time she has left Arbor Loren, and only the fourth time in our history that one of them will leave us. We'll all feel her go. But she is strong with spirit magic, and it is our sincerest hope that, should the patrol make it to the Dragon's Head, she'll be able to open the Walking Gate and let our forces in behind the Min army. Her name is Jenphinlin."

"Can she open the Gate by herself? I thought it took eight people."

"The elfling race is especially gifted with spirit magic. Any one of them can open a Walking Gate. That is the reason your mother never joined your Keepers. She would have been able to open your Gate by herself."

Brax finally understood now why his mom had always refused to take the trials. "Wait, why are you telling me this?" he asked.

"Because, Brax, we believe you need to accompany her."

"What?" He was shocked at what Bendarren was asking. "You want *me* to travel behind the Min line?"

Bendarren nodded slowly. "I think this path is chosen for you."

Yes, child, we must go, Serene interjected. Brax felt a wave of panic wash over him. He couldn't believe she was agreeing with the elf and that they wanted him to travel into the heart of the Min army. His mind filled with the memory of the attack on Oak Haven.

"I'm sorry." He shook his head. "I want to help. I really do. But I can't go to war. I got my mom's essence safely to her tree and need to stay here with her, and then see Phinlera home. I can't possibly go."

Ruskin made a *hmph* sound. "How long do you think your mother will survive if the Mins burn down the forest?"

Braxton looked at the dwarf, surprised.

Bendarren placed a hand on his shoulder. "Do you not understand, Brax," he said kindly, "that your mother's fate is now bound to Arbor Loren?"

Braxton's stomach turned as he realized that the elf was right. His mother's life lay in the balance of the outcome of this war. If the Mins succeeded, she would die.

"You want me to go to war," he repeated.

That is why I have chosen you, Serene clarified.

But I need to stay here and protect my mom, he argued.

You can remain if you wish and wait for war to come to the forest. For come it will. But if you do, my beloved child, it will be too late, and the sword that is my extension will need to pass to another.

You'd leave me? he asked incredulously.

That is the choice before you.

Braxton thought about what it would mean to lose his connection with Serene and her beautiful, magical energy. It had become such a part of him now that he wasn't sure he could live without it. But traveling with the elves meant facing the Mins, something he feared more than anything. Even more than losing his mom, or Serene. Could he maintain control of his emotions, of his fear, if confronted by those who'd assaulted his village and his family?

I'm not sure I can do this, he said. *Besides, I'm only just learning how to fight properly. I can't possibly stand up to a Min!*

He is going with you.

Who, Ruskin?

The one who is training you.

"Kael is going?" He looked up at Bendarren.

"That is correct. He is leading the patrol."

Tell them we will go.

I'm . . . afraid, Serene. He admitted.

I know, child. She paused a moment. *But this is needed.*

Braxton took a deep breath. "All right," he said at last. "We'll go."

Bendarren smiled, as if he'd known Brax would come to this conclusion. "I have brought you these." He walked over to a small pile of supplies near the table. "The cloaks will allow you to pass unseen, and the boots unheard. Neither will leave any sign of your passage. The packs will store whatever you put in them and still have room for more. These waterskins never empty, and the food I've supplied should last throughout your journey."

"Thanks," Brax said simply, still stunned at what he'd been asked to do.

"What about the pipe leaf?" Ruskin commented.

Bendarren glanced at the dwarf but ignored him and turned to Brax. "The others are waking. They will join us shortly. Gather your possessions and eat quickly. The patrol is readying to leave."

W hen Braxton rejoined them in the main room of the guest oak, he saw that Phinlera, like Ruskin, was dressed in the boots and cloak Bendarren had provided.

"I'm going with you," she said firmly. "Don't try to argue."

He was about to respond but thought better of it. He knew he'd never convince her to stay.

Gavin and Penton were there too, but unlike the others, wore only their normal traveling clothes. They had packs similar to his, which Braxton found always weighed the same, no matter how much he stuffed inside it.

"Aren't you coming?"

Pen shook his head. "Gav and I are going back to Amberdeen with an elven emissary to request aid from King Balan. The elves are hoping he'll send some horsemen."

"So much for needed rest." Gavin smiled wryly.

"You'll be a good diplomat for them, Pen," Brax said. "But I still wish you were coming with us."

"Me too, but I think having us with them might help the elves' chances of the Empire getting involved. Gav's still part of the militia if you remember, and my years of bartering in Amberdeen might come in handy." He grinned.

Brax forced a smile. He knew the road ahead was going to be difficult, more than anything he'd faced before, and wished for his brother's strength of company.

Go to the table, Serene entered his thoughts.

He walked over to the large wooden structure and sat down in front of some parchment that had been laid out.

Take the quill.

Dipping the end into a nearby ink bottle, Brax felt Serene close his eyes and draw something on the parchment. After a moment, he rolled it up. When she released him, he looked at the others.

Bendarren handed him a small scroll tube made of a dark wood carved with an oak tree. Brax slid the parchment inside the tube and secured its top.

Tell your brother to give it to Iban and no other. He is one of our Chosen in your king's city. Tell him to request a Council of Sorrows.

Braxton wasn't sure what she meant but repeated the message, excited to learn the name of one of the King's Squires.

"Yes," Bendarren said quickly. "Iban must be a Wielder."

"A Wielder?" Penton asked. "How would Brax know the name of a Wielder? I thought they were kept secret."

Braxton realized that Penton still didn't know about Serene.

"Never mind that now," Bendarren replied. "If Iban is one of the Chosen, you can ask to speak with him directly. There is a very old custom, one that has been deliberately forgotten by the magistrates of your great city. Any citizen is allowed to ask for help from a Wielder. By requesting a Council of Sorrows, you invoke that right, and the governing council is required to oblige. To ignore this is an affront to the Elhunarie of old and a direct insult to the Wielders themselves. No citizen can be denied."

"Give him this." Brax handed Penton the scroll. "It will help make your case."

Penton looked at him curiously, but he tucked the tube under his belt and tied the leather strap.

"Now," Bendarren said, looking around at each of them. "The time has come for you to leave Arbor Loren. The elven patrol and our emissaries are waiting."

CHAPTER
26

As Braxton and the others left the guest oak, they found Kael and a dozen elven warriors outside. Each wore a forest cloak similar to the guards they'd seen at the entrance to Almon-Sen, with bows strapped to their backs and thin swords by their sides. A young elven girl whom Braxton guessed to be around Phinlera's age, with long blond hair and a gentle face, stood beside Kael.

"Allow me to introduce Jenphinlin," the Blademaster said, inclining his head toward the smaller girl. The elven warriors followed his lead.

"Hello." She smiled at each of them.

It is an honor to walk with a Chosen, she added inside Brax's mind, and he sensed the spirit magic in her connection.

The honor is mine, he replied awkwardly, touching her thoughts. He was amazed at the strength in that touch, as if she had complete control of her emotions and, more importantly, of the energy within them. For a single moment, the spirit magic seemed to emanate from every part of her being. Then it was gone.

Kael introduced the rest of the elves who'd be accompanying them to the Dragon's Head, taking time for each man, explaining his special talents or abilities—tracking, hunting, swordsmanship, or some other extraordinary skill. All were accomplished bowmen. As the elves greeted them, it was clear that the Blademaster knew his companions well and had handpicked the members of their party.

"And this—" Kael stopped at the youngest in their group, a boy who appeared slightly older than Brax, with ash-blond hair and almond-shaped eyes. "This is my son, Laefin. He is, without a doubt, the finest archer in all of Arbor Loren." The others nodded their agreement.

"I've never seen him miss," the Blademaster said. "In fact, I'm not sure he knows how to." He smiled proudly.

The young archer looked down shyly, touched a hand to his heart, and bowed, but unlike the others, said nothing.

When they were done, Jenphinlin walked over to Phinlera and pulled a small sword from under her cloak.

"This is Shelindûhin, 'leaf of the forest.'" She rested the weapon across her upturned palms, looking up at Phin. "It was made for an elf maiden long ago, when the world was still young. I gift her to you now, that you may stand beside your Chosen."

For the first time in his life, Braxton saw Phinlera speechless. Having grown up in a poor family, with very little to call her own, no one had ever given her much consideration. Now she was being honored with an amazing gift by someone she'd only just met.

"Thank you," she said, brushing a long strand of hair behind her ear before accepting the weapon, a little embarrassed by the sudden attention.

"I do not agree with her joining us," Kael interjected, turning to Jenphinlin. "Phinlera is young, of little fighting experience, and would be safer in the forest. I cannot assure her safety."

"I understand." The elfling glanced at the Blademaster. "I assume responsibility for her fate, that you may be free of that burden."

Kael nodded, but remained silent. Brax was surprised that the Blademaster deferred to Jenphinlin, who obviously held a high level of authority.

The sword, Brax noticed, was of incredible craftsmanship. Shorter than most and completely straight, the blade had a slightly curved tip and an intricately inscribed vine that meandered down and around both sides. The long, oak handle could be wielded equally well in either one or both hands. It was the hilt, however, that was the focal point. Made from some unknown metal, it formed a series of overlapping dark green leaves that fanned out around the grip, protecting its wielder's hands. As Phinlera touched Shelindûhin, the leaves shone with an inner glow, and Braxton felt the energy emanating from the weapon.

That is a blessed gift, Serene said, and Jenphinlin smiled in response. It took Brax a moment to realize that the young girl had heard his master.

"The time has come," Bendarren interrupted, causing Braxton to jump. "Each of you must follow a new path. One we hope will bring a quick end to this war. May the blessings of the Elhunarie of old, Arbor Loren, and all our people go with you." He touched both hands to his heart, up to his forehead, and out.

It was still early morning when they parted company. Braxton, Phinlera, and Ruskin followed behind Kael, Jenphinlin, and the elven patrol while Penton, Gavin, and Bear left with Bendarren to find the elven emissary. Brax hugged his brother for a long time before separating. Neither spoke. They just looked at each other and grinned sadly, understanding the silent, bitter sorrow of unspoken words when brothers part.

They left the clearing fronting the guest oak and followed one of the well-defined paths northward. Brax looked back a moment and raised a final hand of farewell to Pen. He wished they'd had more time together and that his brother was going with them. It would take over a week to reach the Dragon's Head, Bendarren had told them. If they moved quickly. Braxton knew it wouldn't be the first time he wished Penton was with him.

"You should arrive at about the same time that the Mins reach Arbor Loren," Bendarren had explained. "Don't worry about the elves," he'd added privately to Brax. "Focus on the task at hand and on your connection with the One who walks with you."

For a long time, Brax, Phinlera, and Ruskin followed the patrol through Almon-Fey, eventually coming within view of three gargantuan oaks, taller than anything they'd seen in Arbor Loren—even those at the entrance to Almon-Sen. These stood apart from the others, proudly reaching up to an open sky. Unlike the rest of the forest, they had white bark and leaves of the most vibrant green, as if forever in bloom. Within the vast spread of their branches, broad platforms supported numerous homes, each a smaller section to an entire elevated community. Dark structures fanned out around their giant bases, as though the roots themselves had risen up to form wooden buildings, and landings wound up the massive trunks to watchtowers looking out above the elven kingdom.

"That is Fey Ethel, the heart of Arbor Loren," Laefin explained, leaning in closer to Brax and Phinlera as they walked together. "It is home to King Eilandoran and the elven council, and the source of the *feil*. So long as the three Silver Towers stand, Arbor Loren is safe. It is those that the Mins will try to destroy. If they do, our people and our kingdom will fall."

Brax and Phin stared in silence at the great elven capital, for it was an impressive sight. They continued past, and the view of the city slowly diminished, until all that remained was an endless sea of green, flowing gently in the warm breeze. For a long time afterward, though, the white bark of Fey Ethel could still be seen shining between the darker pillars of Arbor Loren's numerous trees. Eventually, the dense forest closed in and concealed the Silver Towers, shielding them within the endless embrace of its overlapping branches.

They followed Kael's lead, with Ruskin taking up the very last position, muttering to himself as usual.

"Why does Kael keep raising his hand like that?" Braxton asked Laefin around midday.

"He is the Blademaster," the young archer replied. Then seeing Brax and Phin's confused looks, explained. "Although he wears Balen-Tar"—and the elf dropped his head in shame—"he is still respected by our people."

"I still don't understand why he's raising his hand."

"He is signaling his acknowledgment to the greetings from the elven warriors we're passing. It is our way of replying in kind."

"Who's he talking to?" Brax glanced about. He hadn't seen anyone else nearby.

Laefin smiled, shyly. "We've passed more than a dozen patrols since leaving Almon-Fey. Almost three hundred soldiers. They greet my father when they see him because he is the Blademaster."

"Three hundred!" Braxton exclaimed.

"Yes, but I stopped counting a while back, so it could be more."

"Have you seen that many?" he asked Phin as they continued on behind the young archer, somewhat embarrassed at his lack of observation.

"No, nowhere near that," She shook her head and looked into the forest.

For the remainder of the day, they signaled to each other whenever they saw the elves, watching for Kael's familiar gesture. Most were moving in small groups among the undergrowth or standing beside their path. Occasionally, they'd spot a silhouetted figure in the branches of one of the oaks, a quiet sentry observing their passage. When night came, they'd counted almost fifty more, a vast improvement on their earlier observation, but a far cry still, they guessed, from the real number.

The patrol stopped infrequently, walking late into the night and allowing only brief rests for the outsiders to regain their strength. Occasionally the elves handed food down the line—honey cakes, vegetable bread that smelled like lemons but with a sweet crust, and clumps of nuts and forest grains with sticky, sugary centers, like the ones Kael had provided during Brax's training—encouraging them to eat as they walked.

Ruskin, however, was not impressed. He constantly complained whenever the food arrived, badgering the elves incessantly at the sight of every deer, rabbit, or edible-looking bird, trying unsuccessfully to borrow a bow. The elves pointedly refused, a few of them going so far as to call him a member of a primitive race. Eventually he gave up and took to picking large bunches of dark-purple berries that grew wild along their path or running off whenever he spotted some fruit-laden bush. He'd rejoin them later, carrying handfuls of his pickings and grinning through a stained beard, much to the dislike of the elves who considered the berries sacred.

They stopped at midnight to sleep, Kael permitting a few hours' rest under the spread of some large oaks before waking them and continuing on. The food the elves shared revived them quickly, and the fresh, endless water from the skins Bendarren had provided helped banish their fatigue.

Braxton was glad Phinlera was with him and that Jenphinlin had allowed her to accompany them. He found his fondness for Phin growing stronger each day, holding her hand whenever their path permitted walking together. She returned his affections too, squeezing his palm or putting her arm around him each time she noticed some new animal, flower, or unusual tree that her keen eyes spotted, her excitement for these new discoveries contagious. Having Phin there felt like some small part of home walked beside him, supporting him and encouraging him on. And if not for the looming reminder of the confrontation with the Min army haunting his thoughts, or the numerous elves surrounding them, their journey through Arbor Loren might have seemed like just another trip together. He knew the feeling would be short-lived, though. Once they left the safety of the elven forest, things would change—and not for the better.

They continued searching for the elusive elves, trying to identify their individual forms from the otherwise endless cover of the enveloping green. It had been over an hour since they'd seen their last group, and Brax was about to suggest that they give up when Serene connected with him.

Look for their energy, she said.

What?

Do not look for their physical bodies, child. Look for the energy that radiates from within them. She can do it too, if she holds the Leaf they have gifted her.

Brax relayed Serene's message excitedly to Phin, thrilled at the idea of sharing this with her. He summoned the spirit magic and was amazed at how quickly he could see the elves, the vibrations surrounding their physical forms easily identifying them from among the trees and undergrowth. It was more than that, though. Other woodland creatures—deer, rabbits, squirrels, birds, even smaller rodents—all became visible to him now, as if the covers of the forest had been gently pulled back to reveal the extensive life hidden within it. Even the leaves on the trees and the petals on the abundant flowers along their path were brighter and more vibrant. Every life seemed to emanate some form of the spirit magic, and for a few moments, the world appeared much clearer. But the strain of trying to maintain the high energy while following the elves and not walking into Laefin ahead of him proved challenging, and eventually, Brax's concentration faded. With it so did the luminescence of the forest. But for those brief, uplifting minutes in which he'd connected completely with the energy, time seemed to slow, and Braxton felt as if he'd taken another big step in a much larger world.

Phinlera had experienced it too. Not to the extent or depth to which Braxton had, but for several indescribable seconds, she saw the forest in an entirely new light.

"That was incredible!" she exclaimed, her arm still bent over her shoulder, grasping the hilt of the Leaf. "I can see now why you say this is a part of you, Brax, and that you need to follow this path. It felt like something wonderfully new was being revealed to me. That I was opening my eyes and seeing life properly for the very first time."

"I know," he said simply, pleased that she'd been able to see the energy and for her enthusiastic response. "It gets even better with practice."

"I've never felt anything like that before or even knew it existed," she went on.

The spirit magic dwells within all living things, Serene explained. She confirmed too what Kael had said, that the Unicorn Blade, and even the sword given to Phinlera, were doorways into seeing that energy—portals into a much greater world they were just beginning to understand.

CHAPTER
27

For the next two days, they traveled north through Arbor Loren. Serene spoke often with Braxton, guiding him to maintain sustained periods of connection with the spirit magic, teaching him how to direct the energy inside his body or pass it through his feet and into the earth. She showed him how to use the energy to strengthen his muscles and to sense movement before his eyes could register them. The high energy created moments when the forest seemed to come alive. Other times, it concentrated more within, filling Brax with such an uplifting feeling that he thought he might float off the floor. He began to walk more confidently through the forest, especially at night, instinctively stepping to avoid a broken branch or to soften his already silent footfalls.

Whenever they stopped, Kael taught him how to use the Unicorn Blade in combat, often having him practice fighting with Laefin or one of the other elves. The Blademaster watched Braxton closely, adjusting his stance or grip, showing him how to recognize his opponent's intent, and the best actions to deliver precise strikes in return. Most importantly, he helped Brax connect the energy from his heart center to the spirit sword, and to feel it as a natural extension of his body—all the while reminding him to breathe.

But he never dueled the Blademaster.

Simultaneously, Jenphinlin spoke quietly to Phinlera, helping her to join with Shelindûhin. She showed her how to use the weapon for defense and, to a lesser extent than the Unicorn Blade for Brax, as a source to connect with the spirit magic. Phin was excited to find that if she concentrated her entire thought and emotion on this one single purpose, she could very briefly touch the energy and experience that same radiant vibration she'd felt before. The effort took enormous focus, though, and she soon became drenched with perspiration. Mostly, she learned how to fight with the Leaf, uncovering from her elfling mentor the true secret of the weapon's inner power.

"It has the most amazing ability in combat," she said to Brax but wouldn't elaborate. "I want to surprise you." She smiled and kissed him on the cheek before changing the subject. But she never told him what she'd discovered.

By the time they reached Almon-Tel in the late afternoon of their third day, Braxton could sustain the spirit magic for several hours while walking along their winding path, often going for extended periods without rest. He constantly felt the energy flowing through him, penetrating deep inside and joining his mind and body together. Even Phinlera discovered she could more easily call upon it, summoning the spirit magic for brief moments of awed experience whenever she touched the Leaf, carrying the sword protectively on her back.

Ruskin, though, remained reclusive, disappearing into the forest or following way behind the line. It wasn't until they reached Almon-Tel and gained their first view of the towering peaks of the Dragon's Spine Mountains, looming majestically over the northern edge of the forest, that the dwarf's mood improved considerably. The sight of those ancient and familiar monoliths bathed in sun and towering toward the open azure sky seemed to energize their friend, causing him to move about eagerly or call ahead to their woodland comrades to quicken their pace. The cliffs appeared to awaken in him some long-forgotten memory, returning unexpectedly to his consciousness and bringing with it a palpable desire to be in their company.

Almon-Tel was smaller than any of the other elven towns they'd visited and built entirely within the trees. There were no buildings in open glades.

No eating halls or wooden guesthouses near the base of the oaks, and no outlying homes. One moment they were alone in the forest, and the next, they stood within a large circular perimeter of a few dozen inhabited trees supporting several small, elevated platforms and a single building high up in the canopy. All were connected by suspended walkways, giving Almon-Tel an almost weblike appearance. The outpost had a purposeful feel to it, for protecting the northern edges of Arbor Loren. There were no flower-adorned homes or leaf-thatched buildings, and even the familiar elven singing that graced so many other parts of Arbor Loren was absent. Instead, the elves moved about hastily, running from one tree to the next over the intertwining wooden pathways, clad in forest gear and carrying spears or longbows.

It was the elven aerie, however, that drew their attention—a single giant oak at the center of the perimeter and taller than all others. Huge nests rested among the tree's massive boughs, but it was their occupants that awed them the most—enormous majestic eagles, each the size of a horse, with golden feathers that glistened in the bright afternoon light. Pure-white heads gave the birds a regal look. Their intelligent eyes, in dark contrast to their bright surrounding feathers, looked down at the newcomers' arrival, moving their powerful beaks or stretching their massive curved talons in warning. Most sat in pairs, a few calling out, signaling in a deep, rich cry that echoed throughout the forest.

Brax and Phin stared up in wonderment as their elven companions quickly ascended the oaks. An Almon-Tel soldier ran across a thin tendril to the aerie and swiftly mounted a leather harness attached to one of the gigantic birds. The elf leaned forward and spoke to his mount. The creature let out a high-pitched call that reverberated across the outpost then leaped into the air, pushing off from its perch with two powerfully clawed feet. Spreading its golden wings, the magnificent eagle began to circle skyward. When it reached the canopy, it gave another long call, turned south and disappeared from view, carrying the mounted elf above the trees.

"Wow, that was incredible!" Braxton said.

"They are Talonguard." Laefin dropped down next to them from a nearby oak. "This city is one of several such outposts in Arbor Loren."

"Can *we* take one of those?" Brax asked hopefully. "It'd certainly cut down on our travel to the Dragon's Head."

"My father considered that." The young archer glanced up. "But he decided it was too risky. The goal, if you recall, is to reach the Walking Gate undetected, and flying out across the Breaker Dunes or above the Dragon's Spine for all the Mins to see was not his idea of secrecy."

"Too bad," Phinlera said. "I'd love to have flown one!"

"Ha, not me!" Ruskin folded his arms. "Wouldn't trust my life to one of those stupid creatures. Probably pecks at you whenever it gets hungry. A bit like tying a rabbit to a fox, hey?"

"Actually, they're quite intelligent," Laefin explained, "and they never attack their riders. The soldiers train with them from a very young age, and they adopt each other—rider and mount—in a lifelong partnership in service to the forest."

"Bah!" the dwarf responded, turning back toward the mountains. "Where is your father?"

"He's coming. He's just talking with the captain of the outpost."

It was nearing sunset when Kael and several of the patrol returned. Braxton and Phinlera had spent most of the time watching the eagles, occasionally walking around the clearing to stretch their legs or sitting with Laefin on a fallen log near the edge of the clearing, looking up into the oak.

Ruskin paced incessantly, staring at the mountains or grumbling into his beard. "About time we left," he chided when Kael arrived, puffing his chest to confront the taller Blademaster.

Kael smiled at the scowling dwarf. "Bendarren gave me this to give to you when we parted." He took a small, black leather pouch from his tunic. "But this seems a more fitting time."

"What now?" Ruskin snatched the object from the elf, clearly frustrated. "Probably some stupid elvish lore written down for a dwarven king who couldn't care about such pleasantries." He pulled at the straps. Then stopped short and stared down at his hands, the top flap of the bag folded back to reveal its contents. The dwarf's entire body seemed to ease, releasing all the frustration of the past few weeks. He looked up at Kael.

"Bless you, lad," he said, his eyes softening. "Bless you." He embraced the elf, wrapping his short, powerful arms around the Blademaster's waist.

"What is it?" Braxton asked.

"This," Ruskin replied, holding up the pouch, "is the true wealth of this accursed forest. The one thing that makes this whole damned journey worthwhile."

The elves laughed at his somber remarks, talking to one another in their woodland tongue and gesturing toward the crazy dwarf. Ruskin ignored them, sat down on the makeshift bench, and admired his prize.

"It's pipe leaf," Laefin explained. "Treasured, you can tell, by our dwarven neighbors."

"Oh, this is more than just pipe leaf, my boy." Ruskin kept his eyes on the package. "It's forest bloom, the greatest tobac in all of Andorah. A treasure beyond all the jewels beneath the earth." He extracted his pipe from under his belt and began cleaning it.

"Dwarves believe our forest leaf has healing properties," Laefin added. "And it may, for all we know. Elves never get sick."

"It has medicinal purposes," Ruskin assured them, wiping off the rinsed pipe before discarding Bendarren's waterskin.

Braxton smiled as he watched his gruff friend reopen the pouch, extract the minimum amount of leaf necessary, and place it into the vessel. A moment later, he had it lit and sat back, taking long, soothing draws that he savored before exhaling smoke rings up into the trees.

"Ahh," he sighed.

One of the elves commented something in their native tongue, and the others all laughed and nodded in agreement.

"Baehrin here thinks Kael should've given the pipe leaf to the dwarf two days ago," Laefin whispered. "He says it would've made for a much more peaceful walk."

The sun dipped below the western horizon as they followed Kael and the elven patrol north out of Almon-Tel. Braxton looked back one final time at the eagle aerie, knowing it could be the last he'd ever see of those magnificent birds or the suspended elven village. Within seconds, the dense oaks closed in about them, blocking his view of the outpost and replacing it with the slow, endless sway of the forest.

He looked forward, barely catching a glimpse of Laefin ahead of him, when the floor gave way and he fell into darkness. Something touched him, like a whisper brushing against his skin, intensifying his fear. His body went rigid, and he flailed about in the void, his mind yelling of an impending foe.

Then the blackness vanished, driven away by a brilliant light. Serene stood moving her head, signaling for him to follow. He realized he was no longer falling, and he rushed toward her, returning to the forest, Serene and the void having disappeared.

Kael and the elves watched calmly. Phinlera stumbled past, turning this way and that, before recognizing she was free. They glanced at each other and then at the elves.

"The dwarf is having trouble." The sound of the Blademaster's voice helped Braxton regain his senses.

"I'll help," Jenphinlin offered, heading back in the direction they'd come. It was then that he realized what had happened.

They'd passed through the *feil*.

CHAPTER
28

B raxton knelt by a little stream coming down from a granite rock face when he heard it—the horrifically loud roar of some giant creature right behind him. He froze. The sound chilled his body, and the hairs on the back of his neck stood rigid. It was so close. How could it have gotten there without him hearing or sensing something? He could feel the creature towering over him, an enormous upright presence that seemed to have materialized from the mountain itself, its rasping breath penetrating the early morning air. The Unicorn Blade lay on the wet grass, inches from his right hand. He glanced at the weapon, but knew he'd never make it— the creature would kill him the moment he moved.

Wait, Serene said, banishing his fear. She hadn't spoken to him in several days, and her clear voice calmed him now.

They'd left the forest two days earlier, the ground rising steadily and the soft woodland earth giving way to a rockier floor. Large granite outcroppings, silhouetted against the darkening sky, had appeared between the thinning trees, a powerful testament to the end of the elven kingdom and their entrance into the Dragon's Spine. They'd stopped briefly at the base of a jagged spire when Ruskin had come over.

"Time to go," the dwarf said casually. He had felt Ruskin watching him as Brax shouldered his pack and readied to leave. But when he'd turned back, it was Ruskin who had gone, disappearing into the night and the surrounding limbs of the Dragon's Spine.

For a long time, he wondered why the old badger had left without saying goodbye.

"He never was one for long farewells," Phinlera reminded him. But Brax felt disappointed at their friend's sudden departure, as if a part of him had somehow been lost to the Spine. There was so much he'd wanted to say to him, so much to thank him for, but he knew the dwarf preferred it this way.

They'd continued to climb the southern edge of the mountain without Ruskin, the patrol stopping for longer periods and Kael increasing Brax's training, often late into the night. Phinlera spent more time with Jenphinlin, eager to unlock the secrets of Shelindûhin. Even Serene had withdrawn, telling Braxton that upcoming events needed "looking into." And so he began to feel strangely alone, as though entering the Spine had stripped him of those he'd held closest. Perhaps that was why he'd wanted to get away that morning, to think, leaving in the early predawn hour to wander along the banks of the little stream. Kael and most of the elves had gone, wanting to investigate something the Blademaster said lay behind them. It was easy then for Brax to slip past the lone sentry, using a combination of the spirit magic and his elven cloak to pass unseen. He'd followed the water for several miles, deep in thought, until he came to the spring's source near the base of a rock wall. He'd just finished drinking when the creature had appeared, announcing itself with its penetrating roar.

It stood right behind him now. Braxton lay unmoving, barely daring to breathe, his face mere inches from the mountain stream. Time seemed to slow, and he could hear the animal's uneven breath.

But he waited.

A snarling cry broke the silence as something burst from the bushes on the far side of the river and smashed into the creature, jolting Braxton into action.

Run! Serene's voice echoed in his mind. He grabbed the Unicorn Blade and bolted.

A painful yelp silenced the growling from whatever newcomer had distracted the giant beast. The monstrous creature let out another terrifying roar. Moments later it pursued him, crashing through the mountain forest like some unstoppable mass, snapping everything in its path. Whatever had helped Brax get away was gone—beaten off, he guessed, by this stronger foe.

Now it was after him.

He ran, the creature's approach emphasized by the shuddering earth beneath his feet. It was running on four legs, he realized, with giant thundering paws that propelled it forward. Brax suddenly recognized that he wasn't going to make it. He'd strayed too far from the elven camp.

Then something appeared off to his left, barely noticeable in his peripheral vision. A man, it seemed, running with him, keeping pace with his own frantic strides, but angling toward him as well. He could barely see the other's movements, disappearing at times among the trees and sporadic boulders, only to reappear moments later, closer to Brax. They continued running before the other man disappeared entirely, swallowed up by the underbrush. And with him, Braxton's hopes vanished.

An enormous arm wrapped itself around him, as if the forest itself had come alive and stretched out one huge limb to seize him. He braced himself for the pain he knew would come, lifted off his feet and watching the floor fall away. For a moment, he couldn't move, lost in a dream, a nightmare, until panic screamed at his senses, and he struggled to get free. But whatever held him had him in a vicelike grip. He looked up, expecting to see some grotesque visage of the enormous beast that had pursued him.

Sotchek held him under one arm, running as though the fiery breath of a dragon pursued them. The skilled hunter moved effortlessly among the rocks and trees, jumping across small gullies and leaping from fallen trunks or larger boulders protruding from the mountainous floor. All the while, he carried Braxton like an empty sack. In his other hand, he deftly swung his ax, swiping at branches or cutting down saplings as he ran, clearing the path ahead.

The giant creature pursued them, enraged now by Sotchek's appearance and the escape of its quarry. Gradually it began to fall away, as Sotchek's extraordinary strength and swiftness of foot outpaced their adversary through the terrain that slowed their larger opponent. After what seemed like hours, Sotchek hurled his ax and yelled out a terrible cry that echoed back against the rocks. He pushed off a cliff, the two of them flying out over a ravine. Sotchek's legs flailed beneath them until they landed heavily on the ground of the elven camp, knocking the breath from Brax.

A flurry of sounds broke the air as arrows loosened by the elven warriors whizzed past them. Another roar echoed behind him, and Braxton turned to see the creature that had pursued them. It resembled an enormous bear, but with gray shale-like plates for skin, as though the mountain itself had come alive. The hard surface of its body was covered with patchy clumps of gray or black fur, and its head appeared to be a giant boulder broken away from the Spine. A huge maw covered most of its face, revealing rows of razor-sharp teeth that protruded outward like daggers. It stood on its hind legs, towering above Sotchek and the elves, with enormous granite-like arms extending toward them. The claws at the ends of its paws sliced through the neighboring trees with ease, shredding them like twigs.

Braxton's companions moved about gracefully, almost performing a strange dance with the rock-bear, carefully avoiding its massive swipes as they took turns nicking its sides or shooting arrows into its exposed flesh. Dozens of trickles of blood already ran down the creature's body, draining its life from wherever its opponents had found their mark.

Jenphinlin pulled Braxton to the opposite side of the clearing, hiding him with Phinlera in a clump of nearby trees. Laefin stood above them in the upper branches of a tall pine, eye level with the creature, firing an endless barrage of arrows into its face or down its open maw. The young elf moved effortlessly among the branches, releasing an endless assault upon their foe. Occasionally he'd find an opening between the plates of the beast's granite skin and sent a barbed shaft deep into its shoulder or under its exposed neck. Each time, the monster howled and jolted in response, turning to face the wound, clearly unaccustomed to anything penetrating its thick hide.

It was Kael and Sotchek, though, who were causing it the most pain, opening large rips of flesh in its underbelly whenever it reared up, or cutting away chunks of its fur to expose the flesh into which the elves fired their projectiles. Kael signaled to his son, and two arrows protruded from the creature's left eye. It roared a terrible sound and dropped to its front feet. Instantly the Blademaster was on its back, running down its spine to its enormous head. The bear tried to fling off the intruder, but the elf deftly avoided each attempt. He turned his sword down, grabbed the handle with both hands, and thrust his entire weapon deep into the back of the animal's neck. It rose up onto its hind legs, allowing the Blademaster to easily drop to his feet. Then, with one final long and mournful groan, it crashed to the floor.

For a moment, nobody moved.

Kael extended Sotchek his hand. "We are in your debt for saving our young friend's life."

Sotchek looked at the Blademaster for a moment, then clasped his outstretched arm.

"I guessed it was you following behind." The elf smiled lightly. "It's been a long time, my friend."

"I thought this one might need more protecting." Sotchek glanced at Brax. "Trouble seems to follow him wherever he goes, and today it has cost me dearly."

Braxton didn't understand what he meant, but thanked Sotchek all the same. "I'm glad you appeared when you did, or I'd probably be dead."

"Yes, you would be," the big man agreed. "A full-grown shale bear is no easy opponent, not even for one with your unique abilities."

They gathered their belongings and retrieved what arrows they could from the creature. Sotchek suddenly got up, looked north, and ran back into the trees. He returned a moment later carrying an enormous black wolf in his arms. The animal hung limp, its frame mangled and its breathing irregular. He laid it on the ground and ran his hands over its body, feeling its broken bones and wiping away the blood. Sotchek opened a small pouch at his side and poured some liquid into a few of the open wounds. The wolf whined and bared its teeth.

"Come, Brax." Jenphinlin ran over to kneel beside the mountain man. "Place your hands on its heart, and one here at the base of its spine." She placed both of hers on the animal's head. "Now, raise your energy and pour it into the parts you're touching—quickly, for there's little time left."

Braxton closed his eyes and summoned the full strength of the spirit magic, calling upon Serene to help guide him and heal the wolf's wounds, asking that the favor be returned for saving his life.

She responded, overshadowing his presence with her larger form, blending together. Then Brax saw more than felt her energy flow through him and into the animal, filling it with a deep inner glow—like the light his master projected. His own body grew lighter, but he remained focused on Sotchek's companion. He could see what Serene intended with her energy and then felt the animal's body react to those impressions. Its wounds healed beneath his touch, the bones mending, re-fusing where the powerful blows of the shale bear had split them apart. When they'd finished, he sat back, perspiring. His master's presence withdrew, and a wondrous river of spirit magic coursed through him.

He looked up. Sotchek and the elves were watching.

"You are truly a Chosen of the Elhunarie," Kael said, and the others agreed.

Sotchek nodded. "You are full of surprises, my young friend, and I am in your debt."

His giant friend leaned forward and stroked the sides of the wolf. The animal lay still, taking deep breaths, then sat up slowly and licked Sotchek's face. The big man smiled in spite of himself and rubbed his companion's dark fur.

"It's the least I could do for all your help," Brax said, regaining his own breath. "If not for you, I wouldn't have even made it to Arbor Loren."

CHAPTER

29

They traveled east along the southern edge of the Dragon's Spine for several days. Sotchek and his wolf went with them, spending most of their time away with Tayloren, the elven scout, or occasionally reporting back to Kael. Braxton longed to talk with his big friend, but he never stayed long enough and spoke only with the Blademaster.

Travel was slow in the mountains. Their path continued toward the jagged peaks and the ground turned to rock. Snow lingered in patches behind giant boulders or deep within shadows of sunken ravines, untouched by the sun's arc across the Breaker Dunes. The evenings were cold, and Braxton huddled with Phinlera to stay warm, with the elves permitting only a small cooking fire.

A week after leaving Almon-Fey, Braxton awoke well before sunrise. The camp was packed, and both Sotchek and Tayloren had returned.

"What's going on?" he asked Laefin, as the elf wakened Phinlera.

"We've reached the Neck of the Spine, and there's a large group of Mins stationed in the old ruins. We may need to fight our way past to reach the Dragon's Head."

Braxton's stomach lurched. His inevitable encounter with the Mins had finally arrived. The memory of the attack on his mom flashed through his mind, and he shivered. Taking a deep breath, he tried to steady his nerves.

It is all right, child, Serene said, as if answering his unvoiced call. *Whatever happens, know that I am proud of your coming this far. Today, though, we will triumph.*

Thank you, he replied quietly. *I'm grateful you're with me.*

She didn't respond, but he could feel her overlying presence calming him, and he breathed in the cool mountain air.

"We're going to split up," Kael announced, as Brax and Phin ate a cold breakfast. "Sotchek and the others will attack the Mins and hold them as long as possible. With the advantage of surprise, they should be successful. You two and Jenphinlin will follow me around the base of the ruins and down onto the road that winds south along the ridge. It will take us most of the day running, but we should reach the Dragon's Head by nightfall. Once there, Jenphinlin will open the Gate and bring through our army."

The Blademaster spoke confidently, signaling that the decision was not open for discussion.

They gathered their packs and followed Kael. Sotchek and the elves headed north, deeper into the spine, their elven cloaks concealing them the moment they left camp. Laefin was the last to go. He looked back at Brax and gave a quick smile. Braxton raised a hand in farewell, hoping he'd see the young archer again soon. He'd enjoyed the friendship they were developing and silently wished him well. All the while, Phinlera jostled about excitedly, occasionally rocking back and forth on her feet.

"Would you stop that?" he snapped.

"Sorry, I can't help it. I'm so excited to try out the Leaf."

Braxton wished he could say the same. His nerves were strained, and he wondered if he'd have the strength to face their enemy. The memory of that Min smiling wickedly at him kept resurfacing over and over in his mind, despite his efforts to banish it.

"Come," Kael said, drawing their attention. "From here on out, we don't speak. I'll communicate my intentions by signaling. Watch for my actions, and do as I say without question. Do you understand?"

They nodded.

The Blademaster turned and led them on.

I'll connect with you if needed. Jenphinlin's voice flashed through Braxton's mind, causing him to jump at her unexpected intrusion. She smiled as she passed by him, following after Kael.

The sun had risen far to the east when they came in sight of the old ruins. Large stone buildings, once intricately carved but now weathering away, appeared from among the rocks, cut from the mountain itself. Most were in some form of decay, with portions of their walls scattered about the partially overgrown cobblestone roads or doorways standing where no rooms remained. Giant columns rose in several places, the domed ceilings they once supported crumbling away on the vine-covered floor. Flowers grew prolifically around the perimeter, extending deep into the open courtyards of what Braxton envisioned must have been a grand city long ago. The wall that had once protected the settlement lay leveled, creating a flat walkway among the natural rock.

Kael signaled for them to stop, and Braxton and Phinlera froze, pulling their cloaks about them to hide their presence. A large, seven-foot tall Min appeared from one of the broken outer buildings and stepped up onto the collapsed wall. His bull-like face was covered in thick, black hair, and a pair of large pointed teeth curved upward from his rectangular snout. Short, thick horns, one of which had a broken end, extended from above his brow like the bones of some long-dead animal bleached by the sun. His small eyes, though, showed cunning, and he carried a large ax over one shoulder, exaggerating the creature's already intimidating appearance as he patrolled the wall.

They watched the Min approach. Then, just as it seemed he couldn't miss seeing them among the rocks, he turned and retraced his steps. Kael signaled for the others to go but continued watching from where he was, his bow nocked and ready.

As they reached the outcropping the Blademaster had directed them to, a loud cry broke from the far side of the ruins. Braxton turned instinctively and saw an arrow pierce the back of the Min's neck, the unsuspecting creature falling to its death. A moment later Kael ran past, indicating for them to follow. They sprinted toward a small outbuilding resembling a guard's tower and entered through its crumbling wall. Stopping to catch their breath, they waited for the Blademaster's signal.

A horn blew nearby, followed by the heavy sounds of several Mins running past. Still Kael waited. Then a lone creature stopped and sniffed the air. The Blademaster stepped out and swung his sword in a wide arc. The head of a brown-haired Min fell past their doorway. Kael reappeared and signaled for them to go. Phinlera almost tripped over the decapitated body, which still leaked large quantities of blood among the cobblestones.

Kael was several dozen paces ahead and waved at them to quicken their pace. Jenphinlin sprinted forward, easily passing Brax and Phin, reaching the side of the Blademaster.

They ran down the road for almost an hour, stopping when they saw a pair of Min guards standing watch. No sooner had the creatures noticed them than the smaller of the two fell backward, an arrow protruding from its neck. The other, a large gray-headed beast, charged at Kael, swinging its massive halberd at his head. The Blademaster dodged the blow, and, without slowing, turned and buried his blade deep into the creature's back. The Min staggered, fell to its knees, and collapsed.

By midday, they'd passed several more patrols, each consisting of a pair of Mins stationed roughly the same distance apart from the two before. Kael smiled at the weakness in their defense, allowing him to anticipate their next encounter. Each time, the Blademaster felled one with an arrow and then quickly dropped the other with a few precision strikes from his sword. Occasionally, he wouldn't even bother with his bow and just attacked both together.

He'd defeated two smaller Mins this way, when he stopped.

"You're right," he said, looking at Jenphinlin, then turned to Brax and Phinlera. "Drink quickly and catch your breath."

They drank from their waterskins, grateful for the break. The Blademaster paced the width of the road, looking up and down their path or occasionally glancing below the precipice on the western side of the ridge they followed.

"Eat these." Jenphinlin handed them several small honey cakes from under her cloak.

They consumed the food, feeling their strength return. Taking another quick drink, they were running again, following Kael down the winding cobblestone road.

As late afternoon approached, they rounded a turn between two mountainous peaks and came upon a guard post positioned close by on their right side. Six large Mins patrolled the road. Kael and Jenphinlin froze, their cloaks concealing them against the rocky wall. Phin followed their lead, but Braxton was too far away to gain cover from the cliffs. He dropped to the ground in an effort to hide, but one of the Mins spotted him. It was a huge creature with dark, matted brown hair and long, straight horns. It bellowed to its companions, who readied their weapons and charged toward Brax.

Kael sped forward, drawing their attention and attacking the leader. It took several precise blows from the Blademaster to fell the beast before he could focus on the rest of the group, blocking their attacks and striking back. Clearly no match for the more nimble elf, the Mins got in one another's way as they all tried to attack at once. Kael continued his artful assault, positioning himself between each intended victim and its companions, using its large size to shield himself from the others, allowing him to focus on one or two at a time without being swarmed by his opponents.

Brax and Phin watched in amazement at Kael's ability, then drew their swords and charged. As he ran, Braxton summoned the spirit magic, directing it into the Unicorn Blade before bringing his weapon down upon an unsuspecting Min. The power of that pent-up energy exploded the creature, and a nauseating smell permeated the area. For a moment, no one moved. Kael took quick advantage of the distraction, dropping two more Mins before the others reacted.

One black beast with a streak of white hair down its face thrust a long spear at Phinlera. Brax's stomach lurched. But before the weapon reached her, she appeared behind the Min and plunged the Leaf deep into its back. The creature swung around, dripping blood, knocking Phinlera to the ground with its momentum. It raised its spear, intent on pinning the foolish girl to the floor, but she was on her feet again next to the beast, and the Min's spear struck the road harmlessly. Phinlera thrust her blade into the creature's ribs. There was a sickening crack as the sword broke through flesh and bone. The Min's eyes went wide, then it collapsed.

Kael defeated the last attacker before turning to Brax. "Keep your emotions out of the energy or they could be used to serve the enemy."

"The spirit magic is defined by your feelings," Jenphinlin explained. "That Min was the target of all your hatred toward their race for attacking your home and your family. When you raised your energy into the sword, it took on that hatred and your desire for revenge. The result is what you saw. You destroyed that poor creature in a most terrible way. Nothing deserves that fate, Brax, no matter what it's done."

"I'm . . . sorry." He shook his head. "I didn't mean to—"

"We know," Jenphinlin interrupted kindly.

"I expected as much from your first encounter," Kael said. "Don't be too hard on yourself. Just learn from the experience."

I'm sorry, he repeated to Serene.

It is all right, child, but heed their warning, for they speak the truth. Hold your emotions in check and understand that the true strength of the energy comes from using it while calm and at peace, in balance. Do not let your emotions disrupt that balance, or the outcome may not be as you intended.

He nodded, looking down at the small charred remains of the Min, a sense of remorse overwhelming him.

"Come," Kael called. "The sun is already on its homeward journey, and we still have a long way to go."

They continued their flight south along the small mountain road, pausing briefly for Kael to defeat the remaining, less frequent patrols they encountered. As the sun dipped west, they came upon the small collection of mostly broken and low-lying buildings of the Dragon's Head. The little village appeared to have been a sanctuary once to some long-forgotten deity. Large statues of great warriors on bended knee lined the road, and stone maidens bearing platters of fruits and flowers stood proudly at the entrance to the mountain retreat. Most of the structures were unusable now, and many of the statues were missing parts of their once grand forms. Kael motioned them to one side, crouching low among the remains of a proud and regal man.

"There are Mins ahead," he said. "A lot of them." He pointed toward the damaged buildings, then looked west. "Time is running out. We need to split up. Phinlera and I will distract the Mins while you two go past to the Gate. It's located at the southern end on a plateau overlooking the Dunes."

"No!" Braxton said defiantly. "I'm not leaving Phin."

"All that matters now is opening the Gate," Kael replied, "and Jenphinlin needs your help."

"Why don't we fight the Mins together," Brax suggested. "That way we'll get done quicker and can all go on to the Gate."

"There's no time."

"We have to open it before the sun sets," Jenphinlin clarified. "Otherwise we can't try again until morning."

"And we need the army to enter during the night," Kael added, "or we risk being seen crossing the Dunes. If we don't open it now, we'll have to wait another full day. I don't think Arbor Loren will stand that long."

"It's all right, Brax." Phin touched his arm. "Go with her. I'll be fine." She smiled. "Besides, I have a Blademaster to protect me."

Braxton's heart sank. He looked into Phin's beautiful brown eyes and could see her fear and unwillingness to part from him, but also her strength and desire to help the elves. Reluctantly, he resigned himself to Kael's plan and nodded.

"Wait for my signal," the Blademaster said. Before Braxton could respond, he and Phinlera were moving.

Brax started to follow, but Jenphinlin pulled him back. "Wait. Not yet."

It seemed like an hour passed as he and the elfling girl hid among the broken statues. Then, just when he was about to insist on leaving to find Phinlera, Jenphinlin spoke.

Now we go.

He bolted forward, eager to help the others, and ran through the entrance to the Dragon's Head. Passing beneath the stone maidens, he veered right along the western edge of the village. As he crossed between two ruined buildings that formed part of a circular perimeter around the sanctuary, Braxton stopped.

A dozen large Mins in chainmail vests and thick, heavy boots stood on the opposite end of a grassy clearing ringed by the remaining buildings. Each wore metal helmets from which long, black horns protruded and carried halberds in their gloved hands, much like the beast on the road had wielded. These were no ordinary Mins, Braxton realized. They were elite guards. Kael and Phinlera stood on the far side of the clearing facing them. Several of the creatures lay dead at their feet. Unlike those on the road, however, the rest of these beasts weren't rushing to attack. They had encircled Kael and Phinlera, who struck back at the Mins periodically in an effort to break the enclosing net.

Braxton drew the Unicorn Blade and was about to rush to their aid when an iron grip clamped down firmly on his arm, holding him in place.

No, Brax, Jenphinlin spoke in his mind. *This is not your fate. We need to get to the Gate, or their fight will be for nothing.*

He hesitated, surprised by the power in her hand. He looked at the elfling girl, trying to decide.

Go to the Gate, child, Serene said.

A loud cry broke from the far end of the clearing, and he turned to see Kael and Phin charge into the Mins. A moment later, they disappeared among the large forms.

Braxton wanted to scream. He wanted to attack the Mins. He wanted to do anything that would help save Phinlera, but he knew there was no time. Long shadows already shrouded the village, and they still had to make it to the Walking Gate.

Come. Now! Jenphinlin insisted, pulling him away from the battle.

Reluctantly he let her lead him away. Then he broke from her grip and sprinted toward the Dunes.

CHAPTER
30

The sun was approaching the western horizon when Braxton and Jenphinlin reached the little plateau high upon the Dragon's Head of the Spine, facing south across the Breaker Dunes. Statues similar to those on the road surrounded the clearing, casting long shadows across the hard, smooth floor littered with leaves and other debris. A raised platform with a domed ceiling supported by three white pillars and encircled by marble steps sat on the far end, looking back toward the mountains. Unlike the ruins they'd seen before, the little shrine seemed remarkably well-preserved for its age. Beyond the plateau, stone steps cut their way down the mountainside to the Dunes below.

A man dressed in black armor with a high collar knelt at the center of the shrine. He stood as they entered the clearing.

"So, you've come at last," he said, in a slightly high-pitched voice. "You're much younger than I expected."

He withdrew a wicked-looking curved sword with a jagged edge from across his back and descended the platform. Taller and slimmer than Brax, he appeared to be slightly older, more muscular, and well-developed. His high cheekbones and slightly pointed chin gave his face a lean, youthful look, identifying his elven heritage. But it was his eyes that drew Braxton's attention. Completely black, they created the eerie illusion of two orbs hovering in place.

Braxton's stomach dropped as he realized this was the Dark Child.

Help me! he called out to Serene, feeling her warm, all-encompassing presence.

"You—cannot be here!" the Dark Child yelled, pointing a gloved hand past Braxton.

I must step back now, Serene said slowly. *I cannot interfere.*

But I need your help! I cannot do this alone!

You can, and you must. Use my sword to deflect his energy, keep your emotions balanced, and focus all thoughts on this one task.

She filled him with a beautiful and uplifting energy, greater than anything he'd experienced before, cleansing his fear and calming his mind. His body felt stronger, and he sensed the pure connection between his inner self and the Unicorn Blade, as though an extension of his own form. A wave of exhilaration washed over him. Brax knew what he had to do and was ready to begin.

Good luck, my child, she said as she withdrew.

But the energy remained, coursing through him as if pumped from some unknown source deep within. His mind was clear, save for one thought.

Stepping forward, he held out the spirit sword in both hands, confident, calm, and at peace, ready for this fight. All his practice with Kael had toned his muscles, and the energy accentuated that feeling, pulsating inside him.

The Dark Child looked cautiously, searching for something he'd missed. He raised his sword and walked closer. They circled each other for a moment before the Dark Child suddenly attacked. He moved with a speed that reminded Brax of Kael, and he barely raised his weapon in time to deflect the blow. But in that first strike, those first few seconds of their encounter, Braxton learned his opponent's speed. When the Dark Child struck again, he was ready. He parried a strike toward his left shoulder, blocked a thrust to his stomach, and sidestepped a low swing aimed at his thigh. Then Braxton struck back. He moved fluidly, one with the Unicorn Blade. Over and over, he attacked the Dark Child, knocking him backward and forcing him to retreat across the clearing. Eventually, the elf broke away, breathing hard, but he too had learned Braxton's speed.

They fought repeatedly, moving back and forth across the plateau, each searching for an opportunity to gain leverage over the other. As they continued to clash, a white column of vibrant light burst from the shrine, and, for a brief moment, the two combatants paused. The Dark Child stared at the platform, a look of surprise on his face. Jenphinlin knelt in front of the column, her back toward them and her head bent low, opening the Walking Gate.

Braxton sprang forward and caught the Dark Child off guard, slicing through his mail shirt and into his right shoulder. He struck again, trying to keep his opponent's attention on him, hoping to give Jenphinlin the time she needed. But the elf blocked the attack, steadily retreating until they were in front of the Gate. He raised his left hand and spoke a single word Braxton didn't recognize. A wave of energy smashed into him, flinging Brax back several feet to land heavily on the floor.

With catlike speed, the Dark Child leaped up the stairs and buried his sword deep into Jenphinlin's back. The brilliant light of the Walking Gate vanished, and the young girl let out a low scream that sounded more like a sorrowful howl of disappointment than a reaction to the wound inflicted. For a moment, neither moved, locked in time. Then the Dark Child withdrew his sword, and Jenphinlin's body crumpled to the ground.

"NO!" Braxton screamed, jumping to his feet and rushing toward the sneering elf. As he ran, Brax allowed his anger to surge. He cast aside his calm sense of balance and the single thought of defeating the Dark Child. Instead, a rage burned deep within him, a hatred, a need to avenge Jenphinlin . . . and his mom. When he reached the Gate, Braxton leaped up the steps with both hands wrapped tightly around the Unicorn Blade and struck down at his opponent. But the moment their swords met, their weapons locked, as if the two blades had become one. Then he felt it. The spirit magic slowly being drawn out of him and into the elf. All of his anger, his negative feelings, his desire for revenge were fueling the Dark Child, making him stronger. His body grew larger, powered by the energy stolen from Braxton's emotions. Simultaneously, Brax's own form diminished, his energy weakening as he fed the elf.

He tried to pull free, his hatred replaced now by a palpable fear. For a moment, they remained connected, the Dark Child gaining strength at the cost of Brax's lessening form. The elf pulled away and struck a powerful upward blow that Braxton barely deflected. But the strength overwhelmed him, cutting through his vest, ripping into Brax's chest, and knocking him down the stairs, sending the Unicorn Blade from his hands and across the courtyard.

When he looked up, the Dark Child stood over him, his weapon pointed at Braxton's face.

"You've lost!" he screamed. "Your clever plan to open that Gate has failed. Now you will die."

The elf pulled back his arm and struck. Braxton shut his eyes in anticipation of the blow that would end his life. But instead of the pain he expected, he heard metal striking upon itself. Opening his eyes, another blade hovered inches from his face, blocking the Dark Child's. Kael stood to one side, his sword arm outstretched in front of Braxton, smiling at the dark elf.

"So this is what you've become," he said calmly.

The Dark Child backed away, momentarily surprised by Kael's arrival. Then without warning, he attacked the older elf, but the Blademaster deflected his blow.

"There is still time," Kael said as he walked around, watching his adversary. "Time to let go of your hatred, time to shed this false skin and rejoin your true brethren in the forest."

The Dark Child laughed. "I am destined to rule Andorah and have trained to achieve this goal. Why would I give up my power to become a member of your weaker race?"

"Because, it is who you were meant to be."

This seemed to infuriate the Dark Child, and he attacked Kael with an unnatural ferocity. But the Blademaster calmly blocked each strike.

"If you will not return with me, you will die," Kael continued. "You cannot win."

"I will kill you and destroy your accursed forest!" the dark elf yelled, attacking again.

"Then you have made your choice," Kael said sadly.

The Blademaster attacked, moving around the Dark Child in a dancing blur that Braxton could barely follow, jumping and twirling as he struck repeatedly at the evil elf. Each time, Kael penetrated his opponent's defenses before being deflected away, nicking him here, scratching him there, as if the superior elf was almost playing a game with his younger foe. But the Dark Child was well-trained, and he held the power of all the dark emotions of an entire race awakening within him, strengthened now by the spirit magic stolen from Braxton. He too moved in fluid motion, attacking at every opportunity, forcing Kael to give up one step for every few gained. For a long time, they fought, each attacking or defending in response to the other. But Kael was the Blademaster, and his skill was unsurpassed. With a sudden flurry of blows, he forced the dark elf to block and give ground completely, pushing him back across the clearing. Then, inexplicably, he stopped, ceased his offensive, and retreated. He looked at the setting sun, turned to where Braxton lay watching and nodded, barely enough for him to notice.

The Blademaster leaped forward toward his adversary with a speed that was uncanny, as if he simply disappeared from where he had stood a moment earlier and reappeared in front of his opponent. It caught the Dark Child by such surprise that he barely had time to raise his weapon. Kael anticipated his response and pushed upward with his own blade, catching the movement of the other by the hilt of his sword. He held the dark elf in place, the two combatants mirroring the frozen statues surrounding the clearing. Then, ever so slightly, Kael lowered his wrist. Braxton felt a deep, sinking feeling in the pit of his stomach. The Dark Child reacted instinctively to the vulnerability. In one fluid movement, he stepped back, pulled his weapon free, and thrust forward. The blade disappeared into Kael's stomach, reappearing an instant later, curving up out of the Blademaster's back.

"*Kael!*" Braxton screamed, tears flooding his eyes.

The Dark Child grinned wickedly.

But the fight wasn't over. The Blademaster dropped his weapon and grabbed his opponent's wrists, locking down upon them with a vicelike grip. For a moment the Dark Child hesitated, surprised by Kael's reaction. Then he tried to pull his sword from Kael's body. But the Blademaster held him firm, unflinching, his eyes focused on the dark elf's face.

Now! came Serene's sudden and unexpected voice in Braxton's mind. Her energy shot through him, healing his chest and renewing his strength.

Scrambling to his feet, Brax recovered the Unicorn Blade and rushed toward the combatants still locked together. He yelled as he ran, gripping his weapon in both hands and raising it high above his right shoulder. Reaching the two elves, he struck with all his might, simultaneously focusing the spirit magic into the blade as he brought it down upon Kael's opponent. It hit the Dark Child's collar squarely, sliding through as easily as a stick might pass through water. The momentum of his charge took Brax past the two fighters, and he stopped several paces away, his back toward them. He stood there for a moment, hunched over, breathing hard, the tip of the Unicorn Blade touching the stone floor. Even before he turned, Braxton knew he'd found his mark.

He looked back and rose to his full height, taking a deep breath. The two opponents were frozen, like the statues around them, facing each other— the Dark Child and the Blademaster. A gust of cold wind blew across the clearing, whipping Braxton's cloak around his feet and swirling the leaves about him. His skin prickled as a chill ran over him, warning of some unseen evil. Then a deep silence fell across the ancient sanctuary, as if some unknown source had suddenly sucked all life from the world. Slowly, like watching in a dream, the head of the Dark Child tumbled to the ground.

Braxton ran to Kael, dropping the Unicorn Blade and grabbing his elven mentor, his teacher, his friend, the man he'd come to love and respect over these past few weeks. Brax stared into his deep-blue eyes, and the Blademaster smiled back weakly. Kael glanced down to see the hilt of the sword still penetrating his stomach, then looked up and nodded.

Braxton knew what he had to do. He placed his hand on the handle of the Dark Child's weapon. An icy-cold malevolence met his touch, and he released his grip as if bitten by a viper. Looking back at Kael, he saw the elf's normally strong eyes reflecting a fading light. In one movement, Brax grabbed the handle and pulled backward, drawing the sword from the Blademaster's body and throwing it away.

Kael exhaled sharply as the blade slid free. He closed his eyes and swayed. Brax helped him to the ground, leaning the elf against a block of broken marble of some long-forgotten warrior. Pulling off his own cloak, he tucked it under Kael's head, cradling him gently in the small of his neck.

"I'll get some water," he said, but the elf grabbed his arm.

"Time for me to leave this world," he replied, smiling weakly.

"No, Kael!" Braxton shouted, shaking his head. "You cannot die!" Tears ran down his face, and a lump filled his throat.

A slight frown crossed the Blademaster's brow. "Why do you seek to keep me here when you know my time has come? Do not weep for my passing, Braxton, for I return to the spirit world. My journey here complete."

"Don't leave me." Braxton's voice broke.

"Death is but a doorway through which we all must pass. I go to see the one who walks with you, who put you in my charge. May she look fondly upon my deeds of late."

Braxton nodded, unable to speak. His throat was so dry, and his remaining resolve was failing rapidly. He tried to smile at Kael, but choked.

"Open the Gate, Braxton. Help my people win this war."

"I will. I won't fail you."

Kael smiled again. "Would you do one last task for me?"

"Anything."

The Blademaster raised his left hand and weakly began untying the knot of the red ribbon of Balen-Tar from around his other arm. Braxton cried as he watched the elf undo the cloth.

"Take this back to King Eilandoran. Tell him I have regained my honor."

"I will," Braxton managed. "I promise."

The elven warrior seemed to draw comfort from Brax's words. He took another ragged breath.

"Thank you, Braxton Prinn. It was a privilege to have known you and an honor to have served you."

"The honor was mine, Kael." But the elf had already closed his eyes.

There was a calm, almost peaceful look on Kael's face. Then the Blademaster was gone.

CHAPTER
31

Braxton sat crying next to his elven master's body, closing himself off within his emotions, shutting out all other sounds and feelings except the long and endless pain he felt at losing the Blademaster.

When he'd cried himself out, he took a deep breath, stood up, and looked down at the face of the elven warrior. "Goodbye, Kael Illyuntarie," he said. "May you find peace."

He watched the elf. Then he closed his eyes and focused his mind, bringing up a barrier of spirit magic around his thoughts, shutting out all feelings and emotions. Delving deep inside himself, he summoned the energy.

What are you doing, child?

But he pushed Serene away, blocking her behind the barrier he'd created in his mind. He focused on gathering the energy, drawing it to him completely from every part of his existence, his very being, until he held a great sphere of spirit magic within him. He could feel his body reacting to what he'd done, pulling at the energy, calling to give back the strength necessary to maintain its life, requiring it, pleading for it. But he rejected its calls, cutting the tendrils in his mind that it sent looking for the life force it so desperately needed.

When he was sure he'd pulled from every part of himself, from every corner of his body, until there was nothing left to give, he opened his eyes. Walking over to the platform, he shot the spirit magic out through his heart center and into the Gate. The portal burst in a brilliant golden light that encircled the little shrine, forming the Walking Gate. It shone brightly in the fading sunlight, then began to flicker as the life force from which Braxton drew his strength diminished. He stepped closer, thrusting at it with all his might. Every ounce of his mind and body focused on maintaining the Gate, on that one single thought, drawing energy from his very frame, holding his breath. But the strength needed was more than he could give, and his body began to fail, weakening as its parts shut down. He held the connection for a few more moments, watching the golden light within the Gate dance upon the platform, then collapsed to the floor.

He lay facedown on the hard, cold stone of the Dragon's Head, convulsing in pain. His stomach threatened to retch, and he was shivering uncontrollably, but there was nothing left. He was totally spent, broken from inside. He could hear the sounds of a battle in the distance, but didn't care; he knew it was over for him.

"Brax!" Phinlera called out. There was fear in her voice. She dropped down and put her arm around him.

He turned slowly, just enough to look into those eyes. Even now he admired her, the beauty of her face showing through the sweat on her brow and the small trickle of blood from the corner of her mouth. She had a deep wound in her left shoulder, a cut above her eye, and her clothing was damp and torn from fighting.

"Hold on, Brax, it's going to be all right. Help is coming, just hold on."

But the pain was too much, more than his body was designed to endure. He knew he'd pushed too far, that he'd gone beyond his breaking point, beyond the bounds from which anyone could return. He'd been damaged from the inside as a result and knew he wouldn't last much longer.

Smiling weakly at Phin, he closed his eyes.

"I love you, Phinlera," he said quietly. "I love you."

Braxton didn't know if she'd heard him as he began to drift, falling into a deep sleep, gradually letting go of his body. The bonds that held him to the earth broke free, their weight falling away, and he floated.

The rhythmic motion of a horse's movements slowly crept into Brax's senses, the softness of the animal's muscular neck pressing against his face. He was hunched over, as if having fallen asleep while riding. He kept his eyes closed, enjoying a calmness he'd forgotten existed. His body felt light and whole again, the pain gone, and the energy of the spirit magic returned to its source. He breathed in the scent of jasmine mixed with a morning rain and opened his eyes. The blurry form of a green field passed beneath him, small white flowers interspersed among the grass, their centers bursting with purple. He watched them going by before noticing the glow from the horse he rode. It took him a moment to realize where he was. Then he sat up, recognizing that he was riding Serene.

They were in an endless land of vibrant green, sprinkled liberally with the wildflowers, their white petals a vivid contrast to the rolling emerald sea. A clear, midmorning sky extended to the horizon, and the sun's light was warm and uplifting.

Good morning, child. The clear sound of Serene's voice entered his mind.

Brax closed his eyes and breathed deeply, giving himself over to the calming sensation that her companionship provided. Her movements quickened, and Braxton's heart flushed. Reacting to his emotions, her pace increased, and he took another long breath. He sat up straighter, feeling the sun on his face and Serene's spirit magic strengthening his body. She was galloping now, the rushing air breaking upon him like waves of life. Raising his arms to either side, he tilted his head toward the morning sun and drank in its radiance.

When he opened his eyes again, she began to slow, coming to rest next to a small pond. Brax looked down into the tranquil blue waters.

Sunlight sparkled across its surface, and a breeze created little waves of color that swirled in its midst. The pond calmed and his mom's face appeared, bright and smiling. She was singing softly, cradling his infant form in her arms. She stopped and looked up, seeing him watching her for the first time.

"Come back to us, Braxton. It's all right. We're here. Come back."

He shut his eyes tightly, trying to block out the pain of losing her, waiting a while before looking again. His dad was in his workshop, hammering on their anvil, the sound ringing in his ears. He struck it several more times before stopping, becoming aware of something, and looked up at Braxton. Dark circles surrounded his eyes. His face was creased and his hair streaked with white. When he spoke, his voice was old and rough.

"Don't let go, Brax."

The scene changed again. Penton was there, then Bendarren, then groups of elves, and even Ruskin. Each one looked solemn and drawn, calling to him, asking him to return.

"What is this place?" he asked. The images continued to change, showing those he'd once loved or lost.

They are calling to you, wanting you to go back, asking that you not let go of them. Serene's warmth washed over him, easing his pain as he watched the unfolding scenes.

Some are with your body, the body of your human experience. Others are with the memories you left behind. You have a choice to make, my beloved child. Your actions at the Walking Gate demanded a great price from your body, and its light is fading. You must decide whether to go back and save it, or to let it go and stay here with me in the spirit world.

Braxton closed his eyes.

He lifted his face to the sky and bathed in the warm sun. Breathing in the scent of the wildflowers, he savored their intoxicating aroma, listening to the sounds of songbirds in the distance. He drank in the feeling of Serene's energy, enjoying the wonderful exuberance of life that his joining with her provided.

"How can I go back?" he said at last. "How can I return to that world and look in their faces, knowing that I failed them? That I wasn't strong enough to control my emotions or open the Gate? That I couldn't do what they asked?

"It's so beautiful here. The warmth of your presence, Serene, and the soothing beauty of the spirit world is beyond compare. Beyond anything that awaits me back home. I've done my part. I tried and failed. I cannot return. I don't want to go back."

There is more there that awaits you than you know. Look again.

Reluctantly, he looked into the waters, and his heart jumped. Phinlera was walking in the fields outside of Oak Haven on a summer's day. She hummed to herself as she went, smiling at the thoughts he couldn't see. His stomach turned with that same nervous excitement he always felt at seeing her, and smiled despite himself. Watching her flowing movements and graceful youthfulness, she jumped and skipped here and there, enjoying the sunny day, happy to be alive.

Then she stopped and looked at him, and he could see that she'd been crying. Braxton wanted to shout, to jump off Serene and leap into those waters—to hold Phinlera close and tell her it would be all right. But he couldn't move. He couldn't speak. He could only sit there and stare at the scene. He forced his eyes from hers and followed the outline of her face, admiring her smooth, soft skin. Her flowing black hair had been pulled to one side and hung down onto her chest. He remembered its scent. Placing a hand to her lips, Brax felt her brush against him, as though she'd somehow reached across the barrier between their worlds and touched his skin.

"I love you, Braxton Prinn," she said slowly. "I've always loved you."

He closed his eyes. The warmth of those words washed over him, uplifting him, and he listened to her voice echo in his ears.

I love you, Braxton Prinn. I've always loved you.

He replayed it over and over in his mind, drinking in the measure of what that meant to him, surrendering himself completely to it.

If you stay here, you will never again hear those words, or smell her scent, or feel her touch, Serene interjected. *You will only ever look upon her from afar, watch her conceive children with another, and grow old without you. But if you return, my child, you have a lifetime together.*

Braxton didn't answer. He kept his eyes shut for what seemed like hours, repeating Phinlera's words in his mind.

"Then you think I should go back?" he said at last, looking down into the waters.

That choice is yours alone to make, Braxton. I cannot tell you what to do. You must choose it freely for yourself.

It was the first time Serene had ever used his name, and he held onto it like a blanket.

"If I return, will you go with me?"

For a time. While you carry my sword, we will always be connected.

He took another long, slow breath and closed his eyes again. He sat there for a while understanding the choice before him. He knew the failure he'd have to endure if he returned.

"Then I choose to go back," he said. "To be with her."

CHAPTER
32

Braxton Prinn floated through an ever-changing memory of time spent with Serene, and Phinlera and Kael, moving from one experience to the next in an endless array of images, thoughts, and sounds. Sometimes he participated in the events he saw, while in others, he just stood there watching, an invisible bystander to some elaborate play. Each felt like something he'd experienced once and yet different somehow, as if not quite the way he remembered it.

Throughout the experiences, he heard the sound of elves singing nearby but never saw them. He was running, through a dark wood on an island that seemed stranded in an endless sea. Gnarled branches tangled with thick, thorny vines ripped at his clothing. Something was chasing him, something dark and evil that he couldn't see. The elves' song changed to spoken words and became louder as he ran. He was searching for them, he realized, for some memory of the light he once knew existed but now could no longer find. The evil was so close. His mind screamed for him to get away. Where were the elves? Something cold touched his arm, and he pulled away, yelling.

He sat up with a jolt on the stone floor, blinking at the sunlight streaming into the open-sided tent around him. Elven soldiers moved about on the Dragon's Head. A few stood nearby, talking together in small groups. Someone touched his arm, and he jumped again, remembering the dream. Phinlera was beside him. Her clothes were torn and ragged, and her hair was matted down and pulled to one side. Her normally bright eyes were tired and bloodshot, and he could see the tracks of dried tears on her cheeks. But when she smiled, her radiance was still there. He smiled back despite how exhausted he felt, as if seeing her for the first time, and his heart flushed with excitement.

"Don't ever do that to me again!" she said, leaning forward and hugging him tightly. "I thought I'd lost you. They said you might never wake up. But Bendarren told me to wait."

"Bendarren?" He looked around for the elven mentor. "Where is he? How'd all these elves get here?"

"You did it," she said quietly. "You opened the Gate, Brax."

He looked down. "No, I didn't, Phin. I failed. I tried. I really tried. I just couldn't do it." He closed his eyes, ashamed.

"No." She lifted his chin with her delicate fingers and forced him to look into her eyes. "You succeeded."

"I saw the Gate close."

"I know. But what you didn't see was that someone came through."

"What? How is that possible?"

Phinlera grinned. "Bendarren was watching you from Arbor Loren. The moment you opened the Gate, brief as it was, he sent someone through. She saw you fall, Brax. She reopened the Walking Gate for the elves. That's her over there." She pointed to a young elfling girl talking with Laefin.

"Laefin's here?" He looked at the elf, momentarily uplifted at seeing their young friend.

Phin's smile faded. "Tayloren, Baehrin, and Callorin were the only others who made it through. We lost the rest." She looked away. "Sotchek survived, of course. If not for him, I don't think any of us would be here."

"Sotchek?" Braxton asked, looking around again. "Where is he? And what about . . . ?" Then he remembered how Kael had died.

For a while, neither of them spoke.

"They found him by one of the stone statues," Phinlera answered his unfinished question, "with the Dark Child, and Jenphinlin. They burned their bodies at dawn."

"Burned?"

"Some elven ritual that's supposed to help release the spirit." She shook her head. "It wasn't very pleasant, so I'd rather not talk about it."

"Anyway, by late last night, half the elven army had passed through the Gate and down those stone steps into the Dunes. They circled the plateau before they went, saluting you and Kael. It was awe-inspiring." She gave a weak smile.

Braxton didn't respond right away. "It's my fault Phin," he said at last, "that Kael died. I lost control of my emotions while fighting the Dark Child, and Kael paid the price. He died because of me, because I was weak."

"I'm sorry," she said sadly, wrapping her arm around him and pulling him close.

For a long time, they sat quietly together, watching the elves moving about on the Dragon's Head. Neither spoke. Braxton chewed occasionally on some elven cakes and vegetable bread he found in a bowl next to him, disinterested in the taste. Sipping from a cup of water, he held onto it when he was done.

"What's her name?" he asked, wiping his face and looking out.

"Who?"

"The girl who came through the Gate, what's her name?"

"Oh, it's Jenterra."

Braxton nodded. "Why do all their names begin with Jen?"

"It's to honor Jenleah, the first elfling to Arbor Loren," a familiar voice replied. "They're all given her name at birth."

Laefin stood in the tent's doorway, smiling as though on a casual walk. "How are you feeling?"

"Fine," Braxton said unconvincingly.

"Bendarren told me what happened with the Dark Child. But if you're up for it, I'd like to hear it from you."

Braxton looked away, unsure if he wanted to recall the memory, feeling guilty for Kael's death. But then he turned to his friend and nodded. "I owe you as much," he said quietly.

Laefin sat next to Phin. The remaining three elves from the patrol joined them as well, seating themselves on the woven rug that had been laid out inside the tent.

Brax glanced at each of them, sadness reflected in their eyes. He understood the loss they had experienced in the death of Kael and the others during their fight to the Dragon's Head. He drank from his cup. Then slowly he began retelling the events of his fight and of the Blademaster's death. It was a painful experience, one that required him to stop often to control his emotions. The others waited patiently, allowing him time to continue.

When he finished, no one spoke. Phinlera sobbed quietly. Braxton took the red cloth of Balen-Tar from his pocket and handed it to Laefin.

The elf rubbed it between his fingers, as if touching it somehow brought him closer to what he'd lost. "Thank you," he said. "You have allowed my father to find peace and to die with honor. That is a gift I will never forget."

Braxton nodded, unable to speak. "I'm sorry," he said after a few minutes, "for not controlling my emotions better, for not being stronger. That your father died because of me."

"It's all right, Brax," Laefin replied. "I don't blame you. My father made his own choice."

"There's one thing I still don't understand," Brax added. "Why didn't Kael just kill the Dark Child when he had the chance? His skill was clearly superior."

"My father hoped to convince him to return to his elven heritage, to come home with us and be cleansed of his negativity. But he knew it was unlikely. I think from your retelling it's clear that he gave him that choice, as he'd intended, but the Dark Child was unwilling to listen."

"Yes, but why didn't he just kill him? Why'd he have to sacrifice himself like that?"

"Because, Brax," Laefin said slowly, "the Dark Child was my brother."

CHAPTER
33

The sounds outside the tent faded away, sucked into a void as Laefin spoke.

The Dark Child was Kael's son.

It was inconceivable. But then slowly, somehow, in the back of Braxton's mind, it all began to make sense. He could see now how their paths had been linked together, joined in some intricately detailed web.

"My father knew he could never kill my brother," Laefin explained. "But he also knew he couldn't let him live. You, Brax, helped him solve his dilemma and regain his honor. For that I will always be indebted to you."

The young elf stood up, smiled weakly, then turned and walked away, taking the cloth of Balen-Tar with him.

The remaining elves departed quietly as well, leaving Braxton and Phinlera alone. They sat talking together for a long time, imagining what Kael must have experienced at losing his son at birth, knowing he was the Dark Child, and then having to face him again as a grown man, only to watch him die. It was a fate, they thought, that no father should have to endure.

They left the tent an hour later, hoping to find solace in the company of the elves who remained, or at least find out if their armies had engaged the Mins. But the elves on the plateau were soldiers who moved about purposefully or stood guarding their posts, understanding that war had come to their forest. They refused Brax and Phin's questions, politely thanking them for their service and asking after their well-being, but ignoring their more direct requests.

Frustrated, Brax and Phinlera stood at the southern cliff's edge, staring across the Breaker Dunes, watching the twin peaks of Ben-Gar looming out ahead of them. As the sun dipped west, they wondered if the Mins had reached Arbor Loren and whether the forest could withstand the tide of destruction they'd unleash. Had their plan to bring the elven army in behind the Min line swung the balance in their favor? Had others come to help? So many questions remained unanswered, and Braxton had to know.

They looked around for Laefin or any of the others from their original company but found no one they recognized. They'd almost given up when Phin noticed Jenterra cooking by a small fire in the shadow of one of the giant stone pillars across the clearing.

"Perhaps she can help."

The elfling girl was small, like the others of her race, barely reaching Brax's shoulder. *Like my mom*, he thought, but with short brown hair and vibrant green eyes. She bowed deeply when Phin introduced him and thanked Brax for his service to her people, and for the sacrifice she seemed to understand he'd made. She asked much about his health and how he felt inside, although she always seemed to look past his responses, seeing his words as nothing more than a screen to the truth hidden within. He let her probe his body with her energy, understanding her desire to provide some recompense for the service she seemed to think he'd provided, some assurance that no remnant of the evil remained from his encounter with the Dark Child.

It was when she touched his emotional resolve, however, that Braxton thought she'd gone too far. He clamped down on her tendril of spirit magic, holding it firmly in the grip of his own energy. He was surprised at the strength he felt in that touch, even more so than with Jenphinlin, and wondered if he could hold back her power should she choose to resist. But she seemed to understand his reaction and calmly withdrew her invisible connection, detaching from him completely. She inclined her head, acknowledging the extent to which he'd allowed her to go.

Laefin joined them, returning from the southern end of the camp. He grinned as usual when he arrived.

"Can you walk with me?" he asked. "I have much to tell you."

They left the little plateau together, walking back up into the village, carrying with them some honey cakes and a waterskin Jenterra insisted they take. They wandered across the clearing where Braxton had seen Phin and Kael charge into the elite Mins, but which now served as a base camp for the elves remaining in the mountains. Crossing the threshold of the Dragon's Head, they went out onto the cobblestone road. Braxton felt an unexpected sense of relief at finally being able to let go of the experiences he'd endured. Leaving the place where Kael died somehow made it easier to accept, and he exhaled fully. Phinlera seemed to understand his emotions and put her arm around him. Laefin recognized it too and began humming to himself.

The road through the mountain was different now from what Brax remembered. There were no Mins to watch out for around every bend, no one to fight or to hide from, and the kneeling statues that lined their path seemed polished and whole again, bathed in a beautiful golden light from the setting sun.

"I visited our encampment in the Dunes today, and our armies have taken Ben-Gar," Laefin said proudly. "They marched through the night and moved across the Dunes with great speed. At dawn, they assaulted the rear guard of our enemy and pushed them back all the way to their encampment in the twin peaks. For most of the day, we fought at their base camp, and a few hours ago, our forces finally broke through." He ate a honey cake Phinlera handed him and washed it down with some water. Seeing Braxton and Phinlera's blank stares, he continued, "This is good news. The Mins were not expecting a rear assault, and all of their attention was focused to the west, so their main camp was lightly guarded.

Now that we have taken hold of it, our soldiers can use it to launch further attacks against the rear of our army—which, I regret to report, reached Arbor Loren yesterday." Laefin's smile faded. "We still don't yet know how long the great forest can stand against the more than ten thousand that now march on my homeland. But our taking of Ben-Gar is a small victory among this otherwise dark storm.

"We'll know more tomorrow. Our few thousand home guard seem to be stopping the first waves of Mins breaking upon Arbor Loren, and the *feil* is holding for now. If our luck continues, our soldiers moving from the twin peaks should engage the rear of their force, slowing the Min advance on our forest and allowing us to battle them on two fronts. This should buy us much-needed time until help arrives. I only hope it will reach us before our need is too great."

T he following day, Braxton woke to the sound of Serene's voice calling to him.

Awaken, child. It was the first time she'd spoken to him since opening the Walking Gate. *Find the gifted archer.*

Braxton dressed quickly. He nudged Phinlera in the bedroll beside him as he pulled on his boots.

"Phin," he called. "Time to go."

She woke and jumped to her feet as if in anticipation of some new adventure they'd been planning for weeks.

Braxton smiled at her enthusiasm. She tied her hair back and pulled on her cloak, then grabbed Shelindûhin and strapped it to her side.

"What?" she asked, seeing him stare.

"Nothing." He looked away and picked up the Unicorn Blade. "Serene wants us to find Laefin."

They left the little tent they'd shared near the center of the grassy clearing in the village of the Dragon's Head, passing by the elven shelters that seemed to blend in naturally with the landscape. Following the familiar path to the plateau, they arrived just as dawn broke from the east and cast its light across the ancient sanctuary.

Laefin stood near the stairs leading down to the Breaker Dunes.

"Morning," Brax said, as they approached.

"Hello." The archer looked worried.

"What's the matter?"

"Bendarren is considering awakening the trees to fight."

"Isn't that a good thing?" Phin asked.

Laefin nodded. "Yes, but no one has awoken the forest in many centuries, and it is a great shame upon my people that we should need to awaken those whom we dedicate our lives to protect."

"Isn't it better to awaken the trees than to let them die?"

"Indeed it is. But it saddens my heart that we would need the forest to help us in this fight—that we've failed to keep her safe."

Tell him, that the mountain moves its feet and that purple banners ride from the west.

Brax relayed the message. Laefin seemed to understand and became excited by the news.

The feil will not last, Serene continued. *The one you call Bendarren is wise to have the child race awaken the trees. Tell him the arrow that will pierce the breast of your enemy will come from the south. But if it should arrive too late, he should sound the Horn of the White Wood.*

Brax repeated her words.

"She must mean the knights of the Empire will come around the southern tip of Arbor Loren," Phinlera said excitedly, "and crush our enemy!"

Laefin, however, looked stunned.

"What is it?" Brax asked.

"The White Horn has not been heard in the memory of my people. I . . . don't know if this can be done."

Bendarren will remember. For he was there when the trees found their home.

Laefin nodded in silent understanding. "I will report immediately and return as soon as I can. Thank you, Braxton." He bowed, turned, and walked quickly to the Gate.

They watched him speak with Jenterra. The elfling girl looked back at Braxton, fear reflected in her normally calm face. Then she guided Laefin up onto the platform and opened the Walking Gate just long enough for him to pass through.

For the remainder of the morning, they wandered around the quiet Dragon's Head, talking about what Serene had said. They ate a late breakfast with Jenterra and a few of the elven soldiers stationed at the camp who left to pursue their duties, leaving Brax and Phin alone with Jenterra.

"Who are the child race?" Braxton asked her.

"They are the elfling people, of which I am one," she said. "The 'child race' was the name given to us by the Elhunarie of old, when they walked among us. But unlike the rest of the elves, who, as I think you know, grow to be in their midthirties by human standards before ceasing to age, the elflings are fully grown in what you'd consider their teenage years. I myself have lived in Arbor Loren for almost nine centuries." She smiled at their surprised faces.

"What about my mom? She was much older."

"That took a lot of work from Bendarren before she left. But inside, your mom is the same as what you see in me—and the others of my people. Only when she returned to the tree from which she came, like we all do in time, did she revert back to her true and natural self."

Braxton looked skeptical but didn't say anything.

"Are you the ones who can awaken the trees?" Phinlera asked cautiously.

"We are," Jenterra replied, smiling at Phin's tact. "We're Arbor Weavers or Tree Singers, as some call us. Although primarily responsible for healing the forest with our song, we also have the gift to rouse the woods from their eternal sleep, awakening them in times of great need, that they may move or even fight for our world."

"What's the White Horn?" Brax asked.

"Something that has not been heard in almost five thousand years," Jenterra said sadly. "Not since before the coming of humans to this world. It is an ill omen, I fear, that we would need to awaken the spirit of the forest in order to protect our homeland."

"If it means saving Arbor Loren, why wouldn't you call upon all the help you can?" Phinlera interjected.

"Because I worry that waking the Fey of the woods will change Andorah forever. It is an ancient magic that holds life within those great boughs, a spirit force that has not moved upon this earth since the making of the world. All the trees—not only those in Arbor Loren—are connected to its source, and awakening that energy could have a profound impact on nature's balance. It is an enormous power."

"Is it connected to the oaks of Fey Ethel?" Brax continued, eager to know more.

"Yes." Jenterra said. "The Silver Towers are the physical embodiment of the Fey within Arbor Loren. It is the source of the *feil* that protects our woodland realm, the heart of the elven kingdom, and the home of the White Horn itself. But if Fey Ethel is ever destroyed, Braxton, then the elven people will begin to age and will ultimately diminish and pass from this world. The Silver Towers are therefore both our greatest strength and our biggest weakness."

"I see now why the Mins would seek to destroy it." Brax glanced at Phin.

"Indeed they will," Jentrerra continued. "If the Silver Towers fall and the elves pass from this world, there would be no one left to care for the forests in their endless sleep. In time, the trees would begin to fade, and eventually all of Arbor Loren would cease to exist. This is why the one who walks with you would risk waking the Fey to hold back the Min assault."

Brax and Phinlera spent the rest of the day talking about the attack on the elves, the Mins, and all they'd learned. They walked back up the cobblestone road, along the Neck of the Spine, stopping to look down at the river on the eastern edge or off the ravine to the west. The day seemed to drag on without end, and Braxton anxiously wanted to travel to the battlefront or at least visit the elven base camp in the Breaker Dunes. But the elves refused to permit it, blocking his way to the staircase that led down to the plains whenever he tried to leave. He spoke to Serene about slipping past them unnoticed, but she always gave him the same response.

Be patient and regain your strength. That time will come.

They returned to the mountain village as night fell and found Laefin speaking to several Talonguard who had joined their camp. Their great golden mounts stood nearby, preening themselves by the cliff's edge.

"Our forces and the *feil* are holding," the young elf reported when he saw them. "And the trees have begun to awaken. We've created a small outpost at the top of Ben-Gar from which our scouts are flying over the battlefield to communicate events back to Arbor Loren." He pointed to the aerial riders. "Tomorrow I will go out with them on patrol." He smiled broadly. "And they've agreed to take you with us."

CHAPTER
34

Dampness from the morning air broke upon his face, and beads of water crept in through his long white shirt, chilling his skin. Braxton shivered, pulling his wool-lined cloak closer around him. He was high up in the clouds, flying on some giant creature whose powerful presence he could feel but never saw. He listened to its wings flapping rhythmically above the cry of the wind as they passed through yet another low-hanging cloud, further dampening his clothes. His mount was deliberately flying through them, Brax realized. He looked down, and his stomach dropped at the sight of a dark and turbulent sea far below.

Time to descend. A voice broke into his mind—but it wasn't Serene's. It was an older, rougher sound, yet something else entirely, something not quite human. A huge reptilian face looked up at him from between the clouds, and Braxton jumped.

He awoke to Phinlera shaking him. "Come on, Brax, time to go."

He lay on his bedroll, trying to remember the dream that was rapidly fading away. He was flying, he knew, on a creature he couldn't see. What was it? He desperately wanted to recall the images that evaded him. He knew they meant something. Dreams were always strange that way—lost in the waking, leaving behind only feelings of the experience. He struggled for a few moments before rolling over, frustrated.

Phinlera called again, and he realized they were out on the Dragon's Head, and that today was their flight with the Talonguard he'd so eagerly anticipated. He got up quickly, pulled on his cloak and boots, and strapped the Unicorn Blade to his back. Phinlera was already outside, calling for him to quicken his pace.

"They're readying to leave." She pushed back the flap of their tent to look at him. "Would you hurry up?"

They ran from the camp toward the little plateau and found Laefin waiting with the Talonguard riders. Their giant mounts stood by the cliff's edge, looking regal in the morning light. The elf handed each of them a long root as they arrived and told them to eat slowly.

"It'll help with your stomach," he said. "Best to skip breakfast too. We'll eat something at the outpost."

They chewed on the stringy stems, which tasted somewhat like ginger but had a sharp, pungent flavor. The young archer gave them each a thick, wool-lined cloak, which Brax thought looked vaguely familiar but couldn't place.

Laefin turned to an attractive female elf with long, glistening blond hair and deep forest-green eyes. "This is Bellnella," he said, introducing her. Brax stared at the elf's shapely figure.

"You'll be riding together on Hawk, Brax." Their friend pointed to one of the giant golden mounts. Braxton saw Phinlera's disapproving look. She was definitely not impressed with his rider, but he pretended not to notice.

"And this is Tentalis," the young archer continued, introducing a handsome male elf with shoulder-length brown hair and deep-blue eyes. "Phin, you'll be riding with him on Arrow." He indicated another giant eagle with long, white neck feathers. Braxton felt the same jealous feeling he imagined Phinlera must have experienced a moment ago, but he buried his emotions as he watched the handsome elf bow gracefully before Phin.

"I'll be flying with Neah on Fletcher," Laefin added, ignoring their reactions. The last female rider had long black hair similar to Phin's and green, almond-shaped eyes. "We've paired you with each guard to balance the weight on their mounts. That should make it easier for our birds to maneuver, should the need arise. Now go and learn about their harnesses."

Brax and Phin exchanged quick glances, each signaling to the other the same warning: avoid any emotional attachment to your rider. He followed Bellnella—or "Bell," as she preferred to be called—over to Hawk.

"He's a little cautious of strangers," she said. Her voice was beautiful and clear, but her words made Brax nervous. "Let me go first." She stroked Hawk's long neck feathers before calling Braxton over to join them. The enormous eagle watched him approach with sharp, intelligent eyes. Its huge beak was at least the length of his forearm, and he knew it was capable of ripping off his limb in a single move. He suddenly remembered Ruskin's comment—"A bit like tying a rabbit to a fox, hey?"—and now appreciated the dwarf's sentiments.

Brax lifted his hands away from his sides, hoping the eagle would understand his peaceful intentions. All the while, Bell spoke quietly to her mount in their strange woodland tongue. With the elf's guidance, he was able to raise a hand and stroke the magnificent creature. Eventually, the eagle went back to preening itself, indicating its acceptance of him.

Bell walked around showing Braxton the leather harness strapped to Hawk's thick neck and behind its giant wings. He followed closely, trying to listen to her instructions, but his mind kept wandering to her attractive form and tight-fitting leather outfit. Although he assumed her clothing was designed to reduce wind resistance in flight, it had the added benefit of accentuating her already striking figure. It didn't help that her blond hair shone brilliantly in the sunlight, reflecting a myriad of golden layers whenever she moved, or that her lips were full, pink, and lightly moist. Even her skin was perfect, smooth as silk and radiant. He strained to focus on Hawk but continued returning to Bell, as if transfixed. She seemed to sense his problem and smiled sweetly at his childish human emotions. She said nothing, though, and calmly reiterated her instructions several more times, asking him to repeat back what she'd said.

When she was satisfied he knew what he needed, she had him mount Hawk. Brax pulled himself up into the saddle and placed his feet into the small footholds positioned on either side of the eagle's back, just behind its wings. Bell fastened a leather strap around his ankles as well as others behind his knees and over his thighs. Braxton stared down at her from atop the mount, drawn to her radiant beauty and slightly opened top. She secured a single thick cord to the front and back of Braxton's belt, effectively locking him in place from the waist down. She was still attaching the remaining straps when the warm, calm memory of Phinlera gradually crept back into his senses. He closed his eyes, forcing himself to block out the images of Bellnella his mind created. A sudden feeling of guilt washed over him, as though he had betrayed Phinlera somehow.

Turning away from the exquisite elf, he looked across the Dragon's Head to where Phin sat upon Arrow, talking with Tentalis. Seeing her seemed to awaken him from some unnatural dream. He recognized then that it was not just her physical attractiveness that drew him to her. It was her joyful enthusiasm for life and the wonderful sense of excitement she always awoke in him. He loved Phinlera for more than her natural beauty, he loved the person she was. Or more importantly, he thought, the person he had become because of her. He smiled and breathed in a deep sense of contentment.

"You are well-suited for each other," Bell said, drawing his attention. "You have remembered her and have passed the test we laid out before you." She smiled at his confusion. "We are Heartholders," she explained. "Tentalis and me. To recall the one you love in our presence is a great gift you give them. She is lucky to have found you, and you, her."

Braxton turned back to Phinlera. She was watching him now, having passed her own test. He wanted to leap out of the harness and run over to her, to tell her how much he loved her, but the leather straps held him securely in place. He was about to wave when Bellnella spoke.

"Time to go." Sitting atop Hawk's neck, she held a single leather strap attached to the eagle's giant beak. She gave a short whistle. The enormous bird took two large hops toward the edge of the plateau, and then with one powerful thrust, leaped from the precipice.

CHAPTER
35

A rush of cold morning air struck Braxton's face, and his stomach jumped into his throat as the magnificent eagle dropped from the Dragon's Head like a stone tossed off the mountainside. He let out a long "Woooo!" as they fell, grasping the harness with both hands as if the strength of his grip somehow controlled the rate of their fall. A moment later, Hawk opened his giant wings, catching an updraft along the edge of the Spine, lifting them gracefully above the plateau. For a brief moment, Braxton knew what it was like for those few creatures lucky enough to fly on the winds of the world. He let go of the strap and held his arms down alongside the eagle, trusting in the harness. The damp morning air blew against his palms as the massive bird flapped its wings, propelling them toward the sky. Braxton looked back at the others and waved at Phinlera, but his movements were cut short by the wind. She smiled from atop Arrow and signaled back with the same excitement.

Brax gazed at the distant scrublands of the Dunes far below and the edge of the Dragon's Spine melting away. *I'm flying. I'm actually flying.* He had never imagined this possible. And yet there he was on the back of a majestic golden eagle, soaring high above the mountains in a far-off land, weightless and free.

They leveled out and turned southwest toward Ben-Gar. The mountain spires stood ominously ahead of them in the Breaker Dunes, two giant sentinels witnessing the war in the plains.

Braxton realized how easy it was to travel this way. There were no forests or mountains to traverse, no rivers to wade through or block their path, no lakes to circumvent or marshes to cross. The open sky was free of the numerous obstacles he'd become so accustomed to on land. Miles passed quickly, and they crossed the Dunes in a few hours, nearing Ben-Gar at midday.

As they approached the monoliths, Braxton caught his first sight of the war. Flocks of small bat-like creatures with long pointed tails attacked Talonguard.

"What are those?" he called up to Bellnella as she guided Hawk away from the battle.

"Vipers," she said over her shoulder. "We need to avoid them."

"No, we need to help," he yelled into the wind, but she shook her head and turned her eagle farther west.

Braxton looked back anxiously as he and Phinlera flew away from the fight while Laefin and Neah stayed to their original course, drawing their bows and heading toward the vipers.

"No!" he insisted, but Bell continued to ignore him, tapping her mount with the leather strap and leading him away.

Twisting and turning in the harness, he tried to see over one should then the other, eager to participate in the aerial battle he knew was taking place behind him. As he rotated left, Brax froze, seeing on the distant plains the full extent of the massive invasion. Ten thousand Mins covered the Gap of Dunes, like an enormous dark plague spreading along the fringes of Arbor Loren.

So many, he thought. *We can't win, there's no hope.*

There is always hope, Serene said calmly.

But there are so many!

Even the greatest tide can be divided by a single tree. Look to the south. Help will come.

He stared into the distance, hoping to see what his master alluded to, but saw nothing beyond the mass of Mins covering the Dunes.

Focus on the present, she added, then pulled away.

He thought for a minute.

Turn back! he yelled directly into Bellnella's mind, pushing his will deep into her thoughts, using the spirit magic to enter her consciousness. He held there for a brief moment before letting her push him away, beyond the shield she created to block him out. But he had sensed her surprise at his ability to connect with her so easily, and she seemed to understand his need to participate in this fight. She turned Hawk around, circling back toward Ben-Gar, signaling for Tentalis to follow.

When the battle came back into view, Laefin and the other riders were firing arrows into the vipers. The young archer moved so quickly that his actions were a blur. He'd climbed out of his harness—or perhaps was never strapped in—and stood on Fletcher's back, releasing projectiles in every direction. Vipers fell like stones to Laefin's deadly aim, pierced by a woodland arrow. But the dark creatures continued in swarms. Brax could see how they used their barbed tails like spears, attempting to impale the elves or their giant mounts. The eagles were much stronger though and often snatched them out of midair, crushing them with their talons or snapping them with razor-sharp beaks. But the smaller vipers were more maneuverable, and many had already driven their venomous barbs deep into the eagles' sides or bellies, further attaching themselves with pointed teeth or the hooked claws at the ends of their leathery wings. Several eagles and their riders were falling, a half-dozen vipers pulling them down toward the jagged rocks below.

Bellnella guided Hawk toward the fight, and Braxton drew the Unicorn Blade, adjusting his grip several times as they neared. He ventured a quick glance over at Arrow and saw Phinlera holding the Leaf. Tentalis, like Bell, had discarded his reins for a bow, relying on the lifelong partnership with his mount to maneuver them in battle.

A group of vipers turned toward them, seeing new prey, and darted ahead like projectiles. When the creatures were a dozen yards away, Bellnella and Tentalis dropped several with their arrows. Yet still more came on. Some headed toward Braxton while others went for Phin and her rider. Brax raised the Unicorn Blade to his shoulder and summoned the spirit magic to guide him in his first strike. When the lead viper bent its tail forward to pierce his body, he brought his weapon around in a quick arc, fueling his blow with the power of the spirit magic. He sliced through the creature as the sword found its mark, the pent-up energy extending outward like a shock wave into the remaining group, disintegrating them.

Everything disappeared, and Braxton stood in a thick gray fog. Two hooded figures materialized from among the shadows. They sat hunched over a table, facing each other. Slowly one of them turned and looked at him. He couldn't see into their cowl, and only a deep and penetrating darkness stared back at him.

Then, just as quickly as it had appeared, the image vanished, and he was atop Hawk again, flying in the aerial fight around Ben-Gar. Eagles and vipers were everywhere. Arrows whizzed by, a few passing dangerously close, dropping black creatures Brax never saw coming. Bellnella was calling to him, but he couldn't make out her words.

"I'm fine," he yelled against the noise of the wind and battle. "Keep going."

She seemed to hear his response and turned Hawk sharply, concentrating again on the vipers as they continued their attack.

Braxton looked about for Phin but couldn't see her or Arrow. Frantically he looked down, panicked.

Focus on the present. Serene repeated in his mind.

He looked up as a viper turned its tail directly toward him and charged. Dropping back along Hawk's body, he brought the Unicorn Blade across his chest in a whipping action, slicing off one of the creature's leathery wings and sending it tumbling away. He sat up quickly and summoned the spirit magic, feeling it build inside him.

Control your emotions. Send the energy south.

He focused on the ball of energy growing within. When Hawk wheeled, Brax directed it toward a flock of vipers joining the fight. The spirit magic released, its power spreading out like a wave above Ben-Gar, breaking upon the unsuspecting creatures. They began to fall, squirming as if caught in an invisible net.

All sight and sound disappeared, and, like before, he saw the two hooded figures sitting in the mist. When they turned to look at him, long oily hair hung from under their hoods, black like the night and tangled in loose strands. The vision disappeared, and he was flying again on Hawk.

Scanning about at the remaining vipers, he noticed their numbers being reduced by the Talonguard's assault. The elves seemed to be turning the fight in their favor, dropping more and more of the foul creatures. After more than an hour of fighting, Bellnella guided Hawk toward Ben-Gar and flew them to a small encampment on the taller of the two peaks. She pointed ahead and shouted something he couldn't hear. He looked down as Phin's eagle landed on a small ledge housing the base camp. Phinlera and Tentalis were both on its back. Braxton breathed a deep sigh of relief. They'd made it through. She was safe.

"That was incredible," Phinlera exclaimed when Brax dismounted.

"It was pretty amazing." He stretched his legs. "Of course, it would've been better if not for those vipers."

"Yeah, but we beat 'em off. Although having you blast those first few caught me by surprise."

"I think it was that last wave that swung the battle." Bellnella rubbed down Hawk. "You have a powerful gift there, Braxton. I am honored to have flown with an Elhunarie."

He smiled awkwardly, self-conscious at her sudden change in attitude toward him. He preferred it when she thought him like everyone else—just another human who deserved to have his heart tested in her presence.

"We'll rest there," Bellnella said, pointing to three gray pavilions at the back of the rock shelf that blended into the mountain. Large, makeshift roosts lined the camp, filled with leaves, sticks, and grasses from the mountain crevices. The rest of the area was open, where elves came and went, staying only long enough to report in or to allow their mounts time to rest.

"I'd love to be a Talonguard," Phinlera said excitedly as they sat together in one of the tents. "The wind in my hair, the weightlessness, the diving and maneuvering of the giant birds. How do you become one anyway," she asked Bellnella.

"The eagles choose their rider when they hatch," she explained. "Only children still learning to walk are selected, and we train together as we grow. It's a lifelong partnership."

"Too bad." She laughed. "I'd loved to have joined. What about you Brax?"

He nodded. "Did you see the Min army? It was overwhelming."

"I know it seems impossible," Bellnella acknowledged. "But we will succeed. The elves have always defended the trees. This time will be no different."

But Brax wasn't so sure. He kept remembering the massive horde fronting the eastern edge of Arbor Loren, wondering how long the forest, and his mom, could survive.

They left Bell and returned to the edge of the shelf, overlooking the battlefield and the sea of Mins extending into the Gap of Dunes.

It was past midafternoon when Laefin flew in on Fletcher, standing on the giant eagle behind Neah and holding his bow. He jumped down before the bird landed and ran over to them.

"We need to go west," he said anxiously. "The *feil* is dying."

CHAPTER

36

Thousands of bull-faced Mins stood in regimented block formation facing the elven kingdom and extending for miles north of Almon-Rin when Braxton, Phinlera, and two dozen Talonguard flew out over the Gap of Dunes. Like an endless sea, the thick, hairy creatures covered the ground as if the entire race of muscular beasts had flooded into the plains. Most had weapons of some kind—giant swords, axes, or halberds—while others wielded crossbows too big for a normal man to carry.

The invading army stood back from the forest, out of range of the elven archers concealed beyond the *feil*. Bellnella drove Hawk past the Mins' forward line, and Braxton could see where thousands of them lay dead in their repeated attempts to reach Arbor Loren's protective barrier, pierced by the deadly accuracy of the elves hidden within. The *feil*, he noticed, extended now to the very edge of the forest, blocking all view into Arbor Loren beyond a few outlying trees. But it was clear that its strength was beginning to fade. Large black stains were visible at irregular intervals along its otherwise shimmering surface, patches of the woodland covering devoid of its normal magical life. The Mins had given up on their brute-force approach to defeating the forest's shield or the endless barrage of arrows coming from the trees. Instead, large catapults fired burning pitch into the *feil*, diminishing its strength. The elves seemed defenseless against this new approach, unable to reach the Mins with their arrows and unwilling to leave the protection of their woodland home. All they could do now was watch and wait. It was only a matter of time before the *feil* would fall.

As Braxton and Phinlera circled above, the Talonguard who had flown in with them from Ben-Gar broke to assault the Mins, joining others of their kind already engaged in firing an endless barrage of projectiles into their foe. But the effect was little more than an irritation to the expansive Min army—like biting flies trying to stop a herd of cattle from invading the plains—and the riders' attacks were mostly ineffective. A few dozen of the creatures fired their crossbows back at the giant birds, more out of frustration, though, than any real attempt to hold back their assault.

Catching a sudden updraft, Bellnella turned Hawk north before circling back east toward the Dunes. As they wheeled, Braxton saw for the first time the immense size and full extent of the great Dragon's Spine Mountains, its endless spires and rocky cliffs extending far off into the distant horizon. Admiring their expanse, he began to sense something out of place, changed somehow from what he remembered before. Perhaps it was his new perspective gained from his elevated position? Or the fading light casting shadows on the peaks and causing them to appear different? Then he realized what he'd missed. Miles of broken rock extended from the foot of the Spine and past Almon-Tel, as if a great landslide had come down into the valley, pushing its rocky rubble deep into the Breaker Dunes.

He looked back at the mountains, expecting to see a sheared-off cliff face or some other evidence of where the rocks had given way. But nothing seemed out of place, and the Dragon's Spine stood as unyielding as before, apparently undisturbed by the avalanche he imagined. Even the small forest at its base seemed unaffected. *Wouldn't the trees have been felled when the landslide came through?* Hawk turned south, and they flew back over the Mins' front line, drawing Brax's attention to Arbor Loren and the catapults' barrage against the *feil*. The eastern edge of the forest seemed accentuated now by the flaming shot being cast upon its barrier.

"Take me down to that lead catapult," he shouted to Bell, pulling at her shoulder and summoning the spirit magic.

She nodded. They started to dive, and Brax closed his eyes, drawing upon the power of the energy. When Hawk leveled out, he released the spirit magic into the closest catapult. There was a brief silence in which he thought he'd failed to summon the energy correctly, but then a thunderclap echoed across the Dunes as his target exploded, sending burning pitch and wooden planks flying in every direction. Flames erupted among the Mins, and they scrambled to extinguish the fires. But Braxton didn't see it. He lay slumped over on Hawk, drained from the massive energy release, his body convulsing mildly and his temples throbbing.

He shut his eyes, trying to focus and regain control. Instantly, he saw himself standing in that same hazy grayness he'd experienced twice before. The two figures were hunched over the table facing a large sapphire orb. They turned toward him, one then the other. He could see their pale skin beneath shadowy hoods, their eyes still hidden from him. They looked much like each other—delicate chins of young women who might have been pretty once, but whose cheeks were now drawn and heavily lined, their lips dark and thin. Long, black greasy hair hung down in scraggly strands around their faces. One of them lifted her arm and pointed a bony finger toward him. There was a flash of bright light, and he was back on Hawk, flying above the Mins in the dwindling light of the Breaker Dunes.

Do not do that again, Serene said in his mind. *They are watching for you now.*

Who . . . are they? He still shook from the energy's release.

The Witch Sisters of Dahgmor, ancient and powerful creatures from another time. Do not think of them, my child, and keep your energy close.

He nodded, grateful for any excuse not to summon the spirit magic again. He wanted to retch, and it was all he could do to hold back his stomach. Below him, the catapult he'd destroyed still burned out of control, but others continued firing upon the *feil.*

It is time now, Serene said sadly. *Watch, child, and remember this moment.*

The catapults, which had been previously firing upon numerous points along the *feil,* changed their trajectory to concentrate on a single broad area of the magical barrier. Braxton felt a sadness well up inside him, as if something beautiful had passed from this world. A moment later, the shimmering light of the *feil* ceased its rhythmic flow, and a large, gaping hole appeared within the protective wall surrounding the elven forest. Thunder rippled across the Min line, followed quickly by the braying of many horns.

The *feil*, Braxton realized, had fallen.

The Mins rushed toward Arbor Loren, eager to do battle. A hundred yards away, a single long trumpet sounded from the elven kingdom, as if blown by a lone sentry. Thousands of arrows whizzed through the air, released from archers concealed in the trees. The Mins, running headlong into the defensive firepower of the elves, dropped in droves. But still they came; dozens ready to take the place wherever one of their brethren fell. For almost an hour, waves of arrows flew into the oncoming Min charge. And for a while, the elves held back their foe. But the Min numbers were overwhelming, and they swarmed across the Gap of Dunes toward the gaping hole in the *feil* that beckoned to them like an invitation to the woodland realm. Eventually, they reached the trees and with triumphant roars thundered past the fallen barrier and into the forest. The bowmen continued their attack from the gigantic oaks, dropping vast numbers of the beasts. Still the Mins flooded into Arbor Loren, eager to do battle.

Then a low note sounded through the woods, drawn from the very earth itself, a sad and ancient call, like the moan from something old and long forgotten.

"The White Horn!" Bellnella cried, and a cold shiver ran down Braxton's spine. All of the Talonguard pulled up from the Dunes.

The trees in Arbor Loren seemed to come alive, as if an enormously powerful gust of wind had suddenly blown through them, shaking their branches. Thousands of deathly screams echoed from the woods as the Mins were besieged on all sides by the trees themselves. Those still in the plains stopped short, fearful now of the horrific calls from their dying kin.

For a long time, the forest continued its avenging assault, branches lashing amid the howling that filled the air. Braxton covered his ears in a futile effort to shut out the awful screams.

Then it was silent.

"I need to land!" Bell said anxiously. "Hawk . . . needs rest." But Brax knew it was a weak excuse. Every Talonguard was flying toward the trees. It was clear none of them had expected to hear the call of the White Wood.

Is the Fey waking? he asked Serene.

It stirs deep within the earth. If they should sound the Horn again, it will awaken. It is our hope, child, that this will not come to pass.

Will help come in time?

We shall see. Go with your rider. I need to speak with another.

They flew north and landed in Almon-Roe. Unlike the northern outpost they'd visited before, Almon-Roe was larger, with numerous homes and other buildings high up in its branches and at the base of its enormous oaks. Now, though, the city seemed deserted. The fighting, Brax knew, was closer to Almon-Rin, and the few home guard that remained were mostly sentries, resigned to watching the war from the north.

Bell slipped from Hawk's neck. "There's a guesthouse in the side of that oak beyond the ladder." She pointed to one of the rope bridges extending from their aerial platform. Unfastening the eagle's straps, she spoke a few words to her mount in their native tongue and rubbed him down hurriedly. Then she ran off across the numerous bridges that interweaved among the trees and disappeared into the dense forest, leaving Braxton alone with the giant bird. Hawk eyed him suspiciously, as though considering his edibility, then hopped up into one of the enormous nests filling the surrounding trees, settled down, and began preening himself.

Braxton looked around at the massive oak on which he'd been deposited, a hundred feet off the floor. The tree appeared to be one of several landing posts, with numerous platforms extending out at various intervals among its gigantic branches for the birds to land upon. Many of the nests were filled, with more Talonguard flying in all the time. Each rider jumped from their saddle, rubbed down their mount for a moment, and then ran off across one of the rope bridges into the trees. Arrow landed on an open platform in one of the aeries across from him. Brax called to Phin as soon as she'd dismounted and Tentalis had left, waving his arms to get her attention. She looked around for a way to reach him and shrugged. He indicated the rope ladders pointing to the guest oak Bellnella had shown him.

They crossed the bridges, angling toward each other. Braxton stopped often, occasionally dropping to his knees to keep from falling off the floating walkways, which lacked railings of any kind. He sometimes preferred to crawl rather than risk standing upright. When he reached the guesthouse, he was perspiring profusely. He let out a sigh of relief. Phinlera was already there, equally pleased to be off the bridges, although her nimbleness had allowed her to cross more easily.

"What do you think's going on?" Phin asked, taking a drink from a waterskin she was holding before handing it to him.

"Don't know. Everyone just seemed to run off into the forest after the White Horn sounded."

"Must be some kind of call to arms. Not that they need any more reason to fight."

They ate some grains and fruit they discovered in the guesthouse.

"How do you suppose we get down from here?" Phin looked around, noticing the lack of stairs of any kind.

Brax shook his head.

Laefin came running toward them, crossing the rope walkways, as easily as on the forest floor.

"I'm glad you found your way, and something to eat," he said when he arrived.

"Bell directed me here," Braxton commented. "But I don't understand why everyone just ran off like that."

"Or where they went," Phin added.

"It's the Fey Oath." Laefin shook his head and sat down. "Most elves have never heard the call of the White Horn. It's a defining moment for us. All will go to Fey Ethel and commit their lives in defense of the White Wood. Once we touch the Silver Towers, we dedicate our very existence to saving them. No one will leave Arbor Loren, nor will we flee before our enemies, no matter their number, even in the face of certain death. Every man, woman, and child in the forest will pledge to defend Fey Ethel, or die trying."

The strength in their friend's voice and the intensity in his eyes showed the elves' commitment to their woodland home, beyond anything his words alone could explain.

"Before landing here, Neah flew me over the front line," the elf continued. "It seems the Mins have pulled back for now. They're afraid to enter the forest after losing so many to the trees. I think we've gained a precious moment of reprieve, but only time will tell what they plan to do next." He stood. "Try to get some rest. I'll join you in a few hours, and we'll fly out to see what they're up to."

He thanked them again for their help and then hurried back across the rope bridges, disappearing into the forest.

CHAPTER
37

The barrage began again at midnight. Great flaming balls of burning pitch shot high over the forest, cast out by the Mins' catapults fronting the Breaker Dunes. The blazing projectiles lit up the night sky, blocking out the stars, their tails burning behind them like a shower of suns descending upon the elven kingdom. Braxton and Phinlera watched from the north, saddened by the vicious hatred the Mins seemed to harbor for the elves and their endless desire to destroy their woodland realm. Fires appeared among the trees, and thick plumes of gray smoke writhed above the forest like serpents let loose by the Min attack.

Arbor Loren was burning, Braxton realized. He slumped down on the edge of the platform surrounding their guest oak and dropped his head. "Will it never end?"

"Not until one of us is destroyed, I'm afraid," Laefin said. Braxton looked up at their friend, standing beside him. "We should go and see what they're up to. If you're ready?"

"Definitely!" Braxton got to his feet.

It is time to cut the leash that guides this beast, Serene interjected. *Tell the archer to give me one of his arrows.*

A rush of excitement flooded through Brax at the thought of his master's intervention. He relayed her words quickly.

Laefin unslung his quiver and selected an arrow he thought worthy of the Elhunarie's touch. Beautifully fashioned from some dark, old wood, it was perfectly straight and as smooth as polished stone, with three evenly placed eagle feathers—one tinged with white. The head was flawlessly set, cast from the same unusual metal the elves alone seemed to possess, forming an exact point. Accepting the arrow, Serene guided Brax to sit down and take several breaths. She shut his eyes, joined with his consciousness, and began blending her energy deep inside him.

The spirit magic enveloped Braxton in rhythmic waves, starting slowly, but growing in intensity, connecting with him in an interweaving of human and magical forms. His thoughts cleared, and the recent memories that plagued him became locked away in rooms deep within his mind, their doors shutting to the emotions of those lesser experiences. He began to feel stronger, renewed, and bigger in both height and girth. And yet lighter too, that he might drift away among the stars. The sounds of the forest faded, replaced by a low, constant ringing in his ears and the vibration of the energy pulsating through his body.

Serene continued her magical weaving, expanding the spirit magic beyond Brax's form, radiating from within him like a lantern held aloft in the dark. Nothing seemed impossible to him in those moments he connected with his master. Even the Min invasion seemed so much less important now compared to the endless possibilities that seemed laid out before him.

Gradually, he felt her ask him to step aside. He breathed in, drawing in the wondrous sensation of the spirit magic. He remained in the energy for a few more euphoric moments, wallowing in the experience. Then reluctantly he pulled away, drawing himself to one side of his consciousness and releasing the connection to his master, allowing her to fill the vacated space. She focused on the arrow, moving his hands up and down the shaft, feeling its hard, smooth surface. Ever so slowly, Serene began directing the spirit magic through Brax's fingertips and out into the wooden form. She stopped often, he sensed, checking that the brittle timbers hadn't split apart in their reforming with the magic's power. Steadily she increased the strength, allowing the arrow to absorb more and more of her magical touch. All the while, she repeated words in Braxton's mind that he didn't understand but that sounded vaguely familiar to ones he'd heard her say before.

It took only a few minutes for Serene to complete her work. When she released him, he looked down at what he held. The arrow seemed to glisten with an ethereal energy, a brightness in the dark of night. Small silver symbols were burned deep into its wooden surface, and he could sense the spirit magic emanating from them. The feathers and head had been fused into the shaft, so that it was no longer possible to tell where one part of the arrow ended and another began. As he ran his fingers along its markings, Brax's skin tingled, feeling something born of another world. What started as a well-crafted tool had become a weapon of power.

He looked up to see Phinlera and Laefin staring at him. "That was fantastic," Phin said, releasing her breath.

This arrow will now penetrate any defense it encounters, Serene explained. *No bond of metal or skin or magical strength can protect that which it strikes. Tell the gifted archer that I entrust in him its safekeeping, and that no other may fire upon a mark that which I have made.*

Braxton relayed her words, shaking slightly from the energy's withdrawal. Laefin seemed to drink in Serene's message. He raised a hand over his heart, closed his eyes, and breathed in.

"I understand this charge that has been entrusted to me," he said, exhaling. "What must I do?"

There is one among the Mins who communicates the war back to the Witch Sisters through their magical connection. She is a shaman among their kind but born of witch magic. This one is well-guarded deep within the enemy's camp, but tonight, she will move to see the feet of the mountain and ask of her keepers their instructions. When she does, you will have but one chance to fire upon her. Send this arrow deep into her breast, and you will sever the cord through which the Mins are receiving their guidance. Do this and you will gain an advantage.

There was a brief silence after Braxton repeated her words. He felt a strange communication between Serene and the elf, as if one barely brushed past the other, like the gentle touching of a spider's web in the morning fog of an otherwise silent forest.

Laefin took another breath. "I see now the path you have laid out before me," he said. "I accept this task willingly. I am ready."

Several hours before dawn, Braxton, Phinlera, and Laefin flew out from Almon-Roe, accompanied by the Talonguard and their giant mounts. The elves each bore a small white mark upon their cheek, chin, or brow—a symbol, Brax guessed, of the Fey Oath, and their commitment to protect Arbor Loren and the White Wood. The siege had continued throughout the night, and the Gap of Dunes seemed alive now with endless campfires from the Mins below. Flaming projectiles continued assaulting the trees, and bright fires burned in the forest near Almon-Rin. As they flew overhead, Braxton turned away from Arbor Loren, knowing that something beautiful and graceful was going to die.

Serene guided them east from the forest for over an hour before turning south and angling toward the Min camp from above the direction of Ben-Gar. Occasionally, she'd communicate with Brax, telling him to adjust their course one way or another, while other times, he felt her impressions of the direction they should go. Each time he communicated silently with Bell, using only hand signals. The other Talonguard followed, staggered on either side, allowing Braxton to lead them on this journey. They circled high above the Mins for what seemed like hours, searching first one section of the encampment and then another, looking for the shaman.

Turn west! Serene said loudly as they angled again. Brax signaled to his rider, and Hawk turned toward the forest, catching a premorning breeze that blew away from the twin peaks. Braxton indicated to the others the need for silence, and the riders touched their mounts, directing them to avoid calling or making any unnecessary movements.

They glided in the dark above the twinkling of the Mins' campfires, looking for their elusive prey.

There, Serene said to him at last, drawing his attention to a small group of lights moving north. He motioned to Bell and pointed out their target to Laefin. The archer jumped up on Fletcher's back, notching Serene's arrow as his eagle began to dive. Braxton glanced at Phin, flying alongside him with Tentalis, and saw fear reflected in her eyes. He looked back at Laefin and watched as Neah guided her giant mount down toward the patrol, moving steadily away. As Bellnella leveled Hawk into a wide arc, Braxton caught sight of the shaman walking among the Mins, torchlight briefly reflecting off her features. She was noticeably shorter than her protectors and wore a robe as black as night, the cowl thrown back and her face exposed. Unlike the Mins, the shaman had a sheep-like head, with tightly cropped gray hair and small curved horns protruding from her temples. In her right hand she held a staff topped with the bleached skull of some unknown animal. Her other arm was tucked deep inside her robe, clutching something she wished to remain hidden. The patrol joined a larger group of Mins, and the shaman disappeared among the sea of heads around her.

Braxton watched anxiously as Laefin and his Talonguard descended closer and closer to the Mins, almost invisible as they glided toward the immense army. Time seemed to slow as the giant eagle continued to drop, the elf standing frozen on her back like some aerial statue. Then Laefin released the arrow. A shrill cry from some mysterious night bird broke the air followed by a scream that echoed up from the Dunes, making Braxton's skin crawl. Laefin had found his mark.

Bellnella and Tentalis called to their mounts, and their eagles shrieked repeatedly, pulling up from the plains with a flapping of their enormous wings. Braxton, Phinlera, and the two riders fired arrows at the patrol, hoping to increase the Mins' confusion and provide precious time for the still-silent Fletcher to get away. Their plan seemed to work. The shaman's guards fired their crossbows up at Hawk and Arrow, but as Brax had hoped, the Mins had difficulty seeing their eagles in the dark, and their bolts flew wide.

A large patch of inky blackness shot through the sky and smashed into Fletcher, sending Laefin's eagle spinning wildly. The elf dangled below the flailing bird, tethered by a single cord. The panicked eagle screeched in pain, and an evil shriek from some abysmal creature replied.

"Laefin!" Brax called out, but there was no answer.

He watched in horror, as his friend, along with Neah and her injured mount, plummeted toward the Dunes, intertwined, it seemed, with this new attacker. They disappeared moments later, obscured by the brighter lights of the campfires below, swallowed up by the Min army.

"*Laefin!*" Braxton repeated. "We must help him!" He grabbed Bell's shoulder, but she just shook her head and pulled away.

"No!" he shrieked, fumbling with his straps.

Let him go, Serene said. Brax responded in anger. By the time he had his straps undone, Hawk was almost a mile above the ground. Braxton knew he'd never survive the fall. He desperately summoned the spirit magic and drew the Unicorn Blade, calling upon its power to aid Laefin. But Serene quenched his effort, dissipating the energy.

"No!" he yelled again. "I won't lose him!" He struggled to recall the spirit magic.

Let him go, Serene repeated quietly, her calming voice a pillar of reassurance amid the turbulent waters of his panicked mind. *Let him go.*

Braxton woke in the guesthouse of Almon-Roe. Streaks of dried tears covered his face, and he immediately felt the pain of losing yet another friend. Phinlera slept beside him, her breathing regular. He pulled on his boots, slung the Unicorn Blade over his shoulder, and stepped out onto the platform skirting the tree. A bright midmorning sun greeted him, but Braxton ignored it. He wanted nothing more than to shut himself away from the light and crawl back into the shadow of his despair.

When his eyes adjusted, he looked across the elevated city and glimpsed movement in the tree opposite his, reminding him that he wasn't alone. Large plumes of dark black smoke floated over Arbor Loren, drawing his attention to the south and the swath of burning wood coming from Almon-Rin. He rubbed a booted foot against the platform and dropped his head.

"There's no hope. We will never win," he said aloud.

Are you so sure of your fate? Serene asked. *Have you no faith in those you trusted, in those you once loved?*

"All those I've loved have died," he said bitterly. "My mom, Kael, Laefin."

Yet others still walk with you.

He turned to the guest oak. "Am I destined to lose her as well? Will she be the last to go?"

It is a new day, my child, and you should celebrate your night's success. It has helped you far greater than you know, and your loss is not as dark as it seems.

"What can this new day bring that could provide any hope?"

Look to the mountain.

Reluctantly, he glanced at the Dragon's Spine, far to the north. It stood as unyielding as before, unchanged from what he remembered. He scanned the scene for a few listless moments, almost wishing to see something that might give him some hope, but saw nothing, and turned away.

Why do you so easily abandon the faith you once placed in others? Look again, my child.

Brax sighed and looked back at the numerous spires and great peaks of the Spine. For a long time he stared at their endless expanse continuing into the distant horizon, waiting glumly, half expecting something to jump out in front of him and dance in the morning sky. Gradually he followed the path they'd taken from Almon-Tel, crossing the southern ridge to the distant jagged range in the east, and to the Dragon's Head. He retraced the journey from Ben-Gar, pausing at the place where he imagined Laefin had fallen. Feeling dejected at the memory of losing his friend, he dropped his head. His eyes fell on the edge of the Dunes and the landslide of broken rock he'd noticed while flying on Hawk. He was about to dismiss it when he realized he was looking south.

"How can that be?" he said, his mind slowly awakening. The rock now extended well below Almon-Roe.

"Is it moving?" he asked.

Look carefully, child, and remember your walk in the forest.

Reaching over his shoulder, he grasped the handle of the Unicorn Blade. The warmth of the energy seeped into him, calming his emotions and settling over his body, healing his pain. Then he saw them. Row upon row of armor-clad, bearded warriors standing frozen amid the rocks. No, they *were* the rocks. The energy surged in his heart center, pulsating with that same euphoric feeling. Instantly he saw what Serene had been waiting for him to notice. The rocks, the rubble, the debris—the entire landslide that he imagined had come down into the Dunes—was a cover for an immense army.

The dwarves had come.

CHAPTER
38

"Phin, wake up!" Braxton shook her.

"What is it, what's happened?" she answered, startled.

"Get the Leaf. Hurry!"

She grabbed the blade and followed him out onto the platform, pulling on her boots. "What is it?" she repeated. "What's wrong?"

"Hold Shelindûhin and look at that rubble." He pointed to the landslide. "Look past the rocks."

She searched the debris. "What? I don't see anything."

"Keep looking. Call on the energy."

"I don't understand. Just tell me what you see," she pleaded. "I'm not as quick as you. I can't do it that fast. I—" Then she saw them. "*Dwarves?*" Her eyes filled with tears, daring to hope that what she saw was true.

"Yes, Phin," he said calmly. "The dwarven army has come to our aid."

"But how—" She stopped. "That means—"

"Oi!" a sudden gruff voice called from below. They looked down at the forest floor.

"Ruskin!" they yelled together.

The dwarf stood in the clearing at the base of their oak, his gleaming breastplate reflecting the symbol of a large crouching badger, shining brightly in the morning light. His left arm rested atop the head of an enormous ax standing chest-high beside him.

They hurried down the tree and ran over to their friend.

"Well met!" The dwarf extended his right arm, clasping Brax's in return.

"Oh, Ruskin, it's so great to see you!" Phinlera wrapped her arms around his neck, her chest pressing into his bearded face as she kissed him on the bald top of his head.

"Well, yes, ahem." He cleared his throat and pulled away. "Good to see ya both," he said, smiling wryly.

"How'd you get here?" Braxton asked.

"When'd you arrive?" Phinlera added.

"Why haven't we seen you before?" Brax continued.

"We walked. Two days. You were flying," Ruskin answered casually.

Brax frowned. "What've you been doing for two days?"

"Talking with the elves. Lots to be said. We haven't had dealings with 'em in a thousand years, so both sides had to get comfortable with suddenly massing our armies so close together. Been communicating back and forth with Bendarren through these elven runners." He thumbed toward the city. "There were 'conditions' under which King Tharak agreed to fight."

"Like what?"

He rubbed his beard. "Well, when I reached Dûrak-Thûhn, I had to request an audience with the king, which of course took three days while he finished feasting. When I finally got to explain that the Mins were invading, Tharak wasn't too excited about sending out the clans to fight alongside elves."

"Really? Why not?" Phinlera asked. "Surely your king must know that if the Mins destroy Arbor Loren, they'll eventually threaten his kingdom too."

"You understand things pretty well, missy," he said, and Phinlera smiled at the compliment. "For a young'un," he added, and she scowled. "Anyway, Tharak needed a good reason to go to war, and fighting to save elves and a forest didn't seem like one. I finally convinced him by lighting my pipe in his presence, something I'd usually get lashed for, but it worked out. The old boar immediately recognized the scent of elven pipe leaf. And when I told him he'd never again enjoy drawing its flavor if the forest was destroyed, he felt that was reason enough to send out a few battalions to fight, and the rest of the nation eagerly agreed. So here we are."

Braxton smiled at their old guide. "Well, we're glad you came, no matter what the reason."

"There's just one small problem."

"What's that?"

"We've been waiting to fight now for two days. Arming three thousand dwarves and marching them day and night, only to stand around doing nothing, is not our idea of a well-run war."

"Why don't you just attack the Mins then, if you're so anxious to fight?" Phinlera said, still a bit annoyed by the dwarf's earlier comment.

"Nothing would please us more, but Bendarren wants us to wait for the Empire."

"The Empire?" Brax asked.

"Yes, lad. They're coming round the bottom of these damn trees, and we're supposed to wait for 'em before starting in, even though they're taking their sweet time getting here. They're camped out somewhere in the Calindurin—or that's what the elves tell me anyway. If they don't hurry up, we're going to have a riot on our hands. My kinsmen won't wait another day to fight, not when we can *see* the Mins we're supposed to be attacking."

"The Empire's joining the war!" Phinlera exclaimed, excited now. "That's great news."

"The emissary must've convinced them to come. Things are finally looking up," Brax agreed.

"Yeah, well, I need to get back to the clans soon, or they'll start in on themselves again." Ruskin shook his head. "Dwarves don't do well just standing around fully dressed in war gear and drinking ale. We tend to want to bash things, even if it is other dwarves."

They grinned at their friend, happy to have him back, and updated him on all they'd experienced since parting. The dwarf didn't say much until they came to the attack on Laefin. He seemed particularly interested in the creature that had struck him.

It is a wyvern, Serene said.

"A wyvern?" the dwarf repeated with distaste when Braxton relayed the message. "We haven't seen one of those in these parts for almost five hundred years. Evil creatures they are, summoned from the abyss by sorcerers too stupid to know better. It's one of the reasons I hate magic." He spat on the floor. "We'll have to double our night watch when the fighting begins. That thing could cause us some real trouble if we don't prepare for it. Fortunately it only moves at night, but I'd still better pass it along to the clans, so they know what to expect. I'll see you two later." He swung his ax up onto his shoulder and strode off into the trees.

They watched him go, smiling at his grumblings about being back in the forest.

"What's a wyvern?" Phinlera asked after he'd left.

"Dunno, but I bet we're going to find out."

For the remainder of the morning, they wandered around Almon-Roe, waiting for word on the war, but no one came. They ate a cold breakfast outside the guest oak, enjoying the replenished food that always seemed to await their return to the tree, even though they never saw anyone attending to their needs. When they'd finished, Braxton went looking for one of the home guard, anxious to get some news, but every time he approached the elusive elves, they disappeared back into the forest, ignoring his calls. He missed Laefin and how the young archer always took time to inform them on the goings-on in Arbor Loren, thinking about his sunny disposition and feeling guilty at losing him without a fight.

Phinlera tried encouraging him, speaking excitedly about the dwarf and Empire armies joining the battle to hopefully swing this dark tide in their favor.

"Do you think they'll fight separately, or all charge in and crush the Mins?" She punched her fist into her hand.

Brax smiled at her attempts to distract him and at her optimism that the elves could still win this war.

"They'll probably attack together," he said. But he knew his words sounded hollow, even distracted. Now more than ever he feared losing Phin and surviving alone. He knew he could help the elves. He knew Serene and the Unicorn Blade had the ability to make a difference, to tip the scales in their favor. But at what cost? Whenever he thought of going out into the Dunes to fight, his mind fixated on one question. Would Phinlera survive? He wondered what it would be like to be asked to let her go. If the elves might think her death worth saving Arbor Loren, her sacrifice somehow tolerable, even acceptable. Not to him, he thought—never to him. He played it over and over in his mind, the pain he knew he'd feel at losing her and having to return home alone. His heart wrenched at the possibility, at each variation of the nightmarish outcome he imagined.

Why do you live in a future that may never come to pass? Serene said, entering his thoughts and dispersing the gloom. *Live in the moment, child.*

I cannot lose her. I . . . love her.

Love is the greatest ally in your life's experience, but do not waste it like water cast out upon the barren sands of a desert in which you lay down your heart. Believe in her, in her own life's journey, in the possibility that she too has a part to play and a path to walk upon that is guided, like yours, by her own impression of wherein we connect. You do not create her future, nor should you believe that her life's focus is determined by your actions. While you walk together on this path, interwoven in the present, live in the acceptance that your experiences do not govern her fate, but that that *path is driven by a greater awareness than you can possibly imagine.*

Braxton thought about what Serene said, balancing her words against the phantoms that plagued him. He took comfort in her calm reassurance, and, although he struggled to understand the exact meaning, grasped enough of her message to realize what she intended to convey: not to worry about Phinlera, but to enjoy the time they had together. He admired Phin as she sat among the trees, the sunlight catching her hair. He listened to her muse over the coming fight and the events of the past few weeks, focusing more on the sound of her voice than her actual words. Brax wanted so much to be away from here, to be back home with her, just the two of them.

A series of low horns rang out far to the south, and they both looked in that direction, returning to the encroaching war. A dull thumping rose from the Dunes, as though some monstrous creature were beating rhythmically on a massive drum, drowning out all other calls. The sound seemed to suggest something new from the Mins, some change in their attitude toward the forest and their intense focus on its demise.

Phin stared at the trees to the south, half expecting something to come charging out at any moment. "What do you think's going on?"

"Don't know, but something's sure changed."

Within minutes of the sound, Almon-Roe seemed to come alive. Elven runners appeared from the dense forest, passed quickly by, and headed out into the Breaker Dunes. Then scores of archers crossed the rope ladders to the nesting eagles, and the sky above soon filled with Talonguard. Bellnella and Tentalis signaled to them as they mounted their giant birds, landing on the forest floor just long enough for Braxton and Phinlera to strap in before flying out over the edge of the Dunes. They headed south toward Almon-Rin. Brax called up to Bell for some explanation, but she didn't reply, and just pointed farther south, as if that were answer enough. He scanned the horizon, but the smoke hanging over the forest blocked his view. All he could see was the tide of Mins massed in the east.

He looked down at the seemingly endless path of mile-wide rubble that had slid out from the Spine. Brax marveled at how natural the rocks appeared, forming up against the dirt and grassy plains of the Breaker Dunes. A few dozen dwarves were visible among the debris, the huge numbers of armor-clad soldiers having moved farther south. Hawk increased his pace, continuing along the rim of trees until a funnel shape came into view at the end of the rocky formation, spreading out like an open mouth toward the Dunes. A wave of excitement rushed over Braxton at knowing the dwarves were there, hidden among the rocks with Ruskin at their lead, waiting to spring their trap upon their unsuspecting foe. Maybe Phinlera was right. Perhaps they could win this war.

Beyond the landslide, the great Min catapults had ripped up a part of the ancient kingdom, leaving a gaping hole of burning stumps in its wake. The thumping grew louder, and through the smoke still rising above the forest, Brax could see the Mins moving about below. The large, muscular creatures were responding to the drumbeats, turning their distant flank toward the south while keeping their western front facing Arbor Loren.

As they neared Almon-Rin and cleared the smoky haze, Brax felt a sudden rush of exhilaration at seeing in the distance the cause of the change in the Mins' attitude. Far to the south, beyond the reaches of the black tide, stood row upon row of armored cavalry. The horsemen's purple-and-white banners and silver breastplates reflected brilliantly in the afternoon sun. Braxton took a deep breath and released it fully, letting go of all the tension he'd been carrying for so long, seeing at last the hope he feared would never come.

The Empire army had finally arrived.

A loud cheer alongside him caused Braxton to jump. Phinlera beamed and waved her arms above her head, pointing to the thousand or so heavily armored horsemen from their homeland waiting below the Min line.

He smiled back that he too had seen them. The Mins, surprised by the arrival of this unexpected foe, continued turning their massive flank to face the impending threat. Ranks of halberd-wielding Min soldiers marched to the drone of thundering drums as they took up their new formation. Watching the battlefield from the sky, Brax and Phin's giant mounts wheeled north of Almon-Rin, circling above the forest. When they arced back toward the trees, the skies over Arbor Loren were thick with hundreds of Talonguard rising from the canopy. Signaling excitedly to Phinlera, he began to understand the battle plan unfolding before him, and the impending attack.

Do we go down and fight? he asked Serene, drawing the Unicorn Blade from across his back.

Wait, child. That time will come.

Dozens of horns split the air in a single harmonious call, drowning out the Mins and their drums. Twisting south, a chill ran down Brax's spine as row upon row of mounted knights approached the Min line, their lances held upright and their purple banners flapping in the breeze. Bellnella and Tentalis continued circling their eagles, close enough now to watch the unfolding scene. The horsemen began cantering forward in a broad line as the human army advanced upon their larger foe. Another horn sounded, and the cavalry's movements quickened, the line fluidly changing in one graceful motion as if in response to some unknown play, and the horses began to charge.

The sea of muscular brutes in the Dunes readied their crossbows behind forward ranks of larger fighters, waiting for the horsemen to come into range. An extraordinarily loud, single, clear trumpet sounded at the edge of Arbor-Loren. Braxton jumped and looked down. The entire elven nation burst from the protective covering of the ancient forest, yelling and firing arrows as they charged into the surprised Mins. Simultaneously, every Talonguard dove from above the canopy, unleashing a barrage of projectiles into the opposing army.

For a moment, the Mins were caught off guard. Surprised by the sudden offensive of the previously elusive elves, they turned to face the woodland assault. This was exactly what the allied armies had hoped for, Braxton realized, as it bought the galloping knights precious time. By the time the larger beasts recognized the diversion, they fired their volley too late. Scores of mounted soldiers still died from the bolts, but it was not enough to stop the full impact of the charging Empire elite. With their battle cry of *"For the Empire!"* the hardened cavalry smashed into the Min ranks with an impact that drowned out all other sounds, their pointed lances decimating their lighter-armored foe.

An instant later, the forward ranks of the elves reached the Mins. Having discarded their bows now for small, narrow swords in each hand, they nimbly attacked their enemy, sidestepping the slower brute force approach of the big creatures and counterattacking with short, quick double strikes into their opponents' unguarded and vulnerable areas. With surgical precision, the elves crippled the Mins' front line, slashing at their exposed necks or legs as they ran by, dropping the larger enemy in an almost graceful attack. To the surprise of the Mins, however, the elves didn't stop to fight but continued past their injured and bleeding opponents, pushing further into their forward ranks. Simultaneously, the Empire cavalry continued to cut down the Mins to the south, driving a piercing wedge deeper into their enemy's buckling flank. As the Mins turned to pursue the elves, a second wave of woodland soldiers wielding two-handed great swords swept into their front, bringing down the already injured creatures.

The penetrating power of the combined western charge crushed the slower Mins, and for a few precious moments, chaos erupted in the invading army. Instinctively, the Mins turned their northern right flank toward the elves' assault. This was precisely what the dwarves had been waiting for. With a rapid thunder of drums, they sprang their trap. The mountainous rubble and broken rock disappeared, replaced now by thousands of heavily armored dwarf warriors who charged in from only a few dozen yards away. The dwarves hit the northern edge of the Mins like a thunderclap, smashing into the shocked creatures and crushing them in droves beneath their powerful hammer blows. Within moments, the whole forward line of the enemy was surrounded by the combined strength of the western armies who fought the surprised Mins on three sides. In minutes, their vanguard force was slaughtered.

Brax yelled and cheered with excitement at their success. But Serene had him look east, and he was totally deflated. During the counteroffensive, the Mins had divided their force in two, pulling the greater number of their soldiers miles back from their dying brethren, sacrificing their front to provide time for their main army to regroup. They now stood in a broad line across the full width of the combined opposing nations. There would be no flanking this horde, no surprise attack that would take them off guard a second time. The dwarves, elves, and men would have to fight them head on. The greater strength of the Min army still stood thousands strong, untouched in the Gap of Dunes, ready and waiting.

CHAPTER

39

It was after midnight when the warning came. Braxton, Phinlera, Penton, and Gavin, along with Bear, sat together by one of the small fires that littered the allied camps east of Arbor Loren. Brax and Phin had found the others late into the night, and after a brief celebration at seeing one another safe, had eagerly shared their perspectives on the day's victory. The four friends drew as much warmth from their collective company as from the little fire they surrounded.

The war in the plains had reached a tenuous reprieve by the time evening came, neither side willing to engage too quickly in the inevitable confrontation they all knew would come. The Mins had lost thousands in their first fight with the western armies and were cautious now. The Empire was equally willing to wait, needing to regain their strength after the long day's ride, full charge, and intense fighting with the Min army. Tensions ran high in the allied camps as dwarves, elves, and men readied themselves for the fight that would decide the fate of Arbor Loren, and possibly the western nations.

Penton described their journey to Amberdeen with Leylandon, the elven emissary, after having ridden west across the Calindurin Plains.

"Elves never rest," he said wryly, remembering the pace they'd set. It was the meeting with the Empire's king, however, that Braxton found most interesting.

"Took us four days to get an audience with our young leader," Pen explained. "And that was after having the Council of Sorrows and meeting several more times with Iban too."

"King Balan is no older than you are, Brax," Gavin commented, "but I fear he's greatly influenced by the bishop."

Phinlera frowned. "Why do you say that?"

"Well," Penton answered, "Iban and Leylandon pleaded our case to the king. But your friend Zacharias argued strongly against the Empire getting involved."

"Zacharias?" Braxton asked, surprised.

"Yes, I thought you might find that interesting. He was there, along with the bishop, but didn't look too well—all thin and drawn, with his arm in a sling. Looked as if he'd been to the abyss and back." Penton chuckled. "Too bad he survived."

Phinlera turned to Brax. "Leaving him might have been a mistake."

Brax nodded slowly.

"I'm sorry you let him go," Pen agreed. "He spoke eloquently and long about how we shouldn't send aid to the elves. That we no longer needed dealings with 'the wooded race' and that we'd never owed them anything anyway. That we couldn't be sure what they said was true and should wait for our own scouts' confirmation before getting involved."

"The bishop listened quietly most of the time, often nodding his agreement with Zacharias," Gavin added. "It was pretty obvious they knew each other well enough, and although he never spoke openly against the elven emissary, the bishop subtly advised the king that the Empire had much more pressing matters to deal with at home."

Penton took a drink. "Thankfully, Iban's skill well matched Zacharias', but in the end, I think only the fact that he was a Wielder tipped the balance in our favor. King Balan eventually agreed to send a cavalry battalion to see if what the elves said was true."

"When Zacharias and the bishop left the hall, neither seemed too pleased with the decision," Gavin continued. "I think if it weren't for them arguing against us, the Empire might have sent a much larger force."

"Well, we're happy they sent anyone at all," Phin commented.

Braxton said nothing. Letting Zacharias live was proving to be a mistake. He could still see his adversary pinned to the tree by Sotchek's giant bolt.

Then Serene spoke the warning in his mind.

The enemy is moving, child. Alert the others. The battle is about to begin.

"Quiet!" Braxton burst out, interrupting the group's discussion. Bear woke and barked at the sudden sound. The others looked at him in surprise as Brax jumped to his feet. "We need to find the generals. Now!"

Without waiting, he ran toward the main pavilion that had been set up for the military leaders, darting among the numerous tents and patrols that filled the allied camps. Bear jumped excitedly beside him, and Braxton was grateful to see the elkhound, knowing it meant the others had followed. He found the large circular tent, with the banners of the united armies hanging calmly above in the still evening air.

Pushing past the startled guards, he burst inside. "The Mins are attacking!" Brax yelled. The occupants stared at him in surprise. He'd interrupted some intense planning meeting, and a few of the attendees looked annoyed by his sudden intrusion. He recognized the tall, lean figure of the elven general Illian, standing beside Breem, the more muscular Empire commander whom Brax remembered from their journey out of Falderon. There were others too: a few dwarves dressed in full mail, a shorter man with ash-blond hair and small, intense eyes, and several more elves. It was Ruskin, however, who responded first, removing a smoldering pipe from his mouth. "What is it, lad?" He blew a puff of smoke toward the ceiling.

"The Mins are attacking," Braxton repeated. "Where's Bendarren?"

General Illian touched Brax's shoulder. "Bendarren cannot leave the forest," he said. "His life force is bound to the trees. Tell me what you know, and I will act in his stead."

"They're coming," Brax stated. "They'll be here any moment. You need to be ready."

"I know you." Breem pointed a gloved hand at Braxton from across the tent. "You caused me a lot of trouble up in the Vales. Why should we trust you now?"

Illian turned to face the Empire commander. "Because he is a Wielder."

Breem's eyes opened wide, and the other man stared openmouthed as well. Even the dwarves seemed surprised.

"A Wielder?" Breem asked, confused. "This . . . farm boy cannot be a Wielder?"

"Nevertheless, he is," the elf replied.

"We don't have time for this," Ruskin snapped. "You two can decide what you want. I'm going to wake the clans. I suggest you get your horsemen ready." He left the tent with the other dwarves in tow.

General Illian dispatched the elves, but Breem seemed frozen by his disbelief. "He cannot be a Wielder," he said.

"He is, and I'm moving my army." Illian rolled up some parchment and headed toward the flap.

"Wait, Illian!" Breem called. "Are you going to trust your forest, your nation, to this . . . boy?"

The elven general looked first at Brax and then at Breem.

"Yes, I am," he said, then he turned and left the tent.

Breem looked down at Braxton from behind his thick black eyebrows and furrowed brow. He was a large, impressive man.

"You'd better be right about this," he said gruffly, then strode past him. His aide followed, leaving Braxton alone.

The commander had no sooner left the pavilion when a bone-chilling scream echoed across the encampment. Brax knew only one creature that could make that sound.

The wyvern.

He found the others waiting for him outside, held back by the guards. His friends covered their ears, searching for refuge from the evil shadow flying overhead. The soldiers fired arrows at the beast, but they too cowered between shots as the terrifying shrieks drowned out all other sounds. Only Braxton and the few remaining elven warriors seemed unaffected by the wyvern's calls. Breem ran toward the Empire section of the camp, dodging several panicked horses that had broken free of their tethers. The animals bolted every time the wyvern screeched, knocking over everything in their path in a desperate effort to escape.

The wyvern called again, and Braxton looked up, catching a brief glimpse of the creature in the moonlight. Its impenetrable blackness seemed unnatural, blocking out the stars. A hairless, almost shapeless form, it was as long as a dozen men, propelled by two broad, leathery wings with sharp hooks at either end and powerful back legs that ended in curved talons. As it flew, it whipped the barbed tip of its sinuous tail about with an unearthly wail, as if searching the air.

It was the creature's elongated head, however, that captured Brax's attention, sitting atop a serpentine neck with slanted, coal-black eyes that reflected a menacing hatred for all normal life. Its snout angled downward, giving the beast an almost gargoyle-like appearance, and its pointed, razor-sharp teeth protruded haphazardly from snarled black lips. This was a creature designed to hunt and built to kill, with no regard for the natural world. It would track its prey relentlessly.

The wyvern moved past, and Brax followed its trajectory toward Breem. It dove quickly, a silent wraith closing in on its unsuspecting victim. Braxton barely had time to act. He reached over his shoulder and grabbed the Unicorn Blade, simultaneously summoning up the spirit magic. Remembering his experience with Zacharias in Falderon, he released a blast of energy into Breem. It hit the surprised commander with a solid blow, knocking him off his feet and onto a nearby tent, collapsing it. The wyvern gave a haunting scream as it flew by. Unaccustomed to missing its prey, its outstretched claws clutched at the air where Breem had stood a moment earlier. It smashed into a small makeshift structure, sending timbers flying in every direction. The creature was barely a dozen feet above the ground, dragging a ripped canopy that had become entwined around one of its legs, when Breem untangled himself from the tent and jumped to his feet quicker than his large frame would have suggested possible. He drew his sword with an angry, determined look on his face, ready to fight whatever had thrown him, when he saw the wyvern lifting away. He turned back toward Brax and slowly seemed to recognize what had occurred. The veteran soldier relaxed his stance and raised a hand of acknowledgment.

Braxton stabbed at the air with his finger. Breem nodded and gripped the horn strapped to his belt but hesitated, as though deciding whether to trust what he'd seen. Then with one swift motion, the Empire commander pulled the horn free and blew a single long note followed by two pairs of shorter tones. He glanced at Brax, turned, and disappeared among the tents.

As if in response to Breem's call, the sky lit up with flaming pitch cast high above the encampment. But this time, it came from the allied side, near Arbor Loren. Brax looked back at the forest and, in the light of the projectiles, saw that the dwarves had taken over the giant catapults left behind from the previous day's fighting and turned them against the Mins. The clever mountain engineers had modified the siege weapons throughout the night and were using them both to assault their foe and illuminate the Dunes for their human allies. Now the sky blazed with fire.

Braxton wasn't the only one who'd seen them. A dark shadow moved toward the trees, flying high above the flaming shot. He ran, watching the creature as it glided ahead. He didn't notice Phinlera and the others coming toward him until Penton grabbed him.

"We need to get to the front!" his brother yelled above the growing commotion in the camps and the sound of the burning pitch flying overhead.

"No. I need to get to those catapults!" Brax pointed at the wyvern.

His brother nodded without looking up. "We'll meet back at the main pavilion," he shouted, then darted off toward the Dunes with Gavin and Bear.

Braxton watched them go. A strange feeling awoke in the pit of his stomach at seeing them leave.

"Come on." Phinlera pulled at his arm. "It's almost there." She pointed to the wyvern descending upon the closest catapult.

Braxton looked in the direction she indicated. The beast dove from above and hit the side of the war machine with a thunderous blow. Grabbing the crossbeam with its powerful talons, it smashed the rigging and supports with its tail and snout, sending the surprised dwarves diving for cover. It lifted the contraption into the air, dragging with it an unfortunate engineer who'd become trapped in the cords. The creature flew to the next catapult and dropped the remains of the giant war machine onto the second contraption, shattering both structures and killing most of the unsuspecting dwarves. The wyvern gave a resounding scream as if delighting in its attack. Phinlera covered her ears and bent over. Braxton swore under his breath for not getting there in time. Then he sprinted toward the camp's outer perimeter.

The wyvern was circling again when Brax reached the closest of the three remaining catapults. He pulled the Unicorn Blade free and called aloud to Serene.

"How do I defeat this thing?"

There are few who possess the means to penetrate its hide, and most are too far away now. You will need to cripple its flight before you can hope to stop its breath. I will show you.

His vision vanished as if he had shut his eyes, although his head still tilted toward the sky. All sound faded away, drowned out by the high-pitched ringing in his ears. Then a single image flashed through his mind, and with it came the comprehension of how to form the spirit magic. It was complex in its application and yet so simple in its making, as though something he'd always known how to do but never considered somehow. He saw it completely, felt it within every part of his being. All he was seemed filled by this one vision, this one task. The energy surged through him, awakened to its full potential by his understanding of its intent. When the image cleared, he stood in the Breaker Dunes looking up at the sky, the sounds of the surrounding camp flooding back into his senses. The wyvern was exactly where it had been before. It turned toward him and began to dive.

Come, Braxton thought as he watched it charge. *I am ready.*

CHAPTER
40

The wyvern came for him at an incredible speed. Its giant black wings folded back and its legs tucked under its shadowy form, an evil projectile that cut through the air with ease.

Now!

Braxton released the energy. He hadn't held onto the vision quite as completely as he'd have liked but hoped it was enough. The net of the spirit magic spread open and snared the wyvern, wrapping its ethereal tendrils around the creature's body. The beast struggled to break free from the invisible web, then let out a loud scream. Unable to control its dive, it fell the remaining distance toward Brax. He watched it come, frozen in the path of unavoidable death hurtling toward him.

Something smashed into his side, knocking him to the ground and out of the way. An instant later, the wyvern hit the Dunes with a force that reverberated across the plains, covering everything in a layer of dirt.

Brax lay stunned under someone else's weight. Nobody stirred, and the Breaker Dunes seemed surprisingly quiet.

Phinlera groaned. "You could have moved, you know." She got up, stretched, and wiped a hand across her lip, smearing a trickle of blood.

Brax grinned. His left side ached from taking the brunt of their combined weight. When he tried to stand, a sharp pain shot down his leg.

A massive explosion erupted right behind them, knocking Brax and Phin back to the ground and sending the Unicorn Blade flying from his hand.

Braxton lay facedown, dazed by the impact, his head buzzing and a deafening sound ringing in his ears, trying to understand what had happened.

A loud and terrifying scream rang out. Brax curled into a tight ball, burying his face and covering his ears.

"How can it be alive?" Phinlera yelled as they both squirmed about, Braxton no longer protected from the creature's horrific calls.

The sounds stopped, and he turned to look back at what he feared. A dozen yards away, the wyvern reared up on its powerful back legs, towering above them. It flapped its outstretched wings, lifting its long head skyward and tasting the air, its tail whipping about.

It was not the wyvern, however, that caused Braxton to freeze in fear, but the two hooded figures that stood in front of it, one of them stroking the creature affectionately. He recognized them instantly from his visions— pale skin and dark, thin lips hidden beneath cowled hoods from which greasy black hair hung down in loose strands.

The Witch Sisters of Dahgmor.

How can this be? He seemed unable to move. *Serene, help us!*

The closest figure chuckled as she gazed at him from within her dark covering. "*Serene* cannot help you now," she spat out, her voice filled with malice.

The other sister turned toward the catapults and raised a bony hand. Braxton shivered as an evil magical energy surged from inside her and shot out toward the closest war machine, engulfing it in a bright green fire, destroying it in seconds. She flicked her hand, here and there, incinerating tents with the same unnatural flame. Brax jolted with each strike, somehow connected to the source from which she drew her magical power, a strange ripple from the other side of some dark, invisible lake. Within minutes, the allied camps were ablaze in green flame, illuminating the predawn sky with an eerie glow. A group of dwarves and men ran toward the sisters, their weapons drawn. But the witch just spread her fingers in their direction encasing each victim in magical fire, laughing maliciously as she watched them burn.

"You didn't really think we'd continue to ignore your meddling without retribution," the first witch hissed, and she raised her hand toward Braxton. A freezing cold energy surged through him, and he convulsed violently, ignited by an icy fire deep within. He screamed in pain, terrified by the strength of the power that now coursed through his body, enveloping him in a cold, malevolent hatred.

The energy subsided, and the witch let him squirm for a moment, just long enough for a quick reprieve, like a cat toying with its prey. He tried desperately to regain control of his scattered senses, to call upon the energy to protect him. But it was no use. The horrific pain returned, and his terror at the witch's magical ability held him firmly in its grasp.

Through his fear and agony, he noticed a blur of movement at his side.

"Oh, no you don't, girly," the witch hissed.

Phinlera stopped in midstride, the Leaf held aloft. Her body convulsed, then she screamed.

"*Phin!*" he called, but there was no response.

"Listen to her scream," the witch yelled.

Phinlera's voice echoed inside his head, terrified, crying, pleading for the energy to stop. *Help me!* she called. *Braxton, somebody, please!*

"No!" He leaped to his feet, ignoring his own pain. But he too stood paralyzed, held fast by the witch's dark magic. The agony seared through him again. Brax screamed in his mind, and the witch's laughter resounded in his ears.

"So predictable," she said, "so humanly predictable. Now, boy, watch her die."

The pain in his body subsided as she raised her hand. The wyvern leaped forward, awaiting the signal.

"The speed of that accursed sword cannot save you now," the witch spat. In one terrifyingly fluid motion, the wyvern whipped its sinuous tail high above its head and plunged the barbed tip deep into Phinlera's side.

No! Braxton cried, still unable to move. Phinlera had a look of anguish as the color drained from her face. The wyvern pulled its tail free, leaped up into the air, and screeched that same self-satisfied call.

Braxton's heart dropped like the tears from his face. Phinlera's body went limp, slumping over yet still held aloft by the witch's magic. He felt as if *his* heart had been ripped out by the wyvern. The witch's spiteful laughter continued, her magic holding him frozen as he watched Phinlera's breathing slow.

A startling blue light flashed at his side, illuminating the western edge of the Dunes, and Brax turned instinctively. There was Bendarren, cloaked in the same blue robe he remembered from before, holding a thick wooden branch that had been broken off from some old white tree. A calm washed over Brax, and his pain dissipated.

"*You*! You cannot be here!" the first witch shrieked, pointing a long, bony finger at the elf.

"You swore an oath never to leave the forest," the second witch added with loathing, finishing her sister's statement.

"You broke nature's law today, Malicine," Bendarren said calmly to the first hooded figure. "My coming here is nothing more than the natural consequence of that action."

"You dare speak my name?" she said in disgust.

"Your names do not hold power over me. Surely you remember that."

The sisters glanced at each other. Then, in an action faster than Braxton would have imagined possible, they stretched out their hands toward the elf and engulfed him in a ball of blazing green fire, obscuring him from view. Phinlera's body dropped to the ground, the invisible hand that held her in place suddenly letting go.

Phin! Brax called out in his mind, hoping somehow she would hear him, that he could provide some comfort to her even now. But there was no reply. He watched helplessly as the girl he loved lay dying in the Breaker Dunes. Her skin was utterly white from the wyvern's venomous sting. Small beads of sweat formed on her brow and her breathing was slow and ragged. She was going to die, he realized, and there was nothing he could do to save her. Tears ran down his face. His worst fear had come to pass.

Braxton watched her fade away, a silent statue in the Dunes of central Andorah, under the dawning sky. A quiet tribute to a beautiful passing.

The inevitable confrontation between the Mins and the allied western nations had finally come to the Breaker Dunes, Braxton realized. Horns blew in the distance, and the battle cries of armies bent on destroying one another crept into his senses as morning broke over the horizon. Was Phinlera's death the beginning of what was to come for the western world, he wondered?

Another burst of blue light drew his attention from his grief. The evil green fire around Bendarren seemed somewhat diminished, and he could see the elf inside the witches' unnatural flame, sending out waves of his own energy to weaken the green barrier. A column of azure light erupted from the ground beneath each witch, encasing them in a brilliant magical energy that extended up into the morning sky. The green fire around Bendarren evaporated, and a moment later, the two sisters extinguished the elf's light as well, each neutralizing the other's magical power. They faced each other.

"The strength of the White Wood has grown weak, old man," the second witch spat out.

"The endless power beneath Arbor Loren is beyond your comprehension, Belladora," Bendarren replied. "You cannot hope to hold back its strength with the small vessel you now carry."

Bendarren raised his arms, one hand holding the thick white staff aloft. Large roots erupted from the Breaker Dunes and began entangling themselves around the witches' legs and up their torsos. The sisters struggled to get free, igniting the cords with green fire. But the roots seemed unstoppable, and within seconds, they completely encased the hooded figures. In their place stood two giant oaks, their topmost leaves catching the morning sun.

The paralyzing grip on Braxton's body began to wane as the power of the magic that held him, faded. He struggled with renewed strength to get free.

Concentrate. Serene's single word sounded quietly in the far reaches of his mind, no more than an echo of a voice he once knew. But he understood her message and stopped fighting the evil energy, calming his emotions and calling upon the spirit magic he'd neglected deep within him, hidden away in what seemed like a lifetime ago. He took several breaths, allowing the cool morning air to relax his mind. Slowly, deliberately, he searched for the energy's unknown source, willing it to connect with him. He called out to it with a peaceful longing, like a songbird searching for its mate, knowing it would eventually come.

But there was no response.

He probed the depths of his mind, lost in a maze of thoughts and emotions that kept resurfacing, reminding him of his fragile human existence. Painfully he passed through each one, struggling through the cobwebs of his past that sought to weigh him down. He clung to the dwindling memory of his connection to the spirit world and the wondrous sensation of joining with the energy. Forcing himself to continue, he searched for it, not wanting to give up. Gradually the magic began to stir, rising from some long, distant sleep in the catacombs of his mind, listening to the call that had awoken it. A brief wave of exhilaration washed over him as the energy resurfaced, like glimpsing first light at the end of some long, dark tunnel. Brax moved his fingers, realizing that freedom was slowly returning.

A loud creak pulled him back into awareness, and his body jerked. The two large oaks stood rooted in the plains, their trunks shaking as if held by gigantic invisible hands. The sounds emanating from the trees grew louder, and the motion intensified. A moment later, the trees burst apart, sending wood and branches flying in every direction. One bough barely missed Brax's head as he ducked, realizing only then that he could move his neck and shoulders. His elation at gaining some additional movement shattered, though, at the sight of the two Witch Sisters standing in the plains. Their evil laughter sounded from the depths of their cowls.

"Your failure is complete!" Malicine shouted at Bendarren.

"Your magic is weak, and you cannot stop our armies," Belladora added. "Your forest will burn."

"I do not think so," Bendarren replied.

The elf cried out and plunged his wooden staff deep into the dirt before him, his quick movement in vivid contrast to his normally calm demeanor. The ground shook, and Brax could feel the witches' power faltering around him as they fought to keep their balance.

Concentrate. Serene's voice was closer this time. He focused on summoning the spirit magic, closing his eyes and blocking out all sounds of the fight, listening instead for the ringing that always preceded the energy's return. Its power coursed through him, momentarily touching his consciousness. He moved his arms and chest feeling the grip of the sisters' energy diminishing as his own strength grew. But it was difficult focusing on just one thought for more than a few seconds, and images both real and imagined flashed through his mind. Faces of people he once knew appeared, and his emotions faltered, breaking the wall behind which he'd hidden his memories, overwhelming him in their return. Brax struggled to keep them at bay, fighting to rebuild the barrier between his past experiences and present surroundings, pushing behind it the images that assaulted him as he tried to connect with the energy. But it was no use; there was something missing. The sounds of the war to the east flooded into his ears, and the ground moved beneath his feet, throwing him off balance.

An image of a beautiful unicorn flashed through his mind, barely long enough for him to notice, and then Braxton remembered. He needed the spirit sword. It was his only hope for maintaining his concentration and breaking free from the witches' magic that bound him to the plains.

He twisted about, searching for the Unicorn Blade. An enormous white oak stood in Bendarren's place, dwarfing those that had engulfed the Witch

Sisters. Two long, thick roots extended from the ground, giant tentacles that broke apart the parched dirt as easily as pushing through soft clay. The roots had wrapped themselves around the witches, slowly constricting them. Malicine and Belladora fought back, throwing eerie green fire against the cords. But their magic was having little effect as the roots tightened their grip. Their attacks became more frantic, sending endless bursts of green magic against the white tree itself.

Then Belladora called out, a short, strangled sound that seemed a combination of both surprise and pain—something unexpected. Her magical barrage against the tree stopped, and she stood there looking shocked as her sister's unrelenting attack continued.

Malicine turned quickly toward her. "Don't you dare!" she hissed.

Belladora stared at her sister. Then she raised both her hands high above her head and touched her palms together. A swirling green mist appeared around her and hung in the morning air, obscuring her image. When it vanished an instant later, Belladora was gone, and the white cord of the tree dropped limply to the ground.

"No!" Malicine cried in a combination of hatred and rage, before turning and assaulting the oak again with such ferocity that a continuous stream of magical green energy extended from her hands. The tree's leaves began to wither under the onslaught, and small eruptions of green fire appeared, spreading across its upper branches. But when the second white root that had once held her sister began wrapping itself around Malicine, the witch knew she was beaten. For a few, frantic moments, she threw all her remaining power at the oak until its majestic form was completely engulfed in flame, and its limbs showed significant signs of damage. But it was too late. She bent down in pain against the roots surrounding her body, and when she stared up at the tree, her hatred was ferocious and undeniable. She raised her hands above her head and wrapped herself in that same swirling green mist. When it finally cleared, the Witch Sisters of Dahgmor were gone.

CHAPTER
41

Phinlera's breathing was completely inaudible, and only the occasional movements of her chest, faint and erratic, showed she still clung to life. The grip of the witches' magic had disappeared with that green mist, and Brax was finally free, but Phinlera's body was waging a losing battle against the wyvern's sting. He lifted her damp shirt and saw the extent of the venom's reach. Long, dark, purple strands, like fingers of death, extended outward from her bloodied and weeping wound, creeping across her chest, inching ever closer to her fading heart. Braxton couldn't move, he couldn't think; he just stared openmouthed at the damage to her beautiful body. No one could survive this, he knew. No one could recover from a wound that deep, that poisonous.

"You should have gone for the sword first," said a calm voice behind him, as though in a dream, a nightmare, from which some familiar sound was calling for him to return. "Understand, Braxton, that your strength, your magical power, your entire life's force is bound to its purpose; your path intertwined with the fates of many. Do not let yourself separate from it so easily again."

He turned slowly, still in a fog, unable or unwilling to escape from the place where his shocked response to Phinlera's wound had sent him. Bendarren held the Unicorn Blade across his palms. The bright morning sun danced off its unyielding form. The sight of the sword seemed to call to Brax somehow, providing clarity of something he once knew.

"What . . . what did you say?"

"Take up your master's weapon, Braxton. Go to the fight." Bendarren's voice was a ray of hope in Brax's dark and tumultuous emotions that still threatened to consume him.

He reached out, held down by unseen chains, and grasped the shaft of the Unicorn Blade. Its sharp edge cut into his palm. The moment he touched its warm metal surface, his mind awoke, releasing him from the frozen vice in which he'd been trapped. The spirit magic rushed through him, uplifting him, healing and energizing his body.

Awaken, my child, Serene said in a reassuring voice. *We have much to do.*

His mind cleared, like a veil pulled back, revealing the possibilities his connection with his master's sword afforded him. He remembered how to call upon the spirit magic, to hold onto that one thought, to focus on a single vision, and infuse in it the power and will to control its actions. Closing his eyes, he summoned the energy and let it course through him, drinking in the feeling of its return.

He focused his mind on healing Phinlera, on releasing the spirit magic deep into her wound, asking that its power cleanse her infection and renew her body—to return to him this girl he loved so much. But when he looked down, she was gone. The parched ground of the Dunes lay empty and bare. Panicked, Brax searched about. Bendarren moved toward the giant oak, Phinlera's limp body in his arms. The white tree still stood apart from Arbor Loren, its roots returned to normal, and the surrounding dirt undisturbed. The evil green fire no longer covered its branches, and the magnificent oak shone brilliantly, sunlight reflecting off its leaves.

Scrambling to his feet, he ran after their mentor. "Wait!" Brax cried. "I need to heal her!"

"You cannot help her now," Bendarren said, moving quicker as he neared the tree. "There is only one who can, and even then, Phinlera's chances are slim. Go to the front, Braxton. There at least you can be of help."

Brax looked east, to the sounds of the battle beyond the encampments. The intense fighting rang loudly across the Gap of Dunes. When he turned back, Bendarren was gone. Braxton circled the oak, expecting to find him. But there was no sign of the elf or Phinlera. Stunned, he scanned the plains, then moved his hands up and down the warm bark, searching for the entrance he assumed was there but found nothing. He summoned the spirit magic, intending to find the doorway, to locate the path the elf must have taken, but still nothing revealed itself—no sense of opening, no feeling of a direction to follow. He looked toward Arbor Loren. He could run, he thought. It wasn't that far. He could find her. He could still help.

Let her go, child. Go to the east.

Braxton wanted to scream. To tell Serene how much he needed Phinlera, how much she meant to him, that he had to do something to help save her. But he knew it wouldn't do any good. He knew what she'd say—to let Phin go. He stood thinking, trying to calm his emotions, considering the two paths. He glanced toward the fighting. It would take him longer to reach the front. Arbor Loren was closer. Which way?

Go and fight. His master's words sounded stronger in his mind.

He looked at the forest. The giant green oaks seemed so close. Brax stared at those trees, as though seeing home for the first time after a long journey, only to be told he couldn't return. Reluctantly, he turned, picked up Shelindûhin, and sprinted toward the front.

Several hundred yards past the encampments of the allied nations, Braxton crested a small hillock in the plains of central Andorah, a gradual rise in the otherwise unchanging landscape of the expansive Breaker Dunes. But it was enough. Catching his breath, he surveyed the battle between the eastern and western armies. Above the plains, scores of Talonguard fought a vast plague of vipers for control of the skies—a chaotic aerial struggle in which golden streaks moved majestically among a morbid cloud. Below, in the heart of the fighting, the elves continued their masterful swordplay, moving among their slower adversaries in an ever-changing fluid motion, like a river adjusting its course to assault the weaker banks of the hardened Mins, driving ever deeper into their midst.

To the north, the dwarves held fast against the onslaught of a larger host, constantly manifesting their indistinguishable rock barricade in front of the Min warriors, only to collapse it moments later and countercharge with their resolute mountain fighters. But the difference in the two armies' fighting styles was creating a separation between the dwarves and their woodland kin. While the clans held their line, the elves pushed farther and farther into the heart of their foe. Without the protection of their dwarven allies, they'd soon be cut off and vulnerable on their left flank. Looking south, Brax hoped the mounted horsemen of his homeland could provide some support. But there the fighting was most intense. The Empire cavalry charged into a greater enemy, withdrew east or west, re-formed their battle line of purple-and-white banners, and attacked again. He knew they couldn't maintain that pace much longer. Galloping horses grew tired and would eventually cease to run, and lance-armed soldiers were only effective while charging.

Something else, however, awakened his fear. Moving within the Min lines and nearing the front closest to the Empire soldiers, a creature towered above all others. Unlike the Mins, its giant, muscular body seemed covered in black skin, giving it an almost feral appearance. Its face lacked the bull shape of the Min soldiers, and instead an almost human-looking head controlled its actions. Sharp horns extended from its temples above small oval ears, and long, curved teeth protruded from an unnaturally large jaw. While the Mins' human form and bull face were indicative of their mixed-race, this beast seemed made of something else entirely. Almost the reverse of the Mins, a cruel mind controlled its animal's body. In one hand, it wielded an enormous double-edged sword with a hooked tip, that it swung left and right, cutting a wide swath through the men and elves unfortunate enough to cross its path. The creature seemed to revel in its unstoppable power, stirring the Mins around it into a frenzy.

That is Morgaroth, Serene said, *one of the few remaining of its kind. Neither male nor female, it is an evil creature from the shadowy reaches of the spirit realms. It was summoned here through a terrible pact with the*

Dark Child and an unholy ritual performed by the Witch Sisters, diminishing the Dark Child's power and contributing to his defeat in the mountains. The more primitive Mins worship it as a god, believing themselves created in its image. Those closest to it are the most vicious and brutal of their kind, trusting they fight for its will, its dominion of the earth. They see its presence here as the beginning of a new era for their race. Others are driven on by fear, for they cannot oppose it nor combat the vast hordes it now so easily controls.

There are none among you who can defeat it. We had hoped your Blademaster would have taken its breath, for he alone had the skill to challenge it. But he made his choice at the Dragon's Head, and for that, we honor his passing. Now Morgaroth stands unchallenged. It is there, my child, that you must go.

Braxton pained at the mention of Kael. He still felt guilty for the Blademaster's death and for not having controlled his emotions better during his fight with the Dark Child. If he had, Kael might be with them now, and able to help. He stared at the giant creature as it continued to cut down those who opposed it.

"Wait. You want *me* to fight that . . . thing?" he asked in disbelief as Serene's words sank in. He swallowed hard.

You need only stop its advance. Delay it for a brief time, until help arrives.

"I cannot possibly survive against that monster or even get near it!"

You must, child, or the war is lost.

W hen Braxton neared the fighting in the Breaker Dunes, he wanted to retch. The smell of death was everywhere, and the hewn bodies of human and elven soldiers littered the plains by the thousands. Equal numbers of Mins lay among the dead, and the stench of decay sickened him. Here and there, a few broken forms of eagles were amid the carnage, some with their riders still faithfully strapped to their backs. Vipers covered the ground, pierced by Arbor Loren's aerial archers, while others still fought for domination of the skies.

A massive form smashed into Braxton's side, knocking him painfully to the ground. He lay stunned for a moment, trying to catch his breath, spitting out dirt, and wondering what had hit him.

Move! Serene's warning echoed in his mind. He rolled left. A huge ax whizzed past him, barely missing his head, and stuck in the earth. A brown-haired Min towered over him, braying loudly. Its right arm had a nasty gash and hung at its side, its chest leaking blood from several arrows. The creature pulled at the ax with its remaining good arm, trying to free the weapon after the crushing blow it had intended for Braxton's skull. The sight of the Min wrenched Brax from his dazed state, and he scrambled to his feet. Ignoring the pain in his side, he swung the Unicorn Blade underneath the creature's outstretched arm, smashing into the Min's exposed ribs. There was a cracking sound as the spirit sword pierced the animal's thick hide, breaking its bones. When Brax pulled his sword free, he realized he'd almost cut the beast in two. Warm blood gushed from the fatal wound and pooled in the hardened dirt. Brax turned his head and retched.

He wiped the bile from his mouth. The Min must've been lying among the dead, he realized, injured in some previous fight, waiting for some unsuspecting foe. He avoided looking at the creature's severed form and summoned the spirit magic, filling himself with its warm, uplifting presence. Extending the energy outward, he created a warning tendril against anyone else who might try to take him unaware. Brax took a drink from his waterskin, trying to settle his stomach. He could see the maelstrom of fighting ahead and the towering form of Morgaroth a few hundred yards to the south. Breathing deeply, he tried to calm his nerves against the confrontation he knew was coming. He drew Shelindûhin from his belt and looked at it for a moment, wondering if Phinlera had survived the wyvern's attack, then pushed the thought from his mind. Gritting his teeth and gripping both magical weapons, he charged headlong into the battle.

When Braxton flung himself into the fighting between the Mins and the western allies, he was surprised at how attuned his senses were. Everyone around him seemed to move about in a slow, dreamlike state, their actions emphasized by his holding of the Leaf. He realized then the magical ability of Shelindûhin—how it slowed the movements of others, giving its wielder time to adjust to their attack. Combined with the tendril of spirit magic, Braxton could sense whenever someone singled him out, watch their approach, and sidestep their assault before striking back in a way that exploited their weaknesses. Together with Shelindûhin, he swung the Unicorn Blade with masterful precision, striking crippling blows against his larger opponents, as he pressed deeper into the chaotic fighting. But the strain of maintaining the high energy required by both weapons, as well as the spirit magic's tendril, soon overwhelmed him, and he tired fast and sweated profusely. By the time Brax had cut his way to within a few dozen yards of Morgaroth, he could no longer continue. He returned the Leaf to his belt and held the Unicorn Blade in both hands, slowing his pace.

The Mins' worshipped leader towered ahead, continuing its unstoppable rampage through the allied forces. It was the Empire commander, Breem, however, who reached Morgaroth first, emerging from among the purple-and-white banners of Braxton's homeland fighters to stop the creature's zealous advancement. The nearby Min warriors seemed to shy away from this confident newcomer, sensing in Breem a formidable foe and engaging instead the other human soldiers who rallied around their seasoned commander. Morgaroth eyed its smaller opponent eagerly, and for one brief moment, a small clearing formed among the frenzy of the surrounding battle, allowing the two opponents to face off against each other.

Morgaroth made a loud, guttural roar that temporarily drowned out the war around them. It conveyed the distinct impression of some ferocious beast preparing to pounce on its helpless victim, raising the hairs on the back of Brax's neck. Breem, however, seemed unaffected by the sound and slowly nodded his acceptance, his many years of disciplined military experience obviously protecting him from the fear-inducing call. Uninterested in sizing up its opponent, Morgaroth attacked, covering the distance to Breem in a single bound, its speed surprising for its size. It lifted its weapon high above its head, bellowing as it went, intent on crushing its foe. But Breem anticipated the move and raised his sword in both hands, blocking Morgaroth's strike. The strength, though, knocked him to the ground.

Instantly, Morgaroth was upon him, striking another powerful overhand blow. The Empire commander rolled away barely in time, and his enemy's giant weapon hit the plains. Morgaroth reacted in a fluid motion, pulling its sword free and attacking again. Breem deflected the blade, but the hooked end sliced across his left shoulder, ripping through his protective armor and cutting into his flesh. Ignoring the wound with little more than a grimace, he jumped to his feet and swung sideways, aiming for under his opponent's ribs. Morgaroth stopped the attack, exposing its curved teeth in a malicious grin. Then it gave a series of low growls, whether in laughter or some kind of chant, Brax couldn't tell. It allowed Breem a moment's reprieve, as Braxton cut down another Min, trying to get closer.

When Morgaroth struck again, Breem was ready. He stepped aside more quickly and hit Morgaroth against the right thigh, opening a deep gash in its upper leg. The creature didn't even respond to the gaping wound and slashed out sideways with its sword held level to the ground. This time Breem moved a moment too late, expecting some delay from the injury he'd inflicted. The blade hit the Empire commander against his ribs, knocking him back several feet before coming to land among the dirt and debris, his weapon lost. Morgaroth was on him, planting a large foot on Breem's chest and pinning him to the ground. It roared triumphantly. Then its curved claws sliced through Breem's mail and buried themselves into his flesh.

A shrill cry broke from Breem's lips. He groped for his sword, but the beast held him fast. It gave that same eerie laugh and glared at the men looking on in wide-eyed disbelief. One of the Empire soldiers rushed to his commander's aid without regard for his own life, but Morgaroth just hit him with its bare fist, sending the smaller man reeling backward. Another two charged in with their weapons drawn, and the creature cut them down with a broad sweep of its giant sword. It looked around for any other fool who'd dare challenge it, savoring its victory. It kept Breem pinned, tightening its grip and reveling in the pain it was inflicting.

Several yards away, Braxton lashed out with the spirit magic's tendril, converting it into a whip that hit Morgaroth across the face, ripping into its skin. The beast roared in pain and stepped back, covering its wound. Two nearby soldiers grabbed Breem and pulled him to safety as the remaining Empire faithful, their confidence renewed, created a defensive wall around their beloved leader. When the creature looked back, Braxton saw the hatred reflected in its eyes and the deep cut the energy whip had inflicted on its already gruesome face. Without warning, Morgaroth attacked. Speaking some unholy word in its guttural tongue, it sent an intense fire ripping through Braxton. It burned unlike anything he'd felt before, as if ignited from the inside. He collapsed to the ground, writhing in pain, unable to stop the excruciating sensation. Then just as quickly as it started it was gone, leaving him gasping for air. His senses screamed for him to get up. Rolling aside, the huge sword swung down past him, narrowly missing his head and hitting the ground with a tremendous blow. Brax scrambled away, stumbling over several bodies to get to his feet. He panicked at the thought of that pain returning and how close the sword had come to ending his life. Turning, he fled. Morgaroth pursued him, cutting down friend and foe alike in its desire to get at him. Braxton thought of nothing else but escape, his innate need to survive overwhelming his senses and every ounce of remaining strength feeding his flight.

Focus! Serene's single word shot through his mind, and for a moment, the energy returned. But then it was gone, as the pure terror took hold, banishing all other thoughts but that one instinctive desire to flee, to survive, to avoid the certain death that pursued him.

The pain returned, even more excruciating than before, erupting into an explosive molten fire within him. It threw Braxton to the ground, and he rolled around in agony. He wanted to die, to scream, to do anything that would stop the pain. Then, just as quickly as before, it stopped. For a fleeting moment, he felt Serene's warming presence and sensed her light—an echo calling to him to awaken, to stand his ground, to trust her. His desire to flee faltered, and he lay there, still bound by raw terror, petrified of the evil energy and the pain it would bring. Slowly he turned and looked at Morgaroth. The beast was a few feet away, coming for him with a mindless rage, driven to madness by the injury he'd inflicted. It wanted to catch him, to kill him, to rip him apart, and Braxton knew it.

Every sense in his body told him he'd die if he stayed, and all his instincts that had kept him alive hunting in the Vales screamed for him to get up and run, to stay alive at all costs. But there was something else. Somewhere at the edge of his consciousness, in some indefinable place, some calming presence told him to stand, to face his fear, that he could defeat this monster. The instant that he allowed the possibility of another option—something beyond raw fear—Braxton Prinn was free. The chains that bound him to his terror fell away.

Morgaroth was upon him, its sword held high, ready to strike Brax down in a single blow. To end his life. To fulfill its evil desire. Its victory at hand.

When Braxton stood up.

Yes! came Serene's intense voice, and the energy burst from inside him, smashing into Morgaroth, knocking the creature back several paces. Again and again, it poured out of him and into his opponent, causing the beast to retreat farther and farther back, twisting and turning in agony as the pure and radiant light assaulted it. Each time the spirit magic struck, Braxton felt a connection to this demon, to its hatred, its vile existence, and its thirst to enslave all life. Over and over, the connection repeated with each renewed assault until finally, for one brief and fleeting moment, Braxton pitied Morgaroth—its primitive life and what it had chosen to become. And he paused. Instantly Morgaroth struck back, sending endless waves of intense pain searing through Braxton, knocking him to the ground. Brax screamed in agony, squirming in the dirt of the Breaker Dunes like some pitifully small and tortured animal.

Then a strong and intense pressure pushed down on his chest, and Braxton's terror returned. Morgaroth had him pinned, just like it had done with Breem. Its powerful clawed foot pressed Brax into the earth. The pain of the energy ceased, and Braxton looked up through watery eyes at the thing he feared. Morgaroth towered above him, its lips curled away from its yellowed teeth in a leering grin, and its enormous sword mere inches from Braxton's face, ready to strike.

"Die, little thing," it growled.

Time seemed to slow, like holding Shelindûhin. He watched his enemy as the sounds of the battle faded away. Blood pounded in his ears. He thought of all the friends he'd known on this journey and who had fallen before him. They flashed through his mind one after the other. Death had come to him, he knew. His life was over.

Inexplicably a motion caught Braxton's attention, a brief image at the edge of his vision that moved near Morgaroth's side, something he knew wasn't real. He wrenched his eyes from the impending death hovering before him, and looked at it.

Grandpa Ty.

Morgaroth screamed out in pain, and the image of his grandfather disappeared. Brax lay on the ground in the Breaker Dunes, painfully aware of his surroundings. The noise of the ongoing war flooded back into his senses. Morgaroth no longer held him. Slowly, as though waking from some unnatural dream, Braxton lifted his head to see what could have prevented the creature's strike. Morgaroth stood a few feet away, clutching a thick spear that had pierced its chest. Dark, pitch-like blood dripped from the wound.

"It seems I'm destined to help you," came a deep, familiar voice.

Brax twisted to look behind him.

"Sotchek?" he asked incredulously. "Is that you?"

"It is." His big friend knelt and helped him sit up.

Morgaroth gave a shrill call. It pulled Sotchek's bolt from its chest and flung it to the ground. The beast raised its head high and gave another loud and terrifying scream.

"That is for me." Sotchek nodded. "Though this enemy may be well beyond my skill to defeat. It is likely I fight my last today."

"What? No, you can defeat him. You must defeat him!"

"This creature is from another world with different rules. Only there can it be defeated. My only hope is that it'll flee back to its home."

Morgaroth gave another roar and Sotchek stood up. "But that seems unlikely now," he said. Then his gaze fell upon Braxton's waist, and a curious look crossed his brow.

"Is that . . . by chance . . . Shelindûhin?"

"What . . . ? Oh, yes." Brax was surprised that he knew about Phinlera's sword.

Sotchek smiled for the first time. "That weapon would serve me well, if you'd be willing . . . ?"

"Of course." Braxton pulled the Leaf from his belt and handed it over.

"Hope is possible," the mountain man said, almost to himself, then turned and faced Morgaroth.

CHAPTER
42

Braxton scrambled to his feet, anxious to witness the final confrontation between Sotchek and Morgaroth, and to aid his friend in the fight he knew might well determine the outcome of this war. But he stopped short. To the south, a new and immensely large army clustered together in loose groups of a hundred or more powerful-looking fighters, extending the full length of the southern Mins' flank and disappearing into the eastern horizon. Each seemed to hearken from a different clan among their seemingly endless tribes, wearing furs, animal skins, or leather pants that extended to their knees, leaving their muscular chests bare. It was their formidable height, though, that surprised Brax the most, standing a foot taller than the Mins and dwarfing the nearby allied soldiers. Most had icons attached to their skin or carried banners from which totems hung, wielding heavy-looking clubs or long throwing spears. They stood apart from the battle, waiting, it appeared, for some reason to join the fight. The Mins, however, were turning their ranked formations to face yet another new threat. With the return of Sotchek, Braxton realized, the ogre nations had joined the war.

Morgaroth's horrific call jolted Brax's attention back to the confrontation with his friend. The two adversaries faced each other in a circle that had appeared within the fighting. Braxton felt a deep pull from the energy's source, similar to what he'd experienced with the Witch Sisters, like the drawing of a long, full breath. Morgaroth, he realized, was going to use its evil magic to attack Sotchek.

Disrupt it! Serene instructed. Brax called upon the spirit magic closest to his consciousness, sending out another whiplike tendril to hit Morgaroth. It lacked the penetrating power of his original attack but was sufficient enough to break the dark creature's concentration, and he felt Morgaroth's energy subside. The beast looked at him with loathing. Brax knew Morgaroth wanted to break him. He swallowed hard. If Sotchek failed, he would be its next victim.

Sotchek attacked with such incredible speed—fueled by Shelindûhin— that he seemed to disappear from view in front of Morgaroth and reappear behind his opponent, burying his ax deep between the creature's shoulder blades. Bellowing in response, Morgaroth swung around with its sword held level, intending to decapitate Sotchek. It moved at an instinctive pace that seemed so unnatural for its large size that Sotchek barely had time to duck, even while holding the Leaf, and the beast's enormous sword passed swiftly overhead. Taking advantage of the momentum, Brax's friend pulled a knife from his boot and sank it into his enemy's exposed underarm. Morgaroth let out a terrible sound and struck back with its energy. This was an attack Shelindûhin could not foresee, and it hit Sotchek in the chest, knocking him back a dozen paces or more to land heavily on the ground.

He will not long survive those strikes, Serene said. *Feel the pull on the energy and stop them before it lashes out.*

Sotchek was on his feet again, brushing aside the blow that would have stunned a normal man, and attacked. But this time, Morgaroth was waiting for him and struck first with its magic, spinning Sotchek about and sending him hurtling anew. It took Brax's friend a moment to recover, but he was soon up and circling, watching his opponent's every move. Recognizing Sotchek's inability to defend himself against its magical strikes, Morgaroth grinned and summoned a larger amount of its dark power, lashing out with a stronger blast. Braxton felt it, connected somehow to this creature by an invisible cord. He summoned a barrier, awkward and unformed, around Sotchek, blocking Morgaroth's attack. The demon looked at him with hatred, and, for a moment, Brax thought Morgaroth might turn on him.

Sensing the distraction, Sotchek rushed in, angling past his rival's larger weapon, and cut a long swath across his stomach. The elven blade ripped into Morgaroth's black skin, opening a gaping wound. The beast screamed and swung about wildly, anxious to get at Sotchek now. Over and over, it tried to snare him, needing one successful blow to end Sotchek's life. But the skilled mountain warrior, empowered further by the speed of the Leaf, slipped past its attempts, each time delivering back a painful blow. Braxton watched in awe at Sotchek's skill with Shelindûhin and his ability to strike at the precise moment to cause Morgaroth the most pain. The creature lashed out repeatedly with its energy, but Braxton was ready, sensing the pulling sensation an instant before and deflecting its magical power.

Morgaroth suddenly hurled its giant sword at Brax, and he dropped at the last possible moment to avoid being skewered by the massive weapon. But it was the distraction Morgaroth needed. Laying on the ground, Braxton felt an immense pull on the energy's source that he couldn't stop in time. A large dark shadow rushed out of Morgaroth, engulfing Sotchek and hiding them both, blocking all light from the afternoon sun and releasing a chill wind into the Dunes.

No! It is forbidden! Serene's surprisingly masculine voice rang in Braxton's mind, and he cringed at the unusual sound. The shadow changed into a fiery blaze, forcing everyone back. A moment later it disappeared, leaving a burnt ring in the dirt. Braxton's stomach dropped as he stared in disbelief.

Morgaroth and Sotchek were gone.

Bellowing horns drew Braxton's attention to the south and a thunderous vibration reverberated across the Gap of Dunes. With a deafening roar, the ogre nations charged into the southern flank of the Mins like a ferocious storm. For a moment, the surprised Minotaurs stood firm, holding their line in anticipation of the onslaught, but as the wrath of this larger fresh enemy approached, several thousand strong, the bands of Mins faltered. No longer united by the power of Morgaroth, they broke and fled.

Braxton and the allies, weary from hours of fighting, barely had time to avoid being crushed by the ogres' charge into the rear of the routing Mins, cutting them down or trampling them under hardened foot. It seemed the ogres were bent on destroying the Mins now—or perhaps just unable to stop once started. They chased the fleeing invaders with unyielding ferocity toward the Spine. As this giant wave from the south pursued their panicked foe, the combined stalwart strength of the dwarves fighting to the north and the renewed countercharge of the elves and men against their frontal line crushed the Mins. Their remaining numbers scattered into the plains.

By sundown, the war in the Breaker Dunes was over.

CHAPTER
43

Braxton stood in the central Andorah plains surrounded by the aftermath of the war between the western nations and the race of Minotaurs. Piles of carcasses burned every few hundred yards, stacked high with the bodies of elves, humans, dwarves, and Mins. The stench was almost unbearable, and the ash that blew in the warm evening air only served to accentuate the sickening feeling. He looked up as another Talonguard flew low overhead. The keen eyes of the elven mounts searched for survivors among the countless dead. Grim-faced warriors from the defending races moved about stoically, gathering the hewn bodies of both friend and foe, clearing the carnage from the war that had almost destroyed the elven nation. No one spoke beyond what was necessary to complete their task. Arbor Loren had been saved, yes, but at a terrible price. Almost a third of the elves lay dead, along with thousands of dwarves and men. But swords and bows had been set aside now as the warriors helped their fallen comrades find swift passage to the afterworld.

It was the black circle burned deep into the dirt around the final confrontation between Sotchek and Morgaroth, though, that kept Braxton's attention. He replayed the fight over and over in his mind, wondering if he could have done more to have changed the outcome and saved his friend. Sotchek's arrival had signaled the ogre nations joining the war, and their powerful warriors had swung the tide in their favor, but losing another companion to this senseless invasion wore at Braxton's resolve. Victory may have been won for the elves, but it had cost so much.

The thought of Sotchek in Morgaroth's dark, abysmal home, facing some unearthly end, drained Brax of his remaining strength. In time, death came to all, he knew. He could accept that as natural. But the eternal torture that potentially lay ahead for Sotchek haunted him. Even holding the Unicorn Blade now provided little comfort. Serene had left as well, promising to provide whatever protection she could for Sotchek, saying that Morgaroth's actions in breaking the laws of the spirit world had allowed her to intervene, giving her permission to help. But her words seemed hollow. And her departure at this emotional time only added to him feeling small and alone.

The heat and stench of the burning fires filled the air, and his eyes watered. He choked out a dry cough and brushed aside the ash floating in front of his face. Rubbing the toe of his boot against the soot line, Braxton smeared its dark mark, as if breaking the ring Morgaroth had created might somehow change the outcome. He thought about Phinlera and wondered again for the countless time if she'd survived, or if her death awaited him in Arbor Loren. He was desperate to see her again, but for the moment, not knowing her fate was better than the one he feared.

"Ya done well, lad," a gruff voice called to him from some lost and distant past. "Your father would be proud."

Vaguely aware of his actions, he turned toward the sound. Ruskin stood amid the haze of the despoiled plains, leaning heavily on his notched ax, his smoldering pipe emitting white plumes among the more sorrowful gray. Brax smiled at his friend.

"Doesn't look so bad." The dwarf stepped over the scorched line and gazed around unenthusiastically. "Can't see what all the fuss was about, or why it took so long. Probably no dwarves here, eh?"

Braxton nodded. "It's really good to see you," he said. At least Ruskin had survived. At least one of them had made it through.

"Brax!"

He turned in the direction of Penton's voice and grabbed Bear as the elkhound jumped up and licked his face. Braxton grinned, in spite of himself, and rubbed Bear's ears. Pen embraced him warmly, and Brax buried his face deep into his brother's shoulder, hiding his emotions. When they separated, he wiped a hand across his nose and sniffed.

"Where's Gav?"

Penton's smile vanished. He shook his head and turned away, unable to speak. Braxton felt punched in the stomach. His knees gave way, and he dropped to the ground.

"He fought bravely," Pen said after a moment, struggling with his own emotions, "without regard for his life, willing to take on the entire Min army. And for a while he did, cleaving a path through those beasts with a ferocity that seemed unstoppable. Both him and Bear." He chuckled sorrowfully at the memory. "But then a large Min . . ." He choked up.

Ruskin sighed. "It's as I feared. I tried to warn that boy. 'Revenge is a terrible thing,' I told 'im. It consumes you and gives you a false sense of strength, trapping you in its evil seduction. He should've stayed home where he belonged. Now it's too late. What a waste." He spat into the dirt.

They lingered in the Dunes for most of the night, taking comfort in one another's company and providing aid to those few survivors they discovered among the wrecked and broken bodies, bringing hope to fallen comrades who'd already accepted their fate. Caring for the injured and gathering the dead was strangely rewarding, Brax found, a welcome distraction from his guilt at not having done more to save Sotchek. As midnight approached and the smoldering fires shed a ghostly dance under the starlit sky, they began their trek back to Arbor Loren. The elves had left their woodland home and moved about the plains with tiny lanterns held aloft, like fireflies lighting the morbid night, helping those in need or providing food and water to the groups that still littered the Gap of Dunes.

They passed the outer tents of the encampment, seeing shadows moving inside or lying on makeshift cots. Brax remembered the fight between Bendarren and the Witch Sisters. He wanted to tell the others what had happened, how the elven master had come to their aid. How he'd lost Phinlera. But his mind was so exhausted, he just couldn't bring himself to talk about it. Not yet. It took all his concentration to place one foot in front of the other and keep from falling over. He followed Ruskin's lead, a solitary beacon in an otherwise dark and dismal night.

"We'll rest here," he heard Rusk say after a while. They'd stopped in front of an open tent on the western side of the camp, facing the gaping hole that was once Almon-Rin.

"What?" Braxton jerked his head up. "No, we have to go on. We need to get back to the forest. I . . . I have to find her . . ."

"It's late, lad, and we need to sleep. You'll be back by morning, and you can find her then." Without waiting for a response, he turned and disappeared into the tent.

"I need to go." Brax stumbled forward as if half drunk, but Penton grabbed his arm.

"You need to rest, Brax. We all need it. Besides, if Phin's there, she's already asleep. Let it go for tonight, and you can find her in the morning." He gave a weak smile. "Anyway, Bear's already down for the night."

Braxton followed his brother's gaze and saw the elkhound lying at his feet, his chest rising and falling. For a brief moment, he envied the animal's simple life and how easily sleep came to him. He stared at Arbor Loren. It was so close. He could see the few remaining outer trees, brushed in the glow of the campfires. *So close*, he thought. *I can make it.*

"Let her go," Penton repeated, as though reading his mind. "We'll find her tomorrow. I'll even help you look. I promise."

Braxton wanted to force himself to the forest. Now more than ever, he needed to know if Phinlera was all right. If she'd made it through. But his body was so tired, and his feet refused to move. Somehow his brother managed to get him inside the tent. They passed Ruskin, already snoring, before Braxton fell facedown onto a cot. He turned to look at Pen, to say something that needed to be said. But even before he finished moving, he was sound asleep.

Braxton stood in front of Morgaroth. The creature's eyes blazed like red fires, burning dark magic into his body, searing his flesh. He screamed repeatedly and writhed around on the stone floor, unable to stop the pain ignited by some unspeakably hot fire. Sotchek was struggling to get free from thick chains that bound him to the cave's wall. His naked chest showed dark purple blotches from the torture he'd endured. But it was his grim face that haunted Braxton the most, drawn and thin. When Sotchek turned to look at him, his eyes were burned out. Braxton opened his mouth and screamed.

He awoke with a start, sweating profusely, trying to remember where he was. It was dark outside, and he could hear someone snoring nearby. Bear's wet nose touched his arm, and he jumped, pulling away. Then he remembered and shut his eyes. His neck was stiff from lying motionless all night, facedown on the cot and fully dressed. Rolling over, he tried to find relief, scratching Bear's head as the elkhound licked his hand.

He stared up at the canvas ceiling and the faint glow from the moon outside, thinking about the war. Penton breathed deeply nearby, a sound Brax recognized from a lifetime of sharing the loft back home. He tried to block out the dwarf's guttural sounds and recall his dream, focusing on the images he could still remember, holding onto the vision as it slipped away. Was Sotchek being tortured? Had he somehow connected with his friend and witnessed his fate? It felt so real, not like most dreams. He knew better than to dismiss those experiences, having had a few of them before. They always seemed different somehow, more meaningful. And where was Serene? He hadn't seen her helping Sotchek or felt her reassuring presence since the fight with Morgaroth.

Groping about for the Unicorn Blade, he was relieved to find it next to him. He thought of Phinlera and wondered whether Bendarren had reached the aid she'd so desperately needed. Or had he been too late? Could he live with himself knowing he could have saved her but had chosen to go and fight in someone else's war? How could he have abandoned her like that? *She must have survived*, he told himself. *I need to find her.*

He started to get up and froze as the wood frame of his bed creaked loudly. Waiting a moment in the half-light, he listened to the dwarf's monotonous snore. *How could he sleep so deeply?* He tried to hear if Penton was awake, but his brother's familiar deep breathing had stopped. Braxton moved again, trying to keep his weight even. Placing one leg on the dirt floor, he shifted. When he stood up, Bear was waiting for him.

"Where ya going, lad?"

Brax turned toward the dwarf's voice. "I have to get to the forest."

"I'll go with you," Penton said. He got up and pulled on his boots.

Outside, no one stirred. Even the elves, it seemed, had retreated to their forest home. Only the smoldering fires scattered across the plains showed any movement, sending long trails of smoke up to the few remaining stars.

"I need to get back to the clans," Ruskin mentioned, "before they depart for the Spine. I have to send word to Dûrak-Thûhn. Tharak will want to know why so few have returned. I'll catch up with ya's later."

Without waiting, the dwarf headed north, disappearing among the remaining tents and debris of the war they'd endured. Braxton watched him go, thinking of all they'd shared on their journey since leaving Oak Haven. And those they'd lost. *So much death*, he thought. *So much loss to one war.*

He closed his eyes, not wanting to count Phinlera among their number. When he looked back, the dwarf was gone. He glanced at Penton, and his brother nodded, understanding.

"We'll find her," he said reassuringly. Braxton tried to smile. He was amazed at how well Pen knew him.

Turning together, they headed to Arbor Loren and whatever news awaited them.

CHAPTER
44

Sunlight touched the plains as Brax, Penton, and Bear reached the elven forest. The two brothers looked back for a moment, Braxton in awe, as always, at the magnificent sunrise. Like so many others, he thought, yet each one so unique.

"I never tire of that," Penton said. Brax nodded and turned toward the trees. The morning light revealed what he'd been dreading. Black and broken limbs protruded everywhere from the ground, as if some massive, evil creature had awoken beneath the earth, its spines bursting from the underworld, only to be stopped by the light. Gone were the majestic oaks that once heralded Almon-Rin as a vibrant and beautiful city; gone were the intricately carved buildings, ladders, and spires that had formed its elevated forest community. Instead, shattered trunks and burnt snags covered the ground. Even the lush and warming forest floor had been replaced by soot and blackened debris.

Braxton stared in shock at the sight, sickened by the terrible destruction the Mins' catapults had wrought upon the elven kingdom. Then he realized something else was missing. The *feil* was gone. That wondrous living and faerie-like essence had been destroyed, and he no longer felt its pulsating presence or earth-born energy. He closed his eyes, saddened for the loss of something pure that had been taken from this world. Penton's warm hand touched his shoulder, encouraging him. Brax glanced back at the sun, drawing strength from its ability to always revive his spirits. Sniffing, he patted Bear as the elkhound brushed against him.

They stepped into the parched wasteland, taking time to find their footing among the sharp fragments. Scorched twigs snapped beneath their feet, and they tried not to breathe the ash that floated about in the air, disturbed further by their passing. Unlike before, nothing moved. Life no longer existed in this part of the forest, and the elves and other woodland creatures had simply abandoned it to its fate, leaving behind an ugly scar in testament to the Mins' devastation of this once beautiful and vibrant land.

It took over an hour to cross the gaping hole, reaching the green growth and majestic towers of the oaks that had called to them from afar. Moving into the forest felt refreshing, like passing through some invisible barrier. One moment they stood amid the death and destruction of the burned perimeter, and the next, they were surrounded by the brilliant sights, sounds, and feeling of life renewed. Birds sang loudly, and the small white wildflowers that grew prolifically among the sea of green reappeared like earthly stars. Trees swayed overhead, and squirrels, rabbits, and other forest creatures rustled about in the undergrowth, encouraging Bear to chase after them.

They stopped and breathed it in, their senses overwhelmed by the sudden change. The forest seemed to be exaggerating its natural abundance of life in stark defiance to the desolation from the Mins. A dozen yards into the trees, the elves appeared, welcoming them with fruits, breads and honey cakes, and soft leather decanters filled with cool water.

"Can you tell me about Phinlera," Brax asked the first elf he saw. "No thank you, I'm not hungry," he said to another. "Please take me to Bendarren." He tried repeatedly, but the elves refused, lifting the food to his mouth and encouraging him to eat.

Penton, however, consumed large quantities of the cakes and fresh fruit, before draining several goblets of forest berry wine.

Realizing he wasn't going to get anywhere until he'd eaten, Brax swallowed some spicy bread and drank down the water. The meal made him feel alive again, cleansing his weariness from the Dunes and strengthening his body.

The elves guided them through the forest, first in one direction and then another, singing, dancing, and placing small wreaths of wildflowers in their hair. They let themselves be led on by the revelry, a welcome change from their war-soaked melancholy. Brax questioned them again about Phinlera, and they responded by interweaving her name into their song, telling him to go to Almon-Fey. He pleaded for information, but they ignored him, insisting that he eat and drink as they headed toward the capital city.

Hours passed quickly, and Braxton soon lost all sense of time and direction. The food and drink continued to relax him, uplifting his spirits and banishing his fears. By the time they reached Almon-Fey and caught sight of the three enormous white oaks, Braxton felt mildly intoxicated. He had only a vague idea of where he was or why they'd come. The elves continued their celebration, dancing through the capital and joined by hundreds more who led them to a huge clearing where thousands gathered.

Moving among the crowd, Braxton bumped into a man wearing long blue robes.

"I'm sorry," he said, apologizing for his clumsiness, then realized it was Bendarren.

Instantly the festival vanished. Brax, Penton, and Bear stood with Bendarren in the little clearing in front of his tree. They blinked in the bright morning sun. Their elven mentor bore a long white mark on his face, extending from the top of his forehead, along the bridge of his nose and down his right cheek to his jawbone.

"My people's joy can have a powerful effect on those unaccustomed to our ways," he said.

"What?" Brax felt strangely dizzy, and his temples throbbed.

"Where are the elves?" Penton looked around.

"Eat this." Bendarren handed each of them a sprig that smelled like peppermint.

"We were just dancing when . . ." But Braxton couldn't remember.

"Eat," Bendarren repeated, and they began chewing on the stringy plant that had a strong, bitter flavor. Slowly their minds began to clear, and they looked around bewildered, wondering how they'd gone so far into the forest.

"Where's Phinlera?" Braxton blurted out. "Is she all right? Were you able to . . . I need to find her!"

"Where are the elves?" Pen asked again. "There were so many of them."

"Keep eating," The elf handed Penton another sprig.

"I need to know!" Brax insisted, looking into the open doorway of their elven friend's home.

"Drink," he said, handing Penton a silver goblet. Pen drained half the contents before offering it to Brax.

"I'm not thirsty. I just want to know if Phin's alive. Please! Why won't you tell me?"

"Drink first." Bendarren took the goblet from Brax's brother and handed it to him.

"But I just need to . . . oh, fine," he said at last. He took the cup, intending to take a quick sip to appease the elf. But when he finished, he realized he'd emptied the goblet. Surprised, he looked at Bendarren.

"Go to your mother's tree. She will answer all your questions."

"*Please* tell me."

"Go now," he repeated, pointing to the forest.

"But—just—" Brax stammered.

"It's clear he's not going to tell you," Pen said. "There must be a reason for it. Let's find Mom."

Disappointed, Brax let his brother lead him away toward Arbor Glen. He looked back at Bendarren watching them go.

Walking cleared Brax's mind. He breathed in the morning air and began to think out loud. "Why wouldn't he tell us? What does it mean? Is Phin . . . ?" He stopped short, unable to say what he feared.

"Don't think about it," Penton said. "I'm sure she's fine." But Brax could see the worry on his brother's face, unusual for his lighthearted disposition, and his stomach sank. Penton quickened his pace.

Braxton began to run, concerned what Bendarren's refusal might mean.

He couldn't accept that Phinlera might not have survived. He could still hear her screaming from the witch's magic and see the look on her face from the wyvern's sting. It was something he knew he'd never forget. He chided himself for the hundredth time for not being stronger, for not being able to summon the spirit magic better or quicker, for failing to protect her. Now she might be dead. All because of him. Because of his failure. Because he was weak.

By the time they reached Arbor Glen in the early afternoon, Braxton's emotions were at a fever pitch. He crested the little hill fronting their mother's tree and stopped short, his eyes falling on her wooden form.

"What the . . . ?" His thoughts turned to anger at seeing a small structure protruding from her base.

"Who'd build a house in Mom's tree?" Penton asked.

Like so many others in Arbor Loren, the building seemed created from the oak itself, extending out as a natural part of the trunk's larger frame. Low-hanging branches covered the roof, giving the vague impression of the giant tree cloaking the smaller home, overlapping the structure to form a natural porch that wrapped around to one side. A round window faced toward them, its soft curtains closed, blocking their view inside.

Braxton's temper flared. Someone had desecrated his mother's beautiful form, violating her essence by building into her natural shape. He gripped his hands into fists, his nails cutting into his palms. Summoning the energy, he moved his hand over his shoulder and gripped the Unicorn Blade. Whoever did this was going to pay a terrible price.

"Easy, Brax," Pen said. He had almost forgotten his brother was there. Penton shook his head at how fiercely Brax held the spirit sword. For a moment Braxton stared back at him in anger, as if he was the enemy. Penton didn't understand. He could never understand what his mom meant to him, what they'd been through together. The bond they'd created. Building into her tree was a direct assault upon that bond, upon his mom's very essence, and her memory.

Pen touched Braxton's arm. "Let it go. There must be an explanation."

Brax pulled away and drew the sword. But the moment the blade left its sheath, it made an unusual ring, a high-pitched whine, unlike its normal peaceful and rhythmic response to being released. He began to shake. The energy surged through him, sending a cold shiver down his body. With it came an uncomfortable sense of being out of place, of having opened something that should not have been awakened.

He realized then what he'd done—drawing the blade in anger, out of a feeling for revenge, with hatred in his mind. The Unicorn Blade had responded to those emotions. Struggling, he tried to contain the evil sensation, wrestling with the destructive thoughts it evoked. Slowly, very slowly, he managed to move his shaking hand back over his shoulder and sheath the weapon, extinguishing the negative energy.

He stood stunned, breathing hard, drenched in perspiration. He never wanted to feel that side of the spirit magic again. Brax closed his eyes and took several long breaths, practicing the mental exercises Serene and Kael had taught him. Visualizing himself standing in the brilliant light of the sun, he tried to bring his body and mind back into balance. He understood now how the power of the Unicorn Blade had reacted to his emotions, to his dark thoughts and his desire to inflict pain. He at last recognized what he might become if he didn't control his feelings in the face of that power. The magical energy that had intertwined itself with his physical life so completely could be used for good or ill. Through all his experiences on this long journey, it was the first time he'd ever wanted to use the spirit sword in anger: to attack rather than defend, to hurt rather than protect, to destroy rather than heal. The sword's power responded to those emotions, and, if not controlled, they would consume him.

"Let it go," Penton repeated, as if understanding Brax's internal struggle. "We should go inside and talk with mom." He started toward the door.

"Pen!"

His brother turned back to look at him.

"Thanks," Brax said.

Penton smiled. "Come on, little brother."

Hello, Brax! His mom's voice burst into his mind as they approached the tree, feeling her warming presence wrap around him. *I'm so relieved to see you and Pen, returning safely together.*

"Mom!" he cried, and Penton jumped.

I love you both and am so very grateful for all you've done to help me, the elves, and Andorah. Thank you, she said.

So much has happened since we left. Brax connected with her. He took a deep breath and finally let go.

I know. She warmed him in her essence. *We've been watching from afar. Both you and Pen have learned and lost much through this horrible war— things I would not have wished for either of you, but which a mother can no longer protect you from. They will stay with you for a long, long time, these experiences. Now come inside.* She grew more cheerful. *Come and share with us.*

Hopeful that his mom meant Phinlera, Braxton ran to the door and pushed it open.

"Dad!" he said. His father stood in the small room. The house resembled their cottage back home, but with a spiral staircase disappearing up in the center of the tree. Bear trotted past them to the opposite end, wagging his tail as if looking for food.

"Hello, boys!" their dad said, beaming at his sons' safe return. "It's good to see you both so well." Leaning heavily on his cane, he walked over and hugged them together.

Our family is reunited, their mom added.

"This is your home then?" Penton asked when they'd separated. "In Mom's tree." He stepped back and looked around. "I knew there had to be a reason for it being here." He glanced at Brax, who looked away, ashamed.

"It is," their dad replied. "I've decided to live here with Mom, where we can be together in this beautiful place within the forest. My time in Oak Haven has ended. This is where I belong now and will live out my days."

Pen saw their dad's emotional reaction and changed the subject. "When did you arrive? Why didn't we see you before?"

"The elves said I missed you by three days. You both departed Arbor Loren on separate paths but thankfully have returned together. I've been here with Mom ever since, and we've been watching your journey—well, your mom's been doing the watching and tells me what she sees from her connection with the elves. We're very proud of both of you."

Braxton avoided his dad's eyes, still embarrassed by his earlier anger at seeing the house in his mom's tree. He looked around at the wooden table and few chairs, one of which had a footstool in front to it. Their dark polished oak matched the floor, walls, and ceiling, and silk pillows of forest greens covered the chairs. Although sparsely furnished, he recognized a few items from Oak Haven, helping to give the home a welcoming feeling.

"I'm leaving the forge to you," their dad said to Penton. "The family business is yours now. You know it well and have learned much. Oak Haven will be lucky to have you as its smith."

"Thanks, Dad. I'll make you proud," Pen joked.

"You already have," Thadeus replied. "And you, Brax." He turned to face him, leaning on his cane. "We're leaving the cottage to you . . . and Phinlera. We hope you'll be happy there together."

"Phin!" Braxton exclaimed. "Where is she?"

He saw a movement out the corner of his eye, near the central staircase that divided his dad's bedroom with a small kitchen farther back in the tree. Phinlera stood there with Bear, who was wagging his tail.

"You're alive!" He ran over and embraced her warmly, lifting her off her feet.

She cringed. "Careful, Brax, I'm not yet healed." She pulled away and held her side. "But it's really great to see you." She leaned forward and kissed him fully on the mouth. "I missed you," she added more quietly, so the others couldn't hear.

"Me too, Phin, more than you know."

They spent the remainder of the day talking and enjoying the time together, sharing their respective stories. Brax and Pen did most of the talking, retelling their view of the war in the Breaker Dunes, fighting the Mins, and the final confrontation between Sotchek and Morgaroth.

Phinlera wept softly when Penton mentioned Gavin. Brax held her close and swallowed hard, trying to be strong.

"I'm sorry about Sotchek," she said, when the conversation moved on. "I wish I could've been there to help."

"I should've done more for him." Brax shook his head and looked down at the table. "But it all happened so fast. One minute I thought Sotchek was going to win, and the next he was gone. I didn't even have time to react. Morgaroth tricked me, and Sotchek paid the price for my stupidity."

"Don't be se hard on yerself, lad!" Brax looked up and saw Ruskin standing in the doorway. "Ya've done better than ya give yourself credit fer." He took the pipe from his mouth and entered the room. "Good to see you, Thadeus." He shook their dad's hand. "So this is where you ended up, eh? A bit sparse, ain't it?" The dwarf dropped down into the chair with the footstool, put his feet up, and kicked off his boots. "Any chance for a bit of ale and some of Jen's sausages? Muffins would be nice too. The food here is made for birds and mules—all seeds and grasses. I need some real meat!" He took a puff on his dying pipe then looked at it curiously, turned it upside down, and whacked it a few times against the side of his chair. Ashes fell onto the clean floor.

"I'll see what I can do." Thadeus got up and limped toward the kitchen. "Always a pleasure, Ruskin."

"Yours or mine?" He stuck his thumb into the pipe and turned it a few times to clean it. More dead embers fell, and he licked his finger. "There's a council tomorrow," Ruskin said, still looking at his pipe. "We're all supposed to attend—guests of honor or something equally stupid. Anyway, ya'd better be ready for fanfare and boring speeches, the elves are known for it. No 'fense, Jen." He raised his hand toward the ceiling, acknowledging their mom.

None taken, Braxton heard her reply. *Never from you, old friend. Never from you.*

CHAPTER
45

B raxton jumped, hearing something that seemed out of place in the forest. It alerted his senses and brought him quickly awake, scattering the dream he could now no longer remember. He lay in the dark of his little room, high up in the boughs of his mom's tree, a tiny space barely large enough for a single bed. They'd gone to bed late and the strain of exhaustion pulled at him, his body pleading for more rest. But he forced himself to stay up, listening for the sound to come again. He could hear the solitary tune of some nearby songbird and the occasional distant hoot of an owl echoing in the forest, but nothing unusual. He knew that call, he thought. What was it?

Then he remembered. The sound flooded back into his memory as if hearing it for the first time, and a cold shiver ran down his skin. The scream of the wyvern. Stunned, he didn't move. How could it possibly be in Arbor Loren? Had he really heard it, or had it been just another dream? He strained to listen, waiting to see if it repeated, hoping it wasn't real.

What is it? His mom's quiet voice entered his mind, surprising Brax.

Nothing, he said. *I just heard something I didn't expect.*

What was it?

Nothing important. I'm sorry to have woken you.

She laughed quietly. *I no longer sleep. Not the way you think of it, anyway, at least not until winter.*

He nodded.

I don't sense anything unusual, she added after a moment. *Perhaps you were just dreaming?*

Probably.

He got up and pulled on his long shirt to ward off the breeze blowing in from the open end of his room. It was not yet dawn, and he looked out over the forest's canopy, thick with summertime leaves.

I need to tell you something, he said, reaching out again to connect with his mom. *What happened to me during the fight with Morgaroth.*

I am here.

When I stood up and faced it, when I first stood my ground and the spirit magic assaulted it from within me, I connected with Morgaroth as though I was a part of it, and it a part of me. As if we were one. In that moment, our energy seemed to join, and I could feel its hatred and its desire for power and to hurt or enslave everyone around it. It was a terrible experience.

That is a foul creature, his mom replied, as if preferring not to speak of it. *And I am sorry, Braxton, that you had to face it. That you had to feel its negativity, that you were asked to do this for us, for me, for the elves.*

I'm not, he said quickly. *I'm glad to have helped, Mom. What's bothering me is that I saw in it what I could become. As if Morgaroth was a reflection of all the dark parts of myself. Then when I first saw Dad's house built into your tree, I wanted to attack whoever did that to you. I wanted to inflict . . . pain.* He shut his eyes tightly and sat back on his bed, ashamed.

His mom was quiet for a while before responding.

Understand, Braxton, that your life is interwoven now with the spirit magic, and that there are many others like you, connected to it, although it exhibits itself through them in different ways. What you need to know is that what you do with the energy is a choice you have to make. Some will choose to use it for good, to help and to heal themselves and others, to build and create, and to better all life around them. Others, like Morgaroth—she said the name as if it pained her—*choose to use it for power and to control those who have yet to awaken. That, Braxton, is the only thing that separates the two of you, the only difference between light and dark—a simple choice of how you choose to use your energy. It is that choice, given to you freely by the One, that defines your actions and will ultimately determine who and what you'll become.*

"Then I choose to be light," he said aloud.

That is an easy choice to make here and now in the calm and safety of my tree. But will you make that same decision when faced with the opportunity to control the lives of many, or to stop the death of someone you love, or to save our village back home? Would you make that choice, not to hurt or control another and to only use your power for good, if Phinlera's life lay in the balance? That, Braxton, will be your greatest test. Not facing a creature like Morgaroth, but facing yourself.

When she finished speaking, she withdrew.

For a long time, Brax thought about what she'd said—about facing his own dark emotions and overcoming them in the face of the power to influence the lives of many or of the one he loved. Perhaps that was the inevitable test to awakening the spirit magic within him, proving himself worthy. He lifted his shirt and ran his fingers over the Chosen Cross. Those two small interconnected circles burned into his chest had irrevocably changed his life—for better, he knew. Of that there could be no doubt. But to truly master the Unicorn Blade and to become a Wielder like those of old, he would have to do more. He'd need to maintain self-control and mental discipline. He'd have to keep his emotions in check in the power of the spirit magic that had intertwined itself so completely now with the very fabric of his life. He was no longer just a blacksmith's son in some faraway village no one cared about. He'd been given a gift, an opportunity to go beyond what he might otherwise have become, to do more than what was normally expected from everyday life. This energy, this spirit magic that had awakened him, as his mom described it, was dependent upon him making the right choices every day and using its power for the betterment of many. It would take time to master, he knew, and it would be challenging, but the alternative was to become like Morgaroth.

"I can't do this alone," he said, taking a deep breath and letting it out slowly. "I need help." He needed Serene, he realized. He desperately needed her guidance to teach him how to stay calm and in control of his emotions, to help him recognize the consequences of his actions. To be a moral compass by which to measure his life.

He thought about all he'd done, all he'd experienced since leaving Oak Haven—seemingly a lifetime ago. Descending the spiral staircase, he paused outside Phinlera's room and considered waking her, but left her to rest. He needed time to think. He was calmer now, knowing she was safe. He continued down, listening to Ruskin's familiar drone filling the lower boughs of his mom's tree. When he reached the bottom, Brax smiled at the sight of the dwarf still fast asleep in his dad's chair, lying exactly where he'd sat the night before, his face slumped and buried in his thick beard. Bear lifted his head from the rug he was laying on as Brax crossed to the door and watched him go.

Stepping out into the early morning, he found a light mist had settled on the forest. He breathed it in, enjoying its refreshing sensation. Brax always loved early mornings and the calmness they brought. Regardless of what had happened the day before, mornings always offered another chance, a new opportunity to start again. Perhaps this was his opportunity, his chance to start his life again as a Wielder, aware now of his emotions and the need to keep them in balance. To keep his mind at peace.

He wandered among the trees of Arbor Glen, seeing a few attendants moving about the gargantuan oaks in the otherwise seemingly deserted forest. Finding himself moving toward Almon-Fey, he turned away from that path, not wishing to interact with the more numerous elves. Their gratitude and endless offerings wherever he went were becoming overwhelming, and he just wanted some time alone to think. The elves seemed to recognize his need for solitude and kept their distance, some even going so far as to step onto other trails whenever they found themselves approaching along the same path. Braxton was grateful for their understanding. It allowed his mind the freedom to wander, to recall again the fight between Morgaroth and Sotchek. He thought about how the creature had tricked him, breaking his concentration long enough to allow it time to escape. He was past chiding himself for his lack of attention to Morgaroth's ploy, but was not yet ready to be rid of the guilt he felt for not having done more to protect his big friend—someone who'd saved his life on numerous occasions. He carried the weight of that knowledge with him like a tangible backpack.

It was late morning when he returned, watching the light dance among the tree's darkening summer leaves and numerous flowers on the forest floor. He marveled at his mom's exquisite form and the abundant pink roses interspersed among her branches. Several lay at her feet or on the roof of the house, and he was reminded that time was passing. Sooner rather than later, they'd have to make the journey home to Oak Haven. Brax sighed heavily at the thought.

Phinlera came out of the cottage, and his spirits rose as she smiled and waved at him. He jogged down the small rise to where she stood on the porch and kissed her. Embracing, they enjoyed the wonderful sensation of their shared feelings for each other. She flinched when he tried to hug her too tightly, and pulled away, touching her side.

"I need to show you something." She stepped off the porch, drawing his attention away from her wound. "Something you need to know."

"What is it?" He followed her to one side of his mom's tree. Phin moved slower than normal, but he didn't ask about her wound. He knew she was reluctant to talk about it, and he was just happy to be with her again. She looked so pretty in the late morning light. Her lush black hair had been pulled back in an elven ribbon of leaves, a few wisps falling gently to touch her brow, accentuating her beautiful eyes. She led him to the back of the tree, then stopped and pointed up.

Her smile faded.

It is nothing. Pay it no heed, his mom said as she connected with him. *Don't worry yourself over trivial concerns.*

"What is it? I don't see anything." Brax looked up at the oak.

Phinlera pulled him closer, to the very opposite side of where his dad's house was built into the trunk, almost hidden from view.

"Look," she said sadly, pointing to a branch about a dozen feet up.

A dead limb extended from his mom's otherwise life-laden form. The entire branch, as thick as his arm and three times his length, hung limp and brittle. Its leaves, once lush and abundant, were withered and dry, and a black, pitch-like growth covered the branch, spreading out toward its neighbors.

"Mom, what is that?" he called out in alarm. "What's happening to you?"

"Braxton," Phinlera said calmly beside him. "Look at me." She took his face in both hands, her smooth, soft skin touching the sides of his unshaven chin. Slowly she forced him to look into her exquisite brown eyes, droplets forming in their corners.

"It was your mom who healed me." A single perfect tear trickled down her cheek and fell onto her breast. "She was the only one who could." Phin placed a finger on his lips before he could reply. "She drew the wyvern's venom from my body and into her own form, burying it deep within the forest floor, dispersing it through her extensive root system and out into the earth, diluting its strength. Yes, Braxton, your mom saved my life. But . . . at a terrible price." She let go of him and glanced away for a moment, ashamed. Then, determined to go on, she looked back into his surprised face.

"Some of the venom remained in her body and seeped into her branches, and . . . they died." She said it simply, as if telling him the end of something he had not wanted to hear, like closing the book on a chapter in his life.

"Mom!" he yelled, pulling away from Phinlera and looking up into the tree.

It is all right, Braxton. He heard her calm voice. *I knew the risks when I offered to help. It was my choice, and mine alone to make. You and Phinlera have a lifetime ahead of you, and she deserves to be whole and strong. In time, her wound will heal, and it will be but a distant memory that occasionally reminds you of an old experience you once had, long ago.*

You both deserve that life, she said before he could answer. *A life together, whole and complete. Do not let this worry you. It is trivial. It is nothing.*

"Nothing! It isn't nothing that you have poison in your body. That some of your branches are dying. How can you expect me to just ignore that?"

Because, Braxton, my wonderful son, you don't yet understand my life in this new form. Yes, a few of my branches have died, and in time, they will fall from my body, but no more than hairs from yours. Others will grow around them with new life, and my inner core remains strong. It is not necessary for you to anguish over every phase I endure, or you will cry often—with the change of each new season, I expect.

"This isn't a natural change, Mom! Your body is *poisoned!*" He choked on the word.

Braxton! Her voice was strong. *You have to let this go. I'm not dead, not yet anyhow, and I have saved the one you love and whom you are destined to be with. Put aside your grief, and go and live your lives together. It is all right. I will survive.* She pulled away from him.

For a while at least, she added to herself. *For a time.*

CHAPTER
46

They left the house in the early afternoon and headed back toward Almon-Fey for the celebration and elven council Ruskin said they were expected to attend. Braxton was frustrated from his earlier conversation with his mom and still worried about her being poisoned. Having had time to think about their conversation, he reached out to her as they stepped outside.

I'm sorry, he said slowly. *I promised myself I'd balance my emotions better and keep my energy calm and at peace. Yet, at my first testing, I failed.*

It's all right, Brax. You have done so very well. She embraced him in the warmth of their connection. *Do not worry about me. I will always be here for you whenever you return, whenever you need me.*

Thanks, Mom. He smiled, feeling better. *You always know how to make me feel worthwhile somehow, even in my failures.*

You haven't failed, Braxton, not by any man's measure. In contrast, you have achieved much more than you realize. Go and enjoy your time together.

Phinlera waited patiently beside him. She knew what he was doing. He embraced her and pulled her close, feeling her body pressed against his.

"Sorry!" he said quickly, when she winced and put a hand on her side. "I keep forgetting."

"It's fine," she said casually, running her fingers through her hair and flashing him one of her brilliant smiles. He recognized the distraction.

"You all right?" he asked more seriously.

"Yes." She took his hand in hers. Brax could tell she was trying to be strong, not wanting him to feel guilty, trying to hide her pain. "We'd better catch up with the others." She pulled him down the porch stairs before looking away toward the forest trail. "They're already over the rise."

They walked for the rest of the day, allowing their dad to keep pace, and giving Phinlera time for an occasional rest or to stretch her side whenever she thought no one was looking. Each time they stopped, Bear ambled off into the undergrowth to sniff something of interest or chase one of the many surprised squirrels. Ruskin, as usual, grumbled under his breath—at least whenever he wasn't talking to Brax's dad. He went on about stupid ceremonies and how the elves always had to overdo and exaggerate everything.

"Why can't they just go on with their lives?" he asked. "The war's over."

They reached Bendarren's house as the afternoon sun slid toward the horizon. The elf stood outside, waiting for them among the little white wildflowers that grew more prolifically here than in the other parts of the forest they'd seen. He wore a deep-sapphire robe embroidered with silver runes down one side, and his long, straight white hair was beautifully groomed, falling casually onto his chest and over his shoulders. He still bore the white mark of the Fey Oath upon his face. It was his bright blue eyes, however, that captured Braxton's attention as always, conveying the elven master's wisdom.

"Welcome," he said simply, extending his hand from the center of his chest. "I am pleased you will attend our evening festivities. King Eilandoran is looking forward to thanking you personally for your service."

"Oh joy," Ruskin mumbled.

"And I too am eternally grateful," Bendarren continued, ignoring the dwarf, "to each of you, for the sacrifices you have made in saving our forest and her beautiful people." He looked at Penton. "Know that your young friend's death was not in vain. He departed this world thankful for the opportunity to have avenged his family and is at peace with himself and his service to your Empire. He's left you everything he owned, as you know; his family's home and heritage are yours now and will pass to all those who follow in your bloodline."

Braxton looked surprised. "I thought you were going to live with us. With Phin and me."

"No, Brax." His brother took a silver key out of his pocket that was attached to a medallion by a small chain. "I will live in Gavin's house now. The cottage is yours to keep."

"But what about the forge? I haven't the experience to smith for Oak Haven."

"Nor will you need to. I still plan to take my inheritance as Dad has asked and will work the forge and take over our family's business. I only hope I don't wake you too early when I start each morning." He laughed, lightening the mood.

"And I see that your friend here has chosen to live with the two of you," Bendarren added, walking over to pat Bear. "May the three of you be blessed together."

Phin bent down a bit awkwardly and held the elkhound's muzzle, lifting his big head to look into his eyes. "Thank you," she said, and he licked her face.

"Now that that's settled," Bendarren glanced about, "I believe the council is awaiting us." He led them the rest of the way to the elven capital.

They arrived at Almon-Fey as sunset descended upon the majestic woodland city. Every elf throughout the forest seemed to have gathered in celebration, dressed in various forest colors, many with bright ribbons tied to their clothing or intertwined in their hair. All danced joyfully to the festive music that seemed to emanate from the trees themselves. Traversing rope ladders, the elves moved about in the gigantic oaks or along the forest floor, passing through open doors to every home and building throughout the city.

Everyone, Braxton noticed, had a white mark of some kind upon their face—a line here, a symbol there—having pledged their lives to help save

Arbor Loren. Now they sang, danced, and enjoyed the abundant feast of cakes, fruits, hot pies, and steaming vegetables laid out on an endlessly long table that meandered throughout the capital. A veil of tiny sparkling white dust rained down from the canopy, further enhancing the bountiful display and disappearing whenever it touched anything.

"Not a single piece of venison among 'em," Ruskin complained at seeing the food, shaking his head. Bendarren tapped him on the shoulder and pointed to a small cart laden with casks of wine and half-opened barrels of elven pipe leaf.

"Ho!" the dwarf said at seeing this most wondrous sight. He stood there a moment, staring wide-eyed and longingly. Brax even thought he saw a tear forming in his old friend's eye. A moment later, Ruskin sat against a nearby tree with a large tankard in one hand and his smoldering pipe in the other.

"Now that's a contented dwarf!" Pen commented, and the others agreed, pleased to finally see their friend at peace in the forest.

As the sun set in the western sky, a clear note sounded from some unseen trumpet. The elves seemed to recognize the signal and began moving toward the center of the city, crowding around the now enlarged platform where Braxton had first met Kael. The magnificent white throne, carved with inlaid oak leaves and small wildflowers, sat at the far end. Dozens of the high-backed leather chairs lined the court, their polished armrests reflecting a light from the lanterns floating above or in the nearby trees.

Bendarren guided them to a position in the center of the front row of pillow-topped benches that extended back a hundred rows or more. Braxton left a place for Ruskin to join, but doubted they'd see the dwarf. Bear lay down at Phinlera's feet and was soon fast asleep. The chairs began filling up with many of the council leaders they remembered seeing before, and most of the benches were already occupied, with more elves gathering beyond the court, seeking positions in the forest that would afford them the best view. General Illian came over and personally thanked Brax, Phin, Penton, and their dad, saying how much he appreciated their service, their sacrifice, and all they'd done to help Arbor Loren in the war. He spoke with a few other elves before taking his seat in the first chair to the right of the throne. Brax looked at the empty seat beside Illian, remembering it as Kael's position.

Phinlera placed her hand on his, and Braxton flinched. "You all right?" she asked.

"Yeah," he said, sadly. "Just remembering Kael and Laefin."

"I know. I miss them too." She put her arm around him and laid her head on his shoulder.

Another trumpet sounded, and the court quieted down. Breem stepped up onto the platform and took the middle of three open seats next to the council elders on the left side. The human commander sat proudly representing the Empire, his polished metal breastplate reflecting the Imperial Lion, and his rich-purple cloak falling loosely behind him and across his chair. His black hair and thick mustache were neatly groomed, but his strong face seemed drawn and pale.

Several more trumpets brought the assemblage to their feet as King Eilandoran approached from the opposite end of the platform, farthest from his throne. Braxton caught a slight movement near Breem and glanced back to see Ruskin step up out of the crowd and stand in front of the chair to the left of the Empire commander, one seat closer to the throne. The sly badger had taken his position at the last possible moment before the elven king arrived. Brax was surprised to see he held a seat of distinction, expecting him to sit with them. But then it made sense that the elves would afford a place of honor to all their allies, leaving Braxton to wonder why he hadn't thought of it before. He understood now why Ruskin had dreaded attending this council, knowing the dwarf's distaste for such ceremonies.

Ruskin had actually attempted combing his hair—although he hadn't done a very good job of it, removing only the larger leaves and other debris from his head and beard, leaving the smaller fragments behind. The dwarf seemed to realize that he was still smoking and holding a tankard of wine. He stuffed the smoldering pipe deep into his pocket and took a last quick drink. Finding the flask empty, he casually tossed it over his shoulder, much to the surprise of some nearby elves. It was all Braxton could do to stop from laughing aloud.

A moment later, King Eilandoran, escorted by a half-dozen soldiers, walked down the aisle between the benches, crossed the platform in front of the high-backed chairs, and took his place on the throne. The audience, taking their cue from him, sat as well. Eilandoran's deep-green robe was covered by his striking forest cloak of overlapping leaves and long, golden feathers that Braxton now recognized from the eagles of Arbor Loren. His small wreath of tiny white gems accentuated the mark on his face, extending from his forehead and curving around to under his right eye. In his hand, he held a thick wooden staff, about a foot long, made from three distinct woods intertwined together, including a brilliant silver-white that matched his throne.

For a moment, the elven king just looked out at the audience. Then he stood and touched the fingers of his right hand to the center of his chest, to his forehead, and out to his people in the familiar forest greeting. As one the elves rose and repeated the motion back, raising their voices together in a single note that caused the hairs on the back of Braxton's neck to stand on edge and the spirit magic to awaken. Eilandoran raised his hand and the audience fell silent and sat down.

"Beautiful people of Arbor Loren, distinguished guests to our woodland realm, and gathered friends of old," the king said. "Our most beloved and ancient forest home has been saved!" The assembly erupted with singing, applauding, and blaring trumpets everywhere. Braxton became incredibly dizzy, swaying as the energy surged through him in massive waves of such intensity that he felt both euphoric and nauseated. An instant later, the sounds ceased, and silence fell over Almon-Fey, allowing Braxton to keep his stomach.

"We have fulfilled the Fey Oath!" the king announced proudly, and the elves cheered, clapped, and trumpeted again before starting to sing in unison, causing the spirit magic in Braxton to surge anew.

"It is my distinct honor," Eilandoran continued after the tumult had quieted down a bit, "to celebrate with you in this momentous achievement and to thank you for your undying loyalty and service to the White Wood. This was a great time of personal commitment, a time when all Loren's people were called to her aid. You answered that call magnificently, with both honor and distinction." The elves cheered.

The king held up his hand again for silence. "I want to especially thank those who came and sacrificed with us in our great time of need." He extended his arm toward Breem, Ruskin, and the empty chair. "Without their help, I am sure we would not be here today." Silently and as one, the elves stood and made the gesture of recognition, touching their chests and foreheads with both hands, and then extending their arms out toward the allies sitting in their court.

"But of all those who were brought to us," the king said aloud, "it is to the Elhunarie and his Chosen that we are most grateful." He walked over and stood in front of Braxton. "Without their warning, we would have surely been defeated." He extended his hand.

Braxton was so surprised he didn't move. Phinlera nudged him, encouraging him to stand. He got up and shook the king's hand awkwardly. The crowd erupted once more.

"I offer you this token of appreciation for helping to save Fey Ethel." Eilandoran held out the small interwoven staff across his upturned palms. "May it be a symbol of gratitude for your guidance and forever serve as a reminder to our people of your service to Arbor Loren."

"Thank you," Braxton replied. He took the staff and bowed to the king, not knowing what else to do. Eilandoran smiled then turned and thanked Phinlera and Penton, before honoring their dad as well. When he was done, he walked over to Breem and Ruskin.

"To our allies," the elf said in his strong, regal voice, "we are eternally grateful." He shook each of their hands in turn as they stood. Ruskin's pocket leaked an endless stream of faint gray smoke.

"We thank King Balan," Eilandoran announced loudly, "whose youthfulness is surpassed only by his great wisdom for sending his legendary knights and their brave captain to our aid." He turned to an assistant behind him, retrieved a beautiful golden leaf from a silver pillow, and pinned it to Breem's collar. Then he handed him an intricately carved wooden scroll tube. Breem bowed, thanked the king for the gift, and shook his hand again proudly before turning to look at the cheering crowd.

"And to the mighty King Tharak and all his stout warriors from the Spine"—Eilandoran continued, turning toward Ruskin—"we are forever indebted to you for your help." He presented the dwarf with an exquisite pipe made from the same white wood as the throne. For the first time, Braxton saw Ruskin at a loss for words. But his bearded friend reached out with shaking hands and accepted the magnificent gift, as if the elven king were giving him more wealth than all the jewels beneath the earth.

"From the ashes of a fire that almost consumed us," the king said, turning back toward the court and gathered assemblage, "old kinships have awakened. The ancient allegiances with our friends to the north and west are renewed, and even now, new opportunities for cooperation with the ogre people have begun." He indicated the empty chair next to Breem. "May this time serve as a beginning for our world, a new era in which we come together in peace and friendship as in times of old, that all our great nations may once more celebrate in open and supportive collaboration." The applause and cheers began again.

"Now we must turn inward and recognize those within our own borders who served Arbor Loren with special distinction," Eilandoran announced. He went on for more than an hour, thanking various woodland people for their service, recognizing General Illian for leading the charge from the forest that drew the attention of their enemy at a critical moment and awarding him a special distinction. He thanked Bellnella and Tentalis for the assistance of the Talonguard, recognized the skillful accuracy of the elven archers, and commended the masterful swordsmanship of the army's elite. Each time the elves applauded proudly. But it was the gratitude toward the elflings, specifically Jenphinlin and Jenterra, and mentioning Brax's mom by name, that touched Braxton the most. He swallowed hard to maintain his composure.

"And finally," the elven king said, bringing his speech to its natural close, "I wish to recognize Kael Illyuntarie." He announced the name sadly. "Not as your king or as your leader do I say this, but as your friend. For no other throughout our magnificent realm suffered more or lost as much than he and his kin. It is with great sadness that we witness the end of the Illyuntarie line . . . for that branch in our great forest will grow no further." He paused to let the weight of his words settle on the crowd. "May he and his family's name be forever remembered with fondness, with pride, with gratitude, and with the highest level of recognition we can afford them."

For one brief and beautiful moment, the forest went perfectly still. No one moved, no creature stirred, no evening birds sang. Even the wind itself seemed subdued. The starlight dust that had fallen throughout the evening hung suspended in the air as the world around them stopped in silent remembrance.

Beloved child. Serene's voice sounded in Brax's mind, causing him to jump. *Allow me to speak.* She hadn't spoken to him since the fight with Sotchek and Morgaroth, and Brax was excited now to have her return. He had so much to ask her. But he pulled his consciousness aside, allowing her to take over. Standing up, he closed his eyes.

"Children of Arbor Loren," Serene spoke through him, "it is with great pleasure that we see your forest survived, hear your words of recognition for those who have saved and served you so well. In particular, that you would remember this one and his family by name, for you cannot know the suffering he endured in facing and destroying his own son. But all is not lost, nor is it as dark as it would appear." She turned Braxton's body to face the opposite end of the court, his right hand raised high.

"Come," she said.

For a moment nothing happened. No one moved, and the forest again went completely silent, expectant. Then, just as Braxton started doubting whether Serene had actually spoken, a cloaked and hooded figure stepped out of the crowd and up onto the platform. It limped down the court until it came to stand before the king, leaning heavily to one side. Lifting its right hand from under the cloak it held a piece of red cloth toward Eilandoran. Then it reached up and pulled back the hood, and the cloak fell to the ground.

There stood Laefin. His left arm was badly deformed and strapped to a splint made of some broken wood tied together with a piece of his torn and bloodied shirt, his elbow pressed against his ribs to protect them. Dried blood was smeared beneath his broken nose and at the corner of his mouth, and an open wound above his right temple still oozed. But he was alive.

"My father," Laefin said in a strained and parched voice, "has regained his honor."

CHAPTER
47

The elven court erupted with such cheering, celebrating, and trumpets blaring at Laefin's return that Braxton thought his head was going to explode. Elves from every direction came up onto the platform, and together they picked Laefin up and hoisted him on their shoulders for the crowd to see. The poor archer seemed to be enduring a mixture of both excruciating pain from his wounds and joy at returning. When he was finally set down, and King Eilandoran was able to restore order, many of the nearby women were crying, and even a few of the men seemed choked up and unable to speak.

"This . . ." the king said. "This was . . . unforeseen." He reached out and hugged Laefin, welcoming him home. "Your family's name shall indeed be forever cleared of your father's self-imposed discommendation. I henceforth bestow upon it Fey-Anath, Title to the Forest." The crowd trumpeted and applauded loudly. "And I name you Laefin Fey-Illyuntarie," to which the elves cheered their approval and began singing praise to the archer and his family.

When they eventually set Laefin back down on the platform, he limped over to Braxton, refusing aid from those around him. He placed his hand under his shirt and withdrew the arrow Serene had made.

"I return now that which was entrusted to me," he said with a pained smile, "and fulfill the charge of your Elhunarie." He inclined his head in acknowledgment. Braxton took the arrow, and Phinlera flung her arms around the elf, hugging him as tightly as both their wounds would permit. Braxton joined in too, thrilled to see their young friend had survived.

Serene connected with him as they finished embracing.

Give back the arrow. Braxton handed it to the surprised elf. "She says you're to keep it." Then Serene entered his mind.

"That which I have given shall forever bind you to your fate, to your moment of service, and to this manner of your return," she said to the young archer, and those around fell silent. "You and all those who follow in your bloodline shall walk upon this path that you have begun. Remember what I have told of its purpose, and that no other may fire upon a mark that which I have given. It shall be an heirloom to you and your kin, and all those who descend from your father, Kael Illyuntarie, shall be bound to it. Only they shall have the power to use it."

"I understand," Laefin said solemnly, clasping the arrow to his chest. "I receive for myself and my descendants that which you have made, and this path upon which you have placed us. We accept this fate."

"Then let us celebrate together," Eilandoran stated from behind Laefin, startling the young elf. Turning around quickly, he bowed to his king. "Let us all enjoy now the renewed life of Arbor Loren!" Eilandoran adjourned the court so they could dance, feast, and rejoice in the saving of their forest.

Braxton and Phinlera turned to leave when Breem walked over and grasped Brax's arm.

"Thank you," he said, "for your help out there." He nodded in the direction of the Dunes and extended his hand in friendship.

"Of course." Braxton tried not to wince at the man's stronger grip.

"Take this." Breem pulled off his left glove and removed a ring from his little finger.

"Thank you, but it's really not necessary, I was happy to—"

"I insist. I'll be leaving in the morning and don't imagine we'll meet again. I'd like you to have it." The captain looked at the ring fondly, sad to give it up. "In recognition for saving my life."

Accepting the gift, Braxton looked at it closely. The flared silver band came around to form a square base that had two silver horses engraved on the top. Rampant style and facing each other, they supported a shield carved out of a deep-purple gemstone, with a tiny white diamond inlaid at its center.

"Thank you," he repeated, genuinely surprised. "I will wear it proudly." Brax closed his hand around the ring.

Breem gave a weak smile. "Good luck. May your future travels bring you more pleasure than these past days," he said, as though wishing it for himself. Without waiting, the proud Empire commander turned and left the court, leaving Braxton and Phinlera alone on the platform.

It was past midmorning when Braxton awoke. The previous night's festivities had begun right after the elven council ended, with much singing, dancing, and merrymaking going on into the predawn hours. Brax, Phinlera, and Penton stayed most of the night, enjoying the bountiful and legendary hospitality of the elves, their generous company, and their endless and excellent food and drink. He was surprised at how festive the forest people could be, and the wondrous feeling they exuded almost rivaled the euphoric sensation of the spirit magic.

Throughout the celebration, he danced with countless elves, was treated with distinction, and accepted their hospitality, unable to stop himself, despite his usual dislike for attention. Even Phinlera moved about as though her wound were nonexistent, singing along with the crowd and twirling through glades with elven maidens who wrapped themselves in long, bright ribbons interwoven in the dancing lines.

He lay quietly now in the bed of his little room, high up in his mom's tree. He couldn't remember how they had returned to her oak, or when. The bright morning sun streamed in through the open wall. The day started cool and crisp in the forest, but he knew it would warm to be another beautiful late summer's day. He looked out over the sea of green, thinking about the previous night's events, playing over in his mind the council meeting and all that had occurred, putting together the intricate pieces of this puzzle into which he'd strayed.

Turning toward the little nightstand beside him, he picked up the staff King Eilandoran had given him and studied its blended colors—a dark wood, a bright oak, and a gleaming white that reminded him of the Silver Towers. All were masterfully, or perhaps magically, interwoven, as if nature herself had worked the loom. Bendarren said it was the greatest gift an outsider could receive, allowing the bearer to return to the forest whenever he wanted and to obtain unquestionable aid from the elves. Holding the staff, Brax could feel its unnatural warmth, and a faint hum echoed in the recesses of his mind, unidentifiable and yet familiar somehow. Searching for its source, he awakened the spirit magic and sent out a tendril to find it, willing it to uncover and return to him the full light and rhythm of those notes, going so far as to draw the Unicorn Blade to assist him. But despite the bountiful amount of energy he summoned, he was unable to find it. The humming continued, elusive and beyond his grasp.

Slightly frustrated by the experience, he placed the staff back on the table and picked up Breem's ring. It was beautifully formed, not by magic, but rather by man's masterful application of his craft. The silver horses were polished to such perfection that they almost seemed alive, enhancing the depth of the purple-gemstone shield offset by the tiny diamond shining at its center. Rolling the object around in his fingers, Brax noticed some tiny writing encircling the face of the shield. Walking into the sunlight he squinted at the words. When he could finally read them, he realized it was written in a language he didn't know.

From strength of arms comes peace in men.

"Serene!" he exclaimed. "I'm so glad you're back!"

For the moment, she replied, connecting with him. *It is the ancient creed of the knightly orders, written now on the Ring of Arms. It is one of several such rings from your homeland. Whomever wears it has doors opened for them that would otherwise remain shut. Keep it well hidden, my child, for we will have need of it in the future. It will serve us well.*

Thank you, I will. But Braxton was only half-listening. *I have so many questions for you.*

And in time I will answer them. But now you must rise and meet this new day, for time is short.

How is Sotchek? he asked, dressing quickly. *Were you able to help him?*

His strength is holding, and his will is strong. Morgaroth's power has been diminished, but the one you know as Sotchek will not long survive in the shadows. Soon we will need to aid him, but we will talk of that later. Go now, and I will walk with you this day. She withdrew then, ending their connection.

Disappointed at not being able to talk more, Brax pulled on his boots, strapped on the Unicorn Blade, and headed down the stairs. There were so many unanswered questions, so much he wanted to know from his master, but he followed her instructions and let it go—for now.

When he reached the common room, he could tell the others had been up for a while. Their voices drifted in through the half-opened door, and he could see his dad standing on the porch. Leaving the cottage, he found Ruskin leaning against the small wagon Bendarren had shown him the night before, laden now with casks of elven wine and sealed barrels that Brax assumed contained the forest pipe leaf his friend was so fond of. A small, longhaired white pony with dark brown spots on its rump was harnessed to the front. The poor creature looked as though it would be hard-pressed to move the wagon and its precious cargo.

"Finally decided to get up, did ya?" the dwarf grumbled at seeing him. "Thought I was gonna miss ya before going."

"What, you're leaving?" Braxton asked.

"'Fraid so."

"He's in a rush to get back to his people." Phinlera left his dad's side and stood beside Brax, flashing him a bright morning smile.

"Or to smoke and drink the day away," Penton added with a laugh as he secured the wagon's strappings. Bear stood near him, smelling the pony.

"Wouldn't dream of it." The dwarf feigned innocence. "This stuff's for King Tharak." He thumbed toward the cart. "Payment for sending out the clans."

"What's left of it, you mean," Pen clarified.

"Well, now, you can't expect my countrymen to walk all the way back to the Dragon's Spine after such hard fighting without a bit of remuneration, now can you?" Ruskin gave a sly wink.

"Tharak will be lucky to get one flask of wine and a single pipe of leaf when you lot return," Brax's dad commented.

"That wouldn't be my doing."

"I bet," Penton joked.

"Watch it, lad, or you'll find rocks in your smithy." The dwarf made a satisfied grin at the look on Penton's face. "Well, I'm off." He pulled the white pipe King Eilandoran had given him from under his belt, stuffed it full of forest leaf, and lit it cheerfully. Taking a long draw, he exhaled a puff of smoke.

"Wait a minute," Phin said. "Wasn't that a gift for your king?"

"Oh no, lassie," Ruskin said through clenched teeth. "The wagon is fer the Boar. The pipe is fer the Badger." He removed the bit from his mouth and blew a long plume toward her.

"Don't you think he'll be a little suspicious? You arriving home with that gift, I mean?"

"Not at all! Tharak agreed to fight for wine and forest leaf, an arrangement that this now satisfies." Rusk indicated the wagon. "Whatever I get for brokering the deal is fair game. Every dwarf knows this." A smug look crossed his bearded face as he took another draw and blew out toward the trees. Holding the pipe, he stared at the girl as if his logic was undeniable. "There's nothing better than elven leaf drawn through an elven pipe." He placed it back between his teeth and tasted it deliberately. Phinlera shook her head at the shrewd dwarf.

"Much as I'd like to continue educating ya in the ways of the world," Ruskin added, "I best be getting back to see the clans before they start fighting among themselves. Pen, I'll see ya in a month with your first delivery. Hope your cooking's better than your dad's."

"It's not," Phinlera said quickly, and the dwarf groaned. "But mine is, and my specialty is venison sausage stew."

"Heavy on the sausages, light on the stew?"

"You bet."

Ruskin took a deep breath of morning air and looked up at the bright, clear sky. "I reckon I'm gonna be liking this new arrangement." He turned toward the cart. "C'mon, you hairy runt." He slapped the pony on its rump. The surprised creature whinnied, then lurched forward, causing Bear to bolt to one side. The wagon frame creaked under the strain of its cargo.

"See you," Penton called after their friend, but the dwarf didn't bother turning around. He raised the pipe in acknowledgment, and another puff of smoke floated above him.

Brax, Phinlera, and Penton stayed in the forest for several more weeks, enjoying time with their mom and dad, and allowing Phin to regain her strength. They talked often with Laefin, listening to his harrowing account of falling from Fletcher, trying to stay hidden among the Mins, and then hunting down Serene's arrow. Phinlera wrinkled her nose each time at the elf's description of the sheep-faced shaman with her short, curved horns. How he'd found her lying in the Dunes with the arrow still in her breast, and had dug it out with his bare hands. It was a fantastic story and one they enjoyed listening to often. They retold their own tales too, allowing their young friend to put all the pieces together in his mind. Then one cool night after supper, Penton announced he'd be leaving for home. Worried about the backlog of work awaiting him in Oak Haven and the possibility for an early winter, he wanted to get back before the heavy rains started. Braxton reluctantly agreed they should go too.

The following day, the elves brought Obsidian and Cinnamon to the cottage. The big black stallion and auburn mare looked well-fed and groomed to perfection after having been stabled in one of the few paddocks the elves kept. Bear whined when he saw Gavin's horse and lay down on the forest floor, his jaw touching the ground and his ears pulled back.

"I know." Phinlera knelt beside him and rubbed the elkhound's thick fur. "I miss him too."

They spent the next few days preparing supplies, wrapping stores, and packing Obsidian for Pen's long ride back to their village. He planned to stop by Montressa to look in on Cassi, and Brax could see the fondness his brother still held for the young girl he'd saved.

Braxton felt his mom's sadness at their leaving, and she spoke often with each of them, communicating with Penton in a similar way to what Brax had experienced. She seemed to be with them wherever they went in Arbor Glen, as if not wanting to miss a moment together, knowing their time was fading.

He spoke frequently with his dad too, talking in the common room of their cottage late into the night. Brax knew he'd never leave. He had given up his life as a blacksmith in Oak Haven, content to live out his days in the forest.

"This is my home now," he said. "My place is here, with Mom."

Reluctantly, Braxton began to accept that he would live apart from his parents. It was a bitter realization of how time forced events upon him, experiences he may not otherwise have wished for.

"We can come back and visit whenever we want," Penton had told him encouragingly. "It'll be the best of both worlds."

But Braxton wasn't so sure. He was going to miss his family's togetherness. Even Pen would be living apart. Then he'd see Phinlera and realize that while one chapter in his life was ending, another, even brighter, future with her was about to begin.

When the day finally arrived to say their goodbyes, Bendarren was waiting for them outside the cottage. A half-dozen scouts stood with him, offering to accompany Penton as far as the eastern Vales, promising to help protect him from any Hunters who might still be lingering in the Calindurin Plains.

Braxton placed his forehead against his mom's tree and connected with her for the last time. He could feel her weeping softly, sensed her mixed emotions—joy at seeing him grow up, pain at having to let him go. He tried to be strong for her, for himself, but in the end, he could feel his eyes watering.

Penton spoke with their dad, receiving some last-minute instructions for running the forge, even though they'd been over it a dozen times already. When Braxton separated from his mom's rough trunk, he went over and hugged his dad for a long time. He'd always been a pillar of strength in Brax's life, a stable, constant force supporting him, watching over him, ensuring he was safe. He'd no longer be there like before, and already Brax missed him. Growing up, he always dreamed of being on his own, but now that the moment had arrived, he dreaded it. The sand in the hourglass had finally run through, Braxton realized, and it could never be put back.

"You'll be all right," his dad said, as he had for Penton. His boys had grown up, Thadeus knew, and there was nothing more he could do to hold back the time that eventually separates all children from their parents.

"I love you, Dad," Braxton said. His father's dark eyes filled with tears. "You too, Mom," he added, turning toward her tree.

We love you, his mom replied. *And are very proud of you, and Penton, of all you've done and will still accomplish.*

"Always remember that," their dad emphasized.

Phinlera stepped over and hugged Brax's father, holding him tight for a while.

"Thanks," she said softly, "for everything you've done for us." Then she placed her head on the tree, as Brax and Pen had done. "Thank you for welcoming me into your family. I promise to take care of Braxton all my life." She wiped her face somewhat sheepishly, then picked up her pack and began fidgeting with the straps.

Following her lead, Brax shouldered his own pack, adjusting the weight of their gifts and provisions inside, before strapping on the Unicorn Blade.

"Bye," he said simply, raising both hands toward his parents and looking at them for a moment. Then he took Phinlera's palm, squeezed it gently, and called to Bear. They followed Bendarren out of Arbor Glen, Penton riding atop Cinnamon and leading Obsidian. Stopping at the crest of the hill for a final wave back, they turned and disappeared into the forest.

CHAPTER
48

Braxton and Phinlera stood by the Walking Gate in the heart of Almon-Fey, preparing to travel to Falderon, Oak Haven's Gate still having not yet reopened. They said their goodbyes to Laefin and the elves, promising to return in the spring.

"I will forever be in your debt," Brax said to Bendarren. "For all you've done for me, for Phinlera, and for my mom and my family. Thank you so very much." He shook the elf's hand in both of his.

"No, Braxton, my friend," Bendarren replied. "It is I who am eternally grateful for all you have done to save my people, our nation, and this forest. Know that you will always be welcome here, and I shall forever seek to repay your kindness in whatever way I can."

Phinlera hugged the elf, kissing him on the cheek and adding her sentiments as well. He smiled back at the gesture, placing a hand on the spot she'd touched, and inclining his head.

Brax embraced his brother, thinking of all the experiences they'd endured together and the bond between them that no spoken words could explain.

"Be careful," Phin said, leaning up on her toes to hug Pen. "Be safe, and go fast."

Saying their final farewells, Brax and Phinlera turned and, together with Bear, stepped through the Walking Gate.

The sudden hustle and bustle of a new, chilly market day in Falderon burst upon them, an unexpected and dramatic change from the calm of the elves. They looked at each other quickly, already missing Arbor Loren.

"You there," a heavyset official yelled over to them, sitting behind a table, a half-dozen mail-clad guards standing nearby. "No animals allowed." He pointed to Bear on the platform. "Pay your fine."

"Move along," another guard added closer by, urging them forward with all the other travelers arriving through the Gate.

"Sorry," Phinlera replied, flashing the man a quick smile.

They walked over to the guard at the table—who had a thick mop of unruly black hair, an unshaven chin, and smelled heavily of alcohol and dried sweat—and paid the outrageous four-silver fee. Brax jostled their money pouch in his hand for a moment, feeling its lightened weight, then retied it to his belt.

"We'd best find Zambini's soon," he said to Phin, leading her and Bear off the platform.

They wound their way to the inn, where their surprised host welcomed them and insisted that they take a hot bath. After soaking in the waters for a while, they followed Zambini across the courtyard to his whitewashed home. A delighted Brennah overwhelmed them with meat pies and a few glasses of trill, which Brax particularly enjoyed. They spent the day with their friends, sharing the stories of all they'd endured since leaving Falderon. Their two boys, Kudu and Bendwhalie, had grown considerably and were even more rambunctious than before, wrestling and running around the house, often bumping into the furniture. Zambini listened intently to their long tale, considering each event and asking questions whenever he thought additional clarification was needed—in the process gaining much-needed information that his spy network had missed.

"Oh, you poor dears," Brennah exclaimed whenever they described a particular dangerous event. While she continually refilled their mugs, the light in her eyes exposed a much greater intelligence than would have been expected of an innkeeper's wife. Her occasional well-worded questions—

especially when Braxton tried to hide his connection with Serene or the spirit magic—revealed a perceptive mind that often recognized when something was missing. Eventually, they got through their story with sufficient detail to satisfy their hosts, and Brennah stopped asking questions, although Zambini could have gone on forever. Thankfully, Brennah came to their aid, recognizing that they preferred to keep some things private, and she sent her husband back to the inn.

They stayed in Falderon for a few days. Brax, Phin, and Bear wandered among the busy plazas, visiting the stalls and little shops, finding trinkets and other small additions for their cottage back home. Life in the mountain city seemed largely restored, with commerce and trade resuming at its normal pace. Visitors, livestock, and makeshift accommodations no longer filled every road, back alley, or open space. Braxton and Phinlera found they enjoyed the city now, moving about more freely, though they quickly grew tired of the always-noisy streets and cramped bazaars, appreciating the full value of the elves' more tranquil lifestyle. Eventually, they began to miss the simpler life in Oak Haven.

One clear morning, Brax found himself walking hand in hand with Phinlera, heading down the road that led west toward home. Farmers busily worked their fields, trying to catch up from time spent in the city while cows grazed on late summer grasses, fattening up for the coming winter. They stopped often to talk with travelers and spent their evenings sleeping in farmsteads or cottages that dotted the countryside, often talking with their families late into the morning hours.

It gave Braxton a wonderful sense of fulfillment to see the farms working again and to pass merchants on the road pushing carts or leading pack mules laden with goods. He breathed in deeply the scent of hay from the nearby barns and the sweet smell of baked pies or other home cooking that permeated the air. Mostly, though, he loved having Phinlera by his side. It was a drastic contrast to the last time he'd traveled this road with Ruskin and Gavin. There were no dead chickens lying in broken pens or wolf-ravaged livestock decaying in the sun. No unkempt fields or ransacked barnyards. And Phinlera's pleasant company was so much more enjoyable than the prevailing mood of his previous companions.

On the morning of their fourth day, they stood on the west road thanking a farmer's wife for lodging for the night and a warm breakfast in exchange for some chores, when a long line of wagons came rolling by. They stood aside to allow the procession to pass, watching them moving slowly toward their village, and waved at their drivers. Most were workmen moving stores of various kinds or traveling to the local farms. A few, with closed beds, belonged to families who lolled inside or carried possessions after returning home from some easterly travels. The rest were filled with freshly cut hay, with the very last wagon lagging a bit behind the others. Driven by an old man in a broad-brimmed straw hat that filtered light down onto his tanned face, he smiled kindly at Brax and Phin as he passed, and wished them a good morning.

Braxton had an idea. "Wait here," he told Phin. He ran off down the road, calling for the man to stop. A few minutes later, he returned out of breath. "He's delivering hay to Saddler's farm. It took a little persuading, but he agreed to take on a couple of passengers and their dog. For a few coppers, that is." He grinned.

They rode the rest of the morning in the back of the old man's hay wagon, lying together on the soft bedding, talking and looking up at the clear sky, enjoying the summer sun and listening to birds flying overhead. Bear fell asleep as soon as they were moving, taking full advantage of the rest from the previous day's travels. An hour past midday, the wagon train stopped to water the horses by a little brook that ran through a clump of willows. Braxton and Phin sat together with their driver, enjoying a cold lunch. The man shared some fresh fruits and vegetables from a wicker basket he kept under his seat, and they reciprocated with their bread and cheese.

They set off again a little after the last wagon had departed, following a mile or so behind the rest of the procession. The old man removed his hat and wiped his brow with a spotted red handkerchief from his pocket, then mounted up again. He had pure white hair that shone in the afternoon sun but that covered only the sides of his otherwise bald head. His kind face was heavily lined from the passage of time and the years spent outdoors. Brax and Phin smiled at each other at seeing his aged look and offered him a drink from their elven waterskins. He drank deeply before thanking them and setting off again.

It was past sundown when they stopped outside Oak Haven and their driver let them off. They thanked him for his kindness and gladly paid the promised fare, waving as he pulled away toward Saddler's farm.

"What a nice old man," Phinlera said when he'd passed out of earshot. Brax had to agree. He hoisted his pack up onto his shoulders and watched the wagon as it turned down a small lane before veering out of sight.

They walked together through the few back roads of their village, with Bear running alongside or disappearing ahead, only to return a few moments later from a different direction. Turning onto the alleyway that led to the cobblestone street fronting their cottage, they finally came upon the old, familiar sight of Braxton's home and stopped outside the little gate.

"It's good to be back," he said, taking a deep breath and smelling the evening air. He looked into Phin's beautiful eyes, admiring the way the light of the moon enhanced her exquisite features. "I'm glad you're with me."

"Me too." She hugged him, then stood on her toes and kissed him fully. They embraced for a long time before Phin pulled away.

"Come on," she said, "let's get inside. You start a fire, and I'll get some stew going."

Braxton unlatched the gate, and let her in after the excited Bear. He looked back at their village for a moment before stepping off the street and into their little yard. Home at last.

The old man with the straw hat walked around Oak Haven slowly, stopping here and there to look in on its residents. Having long since dismissed the hay wagon and having thanked the big stallion for his service, he meandered through the little streets unseen by most of its inhabitants. A few noticed his passing, smiling kindly in acknowledgment, some even going so far as to offer him a drink or dinner to ward off the night. Pleased by their politeness, he thanked them but continued on his way.

He liked what he saw in the homes of those where he stopped to look in, stretching out his energy to feel the presence of their occupants, reading the lives they'd chosen. Most were of good heart, strong in mind, and faithful to their families and community. A few he nudged, helping them back on path, redirecting their wanderings or lost direction. Some he cured of ailments—those who'd learned from their experiences and could benefit now from the healing sleep he could provide. Most were given a few extra coins, the old man bending his will to manifest the Andorah tender in a purse here or a pocket there. The economy of Oak Haven had suffered much since the closing of their Gate, and he knew their residents could use a little extra help.

He stopped at their Walking Gate and stepped up onto the platform, unnoticed by the two guards standing only a few feet away, and reached out with his mind to feel the power within the portal. Summoning the spirit magic, he reenergized it, cleansing it of the taint from the Mins and the Dark Child. He thought of how the people used the Gates to move about in their little world, still unknowing of their true nature and real potential. Perhaps in time they'd come to realize it.

At last, he came to the Prinn cottage and went into their backyard, passing through the fence without bothering to open the crude gate arrangement. For a long time, he sat on a stump, looking into the home where Braxton and Phinlera lay by the fire. He listened to them talking over all they'd experienced since leaving Oak Haven, pleased with their success. Reaching down, he patted Bear, the elkhound having strolled out of the house to see him. He took a moment to stretch his mind and look at how things might have changed if Penton had been the one to go. He saw where the older brother's choices might have varied, how events would have unfolded differently, and wondered if the final outcome would've been the same.

He focused on the path ahead for this young couple and the direction their new life would take together, all the stronger for their joining. He stopped in places to add refinements, introducing events that would give them opportunities to make choices, to redirect their focus, to test their resolve. He knew what lay ahead and needed their commitment and strength to see things through to the unknown but specific end. The old man looked at those who would join them on their path and set in motion their coming together to help achieve the overall goal. If the shadow of negativity prevailed, it would set back much of what he'd worked for, what he and his brethren had achieved. He knew he couldn't force the path they desired, for that forcing would be worse than the alternative they all hoped to avoid.

Content at last that he'd done what he could, he checked the young couple again, healing their wounds and giving them much-needed rest. Touching the sword with his mind, he infused the spirit magic deep within its familiar form, assuring himself it was adequately prepared. When he was sure everything was as he'd intended, he took a deep breath, smelled the warm evening air and the sweetness that floated in from some distant orchard, wondering why he'd stayed away for so long. After a few moments of savoring the beautiful night, in which time seemed to have slowed, Cathadeus looked back at the house one final time. Then he focused his mind, changed into his favorite form of the white unicorn Serene, and stepped back into the spirit world.

—

The story continues in *Sotchek*,
Book Two of The Walking Gates.

PHONETIC
PRONUNCIATION GUIDE

Amalasia—am-a-lay-she-ah

Andorah—an-door-ah

Baehrin—bay-rin

Belladora—bell-ah-door-ah

Bellnella—bell-nell-ah

Bendarren—ben-daren

Bendwhalie—ben-dwahl-ee

Braxton—brax-tin

Calindurin—kal-en-dur-rin

Callorin—kal-o-rin

Caryle—car-isle

Cassandra—ka-san-dra

Cathadeus—kath-a-day-iss

Dahgmor—dag-mor

Dûrak-Thûhn—do-rack-thuhn

Dynekee—die-nee-key

Eilandoran—ell-en-door-rin

Elestera—el-es-tare-ah

Elhunarie—el-who-nar-ree

Falderon—fal-dah-ron

Gaelen—gay-lin

Gavin—gav-in

Iban—eye-bin

Illian—ill-ee-in

Janson—jan-sin

Jenleah—jen-lay-ah

Jenlyrindien—jen-lah-rin-dee-in

Jenphinlin—jen-fin-lin

Jenterra—jen-tare-ah

Kalendra—ka-len-dra

Karas—ka-rus

Kudu—koo-do

Laefin—lay-ah-fin

Leylandon—lay-lan-din

Malicine—mal-a-scene

Morgaroth—mor-ga-roth

Neah—nay-ah

Penton—pen-tin

Phinlera—fin-lair-ah

Ragi—ra-jee

Ruskin—rus-kin

Shelindûhin—shell-en-doo-in

Sotchek—so-check

Tayloren—tay-lore-en

Tentalis—ten-tell-es

Thadeus—thad-ee-us

Tharak—thar-ak

Tyrrideon—tie-rid-ee-in

Zacharias—zak-ah-rye-es

Zambini—zam-bee-nee

ABOUT THE AUTHOR:

JEFF J. PETERS was born in South Africa and immigrated to the United States as a teenager, where he fell in love with all things fantasy. He obtained degrees in digital electronics and computer science and worked as an IT professional for more than twenty years. In 2014, he left his corporate position to focus full-time on writing. *Cathadeus* is his debut novel. He is currently working on the sequel. Learn more, connect with the author, and follow his blog at www.jeffjpeters.com